SPY, SPY AWAY

Book 7 of the NEVER SAY SPY series

Diane Henders

SPY, SPY AWAY

ISBN 978-1-927460-14-6

PEBKAC Publishing Inc.
P.O. Box 67, Station Main
Qualicum Beach, BC   V9K 1S7
www.pebkacpublishing.com

First printed in paperback December 2013 by PEBKAC Publishing Inc.
v.10

Books in the NEVER SAY SPY series:

More books coming! For a current list, please visit
www.dianehenders.com
Or sign up for my New Book Notification list at
www.dianehenders.com/books

Humour by Diane Henders

Probably Inappropriate

Definitely Inappropriate

Totally Inappropriate

Completely Inappropriate

Unabashedly Inappropriate

Since You Asked...

People frequently ask if my protagonist, Aydan Kelly, is really me.

Yeah, you got me. These novels are an autobiography of my secret life as a government agent, working with highly-classified computer technology... Oh, wait, what's that? You want the *truth*? Um, you do realize fiction writers get paid to lie, don't you?

...well, shit, that's not nearly as much fun. It's also a long story.

I swore I'd never write fiction. "Too personal," I said. "People read novels and automatically assume the author is talking about him/herself."

Well, apparently I lied about the fiction-writing part. One day a story sprang into my head and wouldn't leave. The only way to get it out was to write it down. So I did.

But when I wrote that first book, I never intended to show it to anyone, so I created a character that looked like me just to thumb my nose at the stereotype. I've always had a defective sense of humour, and this time it turned around and bit me in the ass.

Because after I'd written the third novel, I realized I actually wanted other people to read my books. And when I went back to change my main character to *not* look like me, my beta readers wouldn't let me. They rose up against me and said, "No! Aydan is a tall woman with long red hair and brown eyes. End of discussion!"

Jeez, no wonder readers get the idea that authors write about themselves. So no, I'm not Aydan Kelly. I just look like her.

Oh, and the town of Silverside and all secret technologies are products of my imagination. If I'm abducted by grim-faced men wearing dark glasses, or if I die in an unexplained fiery car crash, you'll know I accidentally came a little too close to the truth.

I hope you enjoy the book!

For Phill

Thank you for being my technical advisor and the most tolerant husband ever. Much love!

To my beta readers/editors, especially Carol H., Judy B., and Phill B., with gratitude: Many thanks for all your time and effort in catching my spelling and grammar errors, telling me when I screwed up the plot or the characters' motivations, and generally keeping me honest.

To Rick and Sandy H. at Hand Crafted Images: Your talent makes my covers extra-special, and your sense of humour makes photo sessions fun even for a camera-hater like me. Thank you!

To Steve A. and the staff at The Shooting Edge: Thank you for lending us your excellent facilities for our cover photo sessions. You guys rock!

To everyone else, respectfully:
Canadian English is an unholy hybrid of British and American English, so I apologize if spellings in this book look odd to you. But if you find typos, please send an email to errors@dianehenders.com. Mistakes drive me nuts, and I'm sorry if any slipped through. Please let me know what the error is, and on which page (or at which position in e-versions). I'll make sure it gets fixed as soon as possible. Thanks!

CHAPTER 1

"Well, well. If it isn't Ms. Aydan Kelly. I see your little fraud game is still going nicely." The middle-aged man gave me a smug smile as he slid uninvited into the chair across from me.

My stomach contracted around queasy fear.

"Hibbert." I held my voice level. "If that is actually your real name."

He frowned, projecting righteous affront. "Of course it is." He drew a gold case from his breast pocket and extended one of his cards with a flourish. "And please, do call me Paul. I was hoping you hadn't forgotten me."

Didn't I wish. I'd glimpsed him several times in the past two months, always giving me that sardonic little nod with a smile that just begged to be punched off his face.

I ignored the card and gave him a flat stare. "What do you want?"

The waitress slid a basket of hot chicken wings onto the table in front of me. "Here you go, Aydan. Do you want some more of that hard drink you keep chugging back?"

I forced my stiff lips into a smile and saluted her with my half-empty water glass. "Thanks. Yes, please."

As she hurried away, I turned back to Hibbert. "You're spoiling my lunch. Get lost."

"Miss Widdenback." He pulled a hurt face. "Or do you prefer Miss Cherry? Is that any way to talk to one of your loyal fans? Maybe I just want to compliment you on your latest video. That footage with the Chippendales dancer was amazing. You're very flexible for a woman nearing fifty." He leaned closer, his voice dropping to a purr. "And you used your lovely long hair so... creatively. I've always had a thing for redheads."

I used every ounce of control to prevent myself from recoiling. God damn Stemp for setting me up with that porn star cover story. Even if it wasn't really me in the videos, the thought of this slimeball salivating over them made my stomach turn. And I'd be lucky if salivating was all he'd done.

"Stick it up your ass," I snapped. "And fuck off before I get Eddy to throw you out."

I glanced over as Eddy slid a fresh beer across the bar to one of the regulars, his eyes twinkling while he engaged in his usual banter.

There was no way I'd involve Eddy. Not when I knew Hibbert had a gun tucked under that well-cut suit jacket.

But Hibbert didn't know about the baby Glock cuddled in the waist holster under my sweatshirt, either. Better if he thought I was just a helpless female, depending on Eddy to protect me. Nothing like a few little surprises to keep things fresh.

"Ah, yes, Blue Eddy." Hibbert shot a contemptuous look toward the bar before returning his attention to me. "I'm quaking in my boots. But there's no reason for you to be so hostile. I've come to offer you another business opportunity."

"I told you in October, I'm not interested."

He waved a dismissive hand. "That was small potatoes. An insult to a savvy businesswoman like yourself, and I do apologize. It's clear I underestimated you. My associates would like to propose a more..." He smiled, the expression doing nothing to mask the hardness in his eyes. "...attractive offer."

The waitress arrived with my fresh glass of water, and I used the interruption to surreptitiously draw a deep breath, willing my pounding pulse to slow.

His associates. The ruthless international circle of spies and arms dealers concealed behind the soft, cute smiles of the stuffed toys they imported. If they discovered I truly was Aydan Kelly instead of Arlene Widdenback impersonating Aydan Kelly, my death would be slow and excruciating.

He leaned closer, pitching his voice below the blues music. "I hope you're still enjoying your work at Sirius Dynamics."

I swallowed the tightness in my throat with a sip of water and gave him my best steely stare.

Undeterred by my silence, he continued. "One of my associates is looking for a friend he's lost touch with. The last time they spoke, his friend was working at Sirius Dynamics. I thought of you immediately."

I heaved a theatrically bored sigh and picked up a chicken wing, letting my gaze drift across the room while I devoured the hot, greasy meat and slurped the spicy sauce off my fingers.

His voice deepened. "That's very sexy."

I froze with my thumb in my mouth.

Eeuw.

Fine. Asshole. Stemp was going to owe me for this.

I held eye contact while I withdrew my thumb slowly, sliding my lips down its length. Hibbert swallowed convulsively as I cleaned the last of the sauce off my fingers with little flicks of my tongue before leaning back with another sigh. "Get to the point."

My voice apparently jarred him back from the realm of fantasy. He blinked and shifted in his chair. "It's a small thing, really."

His gaze locked onto my mouth as I went for another wing, and I jabbed the wing at him instead of biting into it. "You have ten seconds. Ten..."

"All we want is a phone list," he said hurriedly. "Just a photocopy of the company directory."

Ennui dripped from my voice. "Why would I bother?"

"You would be compensated, of course."

I waved my chicken wing in a languid 'go on' gesture.

"Two thousand dollars cash right now." He withdrew a fat envelope from his coat pocket. "Three thousand dollars when you deliver the list."

I sneered, hoping I didn't have wing sauce all over my contemptuously curled lip. "Stop insulting me. You offered me a hundred grand a couple of months ago."

"That was for a considerably different item. Which you didn't deliver."

"I didn't see any hundred grand, either. I don't have time to waste on small-time guys like you. Scram." I waved the chicken wing in a shooing gesture before biting into it, ignoring him and trying to be as unsexy as possible.

"*Small-time?*" He sounded as though he was strangling.

I shrugged, patted my lips with my napkin, and attacked another wing.

When I glanced up again, Hibbert's face was an unhealthy shade of burgundy. He drew a slow breath, and the smile he offered was distinctly lopsided. "Most people... most *smart* people would accept this offer with gratitude.

Five thousand dollars for a simple, easily-accessible piece of paper. And if you deliver, it could be the beginning of a lucrative and beneficial relationship."

"Get lost."

"Fine." He slapped another fat envelope atop the first. "Five now, five when you deliver."

I eyed the envelopes as if they contained long-dead fish. "You don't seriously think I'm going to take those with the whole world watching. I'll think about it and be in touch." I trotted out my hard-learned spy lingo with secret satisfaction. "If I accept the deal, I'll expect a dead drop. I don't work with amateurs."

"Amateurs." Hibbert drew another deep breath and cranked on his smile again. "Fine. I'll expect an answer by noon tomorrow. And don't even consider mentioning this to anyone if you want to stay alive." He stuffed the envelopes back in his pocket and stalked out as if he had a hot poker jammed up his ass.

As soon as the door closed behind him, I did my best confident stride to the ladies' room and hid in a cubicle until my knees stopped trembling.

At last, I crept back to finish my unappetizingly cold chicken wings before heading for the back door. I hesitated in the enclosed vestibule.

My nightmares had finally subsided after two long months, but even with all the therapy and mental effort, I couldn't shake my lingering paranoia about emerging through a door when I couldn't see what was on the other side.

I hissed through my teeth. That was probably a good thing. Stemp still thought I was an experienced agent, not a clueless civilian bookkeeper. Maybe a bit of paranoia would help compensate for my total lack of actual spy skills.

I pushed through the door, sidestepping and snapping a quick glance left and right. The glare of sun on snow nearly blinded me after the dimness of the bar, and the frigid December air stole my breath. I sucked in a lungful anyway and headed for my car, surveying its interior for intruders before I slid into the driver's seat.

I replayed Hibbert's last words while I extracted the bug detector from my waist pouch and eyed its reassuring green light.

A whole two months since my last death threat. Well, it had been a nice respite while it lasted.

I blew out a sigh and grabbed one of Stemp's secured cell phones from the glove compartment.

He answered on the first ring, as usual. "Yes."

"It's Aydan."

"Report."

"Paul Hibbert just offered me ten thousand dollars for a copy of the Sirius Dynamics internal phone list. Apparently Fuzzy Bunny is looking for someone at Sirius. I told him I'd think about it. He expects an answer by noon tomorrow."

"Very well. Briefing at fifteen-thirty, your office."

I hung up without offering or receiving a goodbye and drove to Up & Coming, watching the sparse small-town traffic in case anybody was following me.

When I entered the shop, a snort of laughter escaped me. "Lola! You're a sick, sick woman!"

I scanned for the guilty party, shaking a reproving finger when her grin popped up from behind the shelf where she had been stooping to rearrange a display.

"What?" Her wrinkled pixie face was a study in innocence.

"You! Only you would put a Santa hat on Big John the Wonder Horse," I sputtered, trying to hold onto my expression of fake outrage while I indicated the huge black silicone penis with its festive miniature... um... headgear.

She widened her eyes at me. "I thought he should have a nice hat to go with his sack."

I succumbed, doubling over to laugh until tears rolled down my cheeks. "Sick," I wheezed. "You're sick. But funny as hell. Ohmigod, my gut. You made me hurt myself." I massaged my aching belly, still giggling feebly. "What does Linda think of your Christmas decorations?"

Lola smirked. "She bowed to my superior marketing skills. When we hid Big John and started displaying all the tame lingerie and candles up front, everybody asked where he was. He's turned into our mascot."

"And a fine upstanding mascot he is, too," I agreed, doing my best deadpan expression.

"Yes, indeed!" Her wicked grin softened into a smile. "It's good to hear you laugh like that. I was worried about you for a while there."

"Thanks." I suppressed the urge to shuffle my feet and held her gaze with an effort. "The therapy has really helped."

Letting her believe I'd been raped had been the only plausible cover story I could use at the time, but...

I squashed my guilty conscience. It was true that the therapy had helped. That was all she needed to know.

I changed the subject. "What about you?" I searched her face. "Have you recovered from being kidnapped? Are you sleeping all right?"

Lola tossed her head, her spiked hair flashing vivid purple under the display lighting. "It'd take a lot more than that to scare this old broad. If that punk hadn't drugged me,

I'd have kicked his sorry ass."

I grinned down at her diminutive figure, choosing to play along despite the faint tremor in her voice. "Kicked his sorry kneecap, maybe. I doubt if you could've reached his ass."

"Ha. I'm meaner than you think. I could have stood on a chair and kicked him in the head." She looked up at me, her wise eyes seeing too much. "But we were talking about you. You haven't left your house except to go to work for the past two months." She slid a motherly arm around my waist and gave me a squeeze. "It's time to start living again, honey."

I gulped at the memory of how close I'd come to losing her, and hid my rush of emotion with a grin. "I *am* living. I've had a fabulous two months of reading, baking, and working on my '53 Chevy. I feel like I've gotten my life back."

The life I had dreamed of living before I ever knew about Fuzzy Bunny or Canada's clandestine operations.

I hid a sigh.

"It's not healthy for you to spend so much time alone." She gave me the impish grin that always presaged some form of impending personal humiliation for me. "You should make a play for Big John. I bet you could snag him."

I snickered. "It'll be a sad day when I have to work to snag a mechanical boyfriend. Even if he does have his own little Santa hat."

"Very funny. I meant the real Big John." Lola waggled her eyebrows. "Go on, Aydan, wouldn't you like a little hanky-panky with a hunk like him?"

"God, you have no idea." The words were out of my mouth before I could stop them. I backpedalled rapidly. "But I don't want a relationship. Now's just not a good time."

"I know it's tough to learn to trust again, honey, but don't let the fear win." The sympathy in her eyes made my conscience prod me even harder. Before I could come up with an appropriate response, she straightened, her face lighting up. "Hey, Aydan, I just had a great idea!"

"Oh, no." I flung up defensive hands. "Whatever it is, no."

"I promise it has nothing to do with wearing any of our merchandise."

"No dressing up." I eyed her suspiciously.

"No. In fact, the more I think of it, the more I know you'll love it! It's right up your alley!"

"Leave my alley out of this."

She ignored my recalcitrance. "There's a self-defence workshop for women at the rec centre this week. Tomorrow, Thursday, and Friday evening; Saturday and Sunday afternoon. Come with me! It'll be fun."

"Um..."

"Come on, none of my old-fogey friends will go with me, and I really want to go. I want to learn some self-defence moves." She adopted a threatening scowl and swung her tiny fists at the air. "I want to kick some ass."

I clamped down on my smile. "I don't think you'll learn much ass-kicking in five sessions. And... um... do you think it would be... um, safe for you?"

Lola straightened indignantly. "I'm only seventy-three! I go to the gym three times a week, and I'm in damn good shape. And besides, weight-bearing exercise is good for preventing osteoporosis. Come with me. It'll be good for both of us."

I capitulated before I had to lie to her any more. "Okay, you talked me into it. Sign us up." I turned away to make for the office before she could think up any other brilliant ideas. "I'm going to get at that bookkeeping."

My hands trembled when I signed for my fob at the security wicket of Sirius Dynamics a couple of hours later. Clipping the fob on my waistband, I squared my shoulders and strode down the corridor, projecting confidence for all I was worth.

So Hibbert and Fuzzy Bunny were still on my trail. So what. Stemp would probably just tell me to ignore their advances, same as last time. It didn't mean I was going into danger again. I'd be fine. Nothing to worry about.

I repeated my mantra while I climbed the stairs and headed for my second-floor office.

Fine. I'd be fine. I wasn't in any danger...

When I turned the corner into my office, a burst of adrenaline jerked my hand toward my holster.

CHAPTER 2

An instant later, I recognized the stocky bearded man lounging on my couch, feet propped on my coffee table.

"Carl!" Relief weakened my knees and I blew out a shaky breath as Germain rose, smiling. I hurried over to give him a quick hug. "You scared the shit out of me, but it's good to see you!"

He returned my squeeze. "Good to see you, too. You look great."

"Thanks." I grinned as I stepped back. "You look thoroughly disreputable."

That wasn't exactly true. He looked dangerously sexy, his black hair grown out into unruly curls that accented his black brows and keen brown eyes, his muscular frame displayed to advantage in a snug black T-shirt and cargo pants.

He rasped a hand over his whiskered chin, the laugh lines crinkling around his eyes. "I just wrapped up an undercover op. Shave and a haircut are the first things on my list."

"What are you doing here? I thought you were assigned to Calgary." I nodded toward the couch. "Sit, get comfortable."

He sank into the chair instead. "I was supposed to be heading back to Calgary, but Stemp caught me right after my debriefing and asked me to meet you here at three-thirty. That's all I know so far." He glanced at his watch. "We've got a few minutes. Can you update me a bit while we're waiting?"

I slouched onto the couch, stretching out my legs. "What do you know so far?"

"My last update was back in July."

"Okay..." I cast my mind back to the summer. "God, so much has happened since then. Spider is still on the team. Smith turned out to be a spy named Kasper Doytchevsky, and he's dead now."

I declined to elaborate at the sight of Germain's raised eyebrows, still feeling the kick of the gun in my hand, seeing the blood and shattered bone...

"There's a mission report on that," I said firmly. "You can read it later. You never met Sam Kraus, did you?"

"No."

I sighed. "There's another mission report on that. The short version is that Sam is the owner of the civilian research branch of Sirius Dynamics, and also the guy who developed the micro-miniaturized network key that gets me invisibly into the brainwave-driven virtual reality network. Problem was, he didn't invent it for the good of the country. He was going to use me to hack and decrypt digital information so he could sell it, but I caught him at it."

Germain grinned. "Sounds like you've been busy. I presume he's in custody now?"

"Yes." I grimaced. "But he cut a deal with Stemp a couple of months ago. He's been back on my project under heavy supervision ever since. Dr. Honey Travers is supervising Sam's work. You might meet her today; I'm not sure if she'll be sitting in. Oh, and she prefers to be called Jack."

Germain leaned back in the chair to cross his feet on the coffee table again. "Masculine sort?"

I chuckled, anticipating his reaction when he saw her. "Not exactly. And of course, John is still on my project."

"How's he doing? I heard he got shot a couple of months ago, but I couldn't call him while I was undercover."

"He's fine. As far as I know. He's not limping anymore, anyway."

I squirmed, searching for another topic of conversation. For the past couple of months, I had successfully avoided John Kane except for our necessary contact at work. He had responded by treating me with the same friendly professionalism he offered everyone, making no attempt to contact me outside of work or converse about anything other than our daily duties. So that was good.

Just fine.

Excellent.

I drew in a breath of relief when Spider's beanpole figure appeared in the doorway. His youthful face lit up.

"Carl!" He bounded in, shooting out a skinny arm to pump Germain's hand. "Wow, awesome! Long time, no see! How are you?"

"Webb." Germain chuckled and returned the handshake along with an affectionate slap on Spider's bony shoulder. "Good to see you again. I'm fine. You?"

"Great! Are you here to do Kane's requalification?"

"Yes, I was supposed to do that later in the week, but Stemp asked me to sit on in this briefing as well."

"Um... requalification?" I frowned at the two men.

"Yeah." Spider turned to face me. "You know, the annual testing and requalification for agents. Kane was due in January but he has to requalify after his injury anyway, so Stemp moved it up. He'd probably have done it sooner, but Germain wasn't available." He frowned. "I'm surprised you haven't had to do yours yet."

Apprehension tightened my throat. "Um... what exactly would that involve?"

Germain frowned. "And why would she have to?"

Spider turned to Germain, his smile lighting up the room. "Didn't she tell you? Aydan's been promoted to agent!"

Germain's white grin split his dark whiskers. "That's great news! Congratulations, Aydan!"

"Um, thanks..." I shot a pleading look at Spider. "So about this testing..."

"Well, look what the cat dragged in!" Kane's deep baritone interrupted me as he strode in.

"If it isn't the feeble old fart himself! Hope you're ready to get your ass kicked." Germain gripped Kane's extended hand and the two thumped each other on the shoulder, grinning and jostling in a friendly trial of strength.

Kane towered nearly six inches taller than Germain, but the breadth of their powerful shoulders was an even match, making Germain look like a square wall of muscle next to Kane's magnificently proportioned build. I dragged my gaze away from the tasty spectacle as Charles Stemp arrived, swinging the door shut behind him.

Not that I intended to start calling him Charles. Hell, it had only been two months since I'd stopped mentally addressing him as 'Dickhead'.

He directed a piercing gaze toward me and I hurriedly

rerouted my thoughts. God, I'd swear those snake-like eyes could see right through my skull.

"Will Sam and Jack be joining us?" I blurted.

"Later." He eyed the four of us with his customary absence of expression. "This briefing is strictly need-to-know. Kelly has informed me that Paul Hibbert, whom we believe to be one of Fuzzy Bunny's business brokers, has contacted her hoping to obtain a copy of the Sirius Dynamics internal phone listing. This has the earmarks of recruitment, which could prove extremely advantageous to us in infiltrating their organization. I had hoped to set up something of the sort in the new year. This timing forces our hand somewhat, but the opportunity is too good to pass up." Stemp's dispassionate scrutiny stripped me to the bone. "Dr. Rawling informs me that he is satisfied with your progress."

I said nothing, my voice throttled by the icy lump of fear expanding in my chest.

Stemp's gaze snapped to Kane. "And you claim to be back to optimum fitness. Are you mission-ready?"

Kane's expression remained composed as usual, but his grey eyes kindled with predatory fire. "Absolutely."

"Good." Stemp's nod took in Kane, Germain, and me. "Kane, Kelly, you'll both complete your standard physical qualification tomorrow morning at zero nine hundred, followed by your firearms qualification. Kane, Germain will conduct your advanced weapons and hand-to-hand combat qualifications after that. Kelly, tomorrow you'll inform Hibbert that you'll provide the phone list."

Paralyzed, I sat trying to breathe while he continued. "Thanks to Kelly's research over the past several months, we're closer to a comprehensive picture of the extent of Fuzzy Bunny's operations. We've successfully terminated a few espionage and arms deals, but we haven't had sufficient evidence to show involvement of any of their major players." He raised a philosophical shoulder. "Every bit helps. If we can insert an agent, we'll be that much closer."

His tone darkened. "Meanwhile, some of the intel we gained during those ops indicates they have either developed or procured a new weapon which is rumoured to be silent and capable of causing instant death without a visible wound. It's unclear whether it's for mass military deployment or close-quarters use. We don't have any other details."

A sick silence ensued.

"So if they are in fact recruiting Kelly, it may give us a timely tactical advantage," Stemp concluded. "I'll provide all of you with mission reports and analysis of everything to date. Be prepared to meet tomorrow at thirteen-hundred for strategic planning."

He turned his impassive gaze on me. "Depending on how quickly their recruitment proceeds, you may end up devoting considerable time to undercover field work rather than the network surveillance you've been doing to date. With that in mind, I've had Drs. Kraus and Travers recreate Tammy Mellor's network key, and I have recruited Ms. Mellor to replace you."

"But..."

Stemp's voice drowned out my dry croak as he turned to speak to Germain. "I'll provide reports so you can get full detail, but here are the high points. The network key that Kelly uses to decrypt files and hack networks was one of eight in the world, created by a group of scientists calling themselves the Knights of Sirius. Dr. Kraus is the last surviving member of that group. The keys are specially encoded to the brainwave patterns of the woman using the key and to a counterpart of the key used by another person who controls her mind while she's in the network. That made it possible for the Knights to acquire and decrypt data without the key-holder's knowledge."

My heart tried to batter its way through my ribs. Shit, I had bumbled through my first assignment as an agent through sheer dumb luck, but sending me undercover to look for a goddamn death ray was like expecting a first-grader to write the sequel to 'War and Peace'.

I would inevitably fail, dooming myself and my entire team to torture and slow, horrible death.

Germain interrupted my spiralling thoughts. "Wait, so somebody has been controlling Aydan's mind in the network all this time?"

"No, she can't be controlled inside the network." Stemp shot me a grim smile. "It proved fatal to the man who tried."

Hot acid surged into my already-queasy stomach. Bert Cartwright, another one of the lives I'd taken. Eight dead at my hands in less than a year. The body count was burned into my brain.

God help me.

Stemp was still talking, his words floating at the edges of my mind. "Ms. Mellor is one of the eight women, but she is unaware of any of this since she has never entered the network without being under mind control. She will believe she is simply acting as a super-user to power our virtual reality simulations. I'll assign someone with the appropriate security clearance to control her."

Spider's uncertain voice pulled my attention back to the conversation at hand. "But... we'd control her mind? Without telling her?"

"Of course." Stemp didn't let impatience creep into his voice, but his impassive expression became, if possible, even more deadpan.

"But..." Spider's face scrunched into consternation. "But what about her rights? If we just... hijack her mind without her permission, then we're just using her like... like... We're no better than the Knights."

"That's not a relevant comparison," Stemp said smoothly. "We are protecting national security, our agents and clandestine operations, and Ms. Mellor at the same time. As long as she is unaware of the true nature of our department, she can live freely without any of the restrictions and dangers Agent Kelly faces. This is the best possible solution."

Spider subsided, looking unconvinced, and I didn't bother to point out that poor Tammy Mellor would be at exactly the same risk of abduction, torture, and death as I was; the only difference would be that if she got captured, she couldn't tell what she didn't know. Stemp was covering everyone's ass but hers.

Old habits die hard. My brain automatically added 'dickhead' before I could stop it.

Settle down.

Stemp's job was to make the difficult decisions. He had undoubtedly weighed national security and the safety of dozens of personnel against the questionable morality of the situation, and I had to agree that logic was on his side.

But I didn't have to like it, dammit.

"What makes you think she'll agree to work for you at all?" I asked.

Stemp turned his expressionless gaze on me. "Ms. Mellor was devastated when her Knight died. As you said yourself, he was her whole world. In the past two months, I have provided her with counselling sessions, moved her into a furnished apartment, and arranged for a temporary caregiver until she was able to orient herself in her new surroundings. I also sent a couple of agents to befriend her and provide subtle influence if necessary." His reptilian features betrayed none of the smugness he must be feeling. "Needless to say, Ms. Mellor is extremely grateful and eager to help us in any way she can."

Revulsion twisted my guts. "You used her! Took advantage of a blind, helpless, socially isolated woman and manipulated her like... like..."

Like he'd manipulated me.

Rage half-strangled my words. "You fucking *dickhead!*"

His expressionless façade didn't alter. "In my office, Kelly. Now."

CHAPTER 3

I marched down the hall ahead of Stemp, trying to hold onto my anger. Bastard. Using and manipulating a helpless blind woman.

Uncomfortable logic prodded my conscience. Tammy Mellor was utterly alone in the world, thanks to the family who had given her up to Sirius Dynamics at age eight, nearly forty years ago. Stemp had provided her with therapy, housing, transitional care, social contact, and a job. Sure, he had an ulterior motive, but he could just as easily have provided none of those things and forced her to work for him anyway.

Goddammit.

His office door clicked closed behind me, and I blew out a sigh as he strode past me to take a seat behind his desk.

I spoke before he could. "I'm sorry. I was out of line. You did the best you could for Tammy. I'll apologize in front of the others, too."

"That won't be necessary." He inclined his head toward the guest chair. "Please sit."

I sank into the chair, bracing myself for a lecture.

I tensed when he reached into his desk drawer, but relaxed again when he extracted a bug detector and laid it between us on the desk, its indicator light glowing reassuring green. He steepled his fingers and studied me over top of them. The silence lengthened.

Just when my nerves were about to snap, he spoke. "What was the real purpose for your outburst?"

"Um..."

I eyed him in confusion. What the hell was he asking?

He leaned back in his chair, holding me with his flat amber gaze. "Except for those times when you believed I'd harmed one of your friends, the only time you have publicly insulted me is when you need to speak to me urgently and privately. Is that the case, or do I need to remind you of our policies regarding respectful communication?"

I couldn't suppress a sigh. "You don't need to remind me."

God, nothing like hurling names as if I was in second grade. Grow up already. Before I'd gotten snared in this godawful spy's life, I'd have bitten off my tongue before I'd have insulted a co-worker, let alone the director of the department.

"So...?" Stemp eyed me with thinly disguised impatience.

With trembling fingertips, I massaged the incipient headache tightening around my temples. "I can't do this."

"Do what?"

"This mission. Pretending to work with Fuzzy Bunny. I can't do it."

"Why not?"

My fear burst out in its usual angry disguise. "Because I'm a fucking dumb civilian bookkeeper, not a spy! I don't have a fucking clue what to do, they'll spot me right away and then they'll torture all the classified information out of me, and everybody else will be in danger because of me! I can't do this! I won't even pass your qualification tests!"

His silence expanded to fill the room. I clenched my fists around the arms of the chair, my heart pounding in my ears.

At last he spoke. "I notice you said you 'won't pass', not you 'can't pass'."

"I *can't*, for shit's sake! I'm just a bookkeeper."

He blew out a short breath. "Look, Kelly, we both know that's not true."

I resisted the urge to batter my brains out on his desk. "It's *true*, for fucksakes! Hook me up to the lie detector and you can see for yourself."

He slumped lower in his chair, massaging his temples as if his head hurt, too. "I get the point. I know you can't compromise your cover." He eyed me wearily. "Can't you just squeak by with a passing score? Everyone knows you work out frequently and you're a good shot. It would be plausible. There's no need to actually fail the tests."

My voice scraped out between my clenched teeth. "It's not like I have a choice. I'm telling you-"

"I know," he interrupted. He held my gaze. "I opened myself to some undesirable scrutiny when I promoted you to an agent's role in the absence of any formal qualifications or testing. I would consider it a personal favour if you would pass this examination."

My jaw creaked under the strain and I drew a slow, deep breath, easing the tense muscles. Yes, he had put his ass on the line for me, even though he'd had some excellent reasons not to.

Holding my voice level, I asked, "What do I have to do?"

"It's just the standard physical and firearms qualification. Bare minimum."

I unclenched my teeth. Again. "But what does that include? And anyway, whether I pass or fail the qualification isn't the point. The point is if you put me undercover in Fuzzy Bunny, I'll blow it all to hell and take everybody else down with me."

Stemp rose. "Kelly, we believe Fuzzy Bunny is attempting to recruit you, specifically. You are the only person who can do this, and despite your convincing adherence to your cover, I know you're capable. Unless there's something else you want to discuss privately, we need to get back to the briefing."

He strode out, and I had no choice but to trail after him on trembling legs.

When we re-entered my office, Spider was staring at the toe of his running shoe while he scuffed it back and forth, alternately ruffling and smoothing the nap of the carpet. He glanced up, his gaze sliding away to perch in the corner of the room as a flush rose on his cheeks. Kane and Germain broke off their conversation to turn standard-issue neutral cop faces toward us.

Before the tension could increase any more, I spoke. "I owe Director Stemp an apology, and I want to apologize to all of you, too. I was acting childishly. I'm sorry for what I said, and I'm sorry for making everyone uncomfortable. It won't happen again."

"Thank you, Kelly, but as I said in my office, a public apology is unnecessary," Stemp replied. "We all know you've been recovering from some difficult experiences."

As he swept the others with his gaze, I was relieved to see them relax, the air pressure lightening in the room.

"I've asked Drs. Kraus and Travers to join us," Stemp began. A tap on the door interrupted him, and he glanced over to nod at the stunning blue-eyed blonde who leaned into the room, giving us a smile that would make birds sing, flowers bloom, and grown men fall helpless at her feet.

"...at sixteen hundred," Stemp finished, unperturbed.

I turned toward Germain, hiding my gleeful anticipation of his reaction. "Carl, this is Dr. Honey Travers, Jack for short. Jack, Carl Germain."

"Hi, Jack. Nice to meet you." Germain rose with his usual pleasant smile and offered his hand as if meeting brilliant and voluptuous scientists was an everyday occurrence.

"Hi... Carl." A pretty flush stained Jack's flawless complexion, her full lips trembling around his name for an instant before her usual poise returned. "It's nice to meet you, too," she added as she shook hands. "And this is Dr. Sam Kraus." She ushered forward the short, roly-poly man who had hung back in the doorway.

Germain's expression smoothed into watchful appraisal as he nodded. "Dr. Kraus."

"Please call me Sam." Sam shot a pleading glance in my direction. "Hi, Aydan."

"Hi." I couldn't quite summon up a smile to hide the chill of betrayal that still lurked in my heart. I settled for a non-committal twitch of my lips, relieved when Stemp spoke again.

"The doctors have been working on another version of the network key that allows Agent Kelly access to the network. Today they have a prototype to test. Dr. Travers?"

Jack stepped forward, looking unaccountably nervous. Opening her small briefcase on the coffee table in front of me, she lifted out the familiar band of electrodes and settled it around my forehead.

She slipped a tiny box out of her pocket and handed it to me. "Just go into the network and stay there for a few seconds. If that goes well, we'll try a sim, and then maybe some decryptions. But nothing outside our firewall for this first trial."

"Okay." I settled back on the sofa, closing my eyes.

"Wait!" Stemp's bark jerked me upright, my eyes popping open. I eyed him with confusion as he continued, "Kane and Germain, go into the network first. Wait for Kelly to enter. If anything unusual happens, get her out of the portal by any means necessary. Clear?"

Both men nodded, and Kane shot a narrow-eyed glance in Sam's direction. "Do you expect anything unusual?"

"No, no, of course not." Sam's pudgy fingers combed his snowy beard. "Of course not. No, this is just in the interests of... safety..." He trailed off and backed a couple of steps away from Kane's steel-grey stare.

Kane transferred his attention to Jack. "Jack? What's your take on this?"

"I don't see any reason why this should be any different than Aydan's usual access," she soothed.

Kane held eye contact for another second before transferring his attention to me, his voice softening. "Whenever you're ready, Aydan. We'll be there for you."

Despite my attempt to suppress my reaction, the echo of affection in Kane's voice warmed me. I sighed and leaned back on the couch. Forget it. Keep it professional. Safer for everybody.

Kane and Germain exchanged a nod and they both settled into immobility in their chairs, their eyes taking on the thousand-yard stare that indicated they'd entered the brainwave-driven network.

When I mentally stepped into the white void of virtual reality, I smiled at the two muscular avatars encased in combat body armour, submachine guns nestled in the crooks of their bulging arms.

"Are you all right?" Kane demanded, his gaze raking my face.

"Fine. Thanks." I peered up into the blank whiteness. "Hey, Jack, am I supposed to feel any different?"

"No." Her reassuring voice filtered through the external interface. "You shouldn't feel any different at all."

"Okay. How long do you want me to stand here?"

"Just until I get a baseline reading..." Jack sounded abstracted. "Just a minute..."

Kane and Germain bristled with readiness, scanning the void in all directions while I shuffled my feet, feeling foolish. A few long moments later, Jack spoke again.

"All right, try a sim now."

"Anything in particular?"

"Yes, do your mountain simulation. I have baseline data for that one."

"Okay." I materialized the virtual corridor and was about to head for a room when Kane stepped in front of me.

He jerked his chin at Germain. "I'll lead. Germain will cover our six."

They took their places and we moved along the corridor, Kane scouting ahead while Germain brought up the rear, both with their weapons unslung and ready.

Dammit, why all the caution? If Jack had just tossed me the key and said 'Here, try it', I wouldn't have worried at all. I held my face expressionless while nerves twitched in my stomach.

Inside the sim room, I eased out a long breath and

concentrated on the sun and spruce-scented air of my favourite mountain top. It sprang into being in an instant, the wind singing its eternal lullaby through the trees lining the long misty valley. My worries floated away to the distant horizon while diamond-bright spangles glittered on the blue satin of the lake a thousand feet below.

"Aydan!" Kane's voice jerked the tension back into my shoulders. "Can you give us something a little more defensible here?"

He and Germain stood facing outward on opposite sides of me, their weapons sweeping semi-circles around our exposed perch at the summit. A glance at the hard muscles in their jaws indicated that they didn't find the vista nearly as calming as I did.

I sighed and materialized a sheer rock wall behind us.

Both men relaxed visibly, placing their backs to the wall and continuing to scan the mountain and the sky above as if expecting an attack at any moment.

Another sigh leaked out before I could stop it. That constant vigilance was what made them the excellent agents they were. Unlike me, the dumb civilian who would undoubtedly cause them to die horribly.

The gut-wrenching screams of a man in unspeakable agony floated up from the valley below, rapidly gaining volume. Bulging muscles tensed beside me.

Kane shot a split-second glance in my direction before snapping his attention back to the valley. "Aydan? Are you doing that?"

I swallowed hard, willing the memory away. "Sorry. It's okay. Nothing to worry about."

Mountains. Sun. Wind. Open spaces.

Slow yoga breaths. Calm.

Concentrate, dammit.

The screams faded, leaving me trembling with reaction.

"You can come out now." Jack's sultry voice was a welcome sound.

Too wound up to navigate the corridor again, I dissolved the mountain sim and folded sim-space to place all three of us in front of the exit portal. Kane jerked his chin toward it, still watching the void around us, and I stepped gratefully through.

I opened my eyes in physical reality, frowning. "What the hell?"

Judging by my more-or-less unobstructed view of the ceiling, I must be lying on my back. A ring of worried faces hovered above me.

"Don't move yet. Just lie still." That was Jack.

"What happened?" I demanded.

"You lost consciousness. You were out for about thirty seconds." Jack's cool fingers pressed against the pulse point on my wrist. "How do you feel?"

"Fine."

I sat up despite her attempt to press me back onto the sofa. The room whirled once before settling into reassuring stability, and I shook my head experimentally. Nothing untoward happened, so I rose and stretched, elation swelling into my heart.

"Why are you smiling?" Jack peered into my face. "Sit down until I've finished my diagnostics."

I sat obediently, my grin spreading wide enough to make my cheeks protest.

"It didn't hurt." A laugh bubbled up and overflowed my lips. "Don't you get it?" I seized Jack's wrist and shook it gently for emphasis. "It didn't *hurt!* It was painless!"

Her smooth forehead crinkled into a frown. "You were unconscious. That's not an acceptable trade-off."

"Only for a few seconds. And it didn't *hurt*." I resisted the urge to leap up and do a victory dance. "This is great! What did you change from the original key?"

Jack shot a troubled glance at Sam. "We've made a number of changes. And we're nowhere near done testing. Don't celebrate yet."

I tamped down my happiness as best I could, but I couldn't quite wipe the smile off my face. "So let's test! What else do you need me to do? Should I try some decryptions next?"

"No..."

Jack frowned at Sam, who studied the floor, his fingers toying with his beard. When he dragged his gaze up, he eyed Kane fearfully before speaking to me. "You may not like... um... this next part..." He averted his eyes from Kane's frown and extended a hand toward me instead. "Aydan, you know I never meant you any harm, don't you?"

Trepidation crept up my spine on icy feet.

Kane's hard voice made us both twitch. "But you did harm her. Repeatedly."

"I'm sorry, I'm sorry, I didn't mean to..." Sam gave me an imploring look.

"Spit it out, Sam." My voice was as hard as Kane's, and Sam's throat worked as he swallowed, his trembling hands knotting together in front of him.

"I, um..." Sam's gaze darted to Jack's remote expression and glacier-blue eyes before settling on a point just below my chin. "*We*, um... we need you to go back into the network using your original key. Um... under my mind control."

CHAPTER 4

A heavy silence blanketed my office. Sam stood alone in the group, his hands clenching and then releasing to slide down his pant legs as though wiping sweat from his palms. A fine dew of perspiration glistened on his forehead.

"I'm not happy about this, either," he blurted. "You nearly killed me last time. I could die..."

His words faded into a gulp as he apparently realized some members of the team might welcome that outcome.

Stemp remained expressionless, but Kane and Germain eyed him as if viewing some pale and slimy creature slithering from a cesspool.

"No!" Spider's cry was pure dismay. "Aydan, no! Don't trust him!" He shot a wide-eyed glance at Jack. "There has to be another way!"

"I'm afraid not," she said slowly. "But we'll put as many safeguards in place as possible." She inclined her head at Kane and Germain. "That's why you're both here."

"But it won't help, we know it won't!" Spider sprang to his feet, raking his fingers through his hair to leave it standing in untidy peaks. "He just makes her invisible and then he can do whatever he wants and we'll never know!"

At last I managed to unlock my throat without letting a

scream escape.

"No, it's okay, Spider, you'll know." My voice came out in a dry croak, and I cleared my throat before speaking again. "My visible avatar goes silent and stops moving when he takes control." I turned to lock eyes with Sam. "More to the point, I'll know." I did my best threatening growl. "You won't fuck with me, will you, Sam? Because I won't hesitate to fry you like I fried Bert Cartwright."

The greasy smoke of a different cremation strangled me for an instant, but I wrestled the memory into submission. Just put on a good show. I won't have to hurt him if he's too scared to try anything in the first place.

Sam blanched gratifyingly. "I... of course I wouldn't, Aydan, you know I wouldn't... I'd never..."

"Good." I hid my fear in a decisive tone. "Let's do it, then. Jack, do you need me to do anything specific?"

"No, your role this time will be to let Sam control you." Her words sent a wave of claustrophobic terror gushing through my veins, and I clenched my fists and fought the adrenaline with a slow, deep breath. Then another.

Calm. Stay calm.

"Just breathe." Kane knelt beside the sofa, his grey gaze holding me above the sea of fear. "Just breathe," he repeated softly. "We won't let it go on for any longer than absolutely necessary."

Damn Dr. Rawling and his goddamn therapy. I was better at hiding my feelings before he got started on me.

"Thanks. I'm fine." I ignored the heat climbing my face and turned to Jack. "Whenever you're ready."

"All right." She eyed me unhappily. "You'll go into the network using your key as usual. Then Sam will take control..."

I breathed.

"...but he'll only walk you down the virtual corridor to the door of the file repository. That's it. Then he'll release you."

I managed a weak nod.

Stemp's voice cut the silence like a razorblade. "If he deviates from the plan in the slightest, you have full authorization to use deadly force. Kane, Germain, likewise." He drew a small gun, his reptilian features impassive. "I'll supervise Dr. Kraus's physical body here in the real world." His flat eyes evaluated Sam as if measuring him for a coffin. "I'm sure we'll have no problems."

Sam gulped audibly and sank into a chair, his face ashen.

I clenched my fist around the tiny electronic device Jack handed me.

Fine. I was fine. Nothing bad would happen. Just a short test. Nothing, really. Only a few moments. I'd be fine.

"We'll go in first and wait for you." Kane took a seat beside Germain and a moment later their vacant eyes told me it was time to go.

Deep breath.

Fine. I'd be fine.

The void bloomed into existence, ropes already binding my hands. Bars thickened around me, blotting out the light.

"Stop! Aydan, stop!" The cage yielded under the assault of Kane's powerful shoulders. Germain slid through the gap, his arms spread to hold back the bars, his muscles bulging and knotting with the effort.

"Aydan, stop, you control this!" Kane's voice penetrated my blind panic, and a moment later both men staggered at the sudden cessation of their effort when my prison evaporated into smoke.

"Sorry," I panted. "Sorry. I've got it under control now." My heart hammered in my chest. I hunched over to rest my elbows on my trembling knees, grappling for control over the jerky gasps that racked my body.

"Just breathe with me," Kane murmured. "In. Out. Nice and slow."

I straightened, embarrassment heating my face again. "I'm fine." I willed the panic away. Fake it 'til you make it. "Okay, Sam, let's do this."

When the sim turned syrupy around me, I screamed.

Screamed again and again, unable to stop myself while my visible avatar stood motionless and smothered in silence, its face frozen in a macabre mask of serenity.

With every fibre of my being I fought the need to lash out at the inexorable force that carried me away from my avatar, down the corridor toward the file room.

Everything as planned. Don't fight. It's fine. This is necessary.

The screams wouldn't stop.

Despite my efforts to comply, I went rigid, resisting the invisible presence that rode me. The force intensified and I battled it unrestrained, all my will absorbed in clinging to the last shreds of sanity that would prevent me from immolating Sam in the sheer defensive terror of a trapped animal.

The release was so abrupt I tumbled to the floor of the virtual corridor, my suddenly-audible screams tearing the silence. Scrabbling frantically for purchase, I launched myself to my feet in pell-mell flight.

"No! Aydan, no! Stop!" Kane's words made no sense.

As I dove for the portal, he and Germain sprang forward, their arms locking around me.

"Stay calm, we're getting you out!"

Screaming and thrashing against their restraining grasp, a tendril of comprehension reached me at last.

Out.

They were getting me out.

I went limp.

A moment later, the usual pain lanced through my skull when they carried me through the portal.

Back in my physical body, I jerked into a ball, hugging my pounding head. The remaining adrenaline of the panic attack dissipated in sobbing heaves of breath punctuated by my violent swearing.

When the pain subsided enough to allow coherent thought, I groaned and curled tighter on the sofa, wishing I could compress myself enough to vanish between the cushions.

Less than an hour into the briefing and I'd already freaked out like a hysterical child three times. That had to be some kind of personal record. How much more embarrassment could I heap on myself?

Well, hell, the possibilities were endless. Maybe I could top it off by peeing my pants or throwing up. Or doing both simultaneously.

"Aydan?"

I blew out a breath and uncurled to sprawl face down on the sofa for a moment before dragging myself upright. "I'm fine. Sorry, I was just stupid. I panicked."

I pried my eyes open and my heart contracted sharply at the sight of Sam's motionless body on the floor. My voice came out in a dry whisper. "Shit, is he dead?"

Stemp looked up from where he knelt at Sam's head. "No. Should he be?"

"No." I dared to breathe again. "Is he conscious?"

Sam groaned and struggled into sitting position, his normally ruddy face as pale as his snowy beard. "Why did you fight me?" he croaked. "You knew what we were planning to do. You agreed."

"I'm sorry." Shame heated my face. "I'm really sorry, Sam. I just panicked and I couldn't help it. It was all I could do not to kill you."

"...oh." His voice dropped to a tiny quaver. "Thank you, then." He crept to his feet and dropped into his chair again, wiping sweat off his forehead with a shaking hand.

"I'm really sorry," I said again to no one in particular. "What do we need to do next?"

"If you're up to it, we should proceed with the next test as soon as possible," Jack said.

I straightened my spine, ignoring the snivelling of my apparently-not-so-inner child. "Okay. What do I have to do?"

"Take the new key." Jack passed it over, and I relinquished the original with relief. At least I could skip the pain this time.

"We're going to repeat the last test..." she began. I shot a look at Sam, but he looked suspiciously sanguine. "...and this time Spider will be your controller," she finished.

"Wha... no!" I lurched forward on the couch, my heart leaping into my throat. "No! No fucking way! I'm not risking Spider's life. Not for anything."

"I won't control Aydan's mind. That's sick!" Spider's cheeks flushed scarlet, his eyes snapping.

"I'm sorry, but it's necessary." Jack's beautiful face was pale but determined. "Spider, this is only a one-time test. You won't be controlling Aydan on an ongoing basis. And Aydan, there's no reason to believe this will be any riskier for

Spider than it was for Sam."

"I damn near killed Sam! I was barely holding on! I won't do it! No fucking way!"

"I know you won't hurt me." Spider's voice trembled, but he met my gaze, his hazel eyes clear. "I trust you."

"No! No, no, no, goddammit!" I cut myself off with the realization that I was on the verge of adding a temper tantrum to my roster of childishness.

"Just no," I finished with as much dignity as I could muster under the circumstances. "Besides, how can Spider even do it? You said my key was customized to one user and one controller."

"That's not exactly accurate." Jack glanced at Sam. "It's actually a matched pair of keys. One is customized to you, and that's the one you've been using all along. I didn't realize that there's another key, a controller key, that matches it."

"Wait, so there have been two keys all along?" I glared at Sam. "You were hiding the controller key all this time, you-"

"Y-yes," Sam stuttered. "B-but it didn't matter to the operation of your key when you were going into the network by yourself," he added hurriedly.

Jack broke the brittle silence. "So anyway, your new key is customized to you just like the old one, but its matching controller key is customized to Spider."

"But... how?" Spider looked lost. "I didn't... Wait. Last week when you said you needed me for some tests..." His expression crumpled into hurt. "You lied to me!"

"I'm sorry, Spider, it wasn't a lie, we just couldn't tell you all the details-"

"Enough." Stemp's flat voice cut across Jack's apology. "Do the test."

Jack handed Spider a tiny case like the one I clutched in my fist, and he stared at the minuscule cube on his palm, his brow furrowed.

"No," I snapped. "I'm not going to do this."

Stemp's hard voice brooked no argument. "This is not a discussion. If you didn't kill Kraus, you won't kill Webb. You're wasting time. Do it."

Hot rage exploded into my bloodstream, hazing my vision red. Kane caught me as I lunged to my feet, his superior body weight bearing me back to the couch, his powerful hands clamped on my shoulders. Before I could react, he pressed his lips to my ear and breathed, "I love you."

Shock immobilized me, my jaw dangling on slack muscles while cold fear extinguished my anger with an almost-audible sizzle. Kane grinned and released me, stepping back to resume his seat in the opposite chair.

After another moment of ineffectual gaping, I summoned enough presence of mind to close my mouth and attempt an impersonation of normalcy. Before I could marshal my scattered wits into anger again, Spider reached over to squeeze my hand.

"Let's just do it, Aydan. It'll be fine."

Too rattled to even argue, I nodded and subsided onto the cushions.

CHAPTER 5

"Whenever you're ready." Jack's voice penetrated my shock, and I shook my head vigorously.

Get it together.

I glanced at Kane, the laugh lines still crinkled around his eyes even though his smile had smoothed into seriousness.

That lousy bastard. What a rotten, underhanded tactic. The corners of my mouth sneaked into a smile despite my best efforts.

Kane shot me a devilish grin before turning to Germain. "Let's go."

Their faces went blank as they entered the network, and I turned to Spider. "Are you sure?"

His grip tightened on my hand. "It'll be fine. I know you won't hurt me."

I eased out a long breath and stepped into the void.

Kane and Germain eyed me, poised for action. "No cage this time?" Germain inquired lightly.

I let out a short laugh on my whoosh of released breath. "No, I guess we're done with that."

"Aydan, I'm going to give it a try now." Spider's voice floated down from the virtual ceiling. "I don't really know what I'm doing, so I'm just going to see if I can get you to move a couple of steps. I'll try not to hurt you."

"It's okay, Spider, you won't," I reassured him with considerably more confidence than I felt.

The familiar thick stickiness descended, making my heart leap into a rapid drumming. Before I had time to panic, the heaviness dissolved, leaving only a sensation like the cloak of humidity preceding a thunderstorm.

I drew a cautious breath, my pulse still vibrating in my throat. A moment later, a nudge urged me forward a couple of steps. The sensation vanished completely, and I stared back at Kane and Germain from my new position.

"Aydan, are you all right?" Kane snapped.

"I'm... fine..." I drew a long, shaky breath. "Spider, are you okay?"

"I'm fine." His cheery tone weakened my knees with relief. "How was that? Are you okay?"

"Yeah." I straightened, drawing in confidence with another long breath. "Yeah, I'm fine. That was far easier."

"Good. Can you try a longer test now?" Jack asked.

"I'm game if you are, Spider. What do you want to do?"

"Let's just walk to the file room."

"Okay." I shook the tension out of my shoulders. "I'm ready."

Humidity wrapped around me again, and this time the nudge felt more like a gentle pull in the direction of the file room. Holding Spider's blithe smile in my memory for reassurance, I floated down the corridor like a balloon on a string.

The pull stopped outside the file room, and I glanced back to see Germain's sharp gaze riveted on my blank-faced avatar while Kane scanned the void around them, every line of his body broadcasting hyper-alertness.

The thick sensation vanished and I waved. "I'm over here."

Germain's head snapped around from where my avatar had stood only an instant before. "That's spooky."

Kane nodded, grim-faced. "I don't like it at all. What if some unauthorized person was able to take control?"

"That couldn't happen." Jack's voice floated down from the virtual ceiling. "The key pairs are completely unique. They have to be specifically programmed, and it's an extremely complex process that requires substantial baseline data from both subjects."

Kane looked unconvinced, but before he could speak again, Stemp's voice joined the conversation. "Try going outside the firewall now."

"Are you sure that's a good idea?" Kane asked. "Aydan won't have an anchor. I can hold her avatar the way I usually do, but it won't matter because she's not using the avatar at all. I'd only be holding a ghost."

"The person who controls her acts as the anchor." Sam's voice sounded more confident now that Kane's physical body had temporarily ceased to be a threat. "That's how the keys are designed, and that's why it was so risky when Aydan went into the network by herself in the past."

"And it didn't occur to you to mention it at the time," Kane snarled.

"Uh, I... uh..."

Stemp's voice cut in again. "Irrelevant now. Webb, Kelly, are you ready?"

"I'm not sure." Spider sounded nervous again. "I don't know how Aydan goes into the external network. I'm afraid I might accidentally make her visible to intrusion-detection software. And I don't want to force her into the network in case it hurts her."

Sam snorted. "Just push her in. That's why you're the controller. Ride her like a horse."

At least I was pretty sure he'd said 'horse'. If he'd said 'whore' I'd make the little shit eat his words with a side-dish of knuckles.

"That's sick and gross!" Spider's voice shook, and I could imagine the hot flush of indignation on his cheeks. "How could you even say that-"

"Webb." Stemp's voice silenced Spider's incipient tirade. "Kelly, any suggestions?"

"I can't really describe what I do." I tugged at a lock of hair, pondering. "How about... instead of you controlling me, do you think I could tow you along, Spider? The way you towed me to the file room?"

"We could try it," he replied cautiously.

"Whenever you're ready."

The air thickened, and I tried to ask if he was there. When I realized I couldn't speak, I had my answer. I drew a deep breath and let it out slowly, trying to slow the sudden racing of my heart.

Okay, so I couldn't speak. No need to panic.

I sent a mental inquiry toward the vicinity of my forehead, but didn't receive any response. Either I was doing it wrong, or we couldn't communicate while he was linked to me.

I imagined Stemp's voice saying 'irrelevant', and eased out another long breath.

Calm. Stay calm.

Concentrate.

Normally I'd turn myself invisible and simply stretch

into the tunnels of the internet. I was already invisible, so...

I reached.

A moment later, the busy flow of data packets whisked us away like a dry leaf in a rain-swollen stream.

Barely conscious of Spider's extra weight, I rode the exhilarating roller-coaster of data, snooping into emails and sliding through firewalls to browse data the rest of the world naively believed to be secure.

When I turned for home, Spider's presence illuminated the network connections like a beacon, and I navigated the convoluted tunnels with easy confidence.

Slipping back into Sirius's file repository, I hovered waiting, and a moment later the humidity melted away. Spider's laughter was the first thing I heard.

"Awesome! Holy cow, Aydan, that was totally *awesome!* That was so much fun! That was so totally, totally *cool!*" It sounded as though he was jumping up and down. "Holy cow, Aydan! Cool, cool, *cool!*" He burst into laughter again.

Grinning, I asked, "Are we done here?"

Jack's amused voice floated down from overhead. "If Spider can manage to contain himself, we need to do one more test. We need to see if he can fully control you and gather data without your knowledge."

I sobered and gulped, fear chilling my elation. "Okay. Spider?"

"Okay." All traces of laughter were gone from his voice. "Don't worry, I'll just try it for a few seconds."

I tried to swallow the dryness in my throat, but it was already too late. This time the thickness oppressed me, holding me like an insect trapped in amber. My attempt to draw a breath failed, and despite the knowledge that my avatar required neither pulse nor oxygen, my heart battered my ribs in reflexive terror.

Trapped!

My body instinctively fought the control, struggling to flail out, to defend...

Don't fight. Don't hurt Spider.

Trapped *trapped* TRAPPED!

The hold released and I fell to my knees, my frantic panting whistling in my throat. Fists clenched, forehead pressed to the floor, I battled the urge to run screaming again.

Breathe. Just breathe.

In. Out. Slow like ocean waves...

The frenzied pounding of my heart rocked my entire body.

"Aydan!" Spider's fearful voice made me jerk upright just as Kane and Germain burst into the file repository.

"I'm okay," I gasped. "I'm okay."

"Let's go." Kane scooped me up as if I was weightless while Germain scanned our surroundings, his submachine gun at the ready. We hustled down the hallway under Germain's alert defense, and moments later we stepped through the portal.

"Aaaaydaaan..."

"Aaydaan..."

"Aydan..." The distant whispers drew closer, gaining volume and clarity.

"*Aydan!*"

Kane's shout still reverberating in my head, I jerked upright with a grunt, my eyes flying open.

The room whirled into a vortex of colour that made me

clamp my eyes shut again as my stomach heaved. Hands lowered me back to my supine position and something blessedly cool pressed against my forehead.

I breathed carefully through my mouth, willing the nausea away. It subsided rapidly, and I drew a breath of relief. Didn't throw up. Won that one. I eased my eyes open a crack.

When my surroundings remained reassuringly stable, I opened my eyes fully to focus on the ring of worried faces hovering over me.

Déjà vu.

I sighed and groped at my forehead, encountering a cool, moist cloth. "How long was I out this time?"

"Almost five minutes." Jack's hand flew out to restrain me as I attempted to sit up. "Stay there. The ambulance should be here any min-"

She broke off at the sound of running feet and a thump from the corridor. "...now," she finished, stepping back to make way for the first paramedic.

My protests were soundly ignored while they strapped me into the stretcher and whisked me to the waiting ambulance.

In the hospital's small emergency room, Dr. Roth's familiar blonde chignon bobbed through the dark uniforms to my side.

"Hi," I said sheepishly. "Sorry, I think this is a false alarm. I feel fine now."

"I'll tell you when you feel fine," she snapped, her sternness belied by the humour in her eyes. She checked my vital signs with her usual practiced economy of movement before waving the attendants to wheel me down the hall.

I groaned. "Not another MRI. My brain's going start

glowing in the dark."

"The MRI doesn't use radiation." She kept pace with the stretcher, her keen gaze evaluating me. "Dr. Travers sent me your brainwave tracings. You showed a sudden drop in brainwave frequency, which she says corresponded with some tests you were performing at the time. We assume it was strictly a result of the test, but I want to check for anomalies just to be certain."

I sighed as we turned the corner into the MRI lab. "Can you do a quick physical and mammogram while you're at it? I'm due. Might as well make this worthwhile."

She laughed. "Maybe if nothing else has hit the emergency room by the time we're done. It's been eerily quiet today. Just one snowmobiling accident where I taped up some cracked ribs. I'm sure the entire population of Silverside is saving up their crises for Christmas Day."

"You're probably right." I held up a restraining hand as she approached with a gown and scissors. "Don't you dare cut off my clothes. These are my favourite jeans. I'll change."

She glanced over her shoulder at the technician before drawing a curtain around my stretcher. "All right, but stay on the stretcher. And if you lose consciousness on me, this is the last time you get any special treatment."

"Yes, ma'am." I wriggled my arm out of one sleeve of my sweatshirt. "Shit." With chagrin, I eyed the IV the paramedics had inserted in my hand.

"This is why we usually cut clothes off." Dr. Roth gave me a sympathetic smile. "It's okay, just slide your sleeve down and I'll lift the IV bag through."

"Thanks." I peeled off my clothes and donned the gown.

She nodded at my Glock nestled in its waist holster.

"You'll have to leave that here, too."

I gave her a grin. "I'm really glad you have a tiny hospital and a top-level security clearance. I'd hate to have to explain this in Calgary."

"I just don't want to take a chance on you holding me at gunpoint when I try to give you your sedative."

I swallowed. "Let's try it without. You know how much I hate sedatives."

She frowned, shaking her head, but I hurried on before she could speak. "I've been having therapy sessions with Dr. Rawling for the last two months. I think I'm managing my claustrophobia better now. I'd really like to give it a try."

It wasn't a lie. Not really. Well, maybe a little teeny white lie. At least the part about the two months of therapy was the truth.

"All right, we'll try it." She pulled an almost-convincing scowl. "Stubborn. But if I think you need a sedative, you're getting it."

I mirrored her scowl. "Stubborn."

Lying on the table while the technician wedged my head into place with foam blocks, I concentrated on deep, calming yoga breathing.

Slow, steady ocean waves.

The MRI wasn't even closed at the ends. I had been locked in a coffin-like crate and I'd managed not to freak out. I could do this.

I ignored the small internal voice that reminded me I'd knifed a man and thrown a chair across the room immediately after escaping the coffin.

Details. I hadn't freaked out while I was *in* the coffin.

I could do this.

"Aydan, just let me give you the sedative. Your heart rate

and blood pressure are spiking."

"No, I can do this. I know I can."

She sighed. "No, you can't."

The warm fuzziness flowed over me before I could protest again.

CHAPTER 6

I cranked an eyelid open and glared at the blurry Dr. Roth wavering at the foot of my bed. "Damn... sed... tives."

"Rest." She waved her magic wand and vanished.

When I opened my eyes again, she was in sharp focus beside my bed, and her magic wand proved to be a stylus she brandished while she made notes on the computer tablet propped in the crook of her arm.

"Better?" she inquired.

"I really hate sedatives," I croaked, fumbling for the controls to raise the head of the bed.

"Not too high yet," she cautioned. "You know, maybe you should discuss your rampant control issues with Dr. Rawling."

I took the joke as it was intended. "Yeah, look who's talking. Bossy." I gave the bed control another defiant poke, and she grinned.

"I'd love to stand here and watch you go slowly mad, but the paramedics tell me I have a new customer on his way to the ER." She scrolled rapidly through the data on her tablet. "I can't find any physical problem that would cause you to lose consciousness, so I'll agree with Dr. Travers that it was probably caused by your testing. Since she says you were unconscious considerably longer the second time, I'd suggest you limit your testing as much as possible. If the frequency or duration of unconsciousness keeps increasing, you could theoretically slip into a coma."

She peered over her reading glasses to fix me with a stern eye. "I want you here for at least another half an hour to make sure the sedative has dissipated sufficiently. For the next twenty-four hours, no driving, no drinking, no..."

"...operating heavy equipment, making important decisions, yada, yada," I finished. "I hate sedatives."

"Stop complaining and talk to your visitor." She pulled aside the curtain to reveal Spider fidgeting in the corridor. "And behave yourself," she added with a wink before striding away, already absorbed in conversation with an anxious-looking nurse.

Spider sidled into the cubicle and lowered himself into the chair beside my bed.

"How are you feeling?" He didn't quite meet my eyes.

"Fine, just a little dopey from the sedative."

In the silence that followed, he studied the cubicle curtain intently, his knee bouncing with nervous energy. When he started to pick at his cuticles, I laid a hand over his. "Hey, Spider, what's wrong?"

He twitched his bony shoulders, his gaze skittering over to make brief eye contact before sliding back to the curtain again. "Um... Aydan..." He swallowed.

Even through the residual haze of the sedative, nervousness tensed my gut. "What, Spider? Just say it, already!"

"Um..." Colour climbed his neck and set his ears aflame. "I have to tell you something, and I'm afraid you're going to be mad at me," he blurted.

"Spider, have I ever gotten mad at you?"

"Well, no..." He dared a sidelong glance at me before returning his gaze steadfastly to the curtain. "But this is... well..."

He gulped again. "I read your mind. When we were... when I was controlling you. I could see... personal stuff..." He shot me an anguished glance. "I'm sorry, I stopped right away as soon as I realized... but I couldn't help it, it was just there and I..." He hunched his shoulders as if expecting a blow. "I couldn't help it. I'm really, really sorry."

A cold wave swept over me, my heart plummeting to the bottom of my chest.

Oh, God.

All my personal demons and secrets stripped naked and spread-eagled in the harsh light of another's eyes. All the secrets I guarded that weren't even mine to share...

The air refused to enter my lungs.

"I'm really, really sorry!" Spider's agonized apology echoed in the distant buzzing that surrounded my head.

Oh, God.

Oh, *God*.

A torrent of heat made me light-headed, sweat prickling my skin. My ability to think and act returned in a rush and I seized his arm.

"Everything! Tell me everything you saw! Every detail!"

"I'm... sorry..." The words jerked out of him, and I realized I was shaking his arm violently.

With an effort I relinquished my hold and patted his hand instead. "No, I'm sorry, Spider, I'm not mad at you, I'm just really freaked out. Can you please tell me what you saw?"

He blushed to the roots of his hair. "It was... um..." His colour deepened to an unflattering shade of purple. "You and Kane, um..."

Shit, shit, *shit*!

I held my voice under tight control. "What else?"

"That's all, I swear! As soon as I realized, I stopped right away and put up a... a... I don't know, like a shield or something so I couldn't see inside your mind anymore." He hid his face in his hands. "I'm really sorry."

I drew a long, slow breath. "Seriously? That's all you saw?"

"I swear." He gave me a miserable glance through his fingers. "I'm really sorry."

Heedless of Dr. Roth's admonition to lie flat, I jerked up in bed to fling my arms around him. "Spider, you are the best of the best! You are the only person in the world I would trust with this, and you are the only person in the world with enough integrity not only to *not* snoop through my brain, but also to have the guts to tell me about it."

I squeezed him tighter. "You're amazing! You're, you're..." Words failed me and I planted a big smacking kiss on the side of his head, the only place I could reach. "Thank you!"

"Y-you mean... you're not mad?" He straightened slowly, hope rising on his face.

"Spider, you goof, I've never been so not-mad at anybody in my life! You're just..." I hugged him tightly again before releasing him. "You're the best!"

His ugly flush drained away into the pink of pleasure. "Really?" A smile illuminated his face, his eyes clearing. "You really mean that?"

"Abso-fucking-lutely!"

"Thanks, Aydan!" He beamed at me. "I was so scared

you'd hate me. And I promise, I won't say anything to anybody." He leaned closer, his eyes glinting mischief. "I kind of suspected it anyway."

I planted an affectionate elbow in his ribs. "You just shush. And anyway, it's not what you think..." I trailed off. He'd seen inside my mind. It was *exactly* what he thought.

"How much did you see, anyway?"

His blush told me everything I needed to know.

"Never mind," I said firmly. "Forget I asked. In fact, forget we ever had this conversation... *SHIT!*"

Spider twitched violently. "What?"

"Shit, shit, goddamn sonofa-fucking-god-damn-" I stifled myself and clutched his sleeve in a trembling fist. "Do you have a secured phone on you? Call Stemp! It's an emergency!"

At his wide-eyed headshake, I scrambled off the bed and dove for the locker beside the bed, the IV line yanking my hand painfully while I scrabbled at my waist pouch. "Fuck-fuck-fuck-goddamn-fuck!"

The room dipped and swirled around me. I concentrated fiercely while my pouch receded down a darkening tunnel.

On my knees. Head down.

Darkness clearing...

"Aydan, what... oh, sorry!"

I fumbled the phone free and turned as Spider whipped around to stare in the opposite direction. Distantly noting his scarlet ears, I hunched over to keep my head low and stabbed a shaking finger at the phone's speed dial button.

"Yes." Stemp's flat voice was the most beautiful music I'd ever heard.

"Get Sam Kraus locked down, now!"

"Stand by."

The empty line hummed, and I used the intervening seconds to process the combined evidence of Spider's averted gaze and the draftiness in my nether regions.

I was yanking the inadequate gown closed across my ass when Stemp's voice snapped back on the line. "Report."

"Sam read my mind. Everything in my mind! He knows everything I know!"

Stemp barked out an unintelligible word that might have been an expletive. "How do you know?"

"Spider read my mind, too, when he was controlling me with the new network key, but he stopped as soon as he realized what was happening, so he only got the thing I was thinking about right before I went into the network. Which wasn't anything classified, fortunately. He just told me now and I put it all together. I could tell when he was in my mind, it felt..."

I drew a deep breath and slowed my babble, realizing my voice was rising as though I'd been sucking on a helium balloon.

"...It felt heavy, sticky, syrupy, whatever you want to call it. And it lightened up as soon as he shielded himself from me. But when Sam was driving me, he was heavy all the way. And today wasn't the first time. He did it for the first time over two months ago. He's known for two months. That goddamn slimy bastard-"

"Stand by."

A few moments later, Stemp came back on the line. "He's secure. We've been holding him in the minimum-security facility since he was arrested in October. He's being transferred to maximum security now. I'll interrogate him personally. Good work, Kelly." He paused. "Dr. Roth reports you'll be discharged shortly. I'm glad you suffered no lasting ill effects."

I resisted the urge to gape at the phone. "Thanks," I mumbled.

The click of his disconnection was my only reply.

"Aydan...? ...ooohh..."

Spider's voice quavered into silence and I looked up in time to see him slump, his eyelids fluttering closed above chalk-white cheeks.

"Shit!" I sprang to catch him as he began to topple off the chair, the detached end of my IV line drooling a crimson trail across the white floor.

The room whirled again, Spider's skinny form impossibly heavy in my arms.

"Help..." My feeble cry floated into a darkening vacuum. Knees melting...

"What the- *Nurse! Emergency!*"

Strong arms. Flying...

The room stabilized, the bed firm beneath me again.

"What happened?" Kane's frown hovered above me. Scrubs-clad bodies bustled at the edges of my vision, their murmurs underpinning a chorus of electronic beeping.

"Is Spider okay?"

His frown deepened. "I don't know yet. What happened?"

"I just looked up and he was falling off the chair. Did he-"

"The full story," he snapped. "Your IV line was unplugged and the blood trail shows you were on the opposite side of the cubicle. What happened?"

"No, it's okay, that was just..."

I tried to sit up, but his heavy hand landed on my shoulder just as the room did a tricky little sideslip. I let him press me back onto the pillow and clamped my eyes shut until the bed stopped wallowing through space.

When I opened my eyes a few moments later, Kane grasped my shoulders and leaned down, worry and impatience creasing his brow. "Everything. Now," he demanded.

"Spider was just sitting beside me. We were talking when I realized..." I shot a glance around the curtained cubicle and decided on discretion. "...I had to call Stemp. Emergency."

Kane's face tightened, but he didn't interrupt.

"I jumped out of bed to grab a phone from my pouch and I guess that's when the IV line pulled off the bag. I finished my call, and when I looked up, Spider was collapsing."

He released me and straightened, opening his mouth to reply just as Dr. Roth strode in, her white coat decorated with smears of blood. She stuffed an errant wisp of hair behind her ear, further disturbing her formerly tidy chignon, and glowered down at me. "What were you doing out of bed?"

"Sorry, I had an emergency. I-"

"You didn't *have* an emergency; you *were* an emergency." She shot a look at Kane, lines of strain tight around her mouth. "She's to stay in bed, lying flat, for at least half an hour. She's in no danger; she only fainted because she got up too soon. The nurses will check in, but I'm counting on you to keep her under control. I have to go and..." She grimaced and gestured at the bloodstains on her coat before rushing away.

I stared at the still-swaying curtain for a moment, guilt gnawing at me, before directing an imploring gaze up at Kane. "Can you go and check on Spider?"

He frowned. "No. Dr. Roth made it clear you're my responsibility."

A small jab of pain from the IV made me relax the fist I'd clenched. "Come on, John! I promise I'll stay put. I have to know if he's okay."

He was shaking his head when the cubicle curtains parted to admit a tiny brunette in pink scrubs, her glossy ponytail swinging as she hurried in.

I sucked in a breath of relief mingled with fear. "Linda! Is Spider okay?"

"He's fine." Her blue eyes sparkled with mischief. "He just can't stand the sight of blood. When you detached your IV line, the clear solution drained out first so it took a few seconds before your blood started to escape. But as soon as he saw blood on the floor, he fainted."

"Oh." I blew out a breath I hadn't realized I'd been holding. "Oh, thank God." The tension melted from my muscles, leaving me trembling.

I waited until she'd finished checking the monitors before speaking again. "When you get a minute, could you please tell Dr. Roth I'm sorry? I didn't mean to make her mad."

She patted my hand. "I will, but don't worry, she's not mad. It's just that a little boy came in with a bad cut that needed suturing, but your security level makes you top priority. She was just stressed out because she had to leave him while she made sure you were okay."

"I'm really sorry."

"Hey, it's okay. Stuff happens." She gave me her radiant smile. "That's why they pay us the big bucks. Not. See you later." She bounced out, leaving me alone with Kane.

Oh God.

"Are you all right?" He hovered over the bed, eyeing me worriedly.

"I'm fine."

"Then why did you just groan?"

I converted my next groan into a sigh and beckoned him closer. His brows snapped together and he shot a glance over his shoulder before leaning in. I whispered, "Can you drive me home when they let me out? We need to talk."

His frown deepened. "That doesn't sound good."

I squeezed my eyes shut. "It's not."

CHAPTER 7

By the time Dr. Roth pronounced me free to go, my stomach was knotted despite the residual effects of the sedative. My nerves had slowly frayed while Kane and I made stilted conversation, and at last I had closed my eyes and feigned sleep, probably unconvincingly.

When I was finally installed in the passenger seat of Kane's Expedition, I read tension in the set of his jaw as we pulled out of the parking lot.

Before he could speak, I held up a warning hand and extracted my bug detector from my pouch, scanning the interior of the SUV while he drove in silence.

The sight of the steady green light didn't make me relax.

Shit, I didn't want to have this conversation. Ever.

Kane shot an impatient glance at me. "What is it?" he demanded. "What's wrong?"

I sank my head into my hands to avoid his gaze and vented the groan that had been trying to escape for the last half-hour. "Ask me what's *not* wrong."

"Dammit, Aydan, tell me!"

I couldn't think of a good way to start. "Sam Kraus read my mind. So did Spider."

Out of the corner of my eye, I saw his knuckles whiten on

the steering wheel. "What are you saying?"

I churned my fists in my hair before sitting up to face him. "Sam knows everything. Everything I know. Everything I've ever experienced, everything anybody's ever told me in confidence..." My voice choked into silence, the enormity of the invasion twisting my stomach.

The steering wheel creaked under Kane's grip. "That's bad." His voice was controlled, muscles rippling in his jaw. "I presume that's the reason for the emergency phone call to Stemp."

"Yes. He's probably interrogating Sam right now." My voice rattled in my throat and I wrapped my arms around myself, shivering at the horrible reality.

Everything. Sam knew everything. All the secrets and terrors and weaknesses I'd concealed from the world behind barriers reinforced by long years of defensive habits.

I was naked before him. Worse than naked. He had been inside all my secret places, violating me...

The tremors intensified, rolling through my body in long waves. Nausea clawed at my stomach.

"Aydan? Are you all right?"

I sucked in a deep breath. Say it. Say it all.

"He knows about you... um, us. So does Spider. He knows..." I pulled myself upright, bracing my shaking body against the seat.

Say it.

"He knows you said you love me. He knows we... had sex. Spider won't tell, but if Sam says anything, Stemp will know you lied to him and lied to your entire chain of command during that sexual harassment inquiry." The last of my strength deserted me and I folded over my roiling gut. "I *told* you not to get involved. I *told* you I'd hurt you!

Goddammit, John, *why didn't you listen to me?*"

"Aydan-"

"Stop the truck! I'm going to puke!"

He slammed on the brakes while I clawed at the door. The lock released and I stumbled blindly into the icy darkness, slipping and staggering down into the snow-covered ditch.

I rocked spraddle-legged at the bottom, elbows braced on knees, gulping huge lungfuls of cold air. My trembling legs threatened to give way and I groaned open-mouthed, my stomach heaving.

I groaned again at the squeak of rapid footsteps in the snow behind me.

"Go away." The words abraded my throat.

His touch washed another wave of nausea over me. "Aydan, let me-"

"Don't touch me." I staggered away a couple of steps, hot acid surging in my stomach.

"Aydan..."

"*Leave me alone!*" My legs folded and I fell to my knees, my fists clenching in the snow.

Breathe.

A jerky inhalation, my eyes streaming with involuntary tears.

Breathe.

Kane was mercifully silent behind me. The snow stung my knees through my jeans.

Breathe.

Swallow.

Breathe.

At last I managed two breaths in a row without my stomach heaving.

Three.

Four.

Violent shivers racked my body.

Kane's footsteps approached again. A moment later, his jacket enveloped me, the remains of his body heat warming my back.

"Aydan, I'm going to take you to the truck now," he said firmly. "If you throw up, so be it, but you're getting hypothermic out here. Come on."

At the pressure of his hand under my elbow, I tried to rise. My knees refused to cooperate.

"Come on, Aydan."

"G-g-give me a m-m-minute."

"No more minutes."

His powerful arms closed around me, and while he carried me up to the SUV I distantly reflected that it was one thing to dodge bullets, but it took a truly brave man to risk vomit. And carrying five-foot-ten-inch, 160-pound me up a snowy slope without any visible effort was damn impressive.

He strapped me into the passenger seat, peering anxiously into my face. My teeth chattered uncontrollably, and he frowned. "You're going back to the hospital."

"N-n-no. I'm f-f-fine. Just g-g-get me ho..." I swallowed another heave and breathed. "...home."

The door closed and a moment later he swung into the driver's seat and cranked the heat on high, still frowning at me.

I straightened and summoned every ounce of control I owned. "Really, I'm f-fine. Just upset..." My treacherous voice wavered and I gulped again. "...and chilled. I just need a hot b-bath."

I clenched my teeth and willed my shivering into

stillness under his scrutiny. At last he sighed and put the SUV into gear again, returning his attention to the road. "All right. But if you don't feel better soon, you're going back."

Relief eased the ache in my shoulders and I slumped into the corner of the seat. "Th-thank you."

When we pulled up in front of my farmhouse, I gave him a bright smile. "Th-thanks for the ride. See you tomorrow."

My escape was foiled when I wasted precious seconds trying to open the passenger door before realizing the electric lock was still engaged. By the time I punched the release button and got out, Kane was already standing beside the SUV waiting for me.

"Nice try," he said shortly, offering his arm.

I ignored it and stifled a sigh while I trudged up my front walk.

Inside the entry, I tried again. "Thanks for the ride. See you."

"Aydan." He eyed me with unconcealed exasperation. "In the first place, you just had sedation and you're on the verge of hypothermia. You shouldn't be left alone. And in the second place, we need to talk."

"Nooo..." The whimper escaped me before I could prevent it.

Christ, suck it up.

I stiffened my spine. "I was alone after sedation b-before and nothing happened. I'll hop in the tub right away, and I'll be f-fine. And..."

I bit off my words and fumbled the bug detector out of my waist pouch with still-shaking hands. We both eased out a breath when the light glowed green.

"...and I d-don't really think there's anything more to say," I finished. "We b-both know-"

"Tub. Now," Kane interrupted, steering me through the kitchen with firm hands on my shoulders.

"W-wait..." My protest went unheeded. In the bathroom, he turned on the bathtub taps full blast before turning to reclaim the jacket I still clutched around me.

I tightened my grip. "W-wait just a g-goddamn minute. In the f-first place, I'm perfectly capable of running my own bath. In the second p-place, the analysts saw you on my surveillance cameras, and I d-don't want them thinking we're having anything more than a short c-conversation before you leave. And last b-but not least, you are not g-going to undress me."

"Aydan, for crying out loud!" The bathroom seemed very small as he glowered down at me. "It's nothing I haven't seen before, and this is no time for modesty. You need to get warmed up, and I'm not leaving you unsupervised in a bathtub full of water when you've recently been sedated. Not to mention that you inexplicably lost consciousness not too long ago."

"It wasn't inexplicable, f-for shit's sake! It was just the new k-key." I yanked the jacket out of his grasp and pushed him in the direction of the door with approximately as much effect as if I'd shoved a mountain. "And j-just because you saw me naked before d-doesn't mean you're going to see me naked again," I added with more conviction than I felt. "G-get out of my bathroom and g-go home."

"You've got my jacket," he replied, nodding toward my white-knuckled grip. "And I'm not going anywhere. So you might as well get in the bath before it overflows."

"Oh, f-for..."

The storm-grey of his eyes told me I wouldn't win this argument. I stared up at him in sheer frustration. Getting naked in front of him was a bad idea for many reasons, none of which came immediately to mind. Which pissed me off even more.

"Out!" I snapped, bundling his jacket into his hands. "Unless you want me to file a real sexual harassment charge this time."

His eyes blazed, his jaw hardening before he turned on his heel and strode out, closing the door with more force than necessary.

I blew out a long breath that turned into a sub-vocal whine and twisted the water taps off hard in lieu of throttling him. Or possibly myself.

The hot water seared my icy skin when I crept trembling into the tub, and I sighed and thumped my head against the wall behind me, squeezing my eyes shut.

What a fucking disaster.

Okay, think it through. Maybe it would be okay. Kane hadn't actually lied to his chain of command about our relationship. Shit, it wasn't even a relationship; it was just sex. One time.

Okay, twice, but the first time didn't really count.

My mind wandered unbidden to that first time, generating a rush of heat that had nothing to do with bathwater.

Stop that.

I determinedly rerouted my mind. I'd *told* him it was nothing more than sex, dammit. If he had just let it go the way I'd told him to...

I groaned. That made it even worse. If we actually had a relationship, if I had given him something in return...

But I had given him nothing but heartache. And if Stemp found out that we'd slept together and that Kane had lied about it by omission, Kane would be court-martialed and imprisoned.

His exemplary career, his life, utterly destroyed. And for nothing.

All my goddamn fault.

I groaned again and slithered down in the tub, letting the hot water close over my head and listening to the pulse thumping in my ears. Heartbeats are supposed to go 'lub-dup, lub-dup'. I was pretty sure mine sounded like 'stu-pid, stu-pid'.

The suddenness of the hard hands on my body would have made me shriek if I hadn't been completely submerged. Instead, I inhaled a gout of water and instantly convulsed, choking and flailing. Blinded by tears and chlorine-laced water, I tore at my attacker's grip, raking his hands in feral panic.

"Aydan!"

Kane's voice swept me with a deluge of relief.

Coughing racked my body while he dragged me from the bathtub onto the bathmat, where I lay hacking and gasping. At last, I managed to control my breathing. Struggling onto my knees, I grabbed a wad of toilet tissue to wipe my streaming eyes and nose.

Kane knelt beside me, watching worriedly.

"What the hell?" I croaked. Another paroxysm of coughing seized me and I missed his reply. "Sorry, what?" I tried again.

"What happened? Did you pass out?"

"No, I was just underwater, I-"

His face went expressionless, his usually warm baritone flat. "Were you trying to kill yourself?"

"No! Shit, no! I was just-"

"Just what? Trying to scare the hell out of me? Or were you setting me up for another rape charge?" He made a short, angry gesture at the scratches on his hands. "Nice job. I'll wait in the kitchen while you call the police." He jerked to his feet and strode out.

"What... No, of course not. Wait!" I hauled myself to my feet and hurried after him. "I'm sorry! I didn't know it was you. Jesus, you scared the shit out of me." I tugged him back toward the bathroom, my heart still pounding.

When we rounded the corner into the light I winced at the sight of the livid red scratches. "God, I'm sorry."

"You didn't know it was me?" I glanced up to see his cop face softening.

"Of course not, I'd never attack you! I thought you'd left."

"No, of course not. I told you I wouldn't leave. I was just coming down the hall to check on you when I heard you groan. I tapped on the door and called, but you didn't answer. I was worried, so I peeked in. When I saw you underwater, I thought you had passed out and you were drowning."

"I couldn't hear you underwater. I'm so sorry."

"It's all right." His hands closed around mine. "You're shivering again. And you're dripping everywhere. Get back in the tub."

I hesitated, but it seemed a little silly to quibble over nudity at this point. Besides, I was freezing.

I clutched the edge of the slippery tub, my legs shaking with cold and residual shock. All we needed now was for me to fall and crack my skull open so the paramedics could find Kane standing over my naked, unconscious body. With fresh scratches all over him. Perfect, just perfect.

His hot hand on my elbow made me twitch with the sudden intense awareness of his closeness. "Don't slip," he rumbled. "Here..."

I let him help me into the tub, blushing despite myself. Dammit, so much for my noble vow to keep things professional. Or at least non-naked. I whipped in a liberal slug of bubble bath and scrunched down below the protective bubbles.

He smiled. "That's better. It's nice when you cooperate. Rare, but nice." Before I could retort, he added, "Do you have any antiseptic?"

"Peroxide in the second drawer. There are bandages in there, too."

"Just the peroxide is fine. You only broke the skin in a couple of places. The rest should fade pretty fast." He extracted the bottle and lowered himself cautiously onto the toilet lid. The plastic creaked beneath his weight, but held, and he began to dab peroxide on the scratches.

After a few moments he shot me a glance, his gaze coasting over the bubbles before meeting my eyes. He sighed and leaned back against the toilet tank. "So Kraus and Webb both know."

"Yes. I'm not worried about Spider, but Sam..." I couldn't control a shudder as the nausea seized me again.

"Just breathe." He stroked my hair. "It's not that bad-"

I bolted upright, sloshing water and bubbles over the side of the tub. "Hell, yes, it's that bad! It's worse! You don't know what it's like to have every single part of your... your... *being*... stripped naked. All your personal secrets, everything you've hidden, all the shameful little things you wouldn't want anyone to know..." My breath hitched and I gulped hard. "And it's not just my secrets, it's other people's secrets, too.   Yours.   Everything I know about you. *Everything.*"

The sick look on his face told me he finally got it.

My words poured out.   "Arnie's secrets.   Stemp's. Classified stuff... Oh God, John, if Sam blabbed even some of the stuff I know, an innocent little girl could die!"

"Stop!"   Kane seized my shoulders, giving me a little shake. "Yes, it's bad, but you can't change it. Don't make yourself sick over it. That's just a waste of energy."

"I know, but-"

"No buts. You know I'm right."

I drew a long breath and let it out slowly. "You're right."

"Relax. Calm down. Stay in here until you're warm. We'll talk when you're dry and... dressed." His thumb slid over my bare shoulder as he released me, and his gaze dipped to follow its path before meeting my eyes again. "I'll be in the living room. I'll check on you every few minutes. Call if you need help."

His voice had deepened again, and I swallowed and slid lower in the bubbles, hoping he'd mistake my flush for the warmth of the tub. "Okay. Thanks."

Thank God, he rose and strode out seconds before I could ask him to wash my back. Or anything else.

CHAPTER 8

When I finally emerged pink and pruney from the bathtub, my tremors had subsided and my stomach contents had agreed to stay put. My arms and legs felt like lead while I dragged my clothes on, pondering.

Okay, damage control.

In his interrogation, Stemp would identify any threat to his secret wife and daughter in Bulgaria. If there was any danger, he would make sure Katya and Anna were whisked out of harm's way. Anna wouldn't die.

Combing out my wet hair, I wondered what she looked like. I had a mental image of a cute little six-year-old with straight brown hair and solemn brown eyes, but I'd never seen a photo of her or her mother. Not for the first time, I marvelled at the dedication that kept Stemp here when his loved ones were so far away.

Kane's safety was what really worried me. I knew too much about him. Where he lived, where his father lived, some of his cover identities. Thank God I'd never gotten close enough to know too many personal details. What I already knew would be dangerous enough if it reached the right ears.

Most of my classified information would have been

accessible to Sam anyway through his own security clearance, so that probably wasn't as big a deal as I'd initially thought. And Sam's knowledge of Arnie's and my personal demons wasn't the end of the world. Creepy and mortifying, yes, but not actively dangerous.

And speaking of dangerous…

I let out a long sigh and padded toward the living room. When I poked my head in, Kane was slouched in the big upholstered chair, legs stretched in front of him, arms crossed, chin sunk on his chest. He straightened and gave me a smile that didn't hide the worry in his eyes. "We have to talk."

"Yeah." I flopped onto the couch across from him. "Do you think Sam would have sold what I know about you? Is there any market for that kind of information?"

Kane shrugged. "It would depend on who he talked to. It doesn't matter anyway. I'll take a few extra precautions around my house and condo until we know the results of Stemp's interrogation, but I expect if Kraus was looking for information to sell at a profit, mine would be low on the priority list."

"What about your dad? Could he be in danger?"

"Unlikely."

"You need to warn him, though."

Kane sighed. "I will, but he won't listen. Once a drill sergeant, always a drill sergeant. He thinks he's tougher than anybody on the planet." His laugh lines crinkled in a fond smile. "He may be right. I wouldn't want to tangle with him."

I chuckled, remembering Doug Kane's military bearing and the vigorous gait that belied his wrinkles. "I liked him a lot, even though I met him under bad circumstances."

"He liked you a lot, too."

An awkward silence descended.

"What will you do if Stemp finds out about us?" Kane asked at length.

"What will *I* do?" I frowned at him. "It won't matter to me at all." I cursed my tactlessness when I glimpsed the pain in his eyes. "Sorry, I didn't mean that the way it came out," I added hurriedly. "What I meant was, there likely won't be any consequences for me. I'm worried about you."

"No, I think you meant it exactly the way it came out." His cop face was firmly in place, his tone neutral. "You made it clear that you weren't interested in anything more with me, and you've been avoiding me for the last two months. And when you can't avoid me, you treat me like a casual acquaintance. One you're not overly fond of." The edge of hurt in his words slashed my heart.

"I'm trying to protect you!" My words burst out sounding angrier than I'd intended. "For shit's sake, John, it would've been bad enough if Stemp had found out we'd slept together, even before that whole rape and sexual harassment thing blew up. Now if he ever finds out, you'll get court-martialled for lying in front of your whole chain of command. You'll lose everything. No relationship is worth that!"

"Aydan, I know you have commitment issues-"

I sprang to my feet. "For chrissake, I don't have 'commitment issues'! I was married twice! Been there, done that! Not wanting to do it again does not mean I have 'commitment issues', it just means *I don't fucking want to do it again!*"

Muscles rippled in his jaw, but when he spoke his voice was even. "I didn't mean to imply the problem lay with you or even that there is a problem. I just wanted to point out that I don't happen to share your low opinion of committed relationships, and for reasons that escape me at the moment, my time with you was worth the risk. Is still worth the risk."

"And you're just going to go ahead and risk everything, aren't you? Whisper 'I love you' in the middle of my office-"

"You were about to explode. I needed some shock value to-"

"Right in front of Stemp! Oh, smooth! Really smooth!" With a supreme effort, I managed not to kick the sofa. "If you hadn't done that, I wouldn't have been thinking about screwing your brains out..." I faltered. Re-focus. "...and the only thing Spider would have seen in my mind was my worry about him instead of mental pictures of you naked..."

Goddammit, that wasn't helping.

I was trying to reorganize my thoughts into a coherent argument when Kane rose with that fluid motion that never failed to raise my temperature. He crossed the space between us, moving so close his body heat threatened to melt my resolve. His big hand cupped my jaw, tilting my face up to meet his hungry gaze.

"Tell me more about how you were imagining me naked." His sexy rumble stole my breath.

God, now it wasn't only my resolve that was liquefying.

I pulled away before I could do anything stupid. Well, stupider than remembering Kane's magnificent nakedness while his broad shoulders loomed over me, his bulging biceps stretching the sleeves of that snug black T-shirt...

I stumbled back another step and drew a shaky breath. "That's not the point. The point is, I'm not willing to risk losing you, and it's not fair for you to-" I snapped my mouth shut when I realized what I'd said.

He grinned and stepped closer.

I backed away, fetching up against the wall with a bump. "You really need to leave now."

He closed the gap again and planted his hands on the wall on either side of my shoulders, his hot gaze setting fire to my cheeks. My lips parted involuntarily, gasping a shallow breath as he leaned closer.

Trapped.

I trembled between the need to run screaming and the urge to rip his clothes off. Or both, not necessarily in that order.

Kane smiled down at me. "You're probably right." His voice caressed me like a lover's hands.

Like his hands had caressed me.

I jerked the hot memories to heel as he continued. "But when you finally admit to yourself that you want me, you'll beg me to stay." His smouldering gaze ignited places I'd thought couldn't get any hotter. "And you know how good it will be."

I summoned the last vestiges of my self-control for a light tone that might have been more convincing if I hadn't preceded it with a gulp "Modest, self-effacing fellow, aren't you?"

He stepped back, his wicked grin a vivid reminder of all the mind-blowing pleasure he could deliver. "No. Not at all."

I sucked in some air. "Well, um... thanks for everything. You really need to leave before the analysts get suspicious." My voice was slightly strangled by my heart, which had apparently decided to migrate up to my throat.

His grin dissolved into annoyance. "Aydan-"

"John, please! Just go. I'm fine. I've had sedation

before and I didn't react to it. If I was going to have a reaction, I'm sure it would have happened while I was half-freezing or half-drowning, and anyway I promise I'm not going to do anything more dangerous than puttering around the house tonight. But it's dangerous for you to be here too long, and..."

I flung up a silencing hand when he tried to speak again. "Don't tell me it's worth the risk! You won't think that when you're rotting in jail with your entire career in ruins! You won't think that when you get out and the only job you can get is flipping burgers because nobody will hire a guy with a prison record-"

"Don't tell me what I'll think or feel!" Kane towered over me, his sheer physical presence making my voice shrivel in my throat. He glowered down at me. "I'll decide what constitutes acceptable risk for me."

My faulty emotional wiring translated fear and frustration into anger in an eyeblink and I shoved him hard, his chest like rock under my hands. "Don't pull that dominant-male shit on me! You think I'm just going to fall into your arms and bat my big helpless eyes and say 'yes, dear' because that's the way you say it should be? Fuck that! I've got news for you, Buster-"

"Dammit, Aydan, you know I'm not..." He bit off his words and took a step back, his body easing into his deceptively relaxed combat stance. When he spoke again, his voice was calm. "I know what you're trying to do, and I'm not going to let you drag me into some childish fight just so you can drive me away. Look me in the eye and tell me you don't love me. Tell me you don't want me, and I'll walk away right now. Otherwise, stop trying to make my decisions for me."

I stared up at him.

If I lied to him now, he'd be safe. Safe from the consequences of deceiving his chain of command, and safe from the pain I'd inevitably cause him.

His steady grey gaze held me speechless.

Do the right thing, not the honest thing. Just say the words.

Say it, dammit.

"I..." My throat closed and I cleared it to try again. "I don't..."

He stood silently watching.

I sagged in defeat. "For shit's sake, John, this is stupid. You already know how I feel about you, and you know the reasons why I won't take it any farther."

"I know." His voice was level. "And in case you haven't noticed, I'm not exactly down on bended knee offering you a ring and a future. Even if I thought you wanted that, it's not something I can offer. So why don't you get over your irrational fear of..." He broke off and took a deep breath. "Sorry. I know you have your reasons. But 'I love you' is not a threat or a demand. Why can't you accept that?"

"I..." I gulped down the lump in my throat. "I'm sorry, I just... You're right, I overreacted." I shot a guilty glance at his scratched hands. "To everything. I'm sorry."

He reached for my hand and held it gently. "You don't need to apologize. You're dealing with a lot right now. I know how tough it is to go back after a bad mission."

Goddamn sympathy. I swallowed hard and blinked away the prickling behind my eyes, raising my chin and trying for rueful humour. "'Bad' is a tactful way to put it. More like 'gong show'. I did everything wrong from start to finish, you and Lola nearly died..."

My throat closed.

Not so humorous after all.

"It wasn't your fault, Aydan. Sometimes ops go bad. It's just the way it is. Try to let it go."

I drew a shaky breath and straightened my spine. "I know. Thanks. I'm fine."

"Aydan, it's all right if you're not fine." He dropped his gaze to our clasped hands. When he spoke a moment later, his voice was very quiet. "After I got shot the first time, I… didn't know if I could come back. Physically or mentally."

I squeezed his hand, remembering the small scar on his chest and the puckered devastation that marked the bullet's exit from his back. Another fraction of an inch…

"I did a lot of soul-searching in those first couple of months when I was too weak to do much of anything," he continued. "After I'd rebuilt my strength, I made the decision to come back, but even though I was physically ready for my first mission afterward, I know what you're dealing with mentally." He met my eyes. "You don't have to do it, Aydan. After what you've been through, nobody will disrespect you if you bow out."

"Except me." I gave him a twisted smile. "And Stemp."

"Stemp will push you until you break. Ignore him."

"I can't. I'm the only one who can do this."

Kane's fingertips brushed my cheek as he stroked a strand of hair away from my face. "We have other agents, and we'll get other chances to take Fuzzy Bunny down. You can walk away right now."

I met his gaze squarely. "Would you? Walk away?"

We locked eyes for a long moment before he sighed. "No. I didn't really expect you to, either." His eyes were sad above the small smile he gave me.

My hand flew up to caress his cheek before I could stop it. A rush of memories and emotion made me jerk back, breaking our contact. "What about you?" I asked hurriedly. "How are you dealing with coming back after getting shot this time?"

He moved as if to recapture my touch, but locked his hands behind his back and stood at parade rest instead. "I'm fine." His expression was unreadable.

"Physically fine." I searched his face. "But that's not what I'm asking."

He shrugged, an easy gesture I'd seen him fake convincingly even under intense stress. "I made my peace with mortality a long time ago, and recovery was a lot easier this time. It wasn't a major injury." His lips twisted. "Everything takes a little longer to heal than it used to, though."

I gave up and let him evade the question. "No kidding. But you're in such great shape, nobody would ever believe you're turning forty-nine in April."

Don't think about his shape. I yanked my gaze above his chin, only to find myself admiring the frosting of silver in the short dark hair at his temples. And those sexy laugh lines around his eyes. Yum.

His brows snapped together. "How did you know when my birthday is?"

I dragged my mind back to the conversation at hand. "The first time we discovered I could access the Sirius network, you had me read your personnel file as a test." I shifted under his intense scrutiny and shrugged. "I'm a bookkeeper. Numbers stick in my mind."

His gaze probed deeper. "I've always known you had an excellent memory for detail, but I'm beginning to wonder if you're hiding a memory like Hellhound's."

I laughed. "I wish. No, I'm pretty sure Arnie's photographic memory is one of a kind."

His expression eased, but the crease between his eyebrows remained. "Still, it makes me wonder what else you know that I don't even realize I've revealed. No wonder you were upset at the thought of someone reading your mind." I shivered involuntarily, and he gripped my shoulders with both hands, holding my gaze. "It'll be all right, Aydan. Let it go."

"I know." I stepped back before I could fling myself into his arms and beg him to make it all better. "Thanks."

Standing locked in each other's eyes, the silence stretched.

Kane blew out a long breath. "Aydan..." He hesitated, his gaze searching my face for a long moment before he turned away. "Never mind. I'll go now. Call me if you need anything."

When the door closed behind him, the house felt cold and empty.

CHAPTER 9

Freed from Kane's distracting presence, my worry returned full force. I paced back and forth in the silent living room, groaning and muttering imprecations like a madwoman.

Was Stemp still questioning Sam? What had he learned? Was Kane safely at home, or had he been arrested already, carted off to jail while I vibrated uselessly around my house?

And just in case that wasn't enough to raise my blood pressure, what the hell was I supposed to do about my 'standard physical qualification' in the morning?

I had no doubt I'd fail it. Super-fit guys like Kane and Germain could probably do it in their sleep, but all I did was pump some iron and run. Christ, I was forty-seven years old. Most women were expecting their first grandchildren at my age, not toting guns and doing spy-fitness tests.

Hounded by my yammering fears, I finally fled to my heated garage where I tinkered ineffectually with my half-restored '53 Chevy until bedtime.

After a fitful sleep disturbed by nightmares, I hauled myself through the shower and out to the kitchen in the morning, wondering if Kane was still a free man. When my phone rang at seven-thirty, I started so violently that my spoonful of cereal landed with a splat on the table. Swearing, I hurried to check the call display.

Private number.

I hovered beside the phone, my nerves strung tight while I waited for the message to play. A few moments later, Kane's voice spoke. "Hi Aydan, it's John-"

I snatched up the receiver and squeaked, "Hi." I cleared my throat and tried again. "Are you, um..."

"I'll swing by and pick you up around eight, if that's all right. I want to do some warm-ups before the test, and I thought you probably would, too."

"Oh, uh, yeah." My tired brain registered that my car was still parked in the lot at Sirius Dynamics. I could have driven my truck, but then I'd have two vehicles in town...

I yanked my mind back to the conversation. "Um, great, thanks. See you then."

I returned to my soggy cereal, but it had lost what little appeal it once had. I dumped it down the garbage disposal and went to pack some gym clothes that would be suitable for abject failure.

Perched in Kane's passenger seat, I waited until he put the SUV in gear before broaching my question. "What will we be doing this morning?"

"What do you mean?" He pulled out onto the road, snow squeaking under the tires.

"I mean, what does this qualification involve?"

He shot me a quizzical look. "You mean you've never done a qualification?"

"No! I'm just a bookkeeper."

He blew out an impatient breath. "Aydan, I understand how important it is to maintain your cover, but I really wish you'd drop it when we're alone together."

"John, please!" I squeezed my hands between my knees to keep from waving my arms and shouting. "Could you please just tell me?"

"Fine." He scowled at the road. "The first part is six laps around an obstacle course. There are some jumps and stairs and a controlled fall on each lap. Right after that we do the push-pull, seventy pounds six times each, with some controlled falls in between. We have four minutes for that. Then we do the eighty-pound weight carry."

I swallowed a large lump of nervousness. "How long do we have for the obstacle course?"

He shot me an irritable glance. "Four minutes *total*. For the obstacle course and the push-pull."

"For both?" The squeak was back in my voice. "How long is the obstacle course?"

"About 350 metres."

A tremor joined the squeak. "That's almost a quarter-mile."

He pulled to a stop at the highway and turned to face me, his frown softening. "Aydan, what's wrong? Are you nervous about this?"

I held out my hand to display its tremor. "Christ, what gave me away? I hope your seat covers are waterproof, because I'm about to pee my pants."

He chuckled and pulled onto the highway. "Don't worry, I've seen you work out. I know how strong you are. You won't have any trouble."

"Easy for you to say."

Inside Sirius's cramped time-delay chamber, Kane flattened himself against the opposite wall to give me space and eyed me with concern. "This is what you were really worried about, isn't it?"

"No," I gritted. "If I'd known the tests were going to be underground in the secured area, I'd have just passed out on the spot and saved myself the stress." I glanced at my wristwatch for the third time in fifteen seconds and made an attempt to ease my clenched jaw.

At last the secondary lock released and I lunged for the door. As usual, the narrow concrete stairwell made my heart leap in reflexive terror. My knuckles popped and I eased my deathgrip on my gym bag, wincing at the tingle of returning blood.

Breathe. In. Out. Slow like ocean waves.

I almost succeeded in stifling a small moan.

"Aydan? Are you all right?"

"Fine." I tottered down the stairs as rapidly as my shaking legs would permit and yanked open the door at the bottom.

Resisting the urge to press myself against the wall with my eyes closed until my heart rate stabilized, I gave Kane what I hoped was a casual smile. "Which way?"

"Left. Do you need a minute?"

"No, I'm fine. Lead on."

After a moment of scrutiny, he turned and headed down the long white corridor. I followed his broad shoulders, grateful for the momentary semblance of privacy.

Fresh air. There was lots of nice fresh air down here. I could breathe. I wasn't trapped. I could get out. Nothing bad was happening.

I licked dry lips, my tongue feeling too big for my mouth.

Ocean waves. In. Out. Ocean waves.

Near the end of the corridor, Kane opened a door and waved me forward. The open space and high ceiling of a full-sized gymnasium made me draw an involuntary breath of relief, slightly compromised by the sight of the stairs, barricades, mats, and traffic cones of the obstacle course.

A clean-shaven Germain called a cheerful good morning from the other side of the gym. I returned the greeting abstractedly as he carried a large sack over and swung it to the floor, his apparent effortlessness belied by the flex of the impressive muscles revealed by his gym shorts and T-shirt.

Shit, if that was the 'weight carry', I was doomed. I turned to study the obstacle course. Hell, who was I kidding? I was doomed before I ever got to the carry.

I sighed and headed for the change room.

Kane did the test first, easily running and vaulting through the obstacle course and manipulating the push-pull apparatus as if it was weightless The eighty-pound sack looked like a beanbag when he hoisted it smoothly atop his shoulder and ran the fifty-foot distance. He and Germain whooped and high-fived at his time, under four minutes including the carry.

As much as I appreciated his demonstration from a purely aesthetic standpoint, it did nothing to increase my confidence.

Germain turned to me. "Your turn. Don't let this show-off rattle you." He gave Kane a friendly punch on the shoulder. "I'll take him down a peg or two in the hand-to-hand combat qualification."

"In your dreams," Kane retorted, grinning.

I faced the obstacle course with trepidation. The distance was negligible compared to my usual runs, but with that time limit, I wouldn't have much breath to spare for jumping and climbing. I'd have to pace myself.

"Start whenever you're ready," Germain said.

"Call my lap times." I sucked in a deep breath and began at an easy run.

I stayed on pace for the first couple of laps, but my inadequate sleep and incomplete breakfast sapped my strength. By the last lap, I was drenched in sweat, my heart hammering my ribs.

"Go, go! You're doing fine!"

Kane and Germain shouted encouragement from the sidelines, but I knew I was already lagging.

"Push-pull! Go for it! Come on, Aydan!"

I staggered over to the apparatus, sucking air. Seventy pounds was well within my usual capability, but my body shook uncontrollably and nausea climbed the back of my throat.

"Come on, Aydan, go, go!"

I heaved on the apparatus, my sweat slicking the handgrips. One. Two. Three...

My temples pounded with the thunder of my heart, my strength trickling away like the sweat from my body.

"Come on, Aydan!"

Four...

I knew I'd failed when my cheering section fell silent.

Five...

Dammit, I'd do this if it fucking killed me.

Six.

I collapsed to the mat, heaving for breath.

"Good try, Aydan. You almost made it. You'll get it next time."

Still gasping, I squinted up at Germain. "What... about... the carry?"

"You don't have to do it. The test is over."

"Gonna... do it."

"Okay. Two minutes rest, and then the weight carry." Germain's voice held the sympathy reserved for certain failure.

I nodded, sprawled panting and trembling on the floor. Sweat poured off me. Two minutes of rest. I would do this, dammit. I'd already failed, but I'd damn well give it my best.

"Time." Germain's prompt came far too soon.

I stumbled to my feet and staggered over to the sack. "How much... time... do I have?" My voice was a raw croak, my breathing still ragged.

"It's not timed. You get three tries."

"Fine."

I squatted and gripped the sack. My trembling legs strained, barely straightening under the weight. With the sack hugged awkwardly to my chest, I managed to stagger a couple of steps before it slipped from my grasp and thudded to the floor.

Resisting the urge to lie down beside it and cry, I hunched over, elbows on knees, gasping for air. My head pounded as if it would explode, the metallic taste in the back of my throat nearly gagging me.

Do it.

I grabbed the sack again.

Lift.

Walk, dammit.

When it fell from my shaking arms after a single step, I knew I was done.

"Fuck... you... bastard..." I grated.

I hauled on the sack again, my lips drawing back in a snarl of rage.

The floor jumped up and smacked me.

Drenched in sweat and embarrassment, I sprawled on the hard floor, my body heaving with my struggle to suck in more air.

"Aydan!"

The floor vibrated under the thunder of running footsteps, and a moment later Kane knelt beside me, his face creased with worry.

"'M... okay," I gasped.

Germain appeared on my other side a moment later. "Just lie still. Ambulance is on the way."

"Not... 'nother... fuggin... 'mbulance..." I couldn't seem to catch my breath. I struggled to sit up, but failed when two sets of hands restrained me.

Failed.

Fuck.

I forced my mouth back under control. "Just need... orange juice," I enunciated carefully between gasps. "Be fine... in a... few minutes. Try again."

Kane and Germain exchanged a glance. "I think you'd better get checked..." Germain began.

"Especially since you passed out yesterday," Kane added.

"*Just give me the goddamn orange juice!*" My humiliation burst out in a shout that made both men start.

Kane scowled down at me. "Go and get it yourself."

Germain shot him a worried look. "I don't think that's a good idea-"

"Fine!" I tried to jerk upright and managed a twitch that raised my head and shoulders a couple of inches off the floor and made the room whirl around me. I collapsed back into two pairs of waiting hands and clamped my eyes shut, willing the nausea away.

"Smartass..." I muttered. "Hate it... when you're right..."

"What in heaven's name possessed you to do your qualification less than twenty-four hours after sedation and with no breakfast?" Dr. Roth fixed me with a gimlet eye.

I picked at the edge of the tape holding my IV line. "Sorry," I mumbled. "I thought the sedation would be gone. And the breakfast thing was an accident. I guess I just wasn't thinking."

"Aydan, I don't want you to apologize." She squeezed my hand, and I looked up to read the concern in her eyes. "I know your job description doesn't include words like 'careful' and 'safe', but I just hate to see you push yourself like this."

I shifted uncomfortably under her gaze. "I'll be smarter next time."

She sighed. "All right. I'll get Linda to take out your IV and do your discharge. Your bloodwork is fine, and I can't find anything wrong with you other than an excess of optimism and a severe deficiency in judgement. We'll do another glucose-tolerance test later, but I'm fairly sure it'll come back as normal as the last one we did. Just remember to eat frequent small meals, lots of whole grains..." She trailed off as I nodded. "I know you know all these things. Next time, pay attention to them."

"I will. Thanks. Sorry to bother you again."

"It's all right. That's what I'm here for."

CHAPTER 10

When I pulled aside the curtain of the emergency-room cubicle, Spider rose from the waiting chair to walk beside me, smiling. "I'm glad you're okay."

"Thanks. And thanks for bringing my clothes." I hefted the bag containing my sweat-clammy gym gear. "I wouldn't have wanted to wear this stuff back to the office. Sorry you had to go to all this trouble for me, though."

"I don't mind." We stepped out into the cold sunlight and he shot me a conspiratorial glance as we crunched across the snow of the parking lot. "It was a good excuse to see Linda." A flush rose on his cheeks. "I'm... I'm going to give her a ring for Christmas."

I halted to stare up at him, happiness bubbling up into a grin. "Seriously?" At his pink-faced nod, I flung my arms around him. "Oh, Spider, congratulations!" I gave him a squeeze before releasing him. "That's so great! I'm so happy for you!"

"Don't congratulate me yet." He eyed me anxiously. "What if she says no?"

"She won't. She's crazy about you."

"Don't tell anybody, okay? I want it to be a surprise."

"Of course I won't." I let out a giggle of pure joy. "Oh,

this makes my day!" I sobered as we resumed our walk to his car, remembering exactly what my day had been like so far. "Shit, Spider, I failed my qualification. What do you think Stemp will do?"

"I don't know." He frowned at his feet. "He told me to send you straight to his office when we get back."

"Shit."

"Kraus is dead."

I stiffened, staring at Stemp's impassive features. "What?"

"Kraus died of a heart attack last night. Apparently the strain of the last few days was too much for him."

I sagged into his guest chair, my mind whirling. Those were the last words I had expected to hear when I'd trailed reluctantly into Stemp's office a few moments ago.

Shock congealed into suspicion. "Were you by any chance interrogating him in the sim at the time?"

"No. He died several hours later."

I eyed his inscrutable face and decided not to ask awkward questions. I had other priorities. My heart thudded rapidly in my chest and I drew a deep breath, holding my voice steady. "What did you discover in your interrogation?"

"You were correct. He had been inside your mind. He had accessed all your memories."

My breath stopped. Stemp's face receded slowly and a faint buzzing filled my ears.

"And...?" I barely managed to squeeze the word out through stiff lips.

"And he told no one."

"He... what...? Are you sure?"

"My interrogation was very... thorough. The lie detector corroborated his statements."

"So..." I tried to take another deep breath, forgetting I hadn't released the first one yet. "What did you find out?" My voice came out thin and high-pitched.

He held me with his unsettling amber gaze before responding. "Without knowing exactly what you know, I couldn't press for specifics. The lie detector only evaluates yes or no statements. I simply confirmed that he hadn't leaked information of any sort."

Kane was safe. Thank God.

I let out the breath I'd been holding for hours, trying not to blow the papers off his desk. Only one worry left. "Did you ask about... Bulgaria?"

Stemp's eyes narrowed. "Yes. I was quite insistent about that. He specifically denied sharing that information with anyone at any time. The lie detector confirmed it."

"Thank God." I slumped back in my chair. "Thank God. I was just sick when I thought..."

His face softened. "Thank you for your concern. Unwarranted, fortunately."

I nodded mutely, too drained to respond. Sam, dead. A twisted mixture of relief and sorrow swamped my heart. I still believed he had meant well. Foolish, idealistic, selfish and thoughtless, but ultimately altruistic. May his soul find mercy. And Stemp's soul, too, for the murder I had no doubt he'd recently committed. God forgive me for tacitly accepting that.

Stemp's voice interrupted my uncomfortable reflections. "So you failed the physical qualification."

I jerked my chin up. "I told you I would."

"Residual sedation and low blood sugar due to fasting, the doctor's report says." The corner of his mouth twitched. "I must say I'm impressed with your creativity. Tell me, were you faking unconsciousness yesterday just so you could arrange to be sedated?"

I scowled. "No."

"That's unfortunate." He held me for a moment in his dispassionate gaze. "If I reschedule your qualification in a few weeks, do you think you might pass it then?"

"Probably," I muttered. "If I step up my workouts between now and then, and as long as I eat properly that day."

"And may I assume you'll fail the firearms qualification today as well? Considering that unlike my regular agents, I can't confiscate your weapon pending successful completion of the test?"

"I'll do my best. But yeah, I'll probably fail."

"So I should reschedule that test in several weeks, too, to allow you a plausible amount of practice time in the training range."

"A *reasonable* amount of practice time."

"Of course." The humorous twitch tugged at his mouth again. "Very well. Your dedication to your cover is impressive, if inconvenient. Go and fail your test."

Yeah, I failed.

The test might have been fun under different circumstances. My years of trap shooting made reacting to moving targets an enjoyable challenge, but I was jumpy and disoriented in the darkness and flashing lights. And I had never needed to evaluate the appropriateness of my targets before.

Slinking shamefacedly out of the practice range, I avoided Germain's gaze after blowing away several innocent bystanders as well as all the bad guys in the simulation.

"Nice clean shots," he mumbled. "Sorry, Aydan. You were just nervous, that's all. You'll pass next time."

I sighed. "Thanks, Carl, but I sucked. When can I get back into the range to practice?"

"Any time it's not in use. The schedule is available through the network." He changed the subject with obvious relief and turned with me toward the door. "Let's get going. Stemp's expecting you."

When we stepped into the time-delay chamber I drew a deep, shaky breath, mentally counting down the time delay. I twitched when Germain spoke. "That was some nice shooting."

"Yeah, except for the part where I killed the innocent civilians."

"You must practice a lot."

I spent a moment fervently wishing he'd shut up before realizing he was trying to distract me from my claustrophobia.

I forced my face into a smile. "Yeah, I shoot a lot at home." The lock released and I sprang into the lobby, sucking in a frantic breath of freedom.

Germain eyed me with concern. "You'd better sit down for a minute. You're shaking like a leaf."

"I'm okay." I drew a deep breath and let it out slowly. "It's just that damn coffin-chamber. It always freaks me out."

"All right, if you're sure."

I shot a glance at him as he strode beside me toward the

stairs to the second floor. "You don't need to escort me. I'm fine."

"I know, but Stemp asked me to come up with you after your firearms qualification." Germain gave me a wry twist of his lips. "Your impromptu trip to the hospital threw a bit of a wrench in the works. You've only got half an hour left to call Hibbert before noon, so Stemp asked Kane and me to be there while you make your call. That way we'll be prepared for the briefing at one."

Shit, I'd forgotten about that call. I threw out the first conversational gambit that came to mind, hiding the icy clutch of fear in my stomach. "I'm sorry I threw you off schedule."

"It's okay, you didn't really. We did Kane's hand-to-hand combat qualification while you were at the hospital."

I eyed him cautiously as we mounted the last few steps. He seemed to be favouring his left leg.

"Did he pass?"

Germain let out a rueful laugh. "Oh, hell yes. I'd have been shocked if he didn't. If I'm having a really good day, we're about evenly matched." He gained the top step, wincing. "Today wasn't a really good day."

I dredged up a semblance of tact. "Well, he does have a hell of a lot longer reach than you. You must be really good if you can match him at all. I'll never forget the time I saw him take out three guys at the same time."

He grinned. "Thanks, my ego needed to hear that." He motioned me forward to Stemp's door. "After you."

I drew a deep breath and tapped on the door. At Stemp's 'Come', I swung it open and paused, surveying the room's occupants suspiciously.

Kane and Stemp met my gaze with their usual aplomb,

but Dr. Rawling looked distinctly perturbed.

What the hell was he doing here?

"Um... hi." I shot a questioning glance at the doctor. "Um...?"

He uncrossed his arms and indicated the chair beside him, his features rearranging themselves into their usual placidity. "Hello, Aydan. Please sit." He gave me one of his sympathetic smiles, his kind eyes appraising me.

I sidled into the room and pulled the chair back toward the wall where I could see everyone without having to swivel my head. Kane and Germain shared an amused glance, and I allowed them a small smile in return. They knew me too well.

Stemp shot a look at the doctor. "Dr. Rawling, if you intend to have your say, do it now. We're running out of time."

Rawling leaned toward me, those damn kind eyes seeing more than they should. "Aydan," he said gently. "How do you feel about going back to active duty?"

I shifted in the chair and applied a tremendous effort of will to prevent my gaze from sliding sideways. "Fine."

"Aydan. This is a safe place. You've told me you trust your colleagues. You can trust them with your true feelings." His sorrowing-Buddha expression filled me with my usual intense desire to flee screaming. Or burst into the foulest invective I could muster and watch his ears bleed.

I squirmed again and avoided his gaze, but a glance at Kane and Germain revealed sympathetic expressions on their faces, too.

God*damn* sympathy!

Thank goodness Stemp still wore his usual stone-faced façade. I focused on his unprepossessing features with relief.

"Fuzzy Bunny is recruiting me. I'm the only one who can do this." I emulated Kane's easy shrug. "So, fine."

Stemp nodded. "Very well. In that case-"

"Director Stemp." Dr. Rawling's quiet voice overrode him effortlessly. "As I pointed out earlier, Aydan has been making excellent progress, but returning her to stressful situations prematurely is likely to trigger some undesirable reactions."

I flashed back guiltily to my childish behaviour of the previous day. Name calling and temper tantrums. Is that why Rawling was here? Had Stemp ratted me out?

Probably, the bastard. I was working up a good head of indignation when it occurred to me that Kane had accused me of childishness last night, too.

Shit.

Dr. Rawling turned back to me suddenly, startling me out of my embarrassed recollection. "Aydan, did you sleep well last night?"

"Um..." No escape, short of lying outright. "Not... not great. But I had a lot on my mind."

"Nightmares?"

I scuffed a toe at the carpet, wishing I could burrow into its short pile. "A few. But..." I straightened to meet his eyes squarely. "It doesn't really matter, does it? If we want to take advantage of this, I'm it." I shot a glance at my watch. Fifteen minutes. "And we're running out of time. I'm only agreeing to deliver a piece of paper. It's not like I'm going undercover for the next six months."

"But what if it leads to that?" Dr. Rawling's eyes bored through to my soul. "Are you prepared to deal with the consequences?"

"That would be extremely unlikely." Stemp's flat voice

gave me a welcome excuse to transfer my attention to him. "Typically, recruitment into an organization like Fuzzy Bunny takes months if not years. Requesting a small, ostensibly harmless item like a phone list is merely the first hook. After that, the requests typically escalate slowly as they test their recruit's loyalties. We can stall to give Kelly time."

"Though they did try to get Aydan to deliver a reverse-engineered fob two months ago," Kane put in. "That's definitely non-typical. Maybe they're being more direct than usual because they know about her cover identity's fraud convictions. Since they don't have to test her willingness to break the law, this could go faster than we think."

The cautious relief I'd been nurturing during Stemp's exposition evaporated and dread rushed in to take its place.

Dr. Rawling turned back to Stemp. "I didn't realize you were contemplating this. The only reason I discovered Aydan was taking her qualification tests today was because I received a routine copy of her hospitalization report from Dr. Roth this morning." His tone was distinctly accusing. "Considering that both tests indicated more preparation would be beneficial..."

Trust a shrink to find a nice way to say 'she completely fucked up the tests'. Despite my distaste for euphemisms, I indulged in a moment of gratitude for his tact. And that explained how he'd found out about this mission, too. Stemp hadn't tattled after all.

"...I have to reiterate that in my professional opinion, this mission is inadvisable for Aydan at this time," Dr. Rawling finished. He turned to bathe me in his usual expression of warm sympathy. "Aydan, you're a very strong person, but I know you understand the consequences of pushing yourself too far and too fast."

"Kelly, this is ultimately your decision," Stemp said. "And you need to decide. Now."

Four sets of eyes turned to me and I gulped, my mind racing. I could slink away like a coward and squander the opportunity. Or I could plunge in. Nightmares and panic attacks at best; torture and death at worst.

Fear rose to strangle me with icy fingers, but a moment later hot anger bubbled up to sear its grasp.

Fuzzy Fucking Bunny. Those bastards. What the hell would a little more fear matter to me? I'd been living in fear for months. Always wondering if today was the day they'd capture me. If today was the day they'd torture me and kill me and harm the people I cared about.

No more, goddammit.

Those fucking assholes were going down.

When I spoke, my voice was dead level. "Give me the phone."

My spurt of courage lasted exactly as long as it took for the phone to ring. When Hibbert's fatly satisfied voice spoke on the other end of the line, a stinging rush of adrenaline drove my heart rate into the stratosphere.

"Miss Widdenback. How nice to hear from you."

"Yeah." The word grated from my tight throat just before it closed up completely. Unpleasantly conscious of the four men watching me, I jerked to my feet and turned away to pace on the opposite side of the office.

What the hell was I thinking? I couldn't do this. I was an idiot civilian. And two top agents and the director of clandestine operations were watching me. Christ, now I had a whole new sympathy for performance anxiety.

Hibbert's voice filled the longish silence. "Not very

chatty today, are we?"

"Get to the point." Thank God it came out in a growl instead of a squeak.

He sighed. "Fine. Five thousand down, five on delivery. But you never did thank me for doubling the offer. And for such a trivial piece of paper, too." His voice deepened to an oily purr that made me shift the receiver to the tips of my fingers in pure revulsion. "I was hoping you might show me some... appreciation. I particularly liked that scene where you-"

"The only appreciation you'll get is from your own right hand." My voice still wasn't working quite right, but the anger helped. "It better be clean cash. Remember what I said. I don't work with amateurs."

"You don't know who you're dealing with, do you?" The purr was gone, and his tone would have made me shiver if I hadn't had an audience.

Stay angry.

"No," I snapped. "And I don't want to know. I just want the money."

"Fine. You'll find the envelope inside the toilet tank in the middle stall of the women's washroom at the Hogback Tavern. You can pick it up any time after ten tonight."

He sounded triumphant. That couldn't be good.

"Call me when you have the list," he added.

"Where's the Hogback Tavern?" I was too late. The bastard had already hung up. "Asshole," I added, and turned to face Stemp's inquiring expression. "I'm to pick up the first batch of cash tonight at the Hogback Tavern, wherever that is. Then I have to call him when I have the list."

"I'll have Webb research the tavern." He nodded dismissal. "Briefing in your office at thirteen hundred."

CHAPTER 11

Flopping onto the couch in my office, I suppressed a small belch and winced at the residual fumes. Note to self: When eating Greek salad at the Greenhorn Café, skip the onions.

I popped a couple of breath mints just as Spider walked in, his laptop tucked under his arm as usual. "Hi, Aydan! Oh, hey, can I bum a mint? I had major garlic for lunch." He dropped into the chair opposite me, his hand shielding his mouth.

I passed over the box. "Don't worry, I can't smell a thing. I just finished eating so many onions I think my sinuses are slagged."

As he handed the mints back, Kane and Germain strode in, followed by Stemp. As soon as everyone was seated, Stemp provided a succinct summary of the events to date before turning to Spider. "What do you have on the Hogback Tavern?"

Spider turned his laptop screen to show us a map and sent an anxious glance in my direction. "It's in Calgary." He tapped the red arrow displayed on his screen. "Not a good part of town." He switched to the street view, and I hid my dismay at the sight of the bar. The photo had been taken in summer. The harsh sunlight emphasized the bar's scarred exterior and blazed off the chrome of a long line of Harleys parked in front.

"Hogback. Go figure. It couldn't have been a nice quiet country bar, could it?" I muttered. "Hang on, let me write down the address. Do you have floor plans?"

"Yes." Spider flipped to another screen. I was mentally noting the position of the washrooms and exits when Spider spoke again. "I can print off a copy for you, but... are you sure you should go?" I looked up to see his forehead creased with concern. "It's a really rough place. There have been a couple of gang-related killings there.   You should take somebody with you at least."

"Gang-related killings take place everywhere, including in shopping malls," Stemp countered dryly. "Short of getting caught in the crossfire, they present very little threat to anyone except gang members. And you may recall Kelly infiltrated and blew up an enemy base single-handed. I seriously doubt she needs assistance to retrieve a package from a public bar."

Showed how much he knew. I'd need assistance to find my ass with both hands.

Spider subsided, looking unconvinced, and for an unworthy moment I wondered if he had looked deeper into my mind than he'd admitted.

No. He wouldn't lie about that. He was just being his usual tender-hearted self. I gave him a smile as Stemp spoke again.

"I'll prepare a phone list for you. Go down and collect the money tonight, and you can brief us on any new developments tomorrow at ten-hundred.   Once the transaction is complete, we'll have a better idea where this might lead, but for now let's run some scenarios."

Much later, we all leaned back in our chairs, and I massaged my aching forehead. Of all the possibilities the team had identified, the only one that gave me any comfort was the one I considered least likely: That Hibbert and his bosses would be satisfied with the phone list and bide their time before asking me for anything else. That just seemed too good to be true.

I stiffened my spine. It was better if they moved quickly. Hiding and hoping it would all go away was just plain stupid. And the sooner I started looking for their death ray, the better.

I was breathing through the terror of that thought when Stemp's voice dragged me back to the present. "One more thing, Kelly. If you do end up undercover, we want to make sure we have a good communication system in place. The doctors have completed their testing of the portable brainwave-driven network generator, and it's time for a field test. If it works as expected, it will provide you with an untraceable method of communication via the internet."

His flat gaze encompassed both Spider and me. "Webb, Kelly, please take the portable generator and the network key outside the building to make sure it works outside the range of our internal network. Report as soon as you've completed the test."

"Um..." My hand tightened instinctively on the tiny box. "I thought you didn't want the key to ever be outside the building's security perimeter."

Stemp released a breath I might have called a sigh if it had come from anybody else. "Now that we understand that you are literally the only person in the world who can use it, the chain of command has determined that we are willing to risk it if there are significant potential benefits." He met my eyes steadily. "Obviously, if you are captured with the key and the portable generator, the consequences will be…"

I mentally completed the sentence in the ensuing silence. 'Devastating to national security; agonizing and fatal to me'. If I was very lucky, the 'fatal' part would happen soon after the 'agonizing' part. Somehow I didn't think I'd be that lucky.

Stemp rose, freeing us from the quiet immobility that had gripped us all. "Please complete the test right away." He nodded and left.

"Would you like me to come with you?" Kane asked.

"Yes!"

"Yes, please!"

Spider and I spoke almost in unison. "In fact," I added, "Carl, if you have time, will you come, too?"

"Of course."

We all rose, and Spider and I exchanged an uncertain look. "Do you want to go to the Melted Spoon?" I asked. "I can sit down there so I won't fall over when I access the network, and we can all get a snack."

"I like that," Germain agreed. "The layout is defensible."

Kane nodded. "And it gives us a fallback position."

We all headed for the stairs. When we reached the lobby, Spider headed for the secured area to collect the network generator while I paced in small circles, listening to Kane and Germain discuss their defensive strategy in undertones.

Our procession down the sidewalk probably looked casual to the rest of the world. Germain strolled in front, turning to walk backward frequently in the guise of tossing banter to Kane, who was trailing Spider and me by a few paces. Watching them, I realized they were visually covering every direction, and I gave silent thanks all over again for their expertise.

We gained the fragrant warmth of the Melted Spoon without incident, and I drew a deep, calming breath of the coffee-scented air. Settling in our chairs with steaming cups in front of us, Spider and I exchanged a glance while Kane and Germain kept up their seemingly idle conversation, their surveillance blanketing the small bistro.

Spider plugged the small portable drive into his laptop and poked at a few keys before giving me a nod. I set my tea down and balanced my weight in the chair. Then I closed my eyes, reaching for the familiar void of virtual reality.

Instead, a rush of data swept me into the vast and complex currents of the internet.

A shock of terror galvanized me, and I twisted in the stream to fling myself back against the current, frantically searching for the path I had followed. Long seconds later, I reached the portal and slid through it, praying it was the right one.

"Ow, Christ!" I clutched my aching head with violently trembling hands. "Jesus, shit!" My heart pounded against my ribs, and I propped my elbows on the table, trying to calm my shallow panting.

"Are you okay?" Spider's anxious voice made me straighten and squint my eyes open against the fading pain.

"Yeah." I swallowed and drew a deep breath. "Shit." I clamped both hands around my cup to raise it shakily to my lips. My teeth clattered like maracas against its edge.

"You were only in for a second. What happened?" Spider's eyes were wide in his pale face. Kane and Germain still scanned the room, but they both eyed me worriedly as well.

"Just..." I shot a glance at the few other occupied tables. "Just not quite what I expected." I took another sip of tea and chased it with another calming breath. "Okay, I'm going to try again. I'll be a little longer this time."

My tea safely returned to the table, I closed my eyes for a moment of preparation. Okay, now I knew what to expect. I'd be fine.

When I stepped into the data flow, I held my virtual self stationary, studying the portal from the inside. It was distinctive, but I didn't know whether it was distinctive enough for me to recognize again if I got any distance away.

Okay, so I wouldn't go far. Only to Sirius.

I ignored the frightened little voice reminding me that physical geography was irrelevant to internet connections and I might be travelling to the other side of the world and back again. And I'd also have to breach the network security at Sirius once I got there.

Stay calm. Think.

Data packets rushed past me while I gathered my composure. If I could hitch myself to this node and stretch instead of letting myself get wholly swept up...

A few moments later, I extended my questing consciousness into the data tunnels.

The Sirius network was damn hard to find. When I located it at last, I bobbed in the data flow studying it, tethered by the elastic thread of consciousness that bound me to Spider's portal.

It looked benign.

I knew better.

If it was anywhere near as secure as the Knights' server, my tether would be snapped the instant I tried to get in. And then I'd be lost. Trapped forever in interminable tunnels...

Claustrophobia seized me and I fought the panic with everything I had. I wouldn't be lost forever. If I could find Sirius, I could find my way back to the portable network generator.

Before I could lose my nerve, I flung myself at the server.

It slapped me down like a bug, threshing my consciousness in a maelstrom of rejected packets. Completely disoriented, I flung frantic tendrils in all directions, seeking the relatively solid ground of a data tunnel. A couple of my threads connected, and I hauled myself out of the churning pool and collected myself bit by bit to quiver at the edge.

Lost.

I was lost. My tether was gone.

I clamped down on fear. One thing at a time. Stay calm. Just do this.

It took several terrifying tries before I at last discovered the way in. Shivering in the blessedly quiet corridors of Sirius's virtual network, I tried to pull myself together for the return trip.

It would be easier. I wouldn't get tumbled around. I could just sail smoothly down the data tunnels as usual.

The yammering voice of fear spiralled into a crescendo. Sail down the data tunnels to where? Completely untethered in a trackless maze of constantly-shifting connections?

"Shut up!" I spoke out loud before realizing my avatar was visible in the network. If anybody checked the records, they'd discover me standing here trembling like jelly and talking to myself.

Fabulous. When I died with my consciousness shredded and dispersed over the vastness of the internet, their last memory of me would be of a coward and a nutcase.

I was about to berate myself further when an idea dawned. At least I didn't have to look like a total loser. I ducked into a sim room and composed a short email to Stemp explaining that the test was in progress and detailing my experiences thus far. Then I blew out a long breath and slid back through the firewall into the data stream.

Daunted all over again by the immensity of the task ahead of me, I floated for a moment, gathering myself. Sifting through data packets was such a habit that I found myself doing it without conscious thought, like registering the words of a song playing in the background.

Camels.

Caught by the coincidence, I wished with all my heart I'd told Spider to send search requests over the internet to guide me home like we'd done before. Why hadn't I thought of that? Moron.

Camels. Camels.

A wisp of hope illuminated my heart. It couldn't be. Could it?

Camels-camels-camels-camels...

The searches came thick and fast, and I shot down the data tunnel after them.

Thank you, Spider!

I blessed his brilliance with all my heart while I traced the data stream all the way back to the distinctive portal and slipped thankfully through it.

"God, Jesus! Son of a bitch!" I hugged my head, whimpering in pain and abject gratitude.

"Aydan!" A light female voice penetrated my consciousness. "That's not good. We need to get her to the hospital. Call the ambulance!"

CHAPTER 12

Grounding myself with relief in the wonderfully real-world coffee fragrance of the Melted Spoon, I pried streaming eyes open to focus on Linda.

She was bending over me, her young face taut with worry. "Aydan, can you tell me what day of the week it is?"

I emitted a groan. "It's Wednesday. I'm fine, Linda. Sorry, I just get these really bad tension headaches."

"I've never seen a tension headache that makes you unresponsive." She frowned and extended her forefingers. "Squeeze my fingers."

I manufactured a smile and shoved it onto my aching face. "No way. I haven't fallen for that one since I was a kid."

"I'm not joking, Aydan. Squeeze my fingers! I want to make sure you're not having a stroke."

I grasped a finger in each hand and squeezed. "I'm not having a stroke, Linda, I promise. Ask these guys. They'll all tell you this is normal for me." I shot a significant glare at Spider's frightened face. Kane's and Germain's easy posture might have fooled the rest of the world, but I read their hyper-alertness in the hard lines of their faces and the tension bulging in their muscles.

Beside me, Kane chuckled, sounding perfectly relaxed. "It's all right, Linda. She really does do this all the time." He reached over to knead the base of my skull with his strong fingers. "Sometimes this helps."

I groaned and relaxed into his touch. "It always helps. Thanks." I met Linda's eyes. "I'm sorry. I heard you, it's just that I've got a really bad headache and I was in the middle of some relaxation exercises. I didn't mean to scare you."

She planted her hands on her slim hips, still frowning. "I still think you should be checked. A sudden intense headache like that can be one of the signs of a stroke or aneurysm. And you lost consciousness earlier. You might be having TIAs... mini-strokes," she explained to my uncomprehending frown.

I patted her arm. "But remember, Dr. Roth checked me over, and I was fine. And this really is normal for me. I promise if it gets worse I'll come in again, but there's really nothing to worry about."

She blew out a breath. "All right." Her usual sunny smile returned, but her gaze still probed my face. "You don't take good enough care of yourself. If you won't do it for yourself, do it for the people who care about you." She slid an arm around Spider. "Like this guy." She leaned down to kiss him fondly before turning her smile back in my direction. "And me."

"Thanks, Linda." I spoke around the pleasant lump in my throat. "That means a lot to me."

"I guess we'd better get back to the office," Germain said lightly. "We've been goofing off long enough."

We all rose with various expressions of simulated regret and made a hurried exit.

As soon as we gained the sidewalk, Kane extracted his phone and punched a speed-dial button. A moment later, he said, "She's back. We're coming in." He listened, then said, "Understood", and hung up.

I shot him a questioning look, but he simply said, "Let's go." He and Germain took their places and our procession resumed.

I leaned close to Spider. "What happened?"

He turned a still-pale face to me. "Stemp called me and said you were lost in the network so I started sending out camel searches, hoping you'd remember from when we did it before. Then Linda came in and said hi to everybody and you didn't react. Kane and Germain tried to distract her while I kept doing searches, but she had just leaned over and called your name when you came back. I don't know what we would have done if you hadn't."

When we gained the safety of the lobby at Sirius, Spider collected the network key from me and vanished through the door to the secured area.

Kane, Germain, and I drew a collective breath of relief, and I flopped into one of the chairs, letting my head drop back. "God, I don't know if my nerves can take much more of this."

"Actually..." Kane sounded troubled.

I squeezed my eyes shut. "Oh, God. What?"

"Stemp wants you in his office. Right now. Minutes ago, in fact."

I groaned and hauled myself to my feet.

When I tapped on Stemp's door a few minutes later, he looked up from his computer with his usual lack of expression. "Come in. Close the door."

Aw, shit.

I did as he bade and shuffled over to stand in front of his desk.

"Sit."

I sat.

"What the hell were you thinking?" Coming from a man of his monumental self-control, the sharp demand had the same impact as a full-throated shout.

"Um...?"

"What made you think it was a good idea to dive into the internet when you knew you wouldn't have any way of navigating back?" His tone cut like a scalpel.

"I, um..." There didn't seem to be a good answer to that. I hung my head. "Sorry."

"You're sorry." There was a long silence. When I looked up, he was pinching the bridge of his nose as if trying to push back a headache. At last he spoke. "Don't be *sorry*. Be *careful*. Dismissed."

I rose to slink out, but his voice stopped me with my hand on the doorknob. "Thank you for conducting the test."

"You're welcome," I mumbled, and fled.

In the lobby again, Kane and Germain eyed me with concern. "You look like you just gave a pint of blood," Germain said.

I tottered over to the security wicket to turn in my fob. "You know the expression, 'he tore me a new one'?"

Germain grimaced and nodded.

I turned for the door. "He didn't tear. He sliced with surgical precision."

"Ouch."

"Yeah." I offered them a weak salute. "See you guys tomorrow."

Safely outside, I leaned against the building in the long

rays of the setting sun and breathed the cold air, quieting my mind. As I watched, the glowing orange sliver of sun vanished below the horizon and purple shadows deepened. A glance at my watch made me sigh. Only four-thirty. At least the days would start getting longer soon.

A vibration from my waist pouch startled me out of my reverie, and I thumped my head lightly against the building at the sight of the call display. Shit, I'd forgotten about the damn self-defence workshop. Maybe I could weasel out of it.

I punched the Talk button. "Hi Lola."

"Hi Aydan!" Her bigger-than-life voice made me smile in spite of myself. "I can hardly wait for tonight! Do you want to come over for supper and we can just go from my place?"

Her enthusiasm scuttled my hopes for escape. Damn.

Well, I'd promised.

I summoned up a cheerful tone. "Sure, that sounds great. What time do you want me?"

The rec centre's gym looked like an audition for Hollywood exercise videos. Most of the twenty or so women sported designer workout gear along with perfect hair, nails, and makeup, and perfume scented the air. Jack smiled and waved from the other side of the gym, movie-star gorgeous even in her sweatpants and T-shirt.

I sighed and fiddled with my ponytail, using the motion to sniff surreptitiously in the vicinity of my armpit. The morning's sweat had dried on my T-shirt and sports bra, and they were distinctly gamey. A layer of fresh deodorant had helped a bit, but as soon as I started to sweat again it was going to get nasty.

Lola nudged me, and I straightened as one of the gym's two personal trainers waved for attention from the front of the room. "Ladies!" She waved again, her blond ponytail swinging above her perfect little size two pink crop-top and tights. "Ladies!"

The group quieted and she gave us a megawatt smile, radiating so much bouncy energy that I experienced an overwhelming need to haul my aging decrepitude to a dark corner where I could crumble quietly into dust.

Since the room lacked dark corners, I pulled myself up a little straighter and tried to summon some enthusiasm instead.

She had more than enough to compensate. "Hi everybody, I'm Brianna, Bree for short! Welcome! It's so great to see you! Are we ready to kick some butt?"

A few chirps of agreement made her shake a playful pink-tipped finger at us. "I didn't hear you! Give me a 'hell, yeah'!"

"Hell, yeah," we parroted obediently.

"What did you say?" Brianna cupped a hand behind her ear. "Give me a 'HELL, YEAH'!"

This time the response had a little more volume, but it wasn't good enough for Brianna. "I CAN'T HEAR YOU!" she shouted.

This time the responding bellow rocked the gym, and she let out a whoop, punching a small fist at the air. "RIGHT ON LADIES!"

God, if she got any more enthusiastic, I was going to have to go over there and smack her.

Then again, maybe that was the whole point of a self-defence seminar.

"Ladies, I know you're as excited as I am about this, so I

won't keep you waiting any longer. As you all know, we are soooo lucky to have such a wonderful instructor for this workshop! He's an RCMP officer and martial arts expert..."

A sense of impending doom made me squeeze my eyes shut.

"...so please give a big hand for Officer John Kane!"

My eyes popped open to glare down at Lola. "You set me up. You evil little-"

She returned an expression of wide-eyed innocence. "How could you even think that? I signed you up for a valuable course led by a highly-qualified instructor."

Kane strode to the front of the room to applause followed by whispering and fluttering from the crowd. Hell, I didn't blame them. Standing there with his killer body displayed to advantage in a snug T-shirt and gym shorts, he looked like a dream come true.

A smoking-hot dream with a dangerous edge. Twenty pairs of female eyes drank in the still-visible suture marks on his muscular thigh and the thin white scar that bisected his eyebrow. And if they only knew what was under those clothes...

He smiled, increasing the room temperature by about ten degrees. "Thank you for coming." His velvet baritone caused another small murmur in the crowd, and he waited for our full attention before speaking again. "In an ideal world, you wouldn't need self-defence skills. But since this isn't an ideal world, tonight you're taking an important step toward making the world a safer place for yourselves. I'll be teaching you techniques and strategies that will help you minimize risk, as well as protect yourself if you find yourself in a dangerous situation."

He eyed us gravely for a moment before speaking again.

"I want to emphasize that although it's important and potentially life-saving for you to be aware of risks and proactive about your own safety, it's absolutely not your fault if you have been attacked or if you are attacked in the future. No matter where you go, no matter what you're wearing or what you do or say, an attack against you is a crime and the blame lies solely with the perpetrator. Never forget that."

Lola slid an arm around my waist to give me a quick squeeze and I swallowed a lump in my throat, glancing over the suddenly solemn faces in the room.

Kane continued, "The other thing to remember is that you'll almost never win in a contest of physical strength, so you don't want to let a conflict escalate to that point. May I have a volunteer?"

A flurry of hands waved, but Kane met my eyes over the heads of the crowd. Shit. Why did I always have to be taller than every other woman in the room?

"Lola?" he asked. "Will you help me out?"

A grin split her wrinkled face. "Sure thing, Big John!" She scurried up to the front, pursued by envious glances from the rest of the participants.

When she stood beside him, he smiled down from his nearly two-foot height advantage and engulfed her bird-like wrist in a large hand. Turning to the group, he said, "I've just cornered Lola on a darkened street and grabbed her arm. I outweigh her by more than a hundred pounds. I'm bigger, stronger, and younger. Who's going to win this fight?"

A nervous ripple ran through the audience. Nobody seemed willing to state the obvious.

Kane grinned. "She is."

"RIGHT ON LOLA!" That was Bree, echoed by whoops and hollers from the rest of the group.

Kane waited for the bedlam to die down before sobering. "But she's not going to win with physical strength. First we're going to identify some danger signs and talk about ways to avoid danger in the first place. After that we'll discuss strategies for removing yourself from a potentially dangerous situation as quickly as possible. And tonight you're going to learn and practice some basic wrist locks that can help to deter or disable an assailant. Let's get started."

Kane was an excellent instructor, though I found myself wondering whether he would have received the same rapt attention if he'd been short, fat, and bald.

I shrugged off my cynicism. Despite their fluffy appearance, most of these women were serious about learning as much as they could. They should be damn proud of themselves. I smiled down at Lola, affection warming me.

"What are you smiling at?" She screwed up her face into a threatening scowl. "I'm about to bring you to your knees."

"Just go easy on my thumb," I cautioned as we took the positions Kane had demonstrated. "My arthritis is really kicking up in this cold weather."

"Wimpy old lady," she scoffed, grinning.

As we stepped through the motions, Kane finished coaching the pair of women next to us and moved to Lola's side. "That's good, Lola," he encouraged. "Aydan, I'll take over now."

I rose from the mat and stood aside to watch as he took his position, towering over Lola.

"All right, Lola, take me out."

She sprang into action like a tiny tiger, her hands dwarfed by his bulging forearms.

"Twist it and bend," he encouraged. "Use the arm for leverage. Harder!"

Lola redoubled her efforts, and Kane sank to the mat, tapping her hand to signal her to release him. "Good job, Lola. Aydan, your turn."

I eyed him uncertainly as he rose and faced me, but he didn't give me time to think. His hand shot out and I seized it, tentatively securing the wrist-lock but afraid to apply too much pressure.

His muscles bulged against me. "Harder! Take me right down to the mat!"

Come on, brain, quit with the double entendres. I ignored the rush of heat and pressed a little harder, feeling him going down on me...

Jeez, I wish.

Shut up, brain, just shut up.

His tap made me release him as if his skin had burned me, and I stepped away breathing a little harder than necessary.

"Good job, Aydan." Did his gaze linger for just an instant before he turned away to the next pair of women?

"Holy cats, that was hot!" Lola's whisper echoed my thoughts. She leaned closer, bouncing her eyebrows. "I'd pay good money just to have him on his knees in front of me. Learning self-defence is a bonus."

I shook myself back to reality with a grin. "You're incorrigible."

Shivering in my car after the class, I groaned at the illuminated dashboard clock. Nine-fifteen, pitch dark, freezing cold, and I was about to drive two hours for the privilege of walking alone into a biker bar in the middle of the night.

Well, just give me a 'hell yeah'.

I cranked up the tunes and hit the road.

CHAPTER 13

Belting out an off-key rendition of 'Back In Black' along with the radio in an attempt to bolster my inner badass, I peered out at the grey highway and dirty-white snow unrolling in my headlights. Riding an open road on a bright sunny day was one of my greatest joys, but tonight the oppressive darkness crouched beyond the bubble of light, waiting to swallow me. I shivered despite the warmth of the heater.

The song segued into unidentifiable thrash metal and I pressed the next preset button, hoping for more musical encouragement. Garth Brooks began to sing 'If Tomorrow Never Comes', and I snapped the radio off and growled, "You're not helping, Garth!"

Silence closed around me and my mind crept unwillingly toward the glow of Calgary's streetlights reflected against the cloudy sky, only half an hour ahead.

Maybe it wouldn't be too bad. It was the middle of winter, the middle of the week, and the middle of the night. Surely bikers hibernated in winter, curled up snoring and snuffling in their beards while they dreamed of sunshine and open roads.

The mental image brought a smile to my lips as I

imagined Hellhound in sleep, his quiet snores soothing me like a lullaby.

The smile fled as quickly as it had come.

God, why had I been such a pathetic wimp in front of him? He'd probably had to wash that shirt twice to get all my tears and snot out of it. Better to just let that whole thing end quietly.

I shook myself back to the business at hand. Be alert and avoid conflict. Just get in and get out. I replayed the mechanics of the wrist lock in my mind.

No, don't piss around. Pull the Glock at the first sign of trouble and get the hell out of there.

Fine.

I'd be just fine.

My heart sank when I cruised past the bar. Even with my windows rolled up, the thunder of heavy bass pummelled my ears when the door crashed open to disgorge three large bearded men. They stumbled down the cracked steps, their bellowed obscenities audible even above the din of the music.

Apparently bikers didn't hibernate in winter. They garaged their bikes, got madder and meaner, and went to the bar.

Shit.

I drove on by, thankful I'd stopped at home to exchange my shiny new car for my battered half-ton truck. It fit right in with the broken-down winter beaters that lined the sides of the street.

Parked a block away, I eyed the decrepit building, clutching the steering wheel with shaking hands. Goddamn Hibbert and goddamn my idiot mouth. If I hadn't pissed him off playing high and mighty, I could have just quietly accepted the envelope he had offered in the safety of Blue Eddie's. Now I was being punished for my insolence. No wonder he'd sounded triumphant, the bastard.

I eased out a long breath, trying to slow my pounding heart. Okay, options.

I could just drive away. Phone Hibbert, apologize for my rudeness, and ask him nicely to deliver the money somewhere else.

Yeah, like that would work. Not. He'd make me do penance one way or another, and I was pretty sure what form it would take. He'd want me on my knees, and it wouldn't be to say Hail Marys. And considering my damn porn-star cover, it would be pretty implausible to refuse.

Option two; phone Hellhound and ask him to escort me in.

I sighed. In the first place, it would be cheesy to ask him to risk his skin after avoiding his calls for two months. And in the second place, I didn't want him to take the risk anyway. Alone, I was entertainment, not threat. Hellhound's bulk, tattoos, and fearsome face would up the ante far into the danger zone for both of us. And I didn't want Fuzzy Bunny to even catch a glimpse of him. The farther away he was from me, the better.

Option three; phone Kane and wait two hours or more for him to arrive.

He would come if I asked him. It was his job to deal with dangerous situations. Besides, maybe by two A.M., the denizens of the bar would be getting tired and heading for home.

Yeah, right.

Option four. Pull up my big-girl panties, walk the hell in

there, and get the goddamn money.

Option five...

There had to be an option five, dammit. I was too tired to wait for Kane and too scared to walk in there by myself.

I straightened in the seat. What the hell was I afraid of? So they were bikers. So what? This was just a seedy bar in a big city with a competent police force. I might get hassled, but it wasn't like I was going to get gang-raped and killed. Just because they were bikers didn't mean they were criminals. And even if they were, a dead body was more trouble than they needed.

Probably.

I swallowed.

Minutes ticked by while I sat paralyzed by indecision. Kane's words about mitigating risk and avoiding conflict rang in my ears. If anything happened, how could I face him knowing I'd brought an attack on myself through willful stupidity?

Assuming I was alive to face him at all.

Shit.

Maybe I should just call him.

But dammit, I couldn't expect him to run to my rescue every time Stemp gave me an assignment. He couldn't do his job and mine, too. And Stemp was going to keep giving me assignments, since I obviously hadn't managed to convince him of my incompetence. Yet.

Well, maybe it was time to change that.

I slid my hand under my jacket to touch my Glock and the small trank gun I'd requisitioned, and got out of the truck before I could second-guess myself.

I had only taken a few steps when the flashback ambushed me.

Hard hands pinning me spread-eagled, naked and utterly helpless. Struggling uselessly while the abhorrent touch slid up my leg...

My heart lurched into a choking rhythm, hammering in my throat and temples. I forced my shaking legs to keep moving, rejecting the fear with all my will.

That wouldn't happen again. And if it did, so what? Old news. I dealt with it before; I could deal with it again.

Another wave of memory dragged me into its vicious undertow. That nasal voice was seared in my mind: 'First I'll strip you naked.' The agony of my bonds. The horrible portent of the sex toys laid out on his bed. The red-hot slash of his whip...

I flinched and an involuntary whimper squeezed from my throat.

Cut it out, dammit. Just breathe.

Keep walking.

Kane's voice echoed in my brain. "Listen to your fear. If you're feeling fear, it means you need to remove yourself from the situation, no matter how unreasonable that may seem. Always trust your instincts."

"Yeah, unless you're me," I muttered. "Then it's your stupid job to face your stupid fear."

I tottered closer, forcing my wooden lungs to expand and contract. Belly breathe. In. Out.

Two burly figures exploded from the door of the bar, fists flailing. Even from half a block away, the smell of liquor and stale cigarettes carried on the cold air. I pressed against the building beside me, knees trembling.

One man swung a haymaker, the meaty thud flashing memories of blood and broken bone before my eyes. His victim dropped like a stone.

Roaring, the first man kicked the huddled figure over and over, the thumps of his boots overlaid by his grunts of effort. At last he hunched over the motionless heap, gloating or catching his breath, before lurching away down the sidewalk. A snatch of drunken song floated back to me as he receded.

"Listen to your fear." Kane's voice rang so clearly in my memory that I twitched a glance up and down the street despite the knowledge that I was alone.

The body on the sidewalk lay silent and unmoving.

I fled as fast as my shaking legs would carry me.

Safely locked in my truck again, I leaned my forehead against the steering wheel, panting and quivering. When I finally brought my breathing under control, I peeled stiff fingers off the steering wheel and straightened. The dark bundle still lay on the sidewalk, and it occurred to me that I should probably call the police.

Even as the thought crossed my mind, the fallen man stirred and rolled slowly over to haul himself to hands and knees. He wobbled for a few moments before creeping over to the building to crumple into a semi-seated slump against the wall.

A couple of men emerged from the bar to lean against the front of the building, and cigarette lighters flared. The seated figure groped in his pocket and a moment later he lit up, too. Red embers glowed while the three men apparently enjoyed a convivial smoke and a chat. Several minutes later, the two men ground out their cigarettes and returned to the bar, and the human punching bag staggered to his feet to weave an uncertain path down the sidewalk.

And a good time was had by all.

Shit.

I'd had a brief but happy vision of the police arriving to question everybody in the bar and take my statement, allowing me to plead a long journey and stroll into the women's washroom unmolested. So much for that bright idea.

Three more men came out to smoke, their voices rising in coarse laughter. It seemed incongruous, these rough outlaws obediently observing Calgary's strict indoor smoking ban, but I guessed even the Hogback had to knuckle under to the bureaucracy that granted its license.

Wait a minute.

Spider's floor plans rose in my memory. The washrooms were right next to the back door. And I'd never been in a bar where the smokers didn't slip out the back door and leave it ajar while they had a quick puff.

I put the truck in gear and headed for the convenience store I'd spotted on the way in.

Cigarettes in hand, I scooted around the corner into the dark alley and pressed myself against a garbage dumpster.

Stay calm. This would work.

Old nightmares clawed at the edges of my mind, but I drove them back. No time for that now.

I peeked around the dumpster and drew a breath of relief at the sight of the single bulb that cast a jaundiced glow over the back door of the bar. Male laughter and a female giggle made me draw back as a couple of men and a woman came out. Moments later, the smell of cigarette smoke wafted over.

I hunched against the cold steel, waiting. A few minutes later, the voices receded and the door banged shut.

Showtime.

I scuttled over to the door, fumbling a cigarette out of the pack. The lighter gave me a moment's trouble. How the hell did these things work? Smokers made it look so simple.

After a couple of tries, I managed to generate a flame. I held the cigarette over it. A few wisps of smoke rose, but not the cloud I'd hoped for. Dammit, I needed to smell of fresh smoke just in case a real smoker showed up.

I fitted the filter to my lips and sucked cautiously without inhaling. No time to get caught helplessly hacking up a lung. I blew out smoke and stepped into the cloud. That should do it.

With shaking hands, I stubbed out the cigarette and reached for the door.

Locked.

Son of a bitch.

I hovered, shivering with cold and nerves. Dammit, my destination was only a few feet on the other side of this door. Why didn't they leave the fucking door unlatched?

I was fighting the urge to run back to my truck and drive far, far away when the door swung open, thumping me on the shoulder. To my relief, the man who emerged was shorter than I was. He mumbled what might have been an apology as I grabbed the door and pushed past him.

For a moment, I actually thought I was going to make it.

The door was already swinging shut behind me; the women's washroom only a few steps away when a yank on my sleeve stopped me.

Adrenaline slammed into my veins as I whirled, my hand already seeking my holster.

A familiar miasma of stale cigarette smoke and beer registered along with recognition.

"Jane Crazy-Bitch!" The weedy little slimeball clinging to my sleeve grinned hugely, revealing uneven teeth the colour of tobacco. "I been dreaming about your sweet pussy for months!"

I backpedalled as he stepped closer, invading my personal space to push his face close to my neck and sniff deeply. "Goddamn, you still smell crazy good! You wanna fuck now?"

"Not now, not ever. Back off, Weasel."

Loud thumps inside the men's washroom made me shoot a fearful glance over my shoulder.

"Aw, come on, Jane Crazy. You wanna hit me. Admit it."

"You have no idea." Inspiration bloomed, and I suppressed my disgust to lean close. "I just have to go to the bathroom and then I want to sneak out the back door without anybody seeing me. I promise I'll take you out in the back alley and beat you up if you stand guard for me."

His face lit up. "Awesome, Jane Crazy!" He shoved his hand down his pants. "Mmm, I'm getting hard just thinking about it. Promise you'll whip my ass!"

I backed away, tension winding up in my gut when a large leather-clad man gave me an interested glance before shouldering past to disappear into the men's washroom.

"Okay, fine! Just watch out for me, all right?"

Weasel groaned, his hand movement accelerating into a vigorous tempo. "That's so fucking hot. I'm gonna jizz in my pants right now."

"Don't," I snapped. "Stay alert. If you let me down, I won't lay a finger on you." I followed the dire warning with a ferocious glare and ducked into the women's washroom.

Seconds later the wall shivered under a tremendous thud from the men's room next door. Enraged bellows erupted, and I flinched with the not-too-unreasonable fear that the combatants might crash right through the wall. The shouting and banging continued as I dove for the middle stall only to pull up short.

Occupied.

Goddammit!

I wavered in fear-soaked indecision for a moment before whisking into the adjacent cubicle and closing the door behind me.

A dismal groan from beside me was followed by retching, and the smell of vomit made my stomach lurch.

Great, just great. How long was this going to take?

More groaning and heaving.

I huddled in the stall cursing my luck. What the hell was I supposed to do now, just hang around until she was done? I doubted Weasel had much of an attention span at the best of times, and he was drunk tonight. How long before he lost interest or forgot? Or worse, blabbed to somebody?

The only marginally good news was that I wouldn't have to manufacture an excuse for hanging around. I was pretty sure the occupant of the other stall was too immersed in her own misery to care about me.

The truth of that supposition was brought home only moments later when a wet thud emanated from the next cubicle and a limp arm flopped under the divider.

Shit, now what?

No way I was going to hang around until she came to. Or until somebody came looking for her.

Clenching my teeth, I eased out of the stall and stood staring down at the feet protruding from under the adjacent door. I heaved a long sigh.

"Sorry," I muttered insincerely as I grabbed the

unconscious woman's feet and dragged her out. Fortunately she wasn't large, but I was sweating and out of breath by the time I manoeuvred her flaccid body to a relatively out-of-the-way location beside the grimy sinks. A smear of vomit marked her progress across the floor, and I gulped down nausea while I wrangled her into recovery position with her head turned to the side. At least she wouldn't choke on her own puke.

Turning back toward the stalls, the full horror of the situation dawned on me. The damn cubicle door was locked from the inside.

I hesitated queasily for only a few seconds. This was far beyond my gross-out threshold, but gross was better than dead. I paved the disgusting floor with paper towels and squirmed under the door, arching my back to keep my face as far from the malodorous mess as possible.

Averting my eyes from the revolting spectacle inside the cubicle, I managed to lift the lid off the toilet tank and retrieve the dripping plastic-wrapped envelope with only two dry-heaves. Thank God the water in the tank was clean. It was the only thing in the cubicle that was.

Bursting from the stall holding my breath, I scrubbed my hands compulsively, trying not to look at the nameless grime caking the sink. Copious amounts of soap later, I stowed the envelope in my jacket pocket and turned toward the door, my heart rising with cautious hope.

In a few moments I'd be out. Come on, luck, just hold a little longer...

I cracked the door open and hissed, "Weasel!"

No reply.

I clenched my teeth. Goddamn that slimy little shit.

I poked my head out for a quick reconnaissance and

came face- to-face with Paul Hibbert.

CHAPTER 14

Hibbert smiled and leaned close to yell over the ear-splitting music. "Good evening, Arlene. Or I understand it's Jane tonight?" His eyes glittered dangerously in the dim light of the corridor, and the solid kick of alcohol on his breath did nothing to reassure me.

Goddamn Weasel. Sold me out.

A surge of adrenaline blocked my voice, but I was saved from replying when the fight in the men's room spilled out into the hallway. Two thrashing bodies slammed into the wall and tumbled to the floor at our feet, fists and obscenities flying.

"Can it!" Hibbert shouted, and the combatants froze before scrambling to their feet to hang their heads like chastised children.

"Sorry, Mr. Hibbert," one of them mumbled as they shuffled back in the direction of the bar.

"Now, where was I?" Hibbert turned back to me, his gaze skimming contemptuously over my unclean jacket. "Not flattering, I'm afraid. We'll have to get you out of that."

I found my voice. "No need. I was just leaving."

His arm flew up to bar my way as I turned for the back door, and a vision of Kane's wrist-lock flashed through my mind. My hands were rising as if of their own volition when Hibbert grabbed my arm, twisting viciously.

I let out a yelp and folded at the waist, following the path of the force to prevent my arm from breaking. Bent double, my mind floated up through the fear to distantly note that this must be the arm-bar hold Kane had mentioned we'd learn tomorrow night. Assuming tomorrow ever came for me.

Shut up, Garth.

Something hard/soft pressed against the side of my head. Please don't let that be Hibbert's crotch.

His next slurred words confirmed my fear. "You owe me a thank you."

A shove on my shoulder dropped me to my knees. My cry of pain was lost in the thunder of the music. Concealed by my bent posture, my free hand flew to my Glock.

Through my panic, the voice of reason whispered.

Stop. Think.

I couldn't deliver what he wanted when he was securing my arm this way. He'd have to change his grip. Let me straighten a little...

He grabbed a handful of my hair, jerking my head toward him. I catapulted beyond fear into detachment.

The music would hide the gunshot.

My gun was half-drawn when a second thought stilled my hand. If I killed Hibbert now, my cover would be completely blown with Fuzzy Bunny.

And the consequences would be as bad as blowing Hibbert. Probably worse.

I left the gun in its holster.

Contorting my neck at a painful angle, I met his eyes. "You don't seriously expect me to give you a decent blowjob here in the hallway with these wackos interrupting us, do you?"

He sketched a bow, his sophisticated business veneer not quite hiding the drunken animal behind his eyes. "Where do you want to go? Lady's choice."

I seized the opportunity. "Anywhere but here. Do you have a car?"

"Of course I have a car. But my office upstairs is much more comfortable." He yanked my arm, the jolt of pain jerking me to my feet. "Let's go."

Get out. Just get out of here.

"Do you have a bed in your office?" I blurted in desperation.

"No." He squinted at me.

I summoned the sexiest voice I could manage, considering I had to shout over the music. "You'll get a whole lot more than a blowjob if you take me to a nice hotel. After all, if we're going to have a mutually beneficial relationship, we should start off on the right foot. So to speak."

He shot me a suspicious glance from unfocused eyes. "Why are you being so nice all of a sudden?"

"I have your money now." I patted my pocket with my free hand. "And I got your point. I don't like doing business in places like this. I'm sorry for being such a bitch, and I want to make it up to you."

What a load of shit. If he was sober, he'd see right through me. He hesitated, swaying slightly, while my mind ricocheted through possibilities.

Shooting him was out, but what if I tranked him? The trank guns were classified weaponry, so I'd have to find a way to do it when he wasn't looking. If I could get him alone...

My heart pounded, churning out more adrenaline. The noise of the bar receded into distant buzzing.

His voice sounded too loud in my fear-induced bubble. "Let's go." He spun my arm up behind my back and shoved. My shaking legs barely cooperated while he propelled me through the crowded bar toward the front door.

When we entered the vestibule, a buzzer sounded and a scowling giant of a man rose from behind a scarred counter. When Hibbert patted his chest where I'd seen his concealed holster the previous day, the man's face relaxed and he returned a nod.

Holy shit.

They had a metal detector at the front door. Thank God Hibbert was carrying, or I'd have been busted. And thank God I hadn't blundered in here as I'd originally planned.

My knees weakened at the thought and I stumbled on the uneven floor. Hibbert yanked my arm, jerking a cry of pain out of me.

"If you don't trust me enough to let me go now, I'm not going to be able to do much for you at the hotel." I flung the words over my shoulder, hoping Hibbert could hear me.

I flinched when he spoke beside my ear, his voice heavy with booze and menace. "I know where you live. I know where you work. If you double-cross me, you will be very, very sorry."

He released me so suddenly I nearly fell. Regaining my balance, I turned to face him as he pulled on an expensive-looking wool coat and offered his arm.

I cranked on my best smile and took it.

Hope rose when we stepped out into the cold darkness. Just him and me. I liked those odds a whole lot better.

I was drawing a deep, calming breath when Hibbert yanked me close and pressed hard lips to mine, his thick tongue jamming into my mouth. I jerked back involuntarily, barely restraining the urge to spit and wipe my mouth.

"Whassamatter?" He scowled, his fingers biting into my wrist. "I told you not to jerk me around."

"I'm sorry, you just startled me."

"Well, relax." He kissed me again, forcing my head back while his tongue pushed deeper. His booze-and-cigarettes taste fouled my mouth and I determinedly suppressed my gag reflex.

God, what if he had herpes or something? I pulled away, surreptitiously examining his mouth and panting with fake arousal. "Oh my God, Paul, where's your car? I can't wait to get you into bed."

No visible sores. Thank God. And with that much alcohol on his breath, maybe the bacteria would die. I hoped.

He smirked and led me around the corner of the building to a small parking lot, pressing a button on his key fob. The silver Mercedes in front of us flashed its lights, and he opened the door and handed me into the passenger seat with exaggerated courtliness, staggering slightly.

The gory recollection of my last run-in with a drunk driver rose in front of me, writhing and screaming. I drew a deep breath and shook myself free of the memory, easing my trank gun out of its hiding place as Hibbert crossed in front of the car.

Time to end this.

My gun hand trembled violently and I pressed it between my thigh and the passenger door, my pulse reverberating in my ears.

Hibbert half-fell into the driver's seat and pushed the key in the vicinity of the ignition, finding it on the second try. The door locks clicked shut and he peered at me in the dim illumination of the streetlights for a moment before grabbing a handful of hair at my nape, his nails scoring my scalp.

"I don' trust you." His words were so slurred I couldn't believe he thought he was capable of driving.

I held myself still and put on a hurt face. "How can you say that?"

"Easy. I don' trust you. Gimme a little token of good faith."

He yanked my head down toward his lap, unzipping his pants with his free hand. "Jus' a quickie before we go."

Off balance, I braced against him, trying to catch myself without appearing to pull away.

"Oh God, yes, Paul," I gasped, easing my gun up while he fumbled at his crotch.

As his half-mast erection emerged like a pale slug from the dark recesses of his pants, I sucked in a deep breath and pulled the trigger.

He collapsed, his torso flopping forward to trap my head between him and the steering wheel.

I struggled frantically, unable to get purchase and unwilling to put my hands anywhere near his lap.

Don't breathe. Probably still aerosolized anaesthetic in the air. My pulse hammered in my ears.

Lungs straining, I heaved backward only to be jerked to a halt when his limp fingers snarled in my hair.

"Fuck-fuck-fuck..." The high-pitched obscenities squeezed out on a breath I couldn't hold any longer while I tore myself loose. Red and black pulsed at the edges of my vision.

Clawing at the door, I couldn't find the unfamiliar lock release.

Dammit, the anaesthetic should have dissipated by now.

Just as I found the lock button, my starved lungs made the decision for me.

CHAPTER 15

"Hey, darlin', wake up."

A familiar gravelly voice spoke while a gentle hand patted my cheek. "Come on, Aydan, rise an' shine."

I dragged my eyes open to focus blearily on Hellhound's face floating above me.

Shit, what was he doing here?

I lurched into sitting position, and the snow-covered parking lot rocked and billowed. The passenger door of the Mercedes stood open beside me. Hibbert was still behind the wheel, but the driver's door was open, too, and he had been repositioned leaning back in his seat.

"Fuck!" I clutched Hellhound's arm and hauled myself approximately upright. The ground tossed like an angry ocean and I staggered between the swells, caroming around the front of the car and falling to my knees beside the driver's seat.

"Come on, darlin'. Think you've had a little too much to drink." Hellhound's hand closed on my elbow, but I shook him off.

Hibbert divided into twins and I squeezed one eye shut to make him rejoin.

Come on, body, get with the program. My brain was

working fine, but frustration mounted while my clumsy fingers fumbled into my waist pouch.

"Come on, darlin'. Let's go."

"Gotta finish." My ungainly tongue barely managed the words.

I managed to extract my tinted lip balm just as Hellhound chuckled. "Don't bother, darlin', he's passed out cold. Don't waste a perfectly good blowjob on a guy that can't appreciate it."

I glared up at two Hellhounds before closing an eye again so I knew which one to address. "You seers... seriously think I'd blow this shac... sacka shit?"

I made a circle of my thumb and forefinger and swirled the lip balm around and around inside, applying a thick coat before hunching over Hibbert.

"Jesus, don't puke on him!" Hellhound grabbed my shoulders and dragged me back.

I scowled up at him. "'M not puking. 'M *spitting!*"

I lurched forward again to drool inaccurately above Hibbert, sucking my cheeks to summon up more spit.

"What the hell, Aydan?"

I ignored Hellhound's question, cupping my pink-rimmed hand under my mouth to catch more spit before reaching squeamishly for Hibbert's crotch.

Hellhound's bellow of laughter told me he'd finally figured it out.

A few moments later he helped me up, still chuckling, and leaned in to examine Hibbert. "Best blowjob he never had," he assured me. "That pink lipstick's perfect. An' he's gonna wake up sittin' in a helluva wet spot."

"Great," I mumbled, clinging to the door to prevent my knees from collapsing. "Get t'my truck. Gotta go cut off my hand now."

"Ya ain't drivin', darlin'. You're shit-faced."

"'M *not!* 'S trank. Fine inna minnit."

"Sorry, darlin'." He stooped, and a moment later the parking lot flipped nauseatingly upside down as he lifted me over his shoulder.

"Put me down!" I struggled half-heartedly but gave up after a moment. Better to get out of here as fast as possible. And he was right, I was in no shape to go anywhere under my own power.

As he tucked me into the passenger seat of his SUV, I did some mental calculations. The last time I'd inhaled that tranquilizer, it had taken about ten minutes for me to wake up, and by that time my coordination had returned. If I hadn't gotten a full dose this time, I probably still had a few minutes to go.

I sighed and laid my head back.

Parked behind another garbage dumpster in a deserted industrial park, Hellhound handed me my trank gun and the spent dart. "Thought ya might want these back."

I blew out a breath of relief. "Thank you! I was too stoned to think of that." I pocketed both and turned to face him in the glow of his dashboard lights. "How did you find me?"

"Weasel called an' said ya were in trouble."

"*Weasel* called you?"

"Yeah." Hellhound frowned. "He said ya were tryin' to get outta the bar without anybody seein' ya, but a guy called Hibbert knew ya were there."

"He knows Hibbert?"

"I told ya he was tapped into a buncha shit. That's why I use the little slimeball for my snitch. Who's Hibbert?"

I sagged in the seat, ignoring his question. "Shit. I'm going to have to beat Weasel."

Hellhound eyed me with concern. "Ya know he likes that, right?"

"I know." I leaned my head back and studied the headliner in his SUV. "I promised I'd beat him up if he acted as my lookout. And he did. Just not quite the way I expected." I swivelled my head to give Hellhound an inquiring eyebrow. "Did he rat me out to Hibbert?"

"Nah. He said your guy saw ya on the security cameras." He frowned. "What the hell were ya doin' in there, anyway? That ain't the kinda place ya wanna go for a quiet beer."

"Long story, and I can't tell it to you. But thanks for rescuing me." I shuddered.

Hellhound reached to stroke my hair, his brow still furrowed. "Sorry I didn't do anythin' sooner, darlin'. When I got there, ya were just comin' outta the bar, an' ya looked so friendly I didn't wanna fuck up anythin'. I wasn't sure anythin' was wrong 'til I saw ya pass out."

I shuddered again, fighting an internal battle, but I couldn't hold back any longer. "Did my face touch his dick?" The question burst out of me.

"What?" The corner of his mouth lifted.

"I said, did my face touch his dick? When I passed out?"

Hellhound laughed. "Nah, ya were on the other side of the car."

I rubbed my palm against my jeans, shuddering at the recollection of what I had recently handled. "That was the most disgusting thing I've ever done in my life. Including crawling around on a filthy, puke-covered floor." I shot him a glance of wide-eyed entreaty. "You wouldn't lie to me about something like that, would you?"

He eyed me seriously for a moment. "Actually, I would, just so ya wouldn't rip your own face off. But I ain't lyin' this time. There's no way your face coulda touched his dick."

"Thank God." I scrubbed my palm against my jeans again before reaching into my waist pouch for my hand sanitizer.

"Stop, darlin'." His hand closed around mine. "Ya washed for five minutes at the gas station. Ya used that hand cleaner twice already." He brought my hand to his lips and kissed the palm, his beard and moustache sending tingles through my skin. "Trust me, your hand's clean."

His thumb stroked across my palm, spreading my fingers while he kissed each of my fingertips, one by one. "Your fingers are clean."

He leaned in and his whiskers brushed my forehead before moving to my cheeks, trailing kisses all the way. "Your face's clean."

When his lips touched mine, I sighed and pulled him closer, but he drew away after a light kiss and smiled down at me. "Your lips are clean."

He lowered his lips to mine again and this time he unhurriedly deepened the kiss, teasing me lightly with his magic tongue. I opened gratefully to his skillful touch, letting him eradicate Hibbert's loathsome memory and teasing him in return.

A moment later, Hellhound pulled back, smiling. "An' your mouth's clean," he announced. "But ya had onions for supper."

"Oh!" I clapped a hand over my mouth. "I'm sorry, I forgot! It was for lunch, and they were really strong. I can't believe you can still smell them even after all the rinsing I did at the gas station. I'm sorry."

He chuckled. "Don't apologize, darlin', it doesn't bother me a bit. I like onions. Gimme some more."

I drew back, my hand still covering my mouth. "Wait, let me have some breath mints first."

"Are ya kiddin'? An' spoil those onions? Forget it." He seized my hand and pulled me toward him while I pretended to resist, giggling. He pulled again and I yielded, leaning in to kiss him.

"Now I got ya," he mumbled against my lips.

I purred satisfaction, letting my hand wander. "Is that your console shifter, or are you just really glad to see me?"

He growled low in his throat. "I'm really glad to see ya." His mouth captured mine. Hunger kindled low and hot and I pulled him closer, my pulse accelerating.

His hands found my shoulders and he gently broke the kiss. "Darlin', you're some sweet distraction, but I gotta keep my eyes open here. I'm meetin' a client."

"Oh." I peered at him in the dimness. "I wondered why we were here. I thought you were just driving around until you were sure I'd sobered up."

"Well, that, too." He grinned. "Good excuse to kidnap ya. I been missin' ya, darlin'."

I reached for his hand, tracing his scarred and beautiful musician's fingers. "I missed you, too."

"Then why've ya been avoidin' me?"

"I, uh..." I couldn't keep my gaze from sliding away. "I just hate talking on the phone, that's all."

"And..." he prompted.

I sighed, withdrawing my hand. "I, um... I had a lot on my mind. I was really busy at work and I was doing a lot of therapy sessions with Dr. Rawling."

He watched me patiently. "And..."

I stared out the windshield. The silence stretched.

"An' ya were so freaked out about cryin' in front of me that ya ran scared," he finished softly. "I told ya, darlin', it ain't anythin' to be ashamed of."

I didn't meet his eyes. "So what kind of a client wants to meet in the middle of nowhere at..." I glanced at my watch. "...midnight?"

"Aydan." His fingertips coaxed my chin around to face him. "I ain't gonna make fun of ya just for bein' human."

I dropped my gaze. "I know. Look, I don't want to talk about this."

"You're still runnin' scared." His quiet rasp froze me.

I clenched my fists on my fraying emotions. "I don't want to talk about it. I don't want to think about it. I don't want to remember crying like a big fucking stupid pathetic baby and I don't want to trust you and then watch you laugh while you rip my guts out!"

"Aydan, I ain't gonna-"

"I know! My brain knows that but I... I just can't..." I wrapped my arms around myself and stared at the floor. "Look, I knew things would be weird between us and then you'd be mad because I don't trust you enough, and I just... just..." I swallowed around the tightness in my throat. "Forget it." I groped for the door handle. "I have to go. Thanks for everything. 'Bye."

He leaned across to stop my hand. "Aydan, where d'ya think you're gonna go on foot? We're in the middle of nowhere. An' anyhow..." His gaze searched my face. "We been through a lotta shit together. Will ya at least give me a chance to say my piece?"

I crossed my arms over my heart to face him, stiffening my spine and raising my chin.

He studied me in silence for a long moment. "You're freakin' out 'cause ya think I'm gettin' too close," he said at last. "But ya gotta know I ain't gonna trap ya like your fuckin' asshole ex did, 'cause ya know I ain't ever gonna want commitment. So if ya really think I'm the kinda asshole that'll hurt ya just for kicks, then fine, dump me now. But if ya don't think that, why would ya run?"

He relinquished my hand to cup my face in his palms, looking deeply into my eyes. "Aydan, I promise I ain't mad. An' I ain't gonna treat ya any different than usual, so if ya don't want it to be weird between us, just stop makin' it weird."

His whiskery kiss touched my forehead like a blessing. "That's all I got to say." He released me and sat waiting in silence.

After a couple of hard gulps, I managed a grin. "Well, shit, how stupid would I be to dump a guy who compliments me on my lip gloss when he sees it on another guy's dick?"

He burst into laughter. "Fuck yeah, darlin'. I'm a keeper."

I reached gratefully for his hand. "You're right, I freaked out. The last few months... I was dealing with a lot of shit and I... I just kind of ran from everything and everybody. I'm sorry, Arnie. It was stupid to make a big deal over this."

"It's okay, darlin', ya ain't stupid, you're just a little fucked up." He folded me into his arms. "But I love ya anyway."

I cuddled into his embrace, marvelling at how safe those words sounded when I knew there was no expectation behind them.

He tilted my chin up to study me anxiously. "Ya know what I meant, right? Ya ain't gonna freak out again 'cause I said I love ya?"

I grinned and echoed his words from two months ago. "Well, hell, what's not to love?"

CHAPTER 16

Hellhound consulted his watch, frowning. "She was s'posed to be here ten minutes ago. Hope nothin' happened to her."

"Oho, it's a 'her'," I teased. "Is this business or pleasure?"

He grinned, but his eyes were worried. "Strictly business, darlin'." His smile slipped away. "She phoned me this afternoon, an' she sounded scared as hell. Like she'd been cryin' all day. Said she thought her ex was stalkin' her, an' she needed to know for sure."

His worry transmitted itself to me. "She shouldn't have called you, she should have called the police."

"That's what I told her." His frown deepened. "I gave her the number for the women's shelter an' told her to call the cops, but she said she was scared to call them an' she needed a private investigator." He scanned the empty parking lot again. "Fuck, Aydan, I hope nothin' happened to her."

I squeezed his hand in silence, knowing how close to home his fear was. I was casting about for something encouraging to say when he stiffened. "That's prob'ly her."

A taxi turned into the parking lot and headed in our

direction, pulling in on the other side of the dumpster.

"D'ya mind comin' with me, darlin'?" Hellhound reached for the door handle. "She might feel safer seein' a woman with me. I ain't exactly a nice-lookin' guy."

I eyed his battle-scarred features fondly, but I couldn't argue with the truth. "Sure, let's go."

As we got out of the SUV, the cab pulled away, its rooftop sign illuminated once again.

"She must be waitin' on the other side of the dumpster." Hellhound called softly, "Hey, Miz Smith, it's Arnie Helmand. I got my friend Aydan with me, an' we're comin' around to ya now. Don't be scared."

He received no reply, and we exchanged a look. When we turned the corner a second later, Hellhound jolted to a stop. His arm flew out to push me behind him. "Back to the truck. Lock the doors."

I stared at the man in front of us. His face was deeply lined, but his bulky build still looked powerful despite his age. I was pretty sure I'd never met him, but he looked oddly familiar.

"Fuck, Aydan, go!" Hellhound's shout made me jerk with shock. "Get in the fuckin' truck!"

The old man smiled, revealing several missing teeth. "Damn bitches. Ya just gotta show 'em who's boss. But you're so fuckin' pussy-whipped, ya can't even make the bitches listen." His abrasive voice was a horrible caricature of Hellhound's sexy rasp. "Hi, son. Did ya miss me?"

"Skip the bullshit, ol' man. Where's Miz Smith?"

His father's harsh laugh made a chill crawl down my spine. "Knew you'd come runnin' for some cryin' bitch. Miz Smith. Ha." He snapped his fingers. "Two-bit hooker."

"What'd ya do to her?" Hellhound's voice was level.

"Who gives a shit? Dumb bitches're a dime a dozen."

Hellhound's fists clenched, and his father grated out another laugh. "What, ya actually gonna fight me this time? Don't tell me ya grew a dick since I saw ya last."

Strain bulged in Hellhound's shoulders. "I ain't gonna fight ya. I ain't you, an' I never will be. Go ahead an' take your shot so I can call the cops again an' send ya back to the fuckin' slammer."

The old man spat and wiped his mouth on the back of his hand. "Ya always were a fuckin' disappointment. At least your brothers had balls. Ya were always a fuckin' little pansy-ass mama's boy."

"It ain't gonna work, ol' man. Take your shot."

"Arnie." I laid a hand on his arm, feeling his tension like an electrical current. "Let's go. Just walk away."

"Can't, darlin'." His hard stare never left his father. "We gotta do this every time the ol' fuck gets outta jail. Sooner we do it, sooner he goes back, an' maybe this time somebody'll do the world a favour an' shank the fucker 'fore he gets out again. Fuckin' waste of skin."

Fury flared in his father's eyes, and I felt Arnie's almost-imperceptible tremor.

"Gonna teach ya a lesson this time, boy." His father's voice was thick with rage. "This time ya gotta fight or die. Time to grow some balls." He stepped forward, his big hands clenching into murderous fists.

"Aydan," Hellhound said very softly. "Please go to the truck now."

I hesitated.

Obey him and call the police? Or just pull my gun and end this?

His father spoke again. "If ya won't fight for yourself,

maybe you'll fight for her."

The old man swung so fast I barely had time to recognize the threat. I dodged, but pain exploded in my face and my head rang with hollow metallic thunder. My muscles turned to water and I dropped, pavement slapping the breath out of me.

Pull your gun. Shoot.

My body refused to move.

"*NO!*" Hellhound's bellow reverberated in my skull. I dazedly registered a flurry of motion, my vision blurred by involuntary tears.

A sickening muffled pop.

Hellhound flung the slack body aside like a discarded rag.

"*NO!*" He fell to his knees beside me. "*No, no, no...*" Arms wrapped over his head, he rocked violently while the terrible cries wrenched out of him. "*No, no, no, no...*"

Comprehension arrived along with my ability to move again.

Flashback. The worst day of his life.

I dragged myself onto hands and knees. Blood dripped onto the pavement from my throbbing nose and my body tingled with pins and needles.

"Arnie."

"No, no, no..." Five-year-old Arnie sobbed out his agony and terror.

"Arnie." I rubbed slow, gentle circles on his back. What endearment might his mother have used? "Arnie, it's over, sweetie. It's all over now. He won't hurt anybody, ever again."

The gut-wrenching sobs didn't cease, and tears welled up in my eyes. "Oh, Arnie." I wrapped my arms around him and rocked with him, my heart breaking. "It's okay. You're going to be okay. It's over. I promise it's over now."

Long moments passed while I rocked him and murmured comfort time and again, and gradually his sobs eased. His body vibrated with long tremors, his bulky muscles hard as iron in my arms. The frigid pavement numbed my knees and my own trembling threatened to shake me apart.

"It's over. It's okay. It's over," I soothed. "You're okay, Arnie, it's okay."

He drew a deep, shuddering breath.

"...Aydan?" His voice was a broken remnant.

"I'm here, Arnie. It's okay. It's over."

His arms locked around me, almost crushing my ribs. "Aydan... darlin'..." He pressed his face into my hair. "Aydan..."

"I'm here." I held him tightly, wishing my embrace could heal the terrible wounds in his heart. "I'm here. It's all over. It's okay."

At last he released me and drew away. His ravaged features twisted at the sight of my face. "Aw, darlin'." He raised a trembling hand to touch my cheek, his fingertips barely brushing my skin. "I'm sorry. I'm sorry."

"It's not your fault." Forgetting my bleeding nose, I took his icy hand in both of mine and pressed it to my lips. He stiffened at sight of the crimson smears on his skin, old horrors resurfacing in his eyes.

I hugged his hand to me, wiping the stains away. "It's not your fault," I repeated forcefully. "None of it. Not then, and not now."

He sagged back to sit on the frozen pavement, his stare passing through his father's crumpled body to some invisible hell beyond.

"Yeah, it is my fault. Call the cops." His hollow monotone bespoke utter defeat. "The fuckin' bastard won after all."

I stared at him, unwilling to comprehend.

"Call the cops," he repeated. His barren eyes met mine. "I gotta pay for what I did."

Fury seized me. Violent rage at the monster who had done so much harm in life and even more in death.

"No." I lunged to my feet. My voice vibrated on the edge of explosion. "No. You've been paying all your life. No more. *No fucking more.*"

I yanked open my waist pouch and punched the button on the secured phone. When Stemp's flat 'yes' crackled over the line, I held the phone away from my sluggishly dripping nose and snapped, "I have a body. I need a cleanup."

Arnie's eyes widened and he half-raised a hand, but I shot him a look and he subsided.

"Shots fired?"

"No."

"Wet cleanup?"

"No. Broken neck."

"Tidy." Stemp sounded pleased. "Where?"

I did a rapid mental calculation. "I can meet them anywhere on the east side of town in an hour. You tell me where."

"Stand by."

The heat of anger ebbed while I waited. I shot an anxious glance around the parking lot, shivers racking my body. Arnie slumped in silence, staring blindly into the past.

Pacing on stiff legs, I peeked in the dumpster, evaluating my resources before forcing my skittering mind to concentrate on details and logistics.

Stemp's flat voice came back on the line. "Zero one-thirty, under the bridge at Heritage and Glenmore. Look for a dark blue panel van. Do we need a coverup?"

"No." I shot a hard glance at the body, hatred still boiling in my veins. "Nobody will ever miss him."

A moment of silence greeted that announcement. Then, "I'll expect a full report tomorrow."

I sighed. "Yeah. Oh, and I got the money and Hibbert should be happy."

"Good."

He hung up without ceremony, and I tossed the phone into the dumpster before climbing in after it. Thank God the contents seemed to be mostly discarded packing material. At least it smelled better than the women's washroom at the Hogback.

Ignoring the eye-watering throbbing in my face, I bent to tear open some plastic garbage bags and dump them, thankful for the clotting blood that mostly obstructed my sense of smell.

Bags in hand, I clambered out again and headed for the body. A pool of urine glistened around it, and I caught a whiff of fresh shit. Even though I knew death had given the old man no choice, I muttered, "Yeah, you fucker, you just have to do everything you can to be a prick, don't you?"

By the time I got the bags laid out beside the puddle, the itchy stickiness on my face overrode my reluctance to touch my painful nose. I did a cautious mop-up with the only clean spot I could find on my jacket sleeve before turning to Arnie. "Can you help me move him?"

He stared up at me, shivering.

I wiped my hands on my jeans and knelt to stroke his

face. "I'm sorry, Arnie, I know you're in shock right now and I promise this will all go away, but I just need you to help me for a minute and then we need to get out of here."

He shook his head as if to dislodge the memories, his blank expression firming into the Arnie I knew. "Aydan, ya can't do this," he said. "It ain't right."

I held his face in my palms. "It's too late to argue. I've already done it. You're free, Arnie. It's over."

His eyes squeezed shut and he pressed his forehead against mine for a long moment. Then he pulled away and rose shakily, his hand heavy on my shoulder. He straightened to his full height, squaring his shoulders, and gave me a twisted smile.

"Awright darlin', let's take out the trash."

CHAPTER 17

I leaned back in the passenger seat of Hellhound's SUV, my face pulsing with slow, deep pain.

"Ya sure ya don't wanna go to the hospital?" He frowned concern as he pulled in behind my truck.

"No. I'll see Dr. Roth tomorrow."

"Aydan, ya were knocked out. Ya should get checked tonight."

"I wasn't really knocked out. I just whacked my head on the dumpster when I fell, and it hurt too much to move for a few seconds."

He sighed but offered no further argument as I craned my neck, checking the small parking lot.

Hibbert's car was gone, and I eased out a sigh of relief. With any luck, he wouldn't have noticed my old truck still parked among the rest of the dilapidated vehicles. As far as I knew, he had never seen me drive anything but my new Legacy.

I turned to Hellhound. "Do you remember the access code for Weasel's autobody bay?" I stopped myself from slapping my aching forehead. "Of course you do. Photographic memory, duh. I'll follow you there and we can make the transfer..." I jerked a thumb toward the rear of the

SUV, "...where nobody will see us."

He frowned. "I don't wanna take a chance on Weasel bein' there, an' I still don't think ya should be doin' this."

"Weasel won't be there. He was piss-drunk. The only place he'll go is home for a little quality time with Rosy Palm and her five daughters." I got out and headed for the truck before he could protest again.

When the big overhead door rolled up on Weasel's shop, I drew a breath of relief at the sight of cavernous darkness. Despite my confident words, I had been afraid Weasel would be hard at work on another stolen car.

Safely enclosed in the windowless space, leaden fatigue coursed over my body and I slumped briefly in the driver's seat before forcing myself to get out of the truck.

Hellhound met me at the tailgate, his features haggard in the harsh overhead lighting. My heart contracted with sympathy and I stroked his cheek, wishing I could banish the dark ghosts that haunted his eyes.

"Almost done, Arnie. It's almost over." I lowered the tailgate and climbed in to spread out the polyethylene tarp I always kept in the back.

When I climbed out again, Hellhound laid a hand on my arm. "Aydan, I can't let ya do this. I killed him, I gotta take the consequences. Ya gotta tell Stemp the truth an' call the cops. I ain't gonna let ya take a murder rap for me."

"There isn't going to be a murder charge. Pretty soon there isn't even going to be a body. This never happened." I popped open the rear door of his SUV. "And it's too late to change my story with Stemp. I won't get in trouble for killing somebody, but I'll sure as hell get in trouble if Stemp finds out I lied."

"But Aydan, the ol' man's... he was a big guy. Stemp'll never believe ya took him out on your own."

I sighed. "Trust me, he'll believe it." I eyed the plastic-wrapped body gloomily.   "In fact, I probably couldn't convince him otherwise."

"Aydan..."

"Just help me move him. On three. One, two, *three*..."

The slippery plastic bags shifted when the body thumped onto the tailgate and I shuddered at a glimpse of the face, frozen in a rictus of rage. I hurriedly flipped a fold of the tarp over it and tucked the ends in. "Help me roll him."

A few moments later, the lumpy tarp-wrapped bundle lay inside my truck box, and I clanged the tailgate shut and closed the door of the box topper.   Turning back to Hellhound's SUV, I extracted my reading glasses from my waist pouch to peer closely at the back cargo area. I removed a few shreds of packing material, but there didn't seem to be any incriminating hairs or body fluids.

When I turned, Hellhound was still staring into the back of my truck. As I watched, his hands clenched into slow fists.

"Arnie." I spoke softly so as not to startle him.

When he turned, his expression was unreadable, his eyes bottomless wells of darkness.

Worry gnawed at my gut. "Are you..." I stopped myself from finishing the question with 'okay'. Of course he wasn't okay. "Are you still with me?"

"Yeah." His hard rasp made me shiver.

"All right." I took his icy hands, clasping them between my own and willing warmth into him. "I need you to go home and wait for me. Just go straight home and get warmed up. Don't call anybody. I'll come as soon as I can.

Okay?"

"Okay."

I slid my arms around his rigid body and kissed his cold lips. "Go now. I'll close up here."

"Okay."

He plodded to his SUV like a robot. When I pressed the button to roll up the overhead door, he drove into the night without looking back.

I hauled myself into my truck and leaned my forehead against the steering wheel for a few long breaths. Twenty minutes to make it to the drop point.

No problem.

Much to my surprise, it wasn't a problem. The panel van was already there when I arrived a few minutes early, and two silent men swung the tarp-wrapped bundle into it without ado.

I hesitated for a moment before dipping into my jacket to remove the envelope of cash. Stripping off the filthy blood-smeared garment, I tossed it on top of the body. "Could you get rid of that, too, please?"

They nodded wordlessly and departed. The whole transaction had taken about a minute.

Shivering in the frigid air, I climbed into the truck box to retrieve my sleeping bag from the emergency pack I always carried for winter driving. When I wrapped it around me, its accumulated cold penetrated to my bones.

Huddled in the driver's seat with the heater blasting, I wrapped my arms around myself and shivered until the thick padding warmed. When my fingers skimmed over the old bullet hole, my thoughts drifted back nine months to my first encounter with Kane. At the time, I had been so horrified by a bullet hole in my sleeping bag.

Now it seemed foolishly insignificant.

Reaction set in while I drove through the dark streets toward Hellhound's condo. My nose throbbed with slow bloated pain while my hands trembled on the steering wheel. I gulped, my breath hitching into shaky gasps that wanted to become sobs. The streetlights blurred and I scrubbed a fist across my brimming eyes.

Goddammit, get it together. Yoga breaths. In. Out. Slow like ocean waves.

At last, I parked in one of the visitor's stalls and tottered to the front door, hoping no late-roaming resident would sound the alarm over a dishevelled, blood-smeared woman clad in a bullet-punctured sleeping bag.

I peered carefully through my headache before pressing the call button for Hellhound's apartment. Wouldn't want to wake some poor resident at two in the morning.

Long moments crawled by.

No answer.

Shit, had I hit the wrong button after all? I rechecked the list before pressing the button again.

Still no answer.

Burning worry flooded my stomach. Had he left? Or never returned?

Or...

His haunted eyes stared from my memory.

Had he harmed himself? My heart kicked painfully against my ribs.

I leaned on the button one more time. If he didn't answer in ten seconds, I'd summon his neighbour, Miss Lacey. As much as I hated to wake a ninety-year-old woman in the dead of night, I knew she'd forgive me when I explained why I needed her key to Arnie's apartment. She loved him like a son.

Oh, God, I had to be wrong. He had to be okay.

I was reaching for Miss Lacey's call button when the speaker crackled to life.

"Yeah." Hellhound's rasp made my knees go weak with relief.

"It's Aydan."

The door lock released and I hurried inside, trembling.

Inside his apartment at last, I hugged him fiercely, taking comfort from his reassuring bulk. "I was afraid you weren't going to answer. I was just about to ring Miss Lacey." His arms didn't close around me in return and I drew back to study him worriedly. "Arnie?"

He stared at the floor for a long moment. "I... didn't know if I should let ya in." His voice was almost a whisper. "I'm really fucked up."

I slid my arms around him again and held him close. "Thanks for trusting me."

"It ain't you I don't trust." He took my shoulders and held me away to look into my eyes. "Aydan, will ya promise me somethin'?"

"Probably. What is it?"

"Will ya... Aydan, if I ever get outta control like that again... if... if ya ever think I might... hurt ya... will ya promise to shoot me?"

I jerked back. "No! How could you even... no!"

"Please." The terrible entreaty in his eyes tore a jagged hole in my heart. "Aydan, if ya don't promise, I gotta ask ya to leave an' never come back. If I ever hurt ya, I'd... I couldn't take it. Promise me. Please."

"Arnie, you would never hurt me. I know it like I know the sun will rise every morning."

"Then ya shouldn't have any problem promisin' me."

"Arnie..." I reached for him again, but he held me distant.

"Ya gotta promise now, or I gotta ask ya to leave." Despite the gentleness of his grip, I could feel the strain quivering in his hands.

"Oh, Arnie..."

My throat closed with grief for the broken child and the damaged man. Searching his face, I read his resolve. Promise the unthinkable or lose him forever. And if I left now, he would never dare another friendship like ours.

The lost child implored me from his eyes.

"I promise." My voice shook.

He swallowed, his hands trembling on my shoulders. "Aydan, ya swore you'd never lie to me."

"I'm not lying. I swear to you that if you ever attack me, I will shoot you."

"Shoot to kill." His eyes demanded it.

Tears rose, nearly choking me. "Yes." My voice was a raw whisper.

He crushed me in his arms and pressed his face into my hair. "Thanks," he rasped. "Thanks, Aydan."

I clung to him, unable to speak.

At last, he pulled away and stroked a hand over my hair. "Come on, darlin'." He turned me in the direction of the bathroom. "Get cleaned up an' call it a night."

I let out a long, tremulous breath and wobbled into the bathroom. Shaking with fatigue and emotion, I washed off as much of the dried blood as I could see while my eyelids kept sinking closed in front of the mirror. Eventually I gave up, gulped a couple of painkillers, and sleepwalked out.

Passing through the living room where Arnie hunched on the sofa, I paused. Three empty beer bottles already stood on the coffee table, and he leaned back to salute me with their half-empty companion. "Go on to bed, darlin'. I'm gonna sit up for a while."

"Night owl," I teased, and bent over the back of the sofa to drop a kiss on his lips as if everything was all right. "You musicians are all the same." I reached down to give Hooker the cat a chin-scratch and his purring amplified as he slitted his eyes, stretching luxuriously in Arnie's lap. I hesitated before finally giving in to ask the stupid question. "Are you okay?"

"Yeah."

I wavered, torn between trying to get him to talk and giving him a chance to process his feelings.

I sighed. If I pushed, he might withdraw completely.

"Good night, then."

"G'night." He sucked back another long swallow.

CHAPTER 18

I woke to the sound of Arnie's guitar and lay blinking in the darkness for a moment, vaguely surprised I'd slept without nightmares.

I squinted at the illuminated clock beside the bed. Then again, an hour and a half without nightmares wasn't exactly cause for celebration. I stifled a groan and pressed my face into the pillow, forgetting my nose until it was too late.

The pain jerked me upright, teeth clamped on the frenzied swearing that tried to escape. Involuntary tears streamed down my cheeks and I blotted them with the corner of the sheet, hoping my stupid nose didn't start bleeding again.

Something tickled my upper lip, and I hauled myself out of bed to hurry for the bathroom.

When I stumbled through the living room, Arnie was curled over his beloved guitar, eyes closed while he crooned a poignant wordless melody. A flock of empty beer bottles formed a silent audience on the coffee table.

The bathroom mirror assured me that the tickle was only the watery drainage of tears, and I dabbed cautiously before tiptoeing back to the living room.

Alone in his music, Arnie swayed gently on the sofa, his

gifted fingers summoning heartbreak from the guitar while he comforted it with the tenderness of his voice.

I lowered myself onto the end of the sofa and appropriated one of his hand-crocheted afghans to wrap around myself. His eyes opened and he smiled, a smile so sweet it nearly broke my heart.

"Hey, darlin'," he mumbled.

"That's a beautiful song. What is it?"

He peered down at his guitar as if surprised to find it in his hands. "I dunno. It ain't really a song, I'm just playin'." That sweet smile again, his eyes focused decades away. "Jus' thinkin' 'bout Mom."

I leaned forward to trace my fingertips across the back of his hand. "Don't stop."

"Mm." He closed his eyes again and reunited with the music. Watching him, my heart eased. Thank God for his guitar.

I tucked my cold feet up under me, doing a quick bottle count. That was a hell of a lot of beer in only a couple of hours.

Well, whatever it took. I settled back to listen.

My eyelids were drooping when he spoke at last. "So who's the big fuckin' stupid pathetic baby now?"

I snapped to alertness. He stared down at his guitar, his fingertips barely brushing the strings.

Damn my thoughtless mouth.

"Arnie, you had a horrible flashback. It's totally different."

He looked up, meeting my gaze squarely. "So it's okay if I bawl my eyes out over somethin' that happened forty-odd years ago, but you can't cry even when ya just been tortured by some fuckin' sicko. 'Cause that makes ya a big fuckin' stupid pathetic baby."

The beer was doing its best. His words were slurred, but the strain had returned to his body as soon as his music stopped. He was still a hell of a long way from okay.

"Well, ye... n... I mean... You know what I mean."

"Yeah." He laid the guitar down carefully and reached to gather me against his side. "You're so afraid somebody's gonna beat ya up for bein' weak, ya beat yourself up worse'n anybody else ever would." He stroked my hair with a gentle hand. "Ya can't have it both ways, darlin'. Either cryin' is shameful, or it ain't."

I wrapped my arms around him. "Arnie, it's nothing to be ashamed of."

He dropped a slightly inaccurate kiss on my forehead. "I know, darlin'. That's what I keep tryin' to tell ya."

We sat in silence while I absorbed that.

After a lengthy pause, he spoke again, his gaze fixed on the wall. "Never had one that bad before." His arm tightened around me. "It was just... the ol' man swingin' at ya... seein' ya lying there, an' the blood... all of a sudden, it was Mom lyin' there bleedin' out an' him still whalin' on her..." He shook himself back to the present. "The ol' fucker woulda finished me this time."

A shudder seized me. "You really wouldn't have fought back? You would have just let him beat you?"

"I dunno." He slid down on the couch and leaned his head back to stare at the ceiling, tension coiling his muscles like steel springs. "I swore I'd never be like him." His fists clenched. "All those times I just let him take his shot an' then called the cops. I thought I could do it, Aydan. I really thought..." His voice trailed off into silence.

"How..." I had to clear my throat before I could speak

again. "How many times?"

"Eleven." He spoke emotionlessly to the ceiling, and I shivered. "Assault sentence ain't fuck-all," he added. "He usually only did a few months, never more'n a coupla years. But sometimes it took him a while to find me, after I joined up with the army."

Sickness twisted my stomach. "I would have shot him tonight if he attacked you. You know that, don't you? He would have died tonight no matter what."

"Glad ya didn't, darlin'. Wouldn't wanna put that on ya." Hellhound blew out a long breath and slid lower on the sofa. "I took out guys before, in combat. But I was doin' what I hadta. I was always in control." He examined his fists as if seeing them for the first time, the old scars glowing white across his taut knuckles. "But I was always afraid I'd lose it someday. An' tonight I did."

He slumped forward to hide his face in his hands. "I wanted to be better than him, Aydan. I wanted it so bad." His voice was raw pain.

"You *are* better than him! You're so much better, there's not even a comparison!" I threw my arms around him, laying my head on his bowed back. "Arnie, you're nothing like him. You never have been and you never will be. You're a good person. A gentle person."

His laugh sounded like a sob. "Yeah, gentle. I just killed him with my bare hands. Don't think so, darlin'."

"Arnie." I slid off the couch to kneel in front of him and coaxed his hands away from his face. "You were fighting for your life. And he deserved it."

His face twisted. "Don't, Aydan. Don't say that. That's what he always said. Mom deserved it. We deserved it. He always had a reason." He shook his head. "Ya can't make excuses. Either you're the kinda guy who'll hurt somebody, or ya ain't. I am."

"You're not!"

"Aydan, I snapped his fuckin' neck like he was a fuckin' chicken." He scowled, but even the angry-biker facade couldn't hide his torment. "I'm a fuckin' sick bastard, jus' like him."

"But, Arnie," I pleaded. "You've never hit Hooker, have you?"

"No!" He recoiled, his hand flying protectively to cuddle the somnolent cat beside him. "'Course not!"

"But he can get irritating sometimes, can't he?" I persisted.

Arnie stroked the long fur and Hooker rolled over, stretching and curling a tufted paw over his broad face while his purr boomed like distant thunder.

Arnie's face softened. "Hell, yeah. Sometimes he irritates the piss outta me. Goddam dumbass furball." He caressed the big cat's tattered ears with a tenderness that belied his rough words.

"So even though he irritates the piss out of you, you've never hit him. Believe me, Arnie, if you were like your father, you wouldn't even need an excuse. You'd hurt Hooker and enjoy it. You know I'm right. There are lots of studies that prove it."

"But, Aydan, I lost it. I just..." He held out his hands as if they were defective. "I ain't safe to be around people. What if I do it again?"

"You won't." I rose to sit beside him and slid my arms around him. "It'll never happen again. You said yourself you've never had a flashback that bad before. It was just because he hit me and re-enacted that memory. You'll never see him hit anybody ever again. And I'm willing to bet there's nothing else that can trigger you like that."

The naked pleading in his eyes pierced my heart. "But what if there is?"

"Arnie, how old are you?"

He blinked and frowned. "Forty-nine next month. Ya know that. What's that got to do with anythin'?"

"You've been through things most people don't even want to imagine. Abuse. Combat. Torture." I took his hands and looked deep into his eyes. "You've lived through nearly fifty years of shit without ever losing it on anyone but him, and it took a specific set of events to trigger you. Events that can never happen again. Trust me, there's nothing left in the world that can break you."

His hands tightened on mine, his gaze searching my face. "Ya promised not to lie to me, Aydan. Don't blow sunshine up my ass, just tell me the truth. Ya really think that?"

"Arnie, I don't just think it, I know it."

He held my gaze for a long moment. Then the tension eased from his body on a long breath and he sagged back on the couch, closing his eyes. "Thanks, darlin'."

His eyes opened slowly, his face drawn with exhaustion. He smiled and stroked the hair back from my cheek. "Ya better go back to bed. Ya gotta be bagged." His slurring was more noticeable now.

"Come on." I rose. "You need to sleep, too."

"'M gonna sleep here." He reached for the afghan I had shed.

"No, come to bed. Come on, I'll help you." I stooped and reached for his hands.

He shook his head, wrapping his arms around himself. "Can't. If I hadda nightmare, dunno what I'd do in my sleep.

Can't take th' chance."

"It'll be okay. Come on."

"No."

"Arnie…"

His arms tightened, his powerful muscles bulging with returning tension. "Aydan, no." He squinted up at me as if trying to focus his eyes. "Couldn' take it 'f I hurt ya. Ain' gonna chance it." His words were blurred, but their finality was unmistakable.

I blew out a short breath and sank down beside him. "Okay, then we'll sleep on the couch."

"Fuck, Aydan, you're solvin' th' wrong problem!"

I turned to face him, planting my fists on my hips. "I'm going to sleep in the same bed with you no matter what. And you know how stubborn I am, so you might as well just give up now."

He stared at me for a moment before lurching to his feet. "Gotta take a leak. Go on t'bed. Be righ' there…" He tacked an erratic path toward the bathroom.

The door closed and locked behind him, and I rose to frown at it. What was he up to?

Shortly afterward, the toilet flushed.

I waited.

Some muffled thumps and then silence.

"Nice try," I muttered, and headed for the kitchen to round up a toothpick.

The simple privacy lock was just as easy to bypass as the one in the house where I grew up. When the door swung open, Hellhound scowled blearily up at me from his cramped position in the bathtub, the small bathmat draped inadequately over one shoulder and part of his bulky chest. "Whaddafuck, Aydan?"

I kept my expression bland. "I need to pee. And you're not going to watch me do it, so... out."

Ignoring my extended hand, he slowly levered himself up, swearing mightily. At last, he dragged himself to his feet and stood swaying in the bathtub, his eyelids drooping.

"Fuck," he mumbled. "Don' 'member bathtubs... bein' so fuggen hard..."

I hurriedly reached to steady him as he stumbled out of the tub, rebounding off the wall hard enough to rattle the mirror. A flash of his old humour glinted in his half-closed eyes. "'Course I ain't slept inna tub... in 'bout thirty years..."

I wrapped an arm around his waist and guided him toward the bedroom.

He shook his head vigorously, making us both stagger sideways. "No, Aydan, I ain' gonna..."

"I know, it's okay," I agreed. "Just lie down on the bed for a few minutes. When I'm done in the bathroom you can go back to the couch."

"...'Kay..."

We wove our unsteady way into the bedroom and I helped him struggle out of his T-shirt while he mumbled unintelligible obscenities.

"Stop trying to help." I propped him beside the bed. "Just stand still." I undid the button on his jeans and reached for the zipper.

He made an unsuccessful attempt to catch my hand. "H... Hang on..."

I reached up to give him a quick kiss. "What, you don't want me to undress you? That's a first."

He let out a sleepy chuckle, his eyes drifting closed. "Ya can und...undress me anytime, darlin'." He swayed. "But I th... think you're gonna... be dis'pointed t'night."

I gave him another light kiss before shimmying his jeans down. "I don't have any ulterior motives. I just thought you'd be more comfortable if the boys were free."

"Ahhh... yeah..." He sagged onto the bed and sank back on the pillow as I lifted his feet in and pulled his jeans off. "Jus' f'r a minnit... 'N' then I'm gonna..." The rest of his sentence dissolved in a snore.

CHAPTER 19

Hellhound lunged out of the shadows of the darkened bedroom, roaring with rage. His fist smashed into my face, exploding in lightning bolts of pain. I fell, scrabbling desperately at the bedside table for my gun.

He bellowed and sprang as my gun swung up.

The gun kicked in my hand, once, twice; ear-shattering explosions.

I screamed as he fell in slow motion, his body hitting the floor with a sickening boneless half-bounce that settled into horrible stillness-

"Aydan! Darlin', wake up, 's jus' a dream."

Frozen in the terror between nightmare and reality, I stared up at Hellhound's face hovering above me in the dimness.

A moment later, reality claimed me and I flung my arms around him, half-sobbing with relief. "Oh thank God, Arnie, you're okay. God, what a horrible dream," I babbled against his shoulder. "Oh, thank God you're okay."

"Shhh, darlin', s'okay. Jus' a dream."

I burrowed closer, clinging to him in distress that was part aftermath of the dream and part remembrance of my terrible vow.

"S'okay, darlin'…"   His stroking hand faltered on my hair. "Hang on, what'm I doin' here?"

"Sleeping." I tightened my arms around him.

"No." He gently pried me loose. "I toldja-"

"You were asleep before your head hit the pillow," I interrupted. "And you were fine."

He frowned. "But 'f I hadda nightmare…"

"You did. Several. But you didn't do anything. I woke you up and you went back to sleep and you were fine." I gave him the big brown eyes. "Please don't be mad at me. I knew you'd be fine and this was the best way to convince you."

He groaned and collapsed onto the pillow.   "Dunno whether to kiss ya or kick your ass outta bed."

"Kiss me."

He smiled, his eyelids drooping. "Was gonna do that anyway…" His eyes closed and small snore escaped him. His eyes snapped open again. "Wha' time izzit?"

I leaned up on my elbow to check the bedside clock. "Six."

He groaned and buried his face in the pillow.

I stroked the muscled ridges of his back. "How's your head? Do you want some painkillers?"

"Too soon f'r hangover," he mumbled into the pillow. "Still fuggen wasted."

"I'll get you some anyway. Might as well get a jump on it. It's probably going to be a nasty one."

A groan that might have been acquiescence floated up from the pillow, and I slid out of bed to head for the bathroom. He was asleep again by the time I returned with the pills and a glass of water, so I put the supplies on the bedside table within easy reach and slipped back under the covers.

Hellhound mumbled and dropped a heavy arm over me to snug me close to his warmth before resuming his lullaby of snores. I eased out a long breath and reached for my lost slumber.

It eluded me.

My mind raced like a hamster on a wheel. What would I say in my report to Stemp? How would I deliver the phone list to Hibbert, and where would he give me the final payment? Please, God, not in another biker bar. And while I was at it, please let him believe he'd gotten what he wanted last night.

But he wouldn't have any reason to disbelieve it. Would he?

No. He'd believe it. The 'evidence' should have been convincing.

I eased out another long breath. Relax.

Sleep.

But if Hibbert thought I'd sucked him off last night, what would he expect next time? The memory of his tongue invading my mouth made me shudder so violently that Hellhound roused to sprinkle kisses across my shoulder before sinking back into oblivion.

Okay, no way in hell I'd let Hibbert anywhere near me ever again. I needed a plan.

I blew out a short, irritable breath and gave up on sleep. Extricating myself carefully from Hellhound's embrace, I headed for the bathroom to make free with his shower.

Working the tangles out my wet hair afterward and regretting the lack of conditioner, I leaned close to the mirror, tilting my head to examine the damage.

My nose was still puffy but unless I actually touched it, the dull ache was tolerable. The tender spot where the dumpster had introduced itself to my head had made for an uncomfortable shampooing experience, but the skin didn't seem to be broken.

I squinted critically. Please tell me those shadows under my eyes were from lack of sleep. I really didn't want to have to explain two black eyes.

Pulling on yesterday's clothes with distaste, I made another mental entry in the imaginary spy manual I'd been compiling since October. Always carry a change of underwear. And a clean T-shirt might not be a bad idea, either.

Except I'd had enough difficulty finding space in my crammed waist pouch for the secured phone I'd resolved to carry at all times. No room left for wardrobe items. And it'd be damn embarrassing if I dragged out a lacy little thong along with my wallet in public. I sighed and reluctantly crossed underwear off my mental list.

When I emerged from the bathroom, Hooker opened a single incredulous yellow eye from his blanket-nest on the couch before exposing a pink gullet and gleaming fangs in a yawn. Apparently he liked early mornings as much as Hellhound did. He curled into a ball and tucked his scarred nose under his paw, ignoring me completely.

Scrounging through the kitchen, I found the usual impressive beer supply and very little else. I eyed the pizza box in the fridge with suspicion. It might have been fresh yesterday or it might have been fossilized since October. Hard to tell with cold pizza. And I knew better than to look for bread or fruit.

Screw it. I'd hit a drive-through on my way out of town.

Padding back to the bedroom, I paused in the doorway. I had left the bathroom light on instead of turning on the living room lights, and a soft rectangle of illumination fell across Hellhound in bed. He had rolled over to sprawl on his back, the blankets flung aside to reveal his muscular tattooed arms and torso.

I swallowed.

God, two months of abstinence was about two months too long. Maybe I could hit that magic window between 'too drunk to be able to' and 'too hung over to want to'. Still enough time for a quickie.

I was just starting forward when buzzing from the bedside table made me stiffen. Only one person would text me at seven-thirty in the morning.

Hellhound mumbled and opened sleepy eyes as I pulled my phone out of my waist pouch. Sure enough, it was a two-word text. 'Call home'. Stemp's signal.

When I swore, Hellhound sat up to regard me with concern. "What, darlin'?"

I blew out a short breath. "I have to call Stemp. I only have one other secured phone with me, and it's in the truck. And I have to get back to Silverside. I have a meeting at ten."

"Oh." He looked as disappointed as I felt. "Damn, darlin', can't ya stay for a little while?"

The blankets had fallen aside when he sat up, and I surveyed the tempting scene wistfully.

Definitely not too drunk.

But Stemp would expect an answer right away. And by the time I went down to the truck and dealt with the call and got back up here...

Nothing wrong with 'quick', but 'rushed' wasn't worth it.

"Shit." I stuffed my gun into my holster and snapped on my waist pouch. "I wish I could stay. But I can't." I leaned across the bed to give him a hasty kiss.

He slipped a hand behind my head and turned it into a slow kiss. A long, hot, teasing kiss that set every nerve in my body tingling and begging for more. My hands glided over the hard muscles of his chest, drifting down toward a more enticing hardness.

I pulled away. "Goddammit, I want you. But there's no time to enjoy you."

He sighed and released me. "Okay, darlin'." He rolled out of bed and swayed momentarily, his hand going to his head. "Shit, this's gonna be ugly in a couple hours." He followed me to the door to watch while I donned my boots and wrapped my sleeping bag around me. When I leaned in to kiss him goodbye, he folded me into his arms.

"I dunno what to say, Aydan," he murmured against my hair. He pulled away to look into my eyes. "Thanks doesn't cover it, but... thanks. I owe ya."

I kissed him. "You don't owe me a thing." Pressing closer and circling my hips against him, I purred, "But if you'd care to make a small down-payment the next time I see you..."

He scowled in mock indignation. "Jesus, darlin', it ain't that small."

I laughed. "A large down-payment would be more than welcome, too."

"That's more like it," he growled, grinning. Pulling me closer, he nuzzled my neck, trailing spine-tingling whiskery kisses up to my ear. "Go down an' call Stemp an' then come right back." The hot promise in his sexy rasp made my breath quicken. "Tell him ya got a flat tire or somethin'."

"I c..."

He silenced my protest with his lips, sending heat rushing to all points south.

Jammed between us, my waist pouch vibrated.

Hellhound drew away, eyeing it with resignation. "He ain't gonna quit, is he?"

"No." I released my pent-up lust in a long sigh. "I really have to go."

He echoed my sigh. "Well, prob'ly for the best. Ya deserve better 'n what I can give ya when I'm half-way hung over."

"Are you kidding?" I shot him a grin. "Your worst is better than most guys' best."

"Aw, thanks, darlin'." He sobered and stroked my hair back from my cheek. "Be safe, Aydan. An' if things don't go the way ya planned with Stemp, tell him the truth. I'd rather go to jail for life than have ya suffer." Despite his earlier levity, the dark ghosts still haunted his eyes.

I slipped my arms around him to hold him tightly. "It'll be fine," I reassured us both.

Shivering in the truck a few minutes later, I pressed the speed-dial button on the secured phone. When Stemp answered, I spared no graciousness on him. "It's Aydan."

"What's your ETA?"

"Two hours."

"Report to my office immediately when you arrive."

"Fine." I pressed the disconnect button, wishing I had a receiver to slam down in his ear.

Late, but defying Stemp's orders anyway, I made a short detour to The Melted Spoon to grab a second breakfast when I arrived in Silverside, hoping to soothe the hollow shivering that shook my body. I wolfed down the hot peanut-buttered bagel in the parking lot at Sirius Dynamics before shuffling into the building, hugging a cardboard cup of tea that burned my hand without warming me.

The guard in the security wicket gave me a quizzical scrutiny. "'Morning, Aydan," he said in a tone that sounded like 'what the hell happened to you?'

"'Morning, Leo." I signed for my security fob and turned away without elaborating.

When I gained the second floor, the unflattering lights in the women's washroom revealed Rudolf the Red-Nosed Racoon in the mirror, complete with a puffy pink nose and black-shadowed bags under my eyes. A few spatters of dried blood decorated the front of my grubby T-shirt, and I was pretty sure I still smelled vomit from the vicinity of my boots.

Vanity had prompted me to leave my sleeping bag in the truck, but I might as well have worn it. All I needed to complete my fashion statement was a bottle of rotgut in a dirty paper bag.

I gave my reflection a weary grimace before squaring my shoulders and heading for Stemp's office, my mind buzzing with evasions and excuses.

CHAPTER 20

"Eventful night." Stemp's dispassionate gaze inventoried me from frowsy hair to malodorous boots.

"Yeah." I slumped in the guest chair and regarded him over his desk, hoping without optimism that he wouldn't notice the trembling of my hands. Fat chance. He was far too good to miss something like that.

"Report."

I blew out a long breath, gathering myself. "I went into the bar and got the money." I shoved the plump envelope across his desk. "...but things got complicated." I waved a hand in the direction of my nose "I got attacked. I... um, kind of lost control." Which was technically true. "It was self-defence," I added.

Also true.

Stemp eyed me narrowly. "A broken neck. No other marks on the body. That takes quite a bit of skill."

"It was an accident." I didn't sound convincing even to myself.

"Please don't insult my intelligence."

I slouched lower in the chair. "Sorry. I didn't mean... I just meant it shouldn't have happened. Like I said, things got a little out of control."

Stemp frowned. "Considering your careful adherence to your cover thus far, I'd say it was a considerable loss of control. Why were you up in that industrial area in the first place?"

I stared at him, my mind racing. "You were tracking my phone."

"Of course. As soon as you called for the cleanup crew, I started tracking your location."

Shit!

My brain accelerated into overdrive. He knew where I'd been. If he placed Arnie with me...

But he couldn't. He wouldn't have had any reason to track Arnie's phone, and there was no other way for him to know I wasn't alone.

I carried on with my story as planned. "I ran into one of my, um... informants. At the bar. It wasn't directly related to the mission, but I ended up going to the industrial park to meet this guy. When he attacked me..."

I let the sentence trail off.

So far I hadn't actually lied outright.

"This guy." Stemp's inflection placed air quotes around the words, his expression unreadable. "James Helmand, senior. Your lover's father. Odd coincidence."

Damn, I'd been clinging to the faint hope that they would quietly dispose of the body without identifying it, but I hadn't truly believed it would be that easy. I resisted the urge to gulp and held his gaze while I trotted out the excuse I'd prepared.

"Not really that odd. You know Arnie's brother James was high up in the gang hierarchy when you arrested him, and James Senior has been in and out of the prison system all his life. Gang-related people hang around a gang-related bar. Bad luck he ended up dead, but not really surprising I ran into him."

With an effort I prevented myself from babbling more justifications. "And Arnie's not really my lover," I added. "I told you before, we just have a casual arrangement. I haven't seen him..."

I stopped myself. Stemp knew where I'd been.

"...hadn't seen him for a couple of months," I amended.

"But you saw him last night." Stemp looked relaxed, almost bored, but I knew him too well. He wouldn't miss even the tiniest inconsistency in my story.

I leaned back in the chair, deliberately easing my posture. Open, relaxed body language. No fidgeting. "Yeah, I went to his apartment." I grimaced. "I thought I should go in person. I couldn't really see phoning him in the middle of the night to say 'Hi, how are you, sorry I haven't talked to you in two months, oh, and by the way I just killed your father'."

Still not a lie. I had only said I 'couldn't see' saying that.

Stemp's reptilian features didn't twitch. "And how did he react?"

"He wasn't exactly heart-broken." I took a chance. "You must have seen the police reports on all the times his father assaulted him."

"Which makes it very convenient that you killed his father for him."

Fear exploded as frustration. "It was nothing to do with convenience! I explained that already. What the hell do you want from me?"

He leaned forward, skewering me with a look. "I want to know why I'm doing a cleanup that's apparently unrelated to your current assignment. If this meeting with your informant was part of your other ops, your other chain of command should deal with the fallout. It takes time and resources to make a dead body vanish, even when you dispatch it as neatly and conveniently as this one. I have to justify that cost to my higher-ups."

I tamped down my nervous need to jump up and pace, and held my voice steady. "I told you, it was self-defence. He attacked me. You're always telling me I shouldn't hesitate to shoot someone if necessary, so I don't see why this is a big deal."

"Why didn't you subdue him with the trank gun? It wasn't so long ago that you were trying to convince me you wanted to be able to use non-lethal force."

Stalemate.

I eyed him in silence.

He waited, and the silence thickened.

I cracked first. "I told you, I lost control."

"Yes." His flat amber gaze bored holes in my skull. "Two months ago, you fired seven rounds into Kasper Doytchevsky's face at point-blank range even though he was already incapacitated. Killing him was unnecessary and deprived us of the chance to gain valuable information from interrogating him. At the time, I made allowances because I knew what he had done to you. But now I have another body on my hands. Had Helmand attacked you before, too?"

For a fraction of a second I considered lying, but the threat of the lie detector loomed in the back of my mind. Better if I could honestly say I hadn't lied at all.

"No. I'd never met him before last night."

"How badly are you injured?"

I resisted the urge to touch my aching nose. "Just a punch in the nose and a bruise on the side of my head. I'll go and see Dr. Roth later."

Stemp appraised me in silence for a moment. "I'm having a difficult time believing that a relatively minor injury was sufficient to make you breach a cover that you've maintained so long and so successfully even under extreme duress."

My throat went dry.

Don't gulp. Don't blink. Don't look away.

I held his gaze, my eyes watering with the effort.

Thank God, he misinterpreted the moisture in my eyes. His voice softened. "Did something else happen that triggered your reaction?"

I gulped and blinked and looked away after all. "Well... yeah, I guess..." I cleared my throat and studied the lush potted plant in the corner, incongruous in his otherwise barren office. "I... had a couple of flashbacks..."

My heart rate ratcheted up at the memory, and I drew a calming breath and held my voice steady. "Hibbert thought I should be more appreciative of the fact that he doubled the offer. Thanks to your goddamn porn star cover, he..." I determinedly suppressed a shudder. "I had to pretend to give him a blowjob." I realized I was scrubbing my palm against my jeans again and desisted. "I guess I was a little more wound up than I realized," I finished.

"I'm sorry." His sincere tone shocked me into meeting his eyes. He continued, "When I assigned that cover, I had no idea you would become an agent. If I had known then what I know now, I would have handled it differently."

Was that sympathy in his expression?

"You don't need to do this," he said. "We'll find another way. And you should talk to Dr. Rawling. I'm sorry this has been so traumatic for you."

I closed my gaping mouth. "It's, um... it's okay. I don't want to waste this chance. I'll go ahead with it."

"That's not necessary, and under the circumstances, I don't think it's advisable. Dr. Rawling was right. It's too soon for you to undertake this."

I straightened. "I'll finish it. The hard part's over. All I have to do is give him the list and collect the rest of the money. I didn't go through all that shit last night just to walk away now."

"Agent Kelly, sometimes it's necessary for our agents to give their lives on a mission, but you don't have to renounce your soul. Providing sexual favours to further a transaction is neither necessary nor desirable."

Stemp's usual impassive facade dropped, and I saw the face of a man worn down by duty and sacrifice. When he spoke again, his voice held compassion. "When your work begins to destroy you, it's time to quit. That's why I transferred out of active service. And I've seen far too many excellent female agents damaged by exactly this situation. Walk away now, Aydan. His demands will only escalate. You don't have to prostitute yourself for your country."

My throat tightened at the rare glimpse of the human being behind the mask, and I swallowed hard before replying. "Thanks." My voice came out husky, and I swallowed again before continuing. "I appreciate your concern. But I think I have a way to get out of the situation gracefully and convincingly. And I'd really like to finish this."

He smiled, more resignation than humour. "I expected you'd say that. Should I arrange a hand-to-hand combat qualification for you, too?"

"God, no! Not unless you really want to watch Germain

beat the shit out of me."

"Not particularly." Stemp appraised me in silence for a moment. "So you intend to maintain your bookkeeping cover? You wouldn't fight even for your qualification?"

"Even if I was capable of fighting Germain, I wouldn't. And I'd really appreciate it if nobody ever found out about Helmand."

"A report has to go through the upper chain of command, but I can redact the records so it's strictly need-to-know. Unless there's some administrative reason to access them, that should do it."

"Okay. Thanks." I screwed up my courage. "Um... and... another thing..."

Too much dangerous knowledge in my brain. Too much risk for the people I cared about.

Only one way to protect them.

I hesitated, wondering if I was about to do something profoundly stupid. Well, hell, it wouldn't be the first time.

I drew a deep breath and looked Stemp square in the eye. "I won't risk letting anybody else read my mind. If anybody takes control of me in the sim again, I'll kill them."

He sat back slowly in his chair, his face inscrutable again while he studied me. "Another loss of control?" he asked at length, his tone noncommittal.

I mentally crossed my fingers for luck and made my voice as neutral as his. "Something like that."

Silence swelled between us, stealing the air from the room. His stillness and unblinking gaze reminded me of a statue in a wax museum, and I resisted the idiotic urge to poke him and see if he moved. I did my best to emulate his immobility, but my chest vibrated with the pounding of my heart.

Come on, say something, dammit. Sweat prickled my backbone.

I held myself still. The silence stretched interminably.

"I can't condone that," he said at last.

Shit, I'd read him wrong. A jolt of burning adrenaline seared my veins, my guts twisting with bitterness. Shouldn't have trusted him. Never trust anybody, stupid.

Too late now.

Would he shoot me on the spot or inflict the slow hell of prison in the full knowledge of my claustrophobic terror? I resisted the urge to close my eyes as he reached into his desk drawer.

When he withdrew a bug detector and activated it, the immobility I'd wished for earlier was suddenly bestowed upon me. Frozen, I stared at the green light without breathing.

About a year later, he finally spoke. "Off the record, though, I can thank you for resolving a very difficult dilemma for me."

I managed a shallow breath. "...ah?"

He shrugged. "You must know where my priorities lie. If you defend yourself inside the network, my interests are protected."

Of course. His wife and daughter. It suddenly occurred to me that he might not need me now that he had Tammy to do his decryptions. If Sam's 'heart attack' was his doing, he might have been considering an 'accident' for me, too, to eliminate the risk to Katya and Anna.

I might have just saved my own life. Score one for trust after all.

I drew a slightly deeper breath. "Does anybody else know about...?

"No."

"Not even your chain of command? Why..." I bit back the question. The less I knew, the better. "Never mind."

He dropped the detector back into his drawer and leaned back, his expression as bland as if we'd been discussing the weather. "You'll need to attend anger-management classes."

"Uh... okay...?" I frowned a question at him.

"It protects both of us. Me, from an administrative standpoint, in case you suffer another..." he gave me an ironic tilt of his chin. "...loss of control. In the past months, you have, after all, assaulted nearly everyone you've worked with. Including me. And you've uttered threats and been verbally abusive."

I slid lower in the chair. "Sorry. Those were misunderstandings."

"I know. But if I don't act and someone else dies at your hands, my chain of command will demand answers. And it also protects you." His smile was wry. "If you're working to resolve your anger issues, you'll be deemed less of a risk. And who knows, you may actually benefit from it. I, for one, would be pleased to avoid having your gun jammed in my throat a second time."

I squirmed, too embarrassed to meet his eyes. "Um, yeah. Sorry. Okay, I'll go."

"Good. It's a ten-week series starting after Christmas. I'll contact Dr. Rawling and tell him you'll be joining them."

I suppressed a groan and gave him my best imploring big brown eyes. "Can I go to the next series instead?"

His silence wilted me more effectively than any reply.

"Fine," I muttered. "But I didn't have any fucking anger issues before all this bullshit started."

Amusement tugged at the corner of Stemp's mouth.

"That's the point."

Shit. Nothing like getting angry about being sent to an anger-management class. This time the groan escaped, and I sank my head into my hands.

"Go and see Dr. Roth. Then go home. Rest and eat." The warmth in his voice surprised me. "I'll reschedule the team meeting for thirteen hundred."

When I looked up, he still hadn't resumed his aloof façade. I managed a genuine smile for Charles Stemp, the human being. "Thanks."

CHAPTER 21

Climbing the stairs at Sirius Dynamics a couple of hours later, I eased out a long breath. Clean clothes, a nap, lunch, and an ice pack had made me feel, if not human, at least halfway to simian. Vastly better than the pressed shit I'd felt like earlier, anyway.

When I turned the corner into my office I paused, uneasiness fluttering down to perch in the pit of my stomach. Kane and Stemp stood near the wall, their expressions and posture identically cop-neutral. Spider sat behind my desk as if barricading himself from the group, blotches of angry colour on his cheeks. Jack's usually flawless complexion was blotchy, too, and her pink nose rivalled mine.

"Oh, Aydan!" Jack surveyed my face, tears welling up in her reddened eyes. "You must have just heard, too."

"Uh... I, uh..."

What the hell? I retreated to the safety of the excuse I'd prepared earlier. "Um... allergies..." I made a vague gesture nose-ward. "I was digging for some stuff in my shed and I got a face full of something I really reacted to. Heard what? What's going on?"

"Sam died of a heart attack yesterday. I just found out. I can hardly believe it, it's such a shock."

"Oh." With an effort, I prevented myself from glancing at Stemp. "That's..." I groped for something sincere to say. Not exactly a tragedy. And I could hardly say I was shocked. "...um... sad," I finished weakly.

"Oh, Aydan, I'm sorry, I didn't mean to spring it on you like that. Come and sit down." Jack reached out to guide me to the sofa and laid a sympathetic hand on my shoulder. "Would you like a glass of water?"

"Um, no. Thanks, Jack. I'm fine." I frowned, taking in Spider's rigid posture and flashing eyes. He didn't look shocked or sad. He looked mad as hell. My uneasiness morphed into outright worry. "Hey, Spider, are you-"

"I have to go. I don't feel well." Spider jerked to his feet and strode out, his movements stiff.

I hurried in his wake. "Are you okay? Do you want a ride home?"

He turned to face me in the hallway, feverish colour burning in his cheeks. "No thanks, I'll drive myself," he snapped, and stalked away.

Disconcerted, I trailed back into my office. Stemp's neutral expression hadn't altered, but I had the distinct impression it was taking some effort for him to hold onto it.

Jack gave him an uncomfortable glance. "Well... I guess... I guess I'll go, too, then." She hurried out.

I sank onto my couch, staring after her and wondering what the hell I'd missed.

Stemp cleared his throat and passed me an envelope. "The phone list. Call Hibbert whenever it suits you, and let me know what arrangements you make for delivery."

I hesitated. "Is it okay if I..." I gestured at the open flap of the envelope.

"Of course." Stemp shot me a slightly quizzical look,

which I ignored while I slid the double-spaced photocopied sheets out and examined them.

I recognized very few of the names on the list, but then again, I didn't really hobnob with anybody except my team. I noted Kane's name, and my alias of Arlene Widdenback, but no 'Charles Stemp'. I raised an eyebrow in his direction.

"Most of the list is accurate, but I've seeded it with some names that might be of interest to Fuzzy Bunny, while conveniently omitting a few others," Stemp confirmed. "There's nothing in that list that can't be safely disseminated."

"Okay, good." I tucked it back in the envelope, pretending I hadn't just absorbed an infusion of queasy fear at the thought of facing Hibbert again. "I'll let you know as soon as I talk to him."

"Very well." Stemp glanced at Kane. "The two of you may as well tackle some more decryptions this afternoon. Unless you need Webb for anything?"

"No, I don't think so." I shot a look in Kane's direction. "John? How about you?"

"Not that I can think of," he confirmed. He detached himself from the wall to sit in the chair across from me. "Let's get started. Unless you want to call Hibbert first?"

I tossed the envelope onto the coffee table and laced my fingers in my lap to hide their trembling. "No, I'll do that later. Let's do some decryptions."

The work dragged interminably, our usual process made frustratingly slow without Spider's expert computer skills. When we exited the network a couple of hours later, I ground my raging headache against the back of the sofa, spitting some particularly colourful profanity I usually reserved for special occasions.

Kane's hands immobilized my head, his firm fingertips searching out the red-hot knots in my scalp and massaging them away. I let out a whimper of sheer gratitude and went limp under his ministrations.

The pain subsided rapidly but I kept my eyes closed, wallowing shamelessly in his touch until a small blissful moan escaped despite my best efforts.

I pulled away and sat up to shoot a guilty glance around my office. Fortunately we were the only two present, and I turned to face Kane, hoping the warmth in my cheeks wasn't too noticeable.

"That seemed like a bad one," he observed neutrally, and I gave quick and silent thanks that he was continuing our usual friendly but impersonal business interaction.

"Yeah." I rolled my head and shoulders. "I'm just going to make a quick pit stop, and then we can get back to it."

"I think you need a longer break." A hint of inflection in the remark made me search his face, wondering if I'd imagined it. "Let's go down to the Melted Spoon for a snack," he added. He smiled. "I'd hate to have to pick you up off the floor again."

I returned his smile. "That won't happen. I haven't been working that hard." A fractional narrowing of his eyes prompted me to add, "But I could use a snack anyway. I'm just going to zip to the bathroom, and then I'll meet you in the lobby."

Shivering my way down the sidewalk beside Kane a few minutes later, I retreated deeper into the hood of my parka to evade the icy fingers of wind that slipped through every tiny aperture.

I cast a quizzical glance up at his profile. "Um..."

He silenced me with a small hand movement and kept walking, his hand continuing the gesture into his jacket pocket. A couple of seconds later it emerged again and Kane used the motion to look at his watch, the steady green light of a bug detector glowing briefly from his half-concealed palm before he returned it to his pocket.

"I had a feeling this wasn't just a nice brisk walk out in the filthy freezing cold," I whispered, trying not to move my lips too much.

Kane turned a friendly smile on me. "Did you kill him?" he demanded through his teeth.

My feet forgot how to walk.

Kane's hand shot out to grab my arm as I stumbled, and he leaned closer as if in concern. "You did kill him, didn't you?" he hissed.

Shit!

Protect Arnie.

My brain caught up and booted my mouth into gear. "Y-yes."

Kane let go of me and kept walking. His face was composed, but an arctic storm raged in his eyes. "So that's why you wanted me to leave. So you could sneak back and kill him. You... that's..."

Words apparently failed him, and he jerked his jacket collar tighter, his mouth set in a grim line. The wind whistled between us, not nearly as cold as the frost emanating from Kane's rigid posture.

"I..." I began, but he was already speaking, his voice low and hard.

"You've gone too far, Aydan. Murdering a defenseless old man just to protect me is not only illegal and cold-blooded as hell, it's, it's..." Muscles bulged in his jaw. "It's goddamn insulting! And-"

Answering anger boiled up in my veins. "Fuck *defenseless*! That asshole-"

I clapped my mouth shut as I belatedly processed his words. Kill a defenceless old man to protect Kane...

Shit.

"Um, are you talking about Sam?" I asked meekly. "Because I didn't kill him."

Kane didn't stumble, but he shot me a single wide-eyed glance that for him was tantamount to standing stock-still and gaping at me.

An instant later, his cop face closed down and we walked on in silence for a few moments before he spoke again. "You didn't kill Kraus?"

"No." I crossed my fingers inside my pocket even though I wasn't strictly lying. "As far as I know he had a heart attack."

"So who did you kill?"

I hunched my shoulders and stuffed my fists deeper in my pockets. "I can't tell you."

I dared a peek at the muscles rippling in his jaw. Could I tell him?

No. Nobody could know.

"Sorry," I added.

Several more silent strides.

"You were attacked last night." His grey gaze scoured my face for a moment before turning forward again in a convincing imitation of unconcern. "What happened?"

I grimaced, mentally cursing my lack of control and his powers of observation.

"Yes, I noticed your swollen nose," he confirmed grimly.

"Allergies, my foot. You killed your attacker, didn't you? Who was it? Why didn't Stemp mention anything about this when he briefed us this afternoon?"

"It's, um... it's complicated." I gave him a pleading look. "Could you please forget I said anything about it? Nobody is supposed to know."

His eyes narrowed. "Not even Stemp?"

"Stemp knows. Nobody else."

Kane didn't bother to conceal his sigh of relief, his shoulders relaxing. "So it was one of your other ops. That's why we weren't briefed."

I aimed a kick at an inoffensive lump of snow and spoke before the lie could choke me. "Yeah."

"I'm sorry, Aydan." He spoke quickly as we arrived at the Melted Spoon. "I jumped to a conclusion when I should have trusted you. Can you forgive me?"

The guilt of my lies coiled around my throat. "It's fine. Forget it," I muttered, and yanked open the door of the coffee shop without looking at him.

"I don't blame you for being angry with me." Kane spoke moments after we'd regained the sidewalk, steaming cardboard cups in hand. "I'm sorry I-"

"John, it's fine," I interrupted. "I'm not mad. Just forget it." I clammed up as a heavily-muffled shopper hurried by in the opposite direction. "It was an honest mistake," I added quietly when we were alone on the sidewalk again. "I won't say I'm sorry he's dead, because now you're safe. But it was convenient timing, and I probably would have thought the same in your position."

"It *was* suspiciously good timing..." He hesitated.

"Stemp had finished interrogating him before he died, so the timing wasn't as good as you think. But luckily he didn't tell Stemp about you and me." I met his eyes steadily and answered his unasked question without rancor. "I really didn't kill him."

He nodded, and our walk back to the office was considerably less chilly.

Slouched at my desk a few minutes later, I hugged my cup of tea and eyed the envelope containing Stemp's phone list with no enthusiasm whatsoever.

Blowing out a long breath, I relinquished the tea and reached for the phone. Kane would arrive in moments with the network key, and I'd really prefer to do this without an audience.

I punched in Hibbert's number before I could chicken out and clenched the receiver in a sweaty fist, my prepared script swirling through my brain.

Far too soon, Hibbert's unctuous voice slithered to my ear. "Arlene. What a pleasure."

He gave the word a lewd emphasis, and I reflexively scrubbed my lips with the back of my hand, my guts twisting with the remembered need to gag.

"I have the list." My words choked out, and I drew a deep breath and clamped down on control. "Where should I leave it?" Better this time. Now I sounded cool and confident.

"Why don't we meet?" Slimy satisfaction oozed from his voice. "We can engage in some more... mutual benefits."

"I don't think so." I let 'cool' fade into 'icy'. "The benefits were hardly mutual. You fell asleep right afterward. You got your thank-you, so we're done."

"I wasn't at my best. I'll make it up to you next time."

He spoke with the self-important nonchalance of a man accustomed to slavish cooperation.

I cranked my vocal thermostat down to 'flash-freeze'. "My industry is very highly regulated, and actors rarely take up with people outside it.   Last night's little *episode* reminded me why. There won't be a next time."

"Fine." Scorn barbed his voice. "You weren't such hot shit. I can get better head from a cheap hooker."

I struggled to keep a straight face at that resounding truth, and channeled every disapproving grade-school teacher I'd ever encountered.   "Then I suggest you do so. Now, the list; and my money. Where and when?"

"Tomorrow at the Hogback-"

"No," I snapped.

A contemptuous sigh drifted over the line. "Tomorrow *morning* at eleven A.M., outside the Hogback.   The bar doesn't open until eleven-thirty." The line went dead in my ear.

I was spitting a stream of anatomically impossible instructions to the phone when Kane arrived. He raised an eyebrow as I slapped the receiver back into its cradle.

"...and bite it, you limp-dicked ratfuck!" I finished before transferring my attention to him.

His other eyebrow joined the first. "That didn't sound good."

"Asshole! Hibbert, not you," I qualified hurriedly.

"Problem?"

I blew out a breath and stretched, eliciting a snap-crackle-pop from my tense neck and shoulders. "No. The guy's just a dickhead.   I'll give him the list tomorrow morning and hope I don't have to deal with him again." I reached for the phone again. "I have to report to Stemp, and then I'll be ready to do some more decryptions."

Leaving the network at the end of the day, my usual jolt of pain joined the residual throbbing of my nose to offer a convincing simulation of being punched rhythmically in the face. I hugged my aching skull and keened wordless misery through my teeth.

When Kane's big warm hands began to work their magic on my knotted muscles, I slumped forward, head in hands to hide the moisture that tried to escape my screwed-shut eyes.

The worst of the pain subsided at last, and I regained enough presence of mind to wonder how long Kane would keep massaging if I didn't sit up. Banishing the selfish temptation to find out, I straightened slowly and swallowed my whimper of protest when his touch fell away.

"Do you want to go over to Blue Eddy's and get dinner before the self-defence workshop tonight?" Kane asked.

"I'd like to, but..." I squinted at my watch. "I'm just going to grab something quick and then I want to drop in at Spider's to see how he's feeling."

"All right. Tell him I hope he feels better soon." His sexy laugh lines crinkled. "I'll see you tonight."

He took the network key and strode out, leaving me to wonder if it was only my overactive imagination that had made his words sound like a provocative promise.

CHAPTER 22

Huddling into my parka against the icy wind, I tapped on the door of Spider's small bungalow.

Maybe I should have phoned instead.

After a short wait, I tapped again, unwilling to use the doorbell in case he was asleep.

I was about to give up and go back to my car when the door opened and Linda peeked out.

Renewed concern chilled me. "What are you doing home? Is Spider that sick?"

"No... I mean..." She hovered in the narrow opening and glanced over her shoulder before returning her attention to me. "I just haven't left for work yet. My shift doesn't start until eight."

"What's wrong?" My pulse accelerated when she glanced behind her again, her face pinched with worry. I leaned forward, trying to see into the house without being too obvious. "Tell me what's wrong, Linda. Let me help."

"I..." She hesitated, biting her lip.

"Who is it?" Spider's voice drifted from within.

"Aydan's here to see you." Linda gave me an imploring look, but I couldn't tell whether she wanted me to push my way in or push off.

"Hey, Spider, are you okay?" I called. "What's wrong?"

A moment later he appeared, draping his lanky arms around Linda from behind, his gangling six-foot-two towering over her tiny figure. He dropped a kiss on the top of her head. "Thanks, sweetie. It's okay, Aydan's exactly the person I need to talk to. Come on in, Aydan."

Linda sagged with relief and then stretched up on her tiptoes to collect another kiss before turning her usual impish grin back to me. "You heard the master of the house. Come on in."

After shedding my boots and jacket in their front hall, I followed them into the small living room. "It looks great, Spider. Almost the same as before the fire. Not that I noticed much when I came barrelling through the last time."

He motioned me into a beanbag chair before folding himself onto a red loveseat spattered with large white polka-dots. "Not exactly the same." He smiled and waved a hand that encompassed the bright modern décor. "Linda picked out all the colours and furniture this time."

She curled up next to him, smiling like a satisfied cat, and I grinned. "It suits you both." I very nearly added, 'you'll be happy together here', but bit my tongue at the last second. Too close to spilling the beans. "What happened today at work?" I asked instead. "You weren't really sick, were you, Spider?"

Colour rose on his cheeks, but he met my eyes squarely. "No. I was mad."

"Why?"

He shot a quick glance at Linda and answered cautiously. "I was told to do something I... couldn't. Morally."

I stared at him in confusion for a moment before the light dawned. Stemp wanted Tammy to be controlled inside the network without her knowledge. Jack had programmed Spider into my controller key as a test. I was willing to bet Tammy's controller key was programmed for Spider, too.

"Oh." I raised an eyebrow at him, trying to figure out a way to ask without divulging classified information in front of Linda. "Um... driving?"

His flush deepened, his eyes flashing. "I won't do it. I told Stemp that. It's sick and wrong."

Linda scrunched smaller beside him, looking less like a happy cat and more like a miserable child. "But, sweetie, what are you going to do?"

"I don't know, but I won't do that."

"Can't you tell me what it is?" she pleaded. "Maybe I could help if I knew."

"No," Spider and I said in unison. "I'm sorry," he added, his arm tightening around her. "I'd totally tell you if I could, but I just can't." He turned a troubled face to me. "What should I do, Aydan?"

I slumped on the beanbag. "Shit, Spider, I don't know. I wouldn't ask you to compromise your principles, but I don't see much alternative." At his despairing look, I summoned up the most confident voice I could manage. "I'll think about it. Don't worry, between the two of us we'll come up with something. Tomorrow's Friday anyway, so you can buy some time to think about it over the weekend. I hear the twenty-four-hour stomach flu is pretty nasty."

"Thanks, Aydan, I knew you'd be able to help!"

The bright hope in his face made my own stomach feel distinctly flu-like. I couldn't see any way out, and now he was counting on me. Shit.

Two young faces beamed at me with supreme confidence, and I lurched to my feet. "Well, I have to get going. Lola and I are doing the self-defence workshop again tonight."

"I'm glad you went with her," Linda said. "She needed to go to get her confidence back, but I just couldn't go with her. It makes me feel sick to even think about intentionally hurting another human being."

"Um." I turned away, glad she didn't know how many human beings I'd hurt. Hell, murdered. No point in sugar-coating it.

Her small hand landed on my arm and when I turned, her normally sparkling blue eyes were serious.

"That's why I'm really glad there are brave people like you to protect wimps like me," she said. "Be proud of what you do, Aydan. We need you."

I choked up. After a moment, I managed to mutter 'thanks' as I hurried to the front door and bent to tie my boots.

"Oh, hey, Aydan, I forgot to mention this earlier," Spider said. "We're having a housewarming-slash-Christmas Eve party next Saturday evening. Can you come?"

I looked up, thankful for the distraction, and managed a bright smile. "Thanks, Spider, you bet. I'll look forward to it."

Later as we headed across the parking lot toward the rec centre, Lola nudged me with a suggestive elbow. "So, are you going to make a move on Big John? I'm sure he's got the hots for you. Just give him the old come-hither smile, and he'll be all yours."

I laughed. "You never quit, do you? What makes you think he's got the hots for me?" I kept the question light, but caution bristled my antennae. If Lola had noticed something, others might, too. And that was dangerous.

"Well, he'd be stupid not to, wouldn't he?" She smirked. "You're one hot patootie. If he's got eyes in his head, he has to be looking."

Jack gave us a cheery wave from the building's entrance and waited for us to catch up. I lowered my voice. "Trust me, if he's looking for hot, *that's* hot." I cut my eyes toward Jack's radiant blonde beauty.

Lola sniffed. "She's too young for him. And she's too nice. A man like that needs a mature woman with a little wicked edge."

I gave her a nudge of my own. "Sounds like you're talking about yourself."

"Well, hell yeah, honey." She leered up at me, and we rode our wave of laughter to the door.

A short time later, her teasing echoed in my ears when Kane met my eyes over the heads of the class, looking as delicious as ever in his gym shorts and T-shirt. "Aydan, will you help me with this demonstration, please? I need someone your height."

I swallowed a skittering sensation and threaded my way to the front of the gym. He gave me his usual pleasant smile before turning to the class. "There are several ways to secure an arm-bar hold from the standing position if someone has made an aggressive move toward you. This will look a little different if your attacker is much larger than you, but you should be able to get the idea if I demonstrate it with Aydan."

He turned to face me. "I'll demonstrate the full move first, and then I'll walk through the fundamental mechanics. Aydan, just stay loose and follow the path of the force. I won't put any strength into it, but don't hesitate to tap out if you feel uncomfortable. Go ahead and grab my arm as if you're attacking me now."

I drew a short breath and did as he asked. In an instant, my arm was locked, my torso twisting down to follow the force, and panic ripped through me. Kane's voice was a distant echo. "...pressure at the back of the arm to..."

Hibbert's hard hands forced me down. My tap-out was more like a frantic slap, and I jerked away when Kane released me, my hands flying up aggressively. Nearly hyperventilating, I caught myself at the last moment and dropped my guard, pasting a smile on my face through sheer force of will.

I knew I hadn't fooled Kane. His grey gaze flicked over me, assessing my reaction in a fraction of a second before turning his easy smile to the class. "So you can see it really requires very little strength; it's just a matter of effective leverage. Now I'll need a volunteer who's smaller. Jack, would you help me? I'll walk you through the steps while you put the arm-bar hold on me."

Under the cover of his words, I did a fast fade to the changing room, where I locked myself into a cubicle and schooled myself into slow, steady yoga breaths. A few moments later, a tap on the door heralded Lola's arrival.

"Aydan? Honey, are you okay?"

I emerged, smile in place. "Yeah, fine. I just had to pee."

"Horse hockey."

I slumped against the sink. "Was it that obvious?"

She slid an arm around me and squeezed. "No, hon, I don't think anybody else even noticed. I was just giving you the eagle eye because I was afraid something like that might happen when he called you up there."

I straightened. "Then let's get back out there before

anybody does notice."

"If you're sure you're okay."

"I'm fine."

Lola watched me closely while we practiced the next few holds, but I had prepared myself for my reaction and hid it well. After a while she relaxed, and by the end of the class we were back to our usual unwholesome banter. Jack joined us, blushing over one of Lola's raunchier sallies, and the three of us headed laughing for the exit.

I was almost at the door when Kane's voice stopped me. "Aydan, do you have a minute?"

"Sure." I turned to see him still surrounded by his usual gaggle of admirers.

"I just have to..." He half-gestured to his audience, and I nodded.

"No problem, I'm not in a hurry." I propped myself against the wall to wait.

Lola leaned close to murmur, "Do you want me to stay? Are you okay?"

"I'm fine. Thanks, though."

She scowled. "Does that really mean 'fine', or is this another one of your horse-hockey 'fine's? 'Cause I'm staying if you don't feel safe."

"This is the real deal. I'm fine." I grinned at her ferocious protectiveness. "Thanks, Lola. Good night."

She relaxed into a smile. "Good night, then, hon. See you tomorrow." She leaned closer, bouncing her eyebrows. "Don't forget the come-hither smile."

I gave her an affectionate push. "Get lost."

Nearly ten minutes later, the last member of Kane's fan club finally departed with a wistful backward glance. He stretched and rolled his shoulders, coincidentally offering me a magnificent view of his flexing muscles before coming over with a smile. "It's great to see these women taking charge of their own safety. That kind of interest really makes it rewarding to teach workshops like these."

It seemed crass to point out that the interest was directed at his hard-muscled physique, so I just smiled and nodded.

He sobered. "I owe you an apology. I triggered something for you tonight with that arm-bar, didn't I? I should have checked with you before calling you to volunteer. I'm sorry."

I waved an embarrassed hand. "It's fine. No big deal."

"It looked like a big deal." His face softened, his grey gaze searching my face. "Do you want to talk about it?"

"No."

His remote cop face descended, and I regretted my abruptness. "But..." I blurted, trying to think of a way to make it better. "Um..."

He waited.

"Um, is there a way to escape that arm-bar?" I finished in a blaze of inspiration. "It's great to be able to do it, but it'd be even better to be able to get out of it."

Kane smiled, the warmth returning to his eyes. "There are several ways. I can show you sometime if you'd like."

"How about now? If you have time?"

"I have time." He glanced at his watch. "And the gym is booked until ten, so we've still got twenty minutes."

I relaxed. Bad feelings averted. "Great, let's do it."

We took our positions on the mat, and Kane eyed me with concern. "The problem is, if you want to practice getting out of it, I'll have to put the hold on you in the first place. Are you all right with that?"

"Oh, yeah, I'm fine." His doubtful expression made me add, "It just took me by surprise because it was still too fresh in my memory..." I shut up.

"Fresh, like last night?" he inquired gently.

"Um, yeah." Really didn't want to go there. "But it's fine. It was just the surprise. You could do exactly the same thing right now and it wouldn't bother me a bit."

That was a flat-out lie. When I found myself bent double again, it bothered me a hell of a lot, but I clenched my teeth. Just a reaction. Do it, go through it, and the reaction would fade. No need to panic.

I concentrated on Kane's voice. "Grab my arm like I showed you. Pull. Lock it with your shoulder. That's it, now throw your weight forward." He rolled to the mat. "But you have to be fast. If your assailant is stronger than you, you'll only achieve this with surprise. You can't make it a contest of strength. I'll show you."

He secured the arm-bar on me again and I managed not to panic.

"If I'm expecting it..." His arm flexed next to my face as I pulled on his wrist. "...it's your strength against mine..."

Hello, bicep.

"...and you won't win that."

"Right," I panted, not sure whether I was breathless from exertion or the sudden realization that our naked legs were entwined and my arm was pressed low against his corrugated midsection.

"And this escape only works if you can actually reach his wrist," Kane continued, apparently oblivious to my discomfiture. "Here's another option..."

A couple more rolls and tumbles on the mat, and my earlier panic was obscured by a rising tide of arousal. Why hadn't I considered martial arts before? Cheap opportunity to roll around with a buff guy. Duh.

I squeaked and tapped Kane's hand as he bore down a little too hard. Okay, the pain factor was definitely a drawback. But still...

I shook myself and refocused.

"...most fights end up on the ground," Kane was saying. "If you end up in an arm-bar on the ground..." A flurry of motion and suddenly I lay gasping on my back, my hand locked against his chest. And my arm jammed tightly between his legs.

"If I flex my hips..." He did exactly that, and my brain short-circuited at the memory of that well-endowed portion of his anatomy pressed against other parts of my body.

I missed the rest of his exposition.

He rolled free and lay down on the mat beside me. "I won't get into the mechanics of how to secure this hold in the first place, but I'll show you how to get out of it. Just put one leg over my neck and the other over my chest and hold my arm the way I held yours."

I fumbled into position, acutely conscious of the thickness of his arm between my legs and hoping my shorts weren't as damp as they felt. His five o'clock shadow scuffed against my bare thigh, raising goosebumps all over my body.

"Good, now flex your hips..." He trailed off as our eyes met.

I couldn't help it. There was nothing I could do but watch the train wreck.

My crotch pressed up against his hot, hard muscles.

My hips did a teasing little wiggle.

Kane's eyes went glassy for an instant, then ignited with his wicked grin. His arm flexed against me, and my breath came out in a tiny moan.

Sweet Jesus, please tell me I'm not humping this man's arm in the middle of a public gym.

Oh, yes I am.

I jerked free and scooted backward, my face on fire. My stretchy gym shorts dragged against the mat, conspiring to humiliate me as much as possible by creeping down my hips. I sprang up and yanked them back into place while Kane lay grinning up at me.

He rolled to his feet in a single sinuous movement to smile down from close range. "Here ends the lesson," he rumbled, his eyes devouring me.

"Uh, thanks," I stammered, and fled.

CHAPTER 23

Alternating between waves of residual lust and nervous anticipation of my upcoming meeting with Hibbert, I spent a shitty night tossing and turning. When my alarm blared at six A.M., I hauled myself into the shower, grumbling obscenities foul enough to peel the chrome off the taps.

After a breakfast I didn't taste, I jittered in front of my computer, pecking ineffectually at some of my bookkeeping tasks until it was time to leave.

The trip didn't soothe my nerves one bit. The wind had picked up overnight, and snow sifted across the highway in a lazy, treacherous ground-drift that tried to seduce my tired brain into following it across the centre line and into oncoming traffic.

I cranked the radio a little louder and sang until I couldn't stand myself anymore. At last I gave up and pulled off the road to jog around the car a few times. That helped for only a few minutes before I had to fight the deadly drowsiness again.

By the time I got to the outskirts of Calgary, my head was thumping as though the Hogback's finest were partying behind my eyeballs. I pulled over one more time, peeling my aching fingers off the steering wheel and groaning my stiffened body into a semblance of standing position. A glance at my watch drove the last of my sleepiness away. Hibbert had said eleven.

Too damn many stops along the road, and I still had one more to make. I was going to be late.

Swearing, I flung myself back in the car and stepped on the gas.

When I pulled up in front of the Hogback at eleven-twenty, there was no sign of Hibbert, but several shabby vehicles idled in front of the building. The bearded drivers slouched scowling, obviously waiting for the bar to open. I drove on by without making eye contact, nervously peeking from my peripheral vision. My shiny blue Legacy stood out like the Virgin Mary in a brothel, and I swore again.

I had considered driving my old truck, but the weather had convinced me a modern all-wheel-drive vehicle would be a safer choice. And it would have been, too, if I'd been on time. I pulled a U-turn and cruised back, scouring the parking lot for a silver Mercedes.

Heads turned and hostile eyes tracked my conspicuously new car.

Dammit.

I was almost abreast of the bar when Hibbert stepped out the front door and flagged me down with an imperious gesture. He strode over to the passenger side and I hesitated.

I'd be stupid to let him in my car.

Stupider still to get out and make a blatant exchange in front of a gallery of witnesses who would be delighted to scoop up an easy five grand by mugging me.

Too stupid to live if I parked and followed him into the bar where they would discover and confiscate my weapons, leaving me trapped and helpless.

I decided on garden-variety stupid, and hit the lock release.

Hibbert slid inside, his stale-cigarette smell closing my throat. "You're late," he snapped.

"I'm sorry." The words came out in a croak, and I cleared my throat. "The roads were bad." I swallowed hard, and this time my voice came out only slightly hoarse. "Excuse me. I've been singing for the last two hours, trying to stay awake on the road."

Better than admitting I was scared shitless.

My hands trembled on the wheel, and Hibbert gave me a contemptuous sneer. "You look like hell. Lucky I wasn't planning to fuck you. I'd have to put a bag over your head." He snickered. "A bag for a bag. Drive."

Anger stiffened my spine and heated my blood. I stomped on the accelerator and snapped, "Watch it, Mr. Congeniality. If your associates are looking forward to a beneficial relationship, they're not going to be happy with you if you piss me off and I take my business elsewhere."

"You won't. Give me the list."

I glanced over into the soulless eye of his gun and a burst of adrenaline exploded my mind into momentary white static. I spoke without thinking, my voice ridiculously level. "Give me my money."

"You're not in a position to negotiate."

"Neither are you." Thank God my hands had been shaking before. He wouldn't know how scared I was. My driving skills kicked into autopilot and I shot him what I hoped was a contemptuous sneer. "You don't seriously think I'm stupid enough to bring the list with me."

His growl raised every hair on the back of my neck. "I

think you'd be seriously stupid if you didn't."

"And I think you'd be seriously stupid to double-cross me now, and even stupider to shoot me. Double-cross me and it's the end of your so-called mutually beneficial relationship. Your associates can go fuck themselves, but they're far more likely to fuck you. Up the ass, hard. And they probably won't kiss you first. Shoot me and you're really fucked, because the list is in a safe place and if I'm dead, you'll never get it, or anything else your associates were hoping to get from me."

I managed to deliver the entire speech in a threatening rasp, thanks to my raw throat. A wisp of pride thawed some of my icy fear. I was getting better at this spy stuff.

Another sidelong glance at Hibbert confirmed my evaluation. He looked distinctly pouty.

"Fine," he snapped. "What do you propose?"

"We're going to drive to a location-"

"Where?"

"You'll see. It's a public location, so you won't want to do anything rash with that gun. When we get there, we'll go in together. I'll give you the list. You'll give me the cash. I'll drive away. You'll call a cab or whatever the hell you want, I don't give a shit. We'll both live happily ever after. The end."

Hibbert snorted and stuffed his gun back under his coat. "You're not as dumb as you look."

"Thank you."

When we pulled up in front of the mailbox rental office I'd visited on my way into Calgary, Hibbert snorted again, but it sounded like grudging approval.

We went in together and I opened my newly rented box

to extract the list I'd left there less than an hour before. Money and list changed hands, and I wobbled back to my car and drove away, leaving Hibbert standing on the sidewalk, cell phone pressed to his ear.

When I was certain I was far, far away from Hibbert, I pulled into a strip mall and parked, my stomach churning. Limp and shaking, I rested my head on the steering wheel. Breathe. Just breathe.

Relax. It's over.

I drew a deep breath and carefully reclined my seat. No sudden moves. Keep the breakfast where it belongs.

Breathing slowly and evenly, I worked through some relaxation exercises, easing the tension from my muscles. My nausea faded, leaving a hollow gnawing in my stomach. Several minutes later, the gnawing intensified, and my stomach growled.

I sat up. "Seriously?" I addressed my belly. "Minutes ago you were ready to puke, and now you're hungry?"

Another ravenous growl assured me that it was, and I shrugged and scanned the mall for a restaurant that might offer something bland. A tiny hole-in-the-wall café advertised 'comfort food', and I hauled myself out of the car to check their menu.

Half an hour later, I leaned back in the chair with a sigh. Macaroni and cheese nestled in my stomach, and I pushed the tasty remains around my plate, wishing I could eat more. My eyelids drooped with exhausted satisfaction, and I slid my fingertips into my jacket pocket to touch the envelope of money with a smile.

Safety, a full belly, and a successful mission for Jane Bond, super-spy.

I snickered. Yeah, right. But it felt good to succeed, and

more to the point, succeed unharmed. I left a generous tip and headed for my car to call Stemp.

As usual, he answered the secured phone on its first ring, catching me in the middle of a gaping and audible yawn. "Sorry," I said when I was capable of speech. "The list is delivered and I have the money."

"No... complications?"

I grinned. "No." Another yawn caught me unaware. "Sorry," I said again and glanced at my watch. "I should be able to get back by about three-thirty. Assuming the roads haven't gotten any worse."

"No need to rush," Stemp replied with surprising graciousness. "Webb is still home sick today, so I've postponed Tammy's first session until Monday. If you want to take the rest of the day off, do so. The only briefing I had planned for this afternoon was to inform everyone that I'll be taking a week's vacation, so Brent Dermott will be Acting Director in my stead."

"Oh." I hesitated. "How much does Dermott know about... um... me?"

"He has full access to all your official mission reports."

"And, um... the unofficial ones?"

There was a moment of silence on the line, which puzzled me until Stemp spoke again and I realized he had probably been activating a bug detector.

"No."

I nibbled the inside of my cheek. There were a lot of ways this could go bad. My sudden nervousness surprised me. When had I started counting on Stemp to cover my back?

But nothing should happen. I had delivered the list, the mission was over, and the upcoming week should be nothing but routine decryptions.

"Is there a problem?" Stemp's question jolted me out of my worried reverie.

"Um, no... I don't think so."

What could possibly go wrong?

"Are you, um, travelling for your vacation?" I asked abstractedly, still chewing over the possible repercussions of his absence.

"Yes. Is that relevant?" The almost imperceptible edge in his tone snapped me to attention when I realized what 'travelling' meant. A Christmas visit with Katya and Anna. And he was afraid I was trying to warn him of a possible threat.

"No," I said hurriedly. "Enjoy your trip."

"Thank you." After the slightest hesitation, he hung up.

I got out of the car and wandered over to the nearest garbage can to ditch the secured phone, frowning. Stemp's belief in my nonexistent secret ops gave me a lot of latitude, and I was protected by his legendary reluctance to disseminate any information, no matter how trivial. But who the hell was Brent Dermott, and what if something went wrong?

I stood drumming my fingers on the lid of the garbage can and staring into nothingness until a gust of wind whipped a stinging handful of snow into my face.

I retreated to my car and shook off both snow and foreboding. Stemp would be back in a week. Surely I couldn't fuck up so badly that he couldn't dig me out of trouble when he returned.

I was reaching for the ignition key when my waist pouch vibrated. The sight of 'E. Lacey' on my phone's call display gave me a tingle of anxiety.

I punched the Talk button. "Hello?"

"Hello, is this Aydan Kelly?" Miss Lacey's precise tones would have made me smile if not for the hint of worry in her voice.

"Speaking. Miss Lacey? Is anything wrong?"

Her small sigh made my fingers tighten on the phone. "That's what I was hoping to find out," she replied. "Have you been in touch with Arnold recently?"

I swallowed fear. "Yes, I saw him Wednesday night. Why?"

"Did he seem... like himself?"

"Uh..." How much should I tell her? "He seemed... upset. But he said he was okay. Why?"

Oh, God, she wouldn't be phoning me if there was nothing wrong.

"What's wrong?" I demanded.

"I... hope, nothing." She hesitated. When she spoke again, her voice was firm as if she had arrived at a decision. "I don't know if you're aware that Arnold sometimes engages in dangerous activities."

My heart kicked into a rapid rhythm. "Yes."

"And you know that I take care of John Lee Hooker when Arnold is away."

"Yes."

I mouthed a silent scream. Get to the point already!

"Sometimes when he leaves, I get the impression that he is not certain he'll return. On those occasions, he mentions that if anything ever happens to him, I should be sure to find a good home for John Lee. He said that last evening."

"Oh, God." The words trembled from my lips. "When did he leave? Did he say anything else?"

"No, and as you can imagine, I spent a sleepless night

worrying about him. But I heard him return around eight A.M., at which time I was most relieved."

I drew a shaky breath. "Thank God. So he's okay." Shit, with a lead-up like that, I'd been expecting some horrendous news. I massaged my chest, willing my heart to slow.

"I... am not certain."

"What do you mean?" My words snapped out like the crack of a whip.

"I was hoping that you had been in touch with him this morning. I don't believe he has left his apartment. You know how poorly constructed this condo is, and how sound travels through the hallway. I have heard John Lee crying for the past hour, which is most uncharacteristic. I telephoned Arnold's home and cellular numbers, but he is not answering. I am considering letting myself into his apartment, but I didn't want to invade his privacy if-"

The phone creaked under my clenching fingers. "Invade it! I'll be there in ten minutes!"

I hung up and slammed the car into gear.

CHAPTER 24

I made it to Arnie's condo building in five minutes, thanks to benevolent traffic gods and a reckless disregard for speed limits.

Flinging myself out of the car, I dashed for the front door and leaned on both Arnie's and Miss Lacey's call buttons. The speaker crackled to life with gratifying promptness.

"Yes?" Miss Lacey's crisp voice.

"It's Aydan. Is he all right?"

"My dear child, you must have flown here. I was just leaving my apartment to find out. Come in."

The lock released and I wrenched the door open to rocket up the stairs. God, nearly six minutes since she'd called.

Enough time for a man to die.

I skidded around the corner just as Miss Lacey looked up from Arnie's door handle.

"This looks like blood on the doorknob," she quavered. "Perhaps we should call the police."

"Open it, open it!"

I gasped for air while she fumbled the key into the lock. Hooker's demanding meows rose from the other side of the door.

I sprang inside as soon as the door opened, nearly tripping on Hooker as he bolted out. I slammed my back to the wall, hand on holster, and flung a wild glance around the small apartment.

Nothing out of order. No sign of an intruder.

Miss Lacey called to Hooker in the hallway, her voice thin and tremulous.

Drops of blood on the carpet.

I crossed the room in a couple of strides. Nobody in the bathroom. A wad of bloodstained gauze on the floor.

I whirled, my back tingling. Nobody.

A smear of blood on the wall next to his bedroom door.

Through the door.

My heart stopped.

"Call the police and ambulance!" My voice was so shrill it was unrecognizable.

"I have."

Miss Lacey's faint reply from the hallway faded into insignificance as I hurled myself toward the bed and its bloodied, terrifyingly still occupant.

"Arnie! Arnie!" My hands shook so hard I couldn't hold them on the blood-caked pulse point at his throat.

He grunted and his eyes fought their way half-open against the swelling that distorted his face.

I swallowed a sob of relief. "Arnie, what happened?" I did a rapid inventory of the blood-smeared pillow and rough bandage around his head. His T-shirt and jeans were caked with dirt and dried blood, his knuckles swollen and gashed. Purpling bruises showed under the torn fabric of his shirt.

Afraid to hurt him, I stroked an uninjured place on his arm. "Arnie? Talk to me. What happened?"

His gaze passed through me without recognition.

"Wha...?"

"What happened, Arnie? Who did this to you?"

He mumbled something unintelligible, his eyes frighteningly vacant.

"Arnie!" My voice caught on a sob. "Arnie, wake up and talk to me!"

His lips moved without sound.

"Arnie! Come on, Arnie!"

His hand faltered up to touch my cheek. "Mmm... Mommy?"

I hadn't realized I was crying until his torn knuckles smeared the tears across my cheek.

"Don' cry, Mommy," he mumbled. "Gonna... be... 'kay..."

The whirl of police and questions was mercifully short, since I had nothing useful to contribute. They were still taking Miss Lacey's statement when I left to follow in the wake of the ambulance.

I drove with fierce concentration, my body tensed to numbness and my hands locked on the wheel. Look both ways. Accelerate. Brake. Signal. Turn.

If I paid attention to every little detail, I wouldn't have to think about Arnie's battered face and blank gaze.

Signal.

Turn.

Park.

Suddenly I was standing in Emergency with no recollection of arriving there. I approached the woman behind the desk.

"Arnold Helmand." My voice was a dry croak. "How is he? H-He arrived by ambulance. I... I'm his g... girlfriend."

The word trembled out, and the nurse offered me a sympathetic smile.

"Yes, he's being seen."

"C-can I..."

"You won't be able to see him until the doctors are finished. Just take a seat, and we'll let you know."

Wait? They'd let me know? Was she fucking kidding? I clamped down on the hysterical urge to pull my gun and demand to see him.

Christ, I was losing it.

I gave her my name, stumbled to the nearest chair, and sat.

After several minutes of numb immobility, my brain ground into gear again. I got up and tottered outside where I could talk on my cell phone in relative privacy. Shivering uncontrollably in the icy wind, it took me two tries to hit the single speed-dial button.

"Kane."

At the sound of his strong baritone, my throat closed and only a tiny sob escaped.

"Aydan! Where are you? What's wrong?"

I yanked myself under control. "I'm at the F-Foothills Hospital. Arnie..."

I had to gulp again, and Kane snapped, "What happened? How bad?"

"I d-don't know. They just b-brought him in. He's so b-beat up, John..." Tears rose again. "He d-didn't know m-me..."

"I'm on my way." I heard the sounds of rapid movement in the background. "Did you call the police? What do you know so far?"

His firm decisive voice gave me strength, and I pulled

myself together with a heroic effort.

"The police are talking to Miss Lacey. She was the last to see him. Apparently he went out last night, and Miss Lacey said he hinted that he might not come b-back..." I gulped down tears again. "But she said she heard his door around eight this morning. By the time she phoned me at noon, Hooker had been meowing for an hour, and she had tried to call Arnie on his home and cell but got no answer. I got her to open his door and he was..." Another hard gulp. "...s-semi-conscious. Somebody beat the hell out of him. It looked like he'd gotten home and tried to bandage himself up and then gone to b-bed."

Injured and alone and maybe dying...

"Did you check his apartment?"

I forced my voice level. "Nothing disturbed that I could see. It looks as though whatever trouble he ran into, it wasn't at his apartment." My composure cracked again. "It's a h-head injury, John, a n-neglected head injury..."

Tension vibrated in Kane's voice, but he spoke with certainty. "Aydan, Arnie's tougher than anybody on the planet, including my dad, and you know that's saying a lot. He'll pull through. I'm on the road now. I'll talk to the police and get the latest from them."

I drew a shaky breath of relief, belatedly remembering his cover as an RCMP officer. No gun-waving required.

"You stay there, and call me if you get an update before I arrive. I'll come as soon as I can. If you get to see him, tell him I'm coming down there to kick his sorry ass..." I might have imagined the waver in Kane's voice. When he spoke again, he sounded as firm and confident as ever. "I'll see you soon."

Huddled shivering in the corner of the waiting room, I stared blindly at the constant bustle. Each face was a mask of pain, worry, hope, despair. Crying children, stoic elders, a couple who held each other tightly, casting tearful glances at the door to the ER. Across from me, a wizened old man rocked rhythmically forward and back, forward and back.

The hospital smell clogged my nose. Antiseptic and fear. I wrapped my arms tighter around myself, but the shivering wouldn't stop.

Unable to wait any longer, I went back to the desk to hover while the nurse spoke with another worried-looking woman. When she finished, I moved forward, feeling the same expression of fearful entreaty on my own face.

"The doctors are still with him, dear," she said kindly. "I promise I'll let you know as soon as you can see him."

"But... he's... still okay, isn't he? I mean, not okay, but... is there any way to know how he's doing?"

"The doctor will talk with you as soon as possible. I'm sorry, I don't know anything more." She turned away to deal with the next supplicant, and I stumbled back to my chair in the corner.

"Aydan?"

Kane's voice startled me out of my stupor. He bent to search my face worriedly.

"John!" I wobbled to my feet. "You made it in an hour and a half?"

He gave me a smile that didn't reach his eyes. "Police officer. I used the lights and siren. Not strictly kosher, but..."

He looked so tall and strong and safe it seemed like the most natural thing in the world to hide in his arms. I clung to him for a moment, drawing on his strength before pulling away.

His big warm hands closed around my icy ones. "Any news?"

"N-not yet."

He surveyed me, his brows furrowed. "You need a hot drink. Sit." He lowered me to the chair again and wrapped his jacket around me before striding away. Several minutes later he returned bearing a cardboard cup, and I obediently sipped as instructed.

The hot chocolate tasted like melted crayons with sugar, but I forced it down anyway. A few minutes later, Kane smoothed my hair away from my cheek. "That's better."

His touch reminded me of Arnie's torn knuckles brushing the tears from my face, and I couldn't control the quiver that seized my lips.

Kane's arm closed around my shoulders. "He'll be all right, Aydan. Think good thoughts."

I leaned into him and drew a deep breath to steady my voice. "Did you talk to the police? What did you find out?"

Kane shot a glance around the room and spoke softly. "Apparently he was in an altercation early this morning. He was attacked by three men." Kane's lips quirked in a grim smile. "He incapacitated all three. Called the police and ambulance himself."

"But... why...?"

"It's unclear what started the fight. According to the police report he filed, the attack was unprovoked." Kane shrugged, the thin smile still lingering on his lips. "The other three men are still hospitalized and not in any shape to talk yet."

He sobered. "There's also an ambulance report that details his injuries. Mostly superficial cuts and bruises, but he had a blunt-force head wound. He declined treatment, and according to police and paramedics, he was lucid when they saw him. The paramedics warned him of the potential complications of a head injury and tried to get him to come in, but..."

"But this is Arnie," I finished. "He'd avoid a hospital visit unless he was on the verge of d..."

I shut up and we sat in silence.

CHAPTER 25

Late-afternoon twilight was falling by the time the emergency room nurse called my name. I sprang to my feet and hurried to the desk, my heart thudding double-time in my chest.

"The doctor will see you now." The nurse pointed at a weary-looking man in scrubs emerging from the sliding doors.

"Aydan Kelly?"

I nodded, unable to speak. Kane's hand found my shoulder, providing reassurance or seeking comfort, I wasn't sure which.

"You're Mr. Helmand's wife?"

"G-girlfriend."

Kane's grip tightened on my shoulder, but he said nothing.

The doctor turned to Kane. "And you are...?"

"Arnie's brother," I lied.

The doctor gave a preoccupied nod. "Mr. Helmand is in serious condition, but stable."

A rush of relief blanked out his next words.

"...admit him." The doctor was still talking. "We can't find any evidence of bleeding inside the brain, but swelling apparently developed after he was seen by paramedics early this morning. That seems to have stabilized, and in the absence of any other complications it should subside over the next several hours. If it doesn't subside, or if it increases, we will re-evaluate."

"Can we see him?" I clutched Kane's hand, barely breathing.

I had to see him. If I could see him, he'd be okay. He had to be okay.

"This way." The doctor was already retreating, handing us off to a nurse.

It seemed to take forever to get to the curtained cubicle. Outside it, the nurse offered me a professionally sympathetic smile. "He needs to stay calm and quiet. Only one visitor at a time, and only for a few minutes. A porter will be coming to take him for another scan shortly. I can take you in now."

Kane gave my hand a squeeze before releasing me, and I followed the nurse as she pulled the curtain aside far enough to admit us.

I had braced myself for Arnie's injuries, but I wasn't prepared for the sight of him in a hospital bed. His bulky form dwarfed the narrow stretcher, but the pale gown and bandage on his head made him look frighteningly vulnerable. The dark bruises on his face contrasted shockingly against the white pillow.

"Mr. Helmand." His eyes opened, and the nurse gestured me forward with a smile. "Your girlfriend is here to see you."

"Hi, Arnie." My voice quivered and I bit my lip, stepping forward to take his hand.

Confusion knotted his brow and he stared up at me. "I ain't got a girlfriend." His eyes widened and he pulled his hand from my grasp. "I can't have a girlfriend, it ain't safe. I can't ever have a girlfriend!"

"No, it's okay, Arnie," I soothed, but he struggled higher in the bed as if trying to escape.

"No, you're Aydan! Ya promised no commitments. Didn't ya? Ya didn't... we didn't... I ain't got that movie! Shit, my movies ain't workin'!"

"Arnie, no, it's okay!" I shot a worried glance at the nurse, who had withdrawn but was eyeing his distress through the opening in the curtain as if considering kicking me out. I leaned closer to whisper, "I'm not your girlfriend, I never want commitment, I just lied to the doctors so they'd let me see you."

"Oh, Jesus, darlin'." He went limp, his eyes dropping shut. "Jesus fuckin' Christ, ya scared the shit outta me."

"I'm sorry." I stroked his arm. "I didn't think you'd be lucid enough to realize what was happening. When I found you, you thought I was your mom."

His eyes flew open again, fear flickering in their depths. "I ain't got that movie..."

"The porter is here. You'll need to go now." The nurse's voice startled me.

"No, I need her." Arnie's hand closed around mine.

"She'll be back later. You need to stay calm, and she needs to go now."

It wasn't a suggestion. The nurse moved forward as if to physically disengage our hands.

"No!" Arnie's free hand clenched into a fist, and the nurse shot me a look.

I leaned over to brush a kiss across Arnie's lips before scattering kisses over the uninjured parts of his face. His grip relaxed, and I eased my hand free to stroke his cheek.

"I'll be back. You just have to go for another test, and you need to rest." I silenced his protest with another kiss. "Promise you'll behave until I get back."

"Wait!" His hand captured mine again. "Hooker..."

"He's fine. He's at Miss Lacey's."

"Oh..." He relaxed, his hand falling open. "Thanks, darlin'," he mumbled as his eyes drifted closed.

When I emerged, Kane stood at parade rest, his hands locked behind him as if to prevent himself from fighting his way into the cubicle. Strain vibrated in every line of his body, and my heart squeezed. I had been so absorbed in my own fear, so sure of his calm strength. I'd forgotten he was suffering, too.

"How is he?" he demanded.

We stepped aside to make way for the porter, and I gathered my composure.

"He's..." I hesitated, and Kane's jaw clenched. "He's better," I reassured him hurriedly. "He's still not making perfect sense, but he knew me this time, and he remembered Hooker."

When the nurse came out again, Kane stepped forward, his broad shoulders seeming to fill the hallway. "May I see him?"

The nurse looked up. And up.

"I'm sorry, sir," she said after a moment. "He's being taken for a procedure now. And he needs to remain calm and quiet." The look she gave me wasn't exactly accusing, but guilt suffused me anyway. "It's a lengthy procedure, so it will be a couple of hours," she added.

Kane nodded and turned to go, but the pain in his eyes pierced my heart. I laid a hand on his arm and turned to give the nurse a pleading look. "We don't want to disturb him and I know he has to go, but could you please just tell him that his brother is here? He'd want to know."

Kane turned back, and the nurse's face softened at the sight of the mute entreaty in his face. "I'll tell him. Come and stand where he can see you."

She returned to Arnie's bedside, and Kane and I positioned ourselves outside the curtain. Kane's hand tightened on mine as the nurse bent to speak softly.

"Mr. Helmand, your brother is here."

Arnie's eyes flew open to glower at the nurse, his fists clenching. "That fuckin' asshole! What the hell's he doin' here?"

Kane's grip closed convulsively. The nurse shot us a scowl and turned to make calming gestures at Arnie, who was struggling to sit up, rasping threats and obscenities.

A wave of comprehension broke over me. "Arnie, no, it's John, not James," I called.

His gaze snapped to Kane beside me. "Cap! Thank Christ! I'm pinned down, Cap! Lost my weapon..." His hands skimmed the sheets as if searching for the missing firearm.

Kane took a single step forward, his posture stiffening into military authority. "Helmand!"

"Yessir!"

"The area's secure. Rest. Cooperate. That's an order."

"Yessir." The tension smoothed from Arnie's face as he sagged back on the pillow.

The nurse shot us an eloquent glare, and we retreated.

"Wait..." Arnie's voice was weaker, his eyelids beginning to droop. "Cap... Watch my back..."

Kane leaned into the cubicle, his voice as firm as a warrior's armclasp. "Always do."

A smile ghosted across Arnie's lips and his eyes closed.

The nurse hovered a moment as if to be sure he would stay calm before striding out to herd us away. "You said you were his brother." This time the accusation was plain.

"He's the only brother I have left." Kane spoke quietly, watching as the porter wheeled Arnie away.

"They've been friends since they were six," I added. "Grew up in the same home. Served together in the army. They really are brothers in every way that counts."

Her face softened. "All right. After his scan he'll be transferred up to a ward, so it will be at least two hours before you can see him again. Go and get a coffee or something."

Kane spoke without looking at her, still watching the receding stretcher. "Can we wait where he can see us?" The doors closed behind the porter and his precious cargo, and Kane returned his attention to the nurse. "I promised to watch his back."

Compassion filled her eyes, and she laid a gentle hand on each of our arms. "The less stimulation he has just now, the better. The best thing you can do for yourselves, and for him, is to leave the hospital. Take a break. Rest, eat. You'll be called if there's any change in his condition. You can visit him on the ward in a couple of hours."

Kane's hand found mine again, and he took one more look in the direction the porter had vanished before nodding. "All right. Thank you."

"But, John..." I began.

"She's right," he said gently, and towed me away.

In the lobby, I halted. "I need to call Miss Lacey and let her know what's happening. She'll be worried sick."

Kane nodded and leaned a shoulder against the wall,

extracting his own cell phone while I punched the number into mine.

"Hello?" Miss Lacey answered on the first ring, her voice a thin quaver.

"Hi, Miss Lacey, it's Aydan."

"Yes? How is Arnold?"

I imagined her fragile blue-veined hands trembling on the phone, and put as much reassurance into my voice as possible. "He's better."

"Oh, thank heaven!"

"He's still a little confused, but he knew John and me." I hesitated. "Sorry, do you know John Kane?"

"I have never met him, but he is one of Arnold's emergency contacts. I left a message on his cellular phone but he has not returned my call."

"Oh. Thanks, he already knows, and he's here with me. Arnie knew us both, and he asked after Hooker, so that's a big improvement. And they say he's stable. They just kicked us out for a couple of hours because he was going for a test and then they were going to transfer him to a ward."

"What precisely did the doctors say?" Her usual crisp tones had returned, and I relaxed. Thank God for tough little old ladies. I told her as much as I knew and hung up with a promise to keep her informed.

Kane had already completed his calls, and when I stowed my phone back in my waist pouch, he gave me a questioning look. "I know an excellent northern Italian restaurant not far from here. I just called, and they have a reservation available. Are you interested?"

I blew out a sigh of relief. "That sounds fabulous. I was planning to eat some horrible fast-food crap because I couldn't face making any decisions tonight."

He smiled. "This will be much, much better. Come on. I'll drive."

In the parking garage, I sank into his passenger seat with a sigh and laid my head back, closing my eyes. Either the restaurant was very close, or I fell asleep. Cessation of movement made me drag myself upright. Kane slid out of the driver's seat and strode around to open my door, his brow furrowed with concern.

"Are you all right?" He offered his hand, and for once in my life I gratefully accepted, propping myself against his strength.

"Yeah..." The word came out on a long breath as we made our way slowly to the restaurant. "I'm just..." A mirror in the front entrance reflected my strained white face. I averted my gaze from the unrewarding sight and glanced into the restaurant instead. "...shit, I can't go in here."

"Why not?" Kane stopped beside me, signalling a 'wait' gesture to the smiling maître d' who had approached as soon as we entered.

"Look at me," I hissed, indicating my faded jeans, scuffed boots, and the old parka I'd worn in case of any further misadventures at the Hogback.

"You're fine." Kane slid an arm around my shoulders and turned to the maître d'. "Kane, for two."

The maître d' didn't even blink, his expression of warm welcome unruffled. "This way, madam and sir."

Slinking self-consciously through the small, elegant dining room with its well-dressed patrons, I kept my eyes to the front and my head high. Maybe everybody would think I was some celebrity, too important to dress up. Maybe they'd think this was the cutting edge of fashion. Somewhere.

Yeah, right. Not even in Tuktoyaktuk.

I dropped gracelessly into the chair the maître d' pulled out for me, thankful for the privacy of the table and the cozy dimness. Kane smiled and took the seat across from me with his usual aplomb.

Squinting at the menu, I sighed and extracted my reading glasses, but even with their help the fine script defied my tired eyes in the half-light. I fumbled again in my waist pouch and withdrew my tiny LED flashlight, only to catch the humorous quirk of Kane's lips.

He leaned across the table. "Do you trust me?"

"Um... yeah..." I frowned, not feeling very trusting at all.

He smiled and gently closed my menu. "Let me."

I slumped in the chair and nodded, too tired to even speak.

When the waiter returned, Kane ordered in what appeared to be fluent Italian. I felt my eyes widening while he and the waiter exchanged a flow of incomprehensible words and the waiter departed, smiling and bowing.

I raised my eyebrows at Kane. "So you speak Italian."

"I just exhausted my entire repertoire to order our meal."

I studied his modest smile with skepticism. "How many languages do you speak?"

"English and French, of course." He shrugged as if fluency in Canada's two official languages was the norm. "Russian. Enough Putonghua and Cantonese to get along. Enough Italian, German, and Spanish to order a meal, a drink, and a room for the night."

"Holy shit, you're amazing. Where the hell do they speak Putta-whatever-you-said? Africa?"

Kane chuckled. "No, Putonghua is the standard dialect for mainland China. They have nearly three hundred languages, but that's the one most people can speak and understand enough to function."

"Wow." I absorbed that for a moment while comprehension dawned. "Fluent in Russian and Chinese. Pleasure to meet you, James Bond."

He grinned, and we fell silent as the waiter returned bearing two glasses of wine. When he placed the white in front of me, I eyed it dubiously. "I'd better not. I'm too tired, and I want to be able to drive if I have to."

As I reached to return the glass, Kane gently stopped my hand. "It's all right. You said the first couple of sips are always the best, so enjoy your two sips and leave the rest."

"But it's a waste..."

"It's not a waste if you enjoy it. If you only want two sips, have two sips. If you want to finish it, go ahead. I'm driving." He raised his glass to me. "Just relax and enjoy."

I lifted the glass to my nose. The delicate bouquet tickled my senses and I smiled and acknowledged Kane with the glass before sipping. The fruity, floral notes caressed my palate, and I couldn't restrain a little hum of pleasure, my eyes slipping closed for an instant. When I opened them again, Kane was watching me, smiling.

I returned his smile. "You're a very wise man."

He offered me a half-bow from his seated position. "I know."

We both laughed and turned our attention to food as the waiter arrived with some tiny, rich-looking tarts.

A couple of courses of antipasti later, Kane spoke as I reached for my wine glass again. "Were you planning to finish that?"

"Oh!" I pushed the glass in his direction. "No. Here, take it if you want it."

"No, I didn't mean that. It's just that you said you

weren't going to." He inclined his head at the half-empty glass.

I handed it to him. "I wasn't going to, and I won't. That's why I never even have one drink if I'm driving. It's too easy to keep going. Thanks for stopping me."

He eyed me seriously. "I didn't mean to stop you. Finish it if you want. You don't have to drive." He raised a wicked eyebrow. "Since I talked you into it, though, I didn't want to be accused of contributing to your debauchery."

I laughed. "A glass of wine hardly qualifies as debauchery, but really, I don't want it. I'd rather be in full control of my faculties." I couldn't quite suppress a yawn. "What's left of them, anyway."

He leaned back in his chair, sobering. "You really don't trust anybody, do you?"

My shields sprang up and I deflected the question with a smile. "My trust for you is evident in the fact that I accepted the wine at all. And the way my life has been going lately, who knows when I might have to drive?"

He chuckled, and the subject dropped when the braised beef arrived, its mouthwatering aroma seducing my nose.

Later, I moaned unashamed over a silky chocolate panna cotta. "Oh my God, this is amazing." I spooned up another luscious mouthful. "I'm in pain, but I can't stop. This is so good."

Kane smiled. "I'm glad you're enjoying it. Too rich for my taste." He sipped his espresso, the cup ridiculously tiny in his big hands.

"I don't know how you can drink that rocket fuel. I think my head would explode if I did."

"Then I'm glad you're not drinking it. I couldn't afford the cleaning bill."

"Very funny." I scraped up the last few delectable vestiges of dessert and shot a surreptitious glance at my watch.

Not surreptitious enough. Kane drained his cup and rose. "I was just thinking the same thing. Let's go."

He held my parka for me as if it was a sable coat and I fumbled into it, embarrassed by both the garment and my lack of finesse.

As he turned away from the table, I touched his sleeve. "Wait, we need to pay."

"Already taken care of."

I frowned up at him. "When did you... never mind. How much was it?"

"My treat."

"No, you can't. That was an I-don't-know-how-many-course meal. It must have cost a bomb. Let me get half."

"After you." He smiled and gestured toward the door, and after an exasperated moment, I decided that engaging in a heated debate about splitting the bill while dressed like white trash in the middle of an upscale restaurant was simply more humiliation than I needed.

CHAPTER 26

En route to the hospital again, I leaned back and stifled a groan as I furtively undid the button on my jeans to make room for all that Italian food. When I glanced down to make sure the open waistband was hidden by my sweatshirt, I spied the message light on my phone.

"Shit, I missed a call." Fear rising in my heart, I fumbled the phone free with shaking hands. "Please don't let it be the hospital..." I sagged with relief at the sight of the call display. "Thank God. It was just Lola."

Kane relaxed, too, his grip easing on the wheel. A thought struck me, and I glanced over at him. "We're missing the self-defence workshop. Did you cancel it?"

"No, I got Germain to cover for me. He's bored hanging around Silverside, so he was glad to do it."

"If he's been undercover for months, he must be eager to get home to Calgary." I eyed Kane cautiously. "Do you know why Stemp is keeping him around?"

"Stemp wants him to act as Tammy's guard in the network the same as I do for you."

"Oh. So he might end up having to relocate?"

"Unknown." Kane reached to collect a parking stub from the machine at the parkade entrance before giving me a cautious glance of his own. "Tammy should be in less danger than you are, so it's likely only a temporary measure until Stemp can be sure everything is working well. And if Webb doesn't get over being 'sick' soon..." He gave the word an ironic inflection as he parked. "...Tammy's project will be dead in the water until they can find someone else with the skills and security clearance to take over his role."

"Poor Spider," I said as we got out and headed for the exit. "He's stuck between his own principles and Stemp's orders. Talk about a rock and a hard place."

"I thought it might be something like that."

I stared up at him. "You didn't know. You were fishing. Dammit, you sneaky spy, I shouldn't have said anything." I assumed a severe expression. "Spider is sick with the stomach flu, and don't you forget it."

Kane grinned. "Yes, ma'am."

As we approached the entrance, the weight of worry descended on me again, and I hurried forward.

Kane laid a restraining hand on my arm. "If you're going to call Lola, you should do it now. You can't use your phone inside the hospital."

"She'll be at the self-defence workshop now anyway, so I'll call her later. We've been away too long. Arnie will be wondering where we went."

"Aydan, he'll be all right."

But despite his confident words, I had to hurry to keep up to his long stride as we crossed the lobby.

We found the ward without difficulty, but when we checked in at the nurses' station, the nurse's expression closed a tight band of fear around my heart.

"He's been quite agitated," she cautioned. "You can see him for a few minutes, but if the stimulation is too much for him, you'll have to leave. He needs to stay as calm and relaxed as possible."

Kane's hand closed around mine, and we followed the nurse.

As soon as we entered the room, Hellhound's rasp greeted us. "Aydan. Cap. Fuck, where ya been?"

His rigid shoulders relaxed as we hurried to his bedside. I stroked his hand. "I'm sorry, Arnie. We didn't want to go, but they kicked us out while you had your scan and got moved up here. They said we had to stay away for at least two hours."

"Fuck, I hate hospitals. Lucky ya showed up or I woulda started kickin' ass."

Kane grinned. "Well, we're here now. Leave the ass-kicking to us."

Arnie let out a long breath, the tense lines easing from his face. "Good to have ya back. Pull up a chair."

We did, and were rewarded when he relaxed even further, easing his head back on the pillow with another deep sigh.

Mindful of the nurse's admonition, I leaned close to whisper. "What happened? Who were those guys who attacked you?" Kane leaned in, too, listening intently.

Arnie's gaze darted up to the corner of the ceiling before returning to us. "Just some dumbfucks lookin' for trouble."

"Well, they found it." Kane frowned at him. "What exactly happened?"

Arnie's eyes closed. "Whatever I said in the police report." He opened his eyes again to frown at us. "My movies ain't workin' quite right yet. Doc said that one might not come back." He grinned and squeezed my hand. "Hey, darlin', don't look so worried. I ain't as fucked up as ya think. I never mentioned my movies to ya before, did I?"

"Um... no." I clutched his hand tighter and shot an anxious glance at Kane. To my relief, he didn't look as concerned as I felt.

"It's how my memory works," Arnie explained. "It's like watchin' a movie.   Pictures, numbers, conversations, whatever." He grimaced. "Sometimes smells fuck me up, though. Make me sick. That's why I like it that ya never wear perfume, darlin'."

"Oh." I eased my grip on his hand. "Thank God. I thought you were just babbling. You scared me."

"Sorry, darlin'." He brought my hand to his lips and kissed it, giving me a contrite look.

The nurse reappeared. "That's enough for now-"

"They ain't leavin'." Hellhound stiffened, his grip tightening on my hand. "Ya kick 'em out, an' I'll sign myself right outta this fuckin' joint an'-"

He struggled to sit up, and Kane barked, "Helmand!"

"Ain't gonna work this time, Cap." Hellhound grimaced and levered himself higher.

Kane and I each seized a shoulder. "Arnie, please, just lie down," I begged, trying to press him back onto the bed without hurting him. "You're supposed to stay calm and quiet."

"It's all right, they can stay," the nurse put in hurriedly. "Just relax. They can stay."

Hellhound subsided on the pillow, glaring suspiciously. "They go, I go," he snapped. "Got it?"

"Just relax," the nurse repeated. "There's no need to upset yourself." She made a strategic withdrawal.

Hellhound glowered at the empty doorway a few moments longer as if assuring himself that the threat had passed. Then his eyes slipped closed, his tense muscles slackening under my hands.

"Fuckin' bloodsuckers," he mumbled.

"Just rest," Kane urged. "I've got your back."

Hellhound's face relaxed. "Thanks, Cap. Couldn't close my eyes never knowin' when somebody was gonna be messin' with me." He blew out a long breath and lay in silence for a few moments. Just when I thought he might be falling asleep, his eyes opened again. "Darlin', can ya do me a favour?"

I gulped, remembering the last favour he'd asked of me. "Um..."

"Can ya go to my place an' get me some clothes? They cut mine off when I came in. This goddam gown ain't worth shit."

"Um... they probably won't want you to get dressed," I hedged, hoping not to upset him all over again.

"Yeah." He winked. "An' ya know I don't usually mind flyin' the flesh flag, but..." Despite his grin, I read the appeal in his eyes. "I gotta have pants. In case somethin' happens."

"You won't need-" Kane began, but Hellhound cut him off with a level stare.

"Remember that hospital in Bosnia?"

Kane's face hardened and he nodded once, his eyes reflecting old ghosts.

"I'll get your clothes," I promised.

"Thanks, darlin'." Hellhound glanced around the room, frowning. "My keys were in my pocket." He tensed. "Shit, an' my wallet..."

"It's all right," Kane soothed. "Your things are in a locker. Secured."

"Don't worry, I'll just get Miss Lacey to let me in," I said hurriedly as Hellhound tried to sit up. "I'll just run down to the lobby and call her."

"She'll be home," he assured me, relaxing. "Friday night's her bridge club."

"Okay." I leaned down to kiss him. "Do you want anything else from your place?"

"Toothbrush an' toothpaste. That's it. I ain't stayin' here long enough to need anythin' else."

I backed away from that impending argument. "I'll be back as soon as I can."

At nurses' station, I caught the nurse's eye and she closed the file she was working on and rose. I glanced toward Arnie's door and spoke softly. "He's calmer now. I didn't realize it before, but he's got some traumatic memories associated with a hospital from when he was in combat. I think he'll stay calm if one of us sits with him. He's just afraid to relax in case somebody sneaks up on him."

Her expression lightened. "That explains it. I'll make a note in his chart. Stay with him then. Keeping him calm and quiet is our top priority. And if you can, try to prevent him from overtaxing himself mentally. Don't encourage him to talk or think about anything."

"We'll do our best. I'm just going to get a few things for him from home, but John will stay with him until I'm back."

She nodded, and I made my way down to the lobby.

When I extracted my cell phone, the message light was blinking again, and I punched the voice mail button.

The sound of Hibbert's oily voice made me collapse into the nearest chair. "You're invited to a very exclusive party tomorrow night. You will be *pleased* to attend. Call me for details." His emphasis assured me that my presence was not optional.

My arm dropped nervelessly into my lap, the phone sliding from my slack grip. I rescued it with a frantic grab and slumped back in the chair, clenching the phone until my knuckles glowed bone-white. Hollow fear morphed rapidly into the burning adrenaline rush of a panic attack.

No, no, no! My mind curled into a ball of helpless fear. Stemp had said they would likely move slowly. This couldn't be happening. And Stemp was probably half-way to Bulgaria by now. No backup.

Trapped.

Shit, stop it!

I jerked my spine straight, pulling my chin up to glare sightlessly at the vending machine across from me. A passing woman intercepted the look, flinched, and hurried away with a nervous backward glance. I gave my head a shake and tried to convert both my expression and my attitude into something a little closer to neutral.

Okay, Stemp might be gone, but Dermott wouldn't be Acting Director unless he was competent. I still had Kane in my corner, and Germain, too, if necessary. Two of the top agents in the service. I could do this.

I eased out a shaky breath. It wasn't like I had a choice.

I'd do it and get through it. Or die trying.

I forbade myself to contemplate the high probability of the latter and breathed deeply until I thought I had my voice under control. Just to be on the safe side I called Lola first, knowing I'd get her voice mail.

It was a good decision. My voice trembled while I explained about my injured friend in the hospital and apologized for standing her up, but at least she wouldn't question why I was upset.

After a few more calming breaths, I was ready to call

Miss Lacey. This time my vocal cords cooperated, and I gave her a reassuring report before confirming that she'd be available to let me into Arnie's place. A few minutes later, I was on the road.

CHAPTER 27

When the condo's vestibule door released to the sound of Miss Lacey's brisk 'Come in', I trailed across the lobby and dragged myself upstairs, remembering half-way up that I could have taken the elevator.

I was still mumbling half-hearted expletives when I gained the third floor and turned the corner to find Miss Lacey hovering in her doorway, her gaze darting between me and the interior of her apartment.

"You poor child, you look exhausted. Won't you come in and have a cup of tea?" she inquired, but I could tell that despite her sincere concern for me, her card game came a close second.

I smiled, recognizing the gleam of a bridge fanatic in her eyes. "No, thanks, I'll just get Arnie's things and go."

She was far too polite to look relieved. "Very well. Perhaps you could keep John Lee company for a few moments if you're not in a terrible hurry to return. My bridge partner is quite allergic, so poor John Lee has been relegated to Arnold's apartment for the duration. I'm sure he would appreciate the companionship after such an upsetting day."

Hooker's gravelly meow sounded clearly through

Hellhound's door, and I summoned up a chuckle. "I think he agrees."

She smiled, too, and I assumed catcher's position while she unlocked the door and swung it open. Scooping up the big cat when he made his usual determined bid for freedom, I stepped inside.

"Do take your time, dear," Miss Lacey urged. "I will be up for several hours yet." She hurried back to her game, and I bolted Arnie's door behind me with the sense of locking out all the dark dangers that circled me.

Still hugging Hooker, I leaned against the door and slid slowly down to sit on the doormat. Slumping forward to hide my face in his fur, I mumbled, "Jesus, Hooker, I'm so fucked. What the hell am I going to do?"

He squirmed free and gave me an affronted yellow glare before pacing deliberately toward his food dish. His imperious meow made his advice very clear: "Feed me."

I hauled myself upright. "Nice try, buddy. Miss Lacey wouldn't let you go hungry." Nevertheless, I located the bag of cat food and sprinkled a few crunchy treats into his bowl before heading for Arnie's bedroom.

The blood smear on the wall made my stomach tighten. Unable to bear the sight, I pulled the bloodstained linens off the bed and bundled them into the bathtub to soak in cold water before going in search of a cleaning rag. A disposable dishcloth from an unopened package in the kitchen served the purpose, and I tackled the dried blood on the wall, carpet, and bathroom sink. Deliberately blanking my mind to concentrate on my task, I lost myself in the comforting monotony of scrubbing.

At last, I rinsed out my cloth and hung the wet sheets over the shower rod, feeling calmer. I hesitated in the living room.   Somehow Arnie's absence made me feel like an intruder in his home.

His personality radiated from the walls of shelves sagging under the weight of music CDs and vinyl albums. His guitar was propped within easy reach of his favourite shabby but comfortable chair; his jacket still draped carelessly in its usual place over the half-wall at the entrance. His cozy hand-crocheted afghans were bright spots of warmth and softness in the barren bachelor décor.

With an effort, I resisted the urge to wrap up in one of those afghans and curl into fetal position on the couch. Instead, I squared my shoulders and went to breach the privacy of his bedroom.

I had been in there often enough, but the bed was the only thing that had ever occupied my attention.   I approached his small bureau hesitantly.

Dammit, it was stupid to feel so uncomfortable. If he hadn't wanted me rummaging through here, he would have told me exactly where to find his clothes, or else sent Kane instead.

I pulled open the top drawer. No clothes. Only dozens of small, neatly stacked boxes almost filling the available space. I watched in guilty fascination while my hands eased open one of the boxes despite my better intentions.

A medal gleamed against a dark velvet background.

I snapped the box shut and stood staring at the drawer.

Kane's amused voice came back to me. "He has a drawer full of medals at home."

I ignored my nagging conscience and opened a few more boxes. He really did have a drawer full of medals. I carefully replaced the boxes exactly as they had been and slid the drawer closed, wondering.

The next drawer held socks, neatly paired and folded, and the bottom drawer revealed jeans. I extracted a pair each of socks and jeans and turned for the closet. When the door slid open, I stepped back, my jaw dropping.

I had known he kept his shirts in there. Any time I'd watched him get dressed, he'd simply slid his hand through a narrow gap in the doors and pulled out a T-shirt apparently at random. Now I knew why.

A small array of commemorative concert T-shirts occupied one end, but spotless military gear filled the rest of the closet.

I might have believed the dress uniform was left over from before his retirement from the army, but not the black fatigues that hung beside it. Nor the black body armour; the neatly coiled ropes; what looked like a climbing harness; a black rucksack. A matte black combat helmet perched atop olive-drab cargo bins stacked in the corner.

I backed away and sank onto the bed.

All that gear. Clearly well-used and impeccably maintained. And he had a hell of a lot of medals for a guy who'd ostensibly never made it past the rank of corporal.

Civilian private investigator, my ass.

Hooker's accusing meow startled me out of my abstraction.

"Yeah, I know I'm snooping, big guy," I told him, and hoisted him up to my lap. "But if he didn't trust me with this, he wouldn't have sent me."

The big cat gave me a doubtful look and squirmed free to jump down again, padding over to sniff the wet spot on the carpet where I'd scrubbed away the blood.

"Don't worry, he's coming back," I assured him.

Hooker continued to pace, meowing piteously, and after

a few minutes of futile murmured reassurances my nerves began to fray.

What if he knew something I didn't? What if he had some weird psychic connection to Arnie and something bad was happening?

I shook off the foolish notion. If anything untoward had occurred at the hospital, Kane would have called me. I checked my phone just in case, but there were no missed calls. The sight of Hibbert's number in the call list made a queasy knot in my stomach.

Drawing a deep breath, I closed the closet doors and remade the bed with the single set of sheets I discovered in the tiny linen closet. When I tried to cuddle Hooker one last time, he braced both front paws against my chest in an unequivocal 'put me down' gesture, and I sighed and packed up Arnie's things before crossing the hall to tap on Miss Lacey's door. She locked Arnie's apartment and hurried back to her card game, and I shivered out into the frigid darkness.

The drive back to the hospital gave me far too much time to think about Hibbert. By the time I parked, my cowardly brain had fabricated several possible scenarios for the 'party', each more frightening than the last.

I swore and yanked out my phone. If I was going to be terrified anyway, I might as well be terrified of reality, not imagination. I clenched my teeth and punched in Hibbert's number before I could lose what little nerve I had left.

A couple of rings later, his smug voice came on the line. "Arlene. I'm looking forward to seeing you at the party."

I gave silent thanks that he couldn't see my shudder. "I won't be able to make it. I'm not in a party mood," I snapped.

"I don't think you understood my message. When

Nicholas Parr invites you to a party, you are *always* in a party mood."

I went for cranky and uncooperative. It wasn't much of a stretch. "I've never even heard of Nicholas Parr. Why would he invite me anywhere? And why the hell would I want to go?"

I held my breath. Come on, Hibbert, spill it.

He did. "Nicholas Parr is possibly the most powerful man in Canada, and most parts of the world. When the owner and CEO of Fuzzy Bunny Enterprises says j-" My strangled gasp made him pause. "Is there a problem?"

I released my panic in an explosive snort I sincerely hoped sounded like laughter. "*Fuzzy Bunny?* Does he hop around with a little powder-puff tail and floppy ears tied to his head?"

Hibbert's voice chilled me to the bone. "If you want to live, I suggest you never, ever make that joke again. Fuzzy Bunny imports and exports children's toys, and Mr. Parr has diverse business interests all over the world."

Yeah. Interests like espionage, arms deals, and money laundering. Not to mention torturing and killing anyone he suspected of interfering with his 'business interests'.

The gruesome memories rose like bile. The once-handsome young blond man strapped naked to the bed. His horrific injuries...

The rich Italian food churned in my stomach. I clenched my free hand on the steering wheel and held my voice dead level. "So what?"

"So Mr. Parr was pleased with the phone list you provided. I suggest you make sure he remains pleased."

"What's in it for me?"

"Other than the privilege of continuing to breathe?"

I channelled every tough-chick movie character I'd ever seen. "Yeah. I don't work for free."

Hibbert chuckled. "Your priorities are admirable. If Mr. Parr decides he likes you, the opportunities are considerable." Iron entered his voice. "If you give him a reason to dislike you, well... I suggest you don't. Be at the Crystal Ballroom at the Palliser Hotel at eight o'clock tomorrow night. And try not to dress like a drug-addicted vagrant."

Click.

I took my time loudly itemizing every detail of Hibbert's striking resemblance to certain portions of the male anatomy, along with his illegitimate parentage, deviant sexual preferences, and inadequate penis size. When I had it all out of my system at last, I sat glaring through the windshield for a few minutes, vaguely surprised it hadn't melted under the heat of my invective. Then I drew a deep breath and let it go.

Arnie came first. If he still needed me tomorrow night, Parr and Hibbert could go piss up a rope. Preferably in tandem.

I grabbed Arnie's clothes and headed for the ward.

The knots in my shoulders eased when I peeked into the room to find Arnie snoring softly. Kane smiled from his post beside the bed and nodded at its peaceful occupant, and my lips creaked into what felt like their first real smile all day. Kane rose, making barely a rustle, but Arnie's eyes snapped open.

"It's okay, it's just us," I reassured him, and Arnie relaxed, giving me a smile before his eyes slipped closed again.

A few moments later his snores resumed, and Kane trod

quietly across to where I stood in the doorway. His thumb traced gently across my cheekbone, his eyes softening to warm grey.

"Why don't you let me take the first shift?" he murmured next to my ear. "You must be exhausted. There's no need for both of us to be here at the same time. I'll give you the key to my condo, and you can go and get some sleep."

"No, it's too far away. I'll stay."

Kane followed my gaze to Arnie before he gathered me into his arms and held me as if I was made of glass. "He's stable," he whispered against my cheek. "He's safe here, and the best thing you can do for him is to take care of yourself. Take my key. Get some sleep, and come and spell me off around two if you really feel like you need to be here." His lips brushed my forehead before he tilted my chin up to look into my eyes. "Will you do that for him?"

The fatigue of the day descended all at once, and I sagged in his arms, letting my forehead drop against his broad chest. "Okay."

"Take a cab." He stroked my hair, holding me close. "You're too tired to drive."

I hauled myself upright. "No, I need my car. I'll be okay." I accepted the proffered key. "Thanks."

When I stumbled into Kane's condo nearly an hour later, the austere décor chilled me almost as much as the temperature of the abandoned rooms. Shivering, I turned up the thermostat before appropriating the crocheted afghan from the back of the sofa, the only softness in the apartment. The reassuring clicks of the heating system promised warmth soon, and I huddled into the afghan while I wandered through the almost-empty rooms.

I guessed he hadn't been here in a long while. The air smelled flat and stale, though there was no dust to be seen. He must hire a cleaning service.

I drifted to a halt in front of the cold fireplace, caught once again by the photo of his brother. Daniel's sparkling grey eyes and handsome young face laughed from the frame with such vitality it seemed inconceivable he had been murdered only a couple of weeks after the photo.

Nearly twenty-five years ago.

I shivered again and hurried down the hall to curl into a ball in the big, cold bed.

Promptly at two A.M., I peeped into Arnie's hospital room. Arnie still snored quietly, and Kane still sat in the chair beside the bed. His hands lay loosely on his knees, but despite his apparent relaxation I recognized the alert balance in his solidly planted feet and his instant reaction to my movement in the doorway.

"Just me," I whispered.

He smiled and rose to stretch his arms above his head, twisting his torso right and left and grimacing at the ensuing crack from his back. Arnie didn't wake, and Kane and I exchanged a satisfied glance.

I tiptoed in and handed over his key, and Kane leaned down to whisper, "See you in a few hours. I hope my bed's still warm."

I grinned. "Maybe if you hurry."

He slipped out and I took up his post in the chair, letting out a breath of comfort when his residual body heat warmed my back. Arnie slept on, and I watched the reassuring rise and fall of his chest until his snores lulled me into drowsiness.

I was fighting to keep my eyes open when Arnie mumbled and moved restlessly. I snapped to wakefulness as his hands clenched, his head rolling on the pillow while his mumbles grew louder.

"Arnie?" I reached over the bed rail to stroke his knotted fist. "Arnie, it's okay, just relax."

"No..." His face twisted, his eyes still squeezed shut. "*No...*" His fists jerked by his sides, his breath accelerating into ragged gasps. "NO!"

I sprang to my feet to lean over the rail and shake his shoulders gently. "Arnie, wake up. You're dreaming. It's just a dream. Wake up."

His eyes flew open in a wild stare and his hands clamped around my wrists so hard I let out a cry of shock. He pushed me away, struggling to sit up. "Mom... run!"

"Arnie, no, it's okay! Wake up! It's just a dream!"

He stared blank-faced for another moment before recognition relaxed his features and he fell back on the pillow. "Shit. Sorry, Aydan." He hugged my hands to his chest, trembling. "Shit. Sorry."

"It's okay." I twisted awkwardly over the rail to slide my arms around him, dropping kisses on his cheek and forehead. "Just a dream. You're okay. Everything's okay."

A rustle from the doorway made us both snap our heads around to face the source of the sound. The incoming nurse raised her hands placatingly. "Is everything all right?"

"Yeah," Arnie rasped. "Nightmare. Sorry."

"It's all right." She stepped forward, eyeing my contorted pose. "Here. Let's try this." She lowered the bed rail.

I let out a sigh of relief as my body resumed a more comfortable position. "Thanks."

She withdrew and I stroked the uninjured side of Arnie's face. "You're safe," I murmured. "I'll watch out for you."

"Thanks, darlin'. I'm okay." He spoke with confidence, but when he reached to squeeze my hand, tension quivered in his grip.

I kissed him before nudging the chair closer so I could sit without breaking our contact. "It'll take a few minutes to fade. Just let it go." I caressed his arm with slow, soothing strokes.

He gave me his devil-may-care grin. "I'm just tryin' to look pathetic so I can get in your pants. Is it workin'?"

I grinned and cuddled closer. "Hell, yeah. You've got that angle all figured out."

"Hey, I'm good, darlin'." His arm slid around my shoulders. "Watch me sweet-talk ya into bed now."

I succumbed to his gentle pull and leaned over to lay my head on his chest. His heart still thumped too rapidly beneath my ear and his hand trembled on my hair, but I played along with his act with a giggle and a teasing southward migration of my hand. "I know exactly how good you are."

"Ya ain't seen nothin' yet, darlin'." I could hear the grin in his sexy growl.

"Mmm, I can hardly wait."

His heartbeat was slowing. His tense muscles eased under me as he chuckled. "Spring me from this joint, an' I'll give ya somethin' to remember."

"I'll hold you to that."

"Mmm." His chest rose and fell in a deep sigh, his arm loosening around me.

"Go back to sleep," I whispered.

"Mmhmm…"

CHAPTER 28

"...outta here." Hellhound's quiet rasp drifted into my consciousness.

"Listen, you pig-headed git..."

I opened my eyes at the sound of Kane's growl to see him glowering at the foot of the bed, arms crossed over his chest. I dragged myself up from my uncomfortable slump across Hellhound's chest, massaging my strained back muscles and trying to yawn as quietly as possible while Kane continued.

"The doctor was very clear! No exertion. No stimulation. Calm and quiet. A hospital bed is the best place for you."

"No, it ain't. Now look, ya woke her up." Hellhound shot a glare at Kane before drawing me down for a kiss. "'Mornin', darlin'." As I straightened, he returned to the attack. "Hospitals are for dyin' in, an' I ain't plannin' on dyin' any time soon. If ya want calm an' quiet, I'm gonna be a helluva lot better off at home, an'-"

"And if something happens to you there, who's going to call 911? The cat?" Kane demanded. "The doctor said a second head trauma could be fatal. If you lose your balance or pass out and hit your head-"

"I ain't a fuckin' china doll, an' I ain't a fuckin' idiot. I'll be careful at home, but I ain't stayin' in this fuckin' boneyard, an' that's final!"

His voice was rising, and I stroked his hand. "Arnie, just stay calm. Don't upset yourself."

"I ain't upsettin' myself, this fuckin' place is-"

"Good morning."

We all twitched simultaneously, Kane and I whipping around to face the speaker behind us. The white-coated man took a half-step backward, and I had a feeling he might have paled if his skin hadn't been coffee-coloured to start with.

"I'm Dr. Sanchez," he said firmly. "Is there a problem?"

"No problem," Hellhound rasped. "I'm leavin'. Gimme the papers an' I'll sign myself out."

The doctor hesitated exactly long enough to take in Hellhound's fearsome scowl and clenched fists. "I'll send a nurse with the paperwork," he said calmly. "You'll need to avoid exertion and stimulation for at least the next twenty-four hours. No reading, no computer work, nothing mentally taxing. Lots of rest. Even if you're feeling better today, don't assume your injury has healed. Take it easy for at least a couple of weeks, longer if you're still having symptoms. Brain injuries are known to cause cumulative damage, so don't do anything else that might cause any impact to your head."

Hellhound nodded, the picture of cooperation now that he was getting his own way.

The doctor returned his nod with a slight smile and turned to go. Kane shot Hellhound an exasperated look and followed, and I hurriedly tagged onto the tail end of the parade.

In the corridor, Kane began, "Doctor, do you really think-"

"That discharging him is the ideal course of action? No." The doctor shrugged. "But it is the best course of action for him. We want to avoid sedation after a head injury, and he is becoming increasingly agitated simply from being here. If he stays, he'll need to be sedated. If you can convince him to rest and relax at home, that will ultimately be more beneficial. But someone should stay with him, at least for the next twenty-four hours."

"I'll stay with him. But what if he falls or something?" I asked. "And what should I watch for?"

"If he falls, you call the ambulance. Watch for symptoms like confusion, double vision, dizziness, intense headache, vomiting, excessive drowsiness or loss of consciousness..." The doctor trailed off at the sight of my face and offered me a sympathetic look. "Those things are unlikely unless he reinjures his head. To be truthful, if he stayed in the hospital, we would only be monitoring him anyway. He's not missing any treatment by leaving now."

"All right. Thank you." Kane looked only slightly appeased when we turned back toward the room.

Half an hour later, I hovered nervously beside Arnie while he limped toward the door. Just as we stepped into the corridor, Kane strode up pushing an empty wheelchair.

"Sit," he snapped.

Hellhound bristled, and the two men locked eyes for a long moment before Hellhound gave a tiny nod and sank into the chair. I drew a breath of relief and followed them down the hall. No further debate ensued while we got him installed in Kane's passenger seat, and I returned the wheelchair to the hospital before shivering into my frosty car.

To my surprise, Kane's Expedition was idling in front of

Arnie's condo building when I drove up. I parked in one of the visitor's slots and trotted across the parking lot, worry cinching my empty stomach tight. Kane's window hummed down and he explained, "I want you to stay with him while I park."

"For shit's sake," Hellhound groused. "It ain't like I'm gonna fall down in the ten feet between here an' the door."

"See that you don't," Kane retorted, and jerked his chin toward the passenger side.

I hurried over and slid an arm around Arnie when he stepped cautiously out of the truck. He chuckled. "Darlin', what d'ya think you're gonna do if I fall? You're just gonna get squished when I land on ya."

"As long as I make a soft spot for you to land on, that's good enough for me."

He shook his head, smiling, but his arm was heavy on my shoulders while we moved slowly to the door. We waited in the vestibule while Kane parked and strode back, and when Hellhound unlocked the door, the three of us turned for the elevator without discussion.

At the apartment, I poised myself to thwart Hooker's escape while Hellhound turned the key. I was straightening with a squirming armful of fur when Miss Lacey's door popped open and she hurried across the hall.

"Arnold! Young man, didn't I warn you you'd come to a bad end one day? You need to mend your ways!" Her severity was belied by the brightness in her eyes. She reached up, her lips trembling. He stooped and she touched his cheek with one thin hand, her fragile fingertips like white porcelain against the coarseness of his beard and bruised face. "Oh, Arnold, I am so very glad you're all right," she whispered.

"Thanks, Miz Lacey. Sorry to worry ya." His bulky arms closed around her as delicately as if shielding a butterfly, and I hid the fullness of my own eyes behind Hooker's long fur.

After a moment, Miss Lacey drew herself up into her usual arrow-straight posture. "Well, young man? Where are your manners? Were you planning to introduce us?" She turned regally to face Kane, and Hellhound tossed me a wink behind her back.

"Miz Lacey, this's John Kane. My brother." The word was firmly emphasized, and Kane smiled.

"It's a pleasure to meet you at last, Miss Lacey." He bowed over her hand, and Miss Lacey coloured, her free hand fluttering to her lips.

"How very nice to meet you, too, Mr. Kane," she replied. "I presume you are half-brothers? I see no family resemblance."

"No biological relation," Kane agreed. "But we're brothers in every other sense of the word. And please call me John."

"Thank you, John. And I do hope you'll call me Emma."

"It would be my pleasure, Emma," Kane replied with one of his lady-killer smiles, and Hellhound and I exchanged a secret glance of amusement.

Hooker spoiled the moment with a sudden lunge from my arms, and Arnie nabbed him in midair with practiced ease.

"Come here, ya big dumbass furball," he growled.

Hooker squirmed up his chest, burrowing his nose into Arnie's beard and planting one large paw on either side of his neck. Eyes squeezed shut, his purr rumbled into a rapturous crescendo while he nuzzled deeper, his paws kneading Arnie's shoulders.

Arnie chuckled, gently massaging Hooker's scruff. "Jeez, ya think he missed me?"

"Nope." I grinned. "Not at all."

Inside the apartment at last, Kane shot a commanding look at Hellhound. "Bed."

Hellhound eased out a long breath as he shed his jacket and boots with careful movements. "Don't need to tell me twice."

Kane and I exchanged a worried glance and flanked him as he limped toward the bedroom.

He halted. "Fuck, would ya stop doin' that? You're makin' me nervous."

"Just get into bed, Arnie, please." I took his hand and coaxed him into the bedroom. "Do you want to get undressed?"

Kane stopped in the doorway, eyeing us uncomfortably, and Hellhound withdrew his hand and sank onto the bed. "Nah." He lowered himself to the pillow, crossing his arms over his chest. "I hate not bein' dressed in the middle of the day. Makes me feel like a fuckin' invalid or somethin'."

I refrained from voicing the opinion that maybe he should be an invalid for a while, and caught Kane's eye. "Would you bring one of the afghans from the living room, please?"

He nodded and returned a moment later to shake out one of the bright, soft blankets and spread it over Hellhound.

"Christ, cut it out, already!" Hellhound burst out. "I don't want a fuckin' bedtime story, an' if ya try an' kiss me goodnight I'm gonna slug ya."

Kane grinned. "Actually, I was going to offer to get you some breakfast, but if you don't need anything..." He turned as if to go.

"Wiseass," Hellhound grumbled.   "Yeah, I want breakfast. Two of those egg an' sausage things. An' coffee. Black an' bitter."   He hesitated and his voice softened. "Thanks."

"You're welcome. Aydan, what about you?"

My stomach let out an audible roar of approval, and I clapped a hand over it and nodded. "Yes, please. Sausage and egg sounds good to me, too. But grab me a milk instead of coffee if you don't mind."   I followed him out of the bedroom as he turned to go. "Thanks, John."

He smiled. "You're welcome. I'll be back as soon as I can. Get ready to buzz me in, so tough-guy there doesn't try to get out of bed."

"Will do."

I locked the door behind him before trailing back to the bedroom, trembling with fatigue and weak hunger.

"Come here, darlin'." Hellhound extended his arms, and I slid gratefully under the blanket to snuggle next to his warm bulk.   He pressed his lips against my forehead. "Thanks for cleanin' up the place. An' for gettin' my stuff. An' for not tryin' to keep me in the fuckin' hospital."

"You're welcome."   I leaned up on one elbow to look down into his face. "How are you really feeling?"

He sighed, his eyes closing. "Like three guys just kicked the shit outta me."

"No kidding. You know that's not what I meant."

He opened his eyes again, dropping the bravado. "Still pretty dizzy, an' my head hurts like a motherfucker. Don't tell Kane or he'll haul me back to the fuckin' boneyard."

"I won't, as long as you promise to tell me if your headache or dizziness gets worse."

"I will. Thanks, darlin'. Knew I could count on ya."

"So what really happened?" I demanded. He shrugged and started to answer, but I interrupted. "The truth."

He fell silent, staring at the ceiling. "I had to know," he said at last.

"Had to know what?"

"Had to know I wouldn't lose control." He met my eyes. "An' I didn't."

"You... you... what? You purposely went out and picked a fight with three guys and let them beat you up..." Words failed me and I glared at him in furious disbelief.

"Nah..." His gaze slid away. "Well, not really. I didn't start anythin'."

"But you went looking for it."

"Not really." He still wasn't meeting my eyes.

I turned his chin to face me and held his gaze.

Hellhound sighed. "Okay, I pretty much knew what'd happen if I showed up on their turf. But, darlin', I had to know. I just had to know."

"You could have been killed," I gritted.

"I know, Aydan, an' I'm sorry." He caressed my cheek and looked deep in my eyes. "It was a shitty thing to do to ya, but don't ya get it, darlin'? I couldn't go through life afraid I was gonna lose it again. If I ever hurt ya I'd..." He trailed off before continuing, "At least ya got a gun. What if I lost it on Miz Lacey? She's so... she's just bones. Little bones like sticks. I could snap 'em with two fingers." He shuddered.

"But, Arnie, you wouldn't hurt either of us! I know you wouldn't!" I gave him a little shake, desperate to convince him.

He smiled through his bruises, and when he met my gaze the haunted shadows in his eyes had faded. "I'm a bit closer to believin' that now, darlin'."

"Oh, Arnie." I hid my tears in his chest.

His hand stroked softly over my hair. "Forgive me?"

"Of course. Just... promise you won't ever do anything like that again."

His hand stilled. "Ya know I can't promise ya that."

I pressed my face into his T-shirt to blot the moisture from my eyes and sat up to glance significantly at his closet before returning my gaze to him. "So are you Special Forces? Or something else?"

He met my eyes squarely. "Well, darlin', I promised I'd never lie to ya."

I waited.

"So I won't," he finished.

I waited a few more moments before realizing that was the only answer he would give.

"So that's why, once you decided to take those three guys out, you mopped the floor with them. And why it was so quick with your da- old man," I corrected myself.

"Yeah."

I eyed him cautiously. "Did you tell John about... Wednesday night?"

"No." He crossed his arms over his chest as if he was cold, and I tucked the blanket up over his shoulders. He sighed. "I can't. He's a cop."

"He'd never rat you out."

"He can't know, darlin'. If anybody ever finds out what really happened, it's gonna look like premeditated murder, an' you'll go to jail, too, for helpin' me. An' if Kane knew but didn't do anythin', he'd go down as a crooked cop. Ya know what happens to cops in jail. He can't ever find out." He closed his eyes and let out a long breath. "Wish I'd just called the fuckin' cops in the first place. Then it woulda been just me goin' down."

"Nobody's going down. Nobody can place you at the scene. Nobody has any reason to believe I'd lie about killing him." I kissed him. "Stemp believed me, the body's gone, and the records are redacted. Even if somebody digs into them, I've killed enough people in the past year that they won't question one more." I scrubbed my hands over my face. "God, I can't believe I just said that. Anyway, don't worry. It's over."

"Wish I could believe that."

"Believe it." The buzzer sounded and I kissed him again before heading for the security panel. "Breakfast time."

CHAPTER 29

With our greasy breakfast summarily dispatched and Arnie tucked back into bed, I drew a long breath and finally confronted the issue of Nicholas Parr's party.

Avoidance hadn't improved anything. I sank my head into my hands and breathed through rising fear.

"Are you all right?"

I looked up to meet Kane's concerned gaze across the table. Shooting a quick glance over my shoulder to make sure Arnie was still out of earshot, I leaned in. "I have a problem."

Kane stiffened, pushing aside his coffee cup to lean closer. "What is it?"

I explained while he listened in silence.

"...so I'll have to call Dermott, and see what he wants me to do," I finished. "But I don't want to leave Arnie, I don't want to go to any stupid party, and I sure as hell don't want to go to Fuzzy Bunny's stupid party."

Kane frowned, and I shot him a questioning look. "What do you think he'll say?"

"Only one way to find out."

"You're not helping."

Kane frowned. "What do you want me to say?"

"What do you know about Dermott?"

"Practically nothing. The only times Stemp was away and Dermott took over, I was away on ops, too. I assume he's competent. I've heard the occasional whisper that he's considered reckless, but I've never experienced that first-hand."

"That's not necessarily bad, is it? That's what you said about Stemp last summer, too, but you said he had a huge success rate."

Kane sat back in his chair and circled his coffee cup around and around on the table, watching the dregs swirl. "I said Stemp was ruthless, not reckless. Big difference."

"Hmm." I sighed and massaged the tightening in my temples. "That really doesn't help."

Kane jerked his shoulders impatiently. "Speculation is pointless. Just call him."

"I know, you're right. I'm just procrastinating." I hauled myself to my feet and went to extract a secured phone from my waist pouch, silently congratulating myself for remembering to transfer one from my car's glove compartment.

I was prepared for the usual immediate answer, but the phone rang several times at the other end. I frowned at Kane and he shrugged.

Pacing, I listened to the fifth, then sixth ring. At last, a rough voice snapped, "Dermott!"

He sounded pissed off, and I wondered what I'd interrupted.

"Hi, this is Aydan Kelly-"

"This better not be a social call, Kelly."

I bit back my irritation and laid out my report in clipped sentences.

When I was finished, Dermott said, "Fine. Go. Coordinate with Kane. Get close to Parr and find out what he wants from you. Keep your ears open for anything about that new weapon." The line went dead in my ear.

Kane raised an inquiring eyebrow as I lowered the phone slowly.

I drew a deep breath to steady my voice. "I was kind of hoping for a little more direction than 'Fine, go get close to Parr'."

I sank back into my chair.

"Like what?" Kane asked. "Recon is the only objective. That's what I'll be doing, too."

"You'll be...?" I frowned. "You're going, too?"

"Yes. I received an invitation last night."

"What? When were you planning to tell me?"

"I wasn't." He looked puzzled at my expression of outrage. "Why would I? If Dermott thought it was relevant, you would have been informed."

I opened my mouth to retort and then closed it again while I considered that. Another entry for the spy manual: All missions are strictly need-to-know, even between team members.

"I'm glad you're going, though. It'll be good to have an extra set of eyes," Kane added.

"Uh." I booted my brain back into gear. "Yeah. So why did you get an invitation? Are they just inviting everybody on the phone list?"

"Dermott didn't say. I assume not, since I don't have orders to coordinate with anyone else-" A buzzing sound came from his pocket and he extracted his phone. "...though I expect this is an order to coordinate with you," he finished after a glance at the display. "Excuse me a moment."

He pulled a secured phone from his jacket pocket and punched the button. "It's Kane." He listened for a moment before saying, "Confirmed," and hanging up.

He smiled. "Looks like it's you and me."

I eased out a breath of relief. Thank God. I wouldn't be completely on my own.

"So what are we going to do?" I asked.

Kane frowned. "Standard recon. I'll be watching for any faces I recognize and keeping my ears open. I expect I've been invited because my name flagged somebody's interest, so that means there should be someone there who recognizes me. You've obviously been invited because Parr wants to meet his new informant."

"But... I don't like it that you've been invited."

"I know you're used to running your own ops independently," Kane began, and I detected an edge of hurt in his tone.

"No, no, that's not what I meant. What I meant was, I don't like it that Fuzzy Bunny is interested in you. The only time they heard your name was out at Harchman's last summer. When you got captured and..." I swallowed a surge of nausea at the horrible memory. "...tortured. What if they're just setting a trap for you?"

He gave me a grim smile. "Then I'll be glad you're there."

I reached across the table to clutch his hand. "Don't go. It's too dangerous."

"Aydan." He frowned, withdrawing his hand. "This is my job. You know that."

"But..."

"Do you think I'm happy watching you go into this? But you don't see me trying to prevent you from going."

"Christ, John, I'm not doing it because I want to. I'm scared shitless, and if I had a choice, I'd run so far and so fast-"

"No, you wouldn't." He blew out a short, irritable breath. "Aydan, would you *please* drop your cover for just a few minutes? I know you've been undercover for years. I know you deliberately risked your cover to bring the secret network key to light and eliminate the Knights of Sirius. I know you've gone into dangerous situations again and again, and I know you're an excellent agent because you're still alive after all this time. Will you please just trust me enough to drop your bookkeeper act so we can plan this mission?"

I collapsed forward on the table, giving my forehead a couple of despairing thumps against my folded arms. "I can't," I mumbled hopelessly to the table. "If you're expecting me to be anything but a dumb civilian bookkeeper, you're going to die a horrible death. Please don't."

After a moment of silence, his hand closed gently around mine. "I'm sorry," he said. "That was unfair. You don't get to be a top agent by dropping your cover every time it's inconvenient. I..."

I heard him sit back in his chair, and when I looked up, he was scrubbing his hands through his hair. The grey light from the overcast sky outside emphasized the lines of fatigue carved in his face.

"I'm having a hard time with this," he said slowly. "I've always agreed in principle with the rules against relationships between agents who work together, and now..." He gave me an imploring look. "I hate the thought of you risking your life. I hate knowing I might not be able to help you. I hate knowing you have to keep secrets from me. I hate having to keep secrets from you."

Fear chilled my heart, but I spoke before it could overwhelm me. "Maybe you should tell Dermott we have a conflict and just stay away from the party tonight."

"No. That would be worse."

"But..."

"Let's just plan our strategy."

I sagged in defeat. "Okay. Do we admit we know each other?"

"I think we should definitely admit an acquaintance. It would be implausible that we work in the same building in the same small town without at least having some acquaintance."

"True. Okay."

"But I don't want to appear too friendly. If it turns out to be a trap for me, I don't want you implicated."

Icicles of nausea pierced my stomach at the thought. Kane must have read my face, because he squeezed my hand. "It's unlikely. If they wanted to capture or kill me, they wouldn't bother inviting me to a party. Silverside is a small town and I'm easy to find. If they haven't made a move yet..." He shrugged and rose. "I'm going to go and buy some clothes. I brought an overnight bag, but I don't have a suit jacket with me, and I'm not driving four hours round trip just to get one from home."

I groaned and let my head thump down again. "Clothes. Oh, God."

I could hear the smile in his voice. "I take that to mean you need some."

"Yeah. I wasn't planning to spend the night when I came down yesterday. I don't even have an overnight bag. No shampoo, not even any deodorant." I chanced a sniff in the vicinity of my armpit. "God. Hibbert told me not to dress like a drug-addicted vagrant. Little did he know."

"Do you want me to buy you something?"

I straightened, hope rising. "Seriously? You would shop for me?"

"Of course, if you tell me what you need."

"Oh, that would be heaven..." I trailed off as thorny reality punctured my bubble. "...shit. You can't. I need everything. Even if I buy slacks, I can't wear my hiking boots to a fancy party, and there's no way you'd be able to buy dress boots without me there to try them on."

I slumped again, the last vestiges of optimism sucked out of me at the thought of being forced to shop for party clothes.

"I hate to say it, Aydan, but I don't think slacks are going to cut it," Kane said. "You'll need a dress."

"Oh fuck! Fuck Hibbert and fuck Parr and fuck Fuzzy Bunny right in their pointy ear! It's thirty below outside, and they want me to freeze my *fucking* ass off in some *fucking* little scrap of fabric..." My voice was rising as rapidly as my irritation. Another thought hit me. "Oh, for *Christ's* sake! I'll need makeup and jewellery and a coat and a purse for my gun..."

"I think the gun's out, too," Kane interjected, taking a cautious step backward. "They'll likely have metal detectors set up."

"Well, fine! That's just fucking *fine!*" I bellowed. "Who needs a gun? I'll just rip their fucking nuts off with my bare hands-"

"Aydan?" Hellhound's tentative rasp made me whirl around. He braced himself against the door frame as if expecting an assault. "What's wrong?"

"Oh, Arnie, I'm sorry." I sprang up to steer him back to bed. "I didn't mean to be so loud. Just go and lie down again."

"Don't think so, darlin'. I wanna know whose nuts you're rippin' off."

"Nobody's. I'm just tired and cranky and-"

"Bullshit."

I slumped back into the chair, defeated. "I have to go to a stupid party tonight and I have to buy clothes for it. I hate shopping."

"An' the part about guns and rippin' nuts off?"

"Just me being cranky because I can't take my gun."

"Don't like the sound of that, darlin'."

"Me neither." I rose again to shepherd him in the direction of the bedroom. "Come on. John's going to go out and buy his clothes, and then he'll come back and stay with you...?" I shot an interrogative glance at Kane and he nodded. "...while I go and buy my things," I finished. "We can ask Miss Lacey to stay with you while we're at the party."

"I don't need a fuckin' babysitter," Hellhound growled. "If nothin' happens to me by the time ya leave, it ain't gonna happen this evenin'. I wanna know more about this party that ya can't take your gun to."

"I know; what kind of a lousy party is it if you can't bring your gun?" I joked, still jockeying him toward the bedroom. "See you later, John. We'll order some pizza or something for lunch when you get back."

Kane took the hint and made for the door. As soon as it closed behind him, I turned to Hellhound. "Can we please go to bed now?"

He brightened. "Hell yeah, darlin', why didn't ya say so?"

"To sleep," I added severely as he towed me into the bedroom.

"Well, shit, that ain't any fun." He pulled me closer, nuzzling the sensitive spot near my collarbone and nibbling kisses up my neck. "How about if we sleep afterwards?"

I shivered and swallowed hard as the tempting tingles radiated downward. "No. What part of 'no exertion' did you forget about?"

He sank onto the bed, pulling me toward him with a teasing grin. "I promise I'll follow the doc's orders, darlin'. I'll just lie here an' let ya do all the work."

"Nice try." I let him draw me onto the bed beside him, but planted a chaste kiss on his forehead instead of meeting his lips. "Anything that raises your blood pressure is a bad idea. And if your blood pressure doesn't go up while I'm doing all the work, then I'm doing something wrong."

"Ah, darlin', you're a cruel woman." But he settled on the pillow without further argument and in a few minutes his arm slackened around me, his breathing deepening into sleep.

CHAPTER 30

Buzzing startled me awake and I stared in confusion around the unfamiliar room.

Hellhound stirred beside me. "Call button," he mumbled, and heaved himself up on one elbow, blinking groggily.

"It's okay, I'll get it." I rolled off the bed and hurried to the panel. When a tap at the door sounded shortly thereafter, I opened it to eye Kane's garment bag enviously. "I bet there's a nice warm wool blazer in there. Which you'll wear with warm wool slacks and a nice warm shirt and socks and nice comfortable shoes."

"Yes." He grimaced. "Sorry."

"Not your fault," I assured him gloomily. "What do you want to order for-"

I broke off as he handed over the plastic bag in his other hand. "I got us some Vietnamese noodle soup," he said. "I wasn't in the mood for pizza."

I hugged the hot bag, my spirits rising. "Fabulous! Have I told you lately how much I love you?" The words were out of my mouth before I could stop them, and I cursed myself for the fleeting spasm that crossed his face.

"I'm s..." I clamped my lips shut on the apology and

turned away before I could make things worse. "Hey, Arnie, we've got pho!"

"Pho you, too," he rasped cheerfully as he emerged from the bedroom.

Replete with a bellyful of spicy goodness, I stared out at the naked tree branches clawing the bleak grey clouds. Wind moaned through the snow-covered balcony railing, and I contributed a dismal moan of my own.

"God, I don't want to do this." A glance at the two men who risked their lives on a regular basis made hot shame push me to my feet. "But I guess I'd better get at it," I finished with my best simulation of a positive attitude. "See you guys later."

"See ya, darlin'. Good luck with your shoppin'," Hellhound rasped.

"Drive carefully," Kane added. "The streets are getting slippery."

"Great." I shoved my feet into my boots and yanked on my chabby old parka. "Just great."

I debated my options while I swept the snow off my car and huddled in the driver's seat waiting for the windshield to defrost. If I called my friend Nichele, the burden of decision-making would be lifted and I could simply hand over my credit card while she dressed me.

A wave of wind-driven snow hissed against the window, and I growled and hunched deeper into my parka. Really not in the mood for light conversation. Kicking the shit out of something, maybe. Shooting a big gaping hole in a target, definitely. Social contact?

No.

I growled again and jammed the shifter into gear.

Shopping when I didn't give a shit turned out to be remarkably liberating.   I presented my surly self to a department-store clerk and offered her fifty dollars to find me comfortable fashion boots and an outfit to go with them, as fast as possible, price no object.   Though the final ensemble wasn't remotely like anything I would have chosen, it fit and flattered, and more to the point, the process was quick.   I blitzed the lingerie department for some clean underwear, then whipped out my credit card.

The blood drained from my body at the final total, but I kept up an impassive façade. Dermott could stick the bill up his ass, and I hoped he got paper cuts in the process.

A rapid foray into the drugstore furnished me with some toiletries and I fled the mall only an hour and a half later, laden with bags.

Hellhound let out a slow whistle when I emerged from the bathroom at seven-thirty.   "Jesus, darlin', ya clean up nice. Ya look like a million bucks."

I grimaced. "Over a thousand, anyway. The expense department is going to have a collective coronary."

"Just give 'em a picture of ya in that outfit an' they'll figure it was worth every penny."

I tugged morosely at the short skirt. "I doubt it. They're female."

"Hm. Guess I better show ya some appreciation, then. Dirty job, but somebody's gotta do it." He pulled me into a kiss, his lips tasting mine with sensuous slowness. A small moan of pleasure escaped me and he deepened the kiss, sending molten hunger coursing through my veins. His hand slid down to the hem of my skirt as I pressed closer.

"Sure like those boots an' stockin's, darlin'," he growled. "An' I bet ya got nothin' but one of your little bitty thongs under there." He rumbled satisfaction when his roving hand confirmed his surmise.

I sucked in a breath as his touch ignited a need that threatened to immolate my common sense. "God, Arnie..." I groaned and pulled away. "You know I can't. In the first place, I have to leave in five minutes, and in the second place, you shouldn't exert yourself."

He stepped closer. "Darlin', if I can't put a smile on your face in less than five minutes without breakin' a sweat, I'm losin' my touch." His lips claimed mine again while his hand slipped under my skirt.

He was in no danger of losing his touch. Minutes later, I braced myself against him, my knees trembling. "Now look what you did," I panted. "My lipstick's all messed up."

He grinned. "So are your panties."

"Yeah, and you look really sorry about that." I returned his grin and reached up to kiss him one more time. "I have to go."

His arms wrapped around me. "Ya still got time for another. Kane ain't here yet."

"He's not coming. He was going to change at home and go on his own. We didn't want to arrive together."

He sobered and released me. "Okay, darlin'. Ya comin' back here tonight, or goin' home with Kane?"

I leaned toward the mirror to repair my lipstick, glad he would credit the sudden tremor in my hands to post-orgasmic bliss instead of the pre-party terror I'd been holding back by pretending nothing bad was happening.

I held my voice steady. "I'll be back. How's your head? Are you sure I can't call Miss Lacey?"

"Fine. I ain't dizzy anymore, an' the headache's gettin' better." He shot me a wicked look. "I know what'd fix my headache."

"Well, it might fix the ache in one head," I teased. I touched his forehead. "Probably wouldn't help this one, though."

"Darlin', if the little head's happy, the big head's happy."

"Uh-huh." I blew him a kiss, hiding my renewed surge of fear at the thought of leaving his warm, safe apartment. "Get some rest. You're going to need it when you're healed up enough to play again."

"Promises, promises."

"And... Arnie... if I don't make it back tonight, call Dermott, okay?"

His smile vanished. "Who's Dermott?"

"Acting Director. Stemp's away."

"How long d'ya want me to wait?"

I hesitated. How long would I have to stay? What if things went terribly wrong from the start? My guts twisted into burning knots at the memory of Kane's ravaged body dangling from chained wrists.

But if everything was going well, having a rescue team show up for no reason would be equally disastrous. Assuming Dermott even bothered to send a team. Maybe he'd just write us off as collateral damage. After all, I wasn't irreplaceable anymore.

I blew out a shaky breath. "I don't know. Give me until four A.M."

"Okay." He pulled me into a tight embrace. "Come back

safe, Aydan."

"I will." I slipped out the door before I could dissolve into a puddle of terror in the middle of his floor.

The long drive through dark and slippery streets did nothing to calm my nerves. By the time I parked in the hotel's parkade, my hands were icy and bloodless on the wheel and a tension headache pounded at the base of my skull.

And I had no gun.

The absence of its familiar weight made me feel naked and helpless. If somebody attacked me, what the hell was I going to do? Give them a vicious tongue-lashing and hope they'd burst into tears and run away?

I rested my forehead on the steering wheel and switched to yoga breathing. I'd be fine. I had only carried a gun for five months. I had been all right before that. Got the shit kicked out of me a few times, but...

I firmly diverted my mind from that unhelpful thought. Dammit, why didn't I have super-ninja skills like Kane? He was just as lethal unarmed as he was with a gun.

Of course, now the Department thought I was that lethal, too.

Shit.

But I'd be fine.

Really.

I groaned and got out of the car. Screw positive self-talk. I summoned bad attitude and foul temper instead, and stalked to the elevator.

The hotel lobby was crammed with bejewelled evening gowns and starched penguin-suits. I sidled along the perimeter, wishing I could vanish into the wallpaper. Goddamn Hibbert for not mentioning this was a black-tie event. For once in my life I was fashionably dressed, but formal was definitely beyond the scope of my outfit.

I clenched my teeth and followed the signs for the Crystal Ballroom. Shit, the name alone should have been my first clue.

When I reached the doorway, though, I was relieved to discover that the ornate mouldings and grand draperies of the ballroom were far more formal than its occupants. The sartorial mix ranged from faded jeans to eveningwear, and I was surprised by the sheer number of people milling around. Somehow I had expected a dingy room with a handful of gangsters trading threatening stares and muttering clichés like 'youse guys gonna swim wit' da fishes'.

This looked more like a corporate 'Holiday Party'. In fact, a moment later I realized the string quartet in the corner was sawing out seasonal music, and the decorations on the scattered cocktail tables looked distinctly festive.

I didn't see any metal detectors at the doors, but that didn't mean there weren't any. I hadn't spotted them at the Hogback, either. And there did seem to be large men in ill-fitting suits positioned by each doorway. At least they got that part of the cliché right.

Just as I noted them, one of the gorillas glanced over at me and spoke into his headset.

I tried not to let the rush of adrenaline make me stiffen. Pasting a pleasant smile on my face, I strolled into the crowd, weaving between clusters of chattering people.

The densest concentration of bodies seemed to be around the bar. I angled in that direction, slipping into the lineup to stand behind two tall, dark-suited men.

Maybe they'd block the gorilla's sight line. I let my gaze roam casually across the room and eased out a sigh of relief when all the security men remained in their positions.

Letting the queue carry me forward, I drew a long, slow breath. Come on, heart, stop trying to escape from my chest and flee like the coward you are.

A slow inhale; another slow exhale. In. Out. Just like ocean waves.

Conversations gradually began to penetrate my fear, and I gave myself a mental shake. Jane Bond wouldn't hide, she'd circulate confidently and eavesdrop on every conversation. Maybe even strike up an acquaintance with somebody and pump them for information.

That was beyond the current capability of my paper-dry throat, but at least I could listen.

In front of me, the two young men were snickering. "...should've seen Mortimer when I pulled that Uzi on him. He squealed like a little girl!"

I was gulping air when the second man laughed. "Those super-soakers are the best! I saw him later and he was still drenched. Looked like he'd pissed his pants!"

"I know, did I nail him or what?"

"Yeah, you better watch it, though. One of these days you'll get a suction-cup dart right between the eyes..."

Their conversation died as they stepped up to request their drinks, and I retrieved my smile and reattached it to my stiff lips.

Goddamn it, if my pulse rate didn't slow, I'd have a heart attack right here in the middle of the ballroom. And nothing had even happened yet.

The beleaguered bartender turned a 'hurry-up-and-order' smile toward me, and I barely resisted the urge to toss down a couple of shots just to calm my nerves.

"Cranberry and soda, please."

While he splashed liquid into the glass, I concentrated on the women chatting behind me.

"...and that new Bunny Snookums stuffie is just adorable in pink... oh, look, there's Nick. Isn't he a hunk?"

By the time I registered that 'Nick' might be Nicholas Parr, the bartender was pushing the glass into my hand and the women had stepped up to the bar so I couldn't tell where they'd been looking.

I sidled away to take up a position at the edge of the bar crowd, scanning the room.

Shit. Idiot.

Any agent worth her salt would have at least checked the internet for a photo of Nicholas Parr. A businessman of his prominence would undoubtedly be featured in some news articles.

I scanned the room, hoping I'd be able to identify the big cheese by a retinue of rats, but nobody stood out. It looked just like any other office party. In fact, I even caught sight of the requisite office jerk, already well marinated and wearing a smeary smile while he dangled a sprig of mistletoe over his own head.

Then again, he was pretty easy to spot. I only had to look for the place where the women weren't.

I rubbernecked and eavesdropped a while longer, holding onto my smile and slipping into the crowd whenever anyone made as if to approach me. Dozens of inane conversations reminded me exactly why I loved my solitary bookkeeping practice so much.

God, even Jane Bond would have been discouraged.

I smothered a groan as the embarrassing magnitude of my own naïveté slowly dawned on me. 'Fuzzy Bunny's going down.' Thank God I hadn't uttered that profoundly improbable resolution out loud in front of Kane and Stemp.

Parr obviously had contacts high up in government and business. I identified a few politicians and local bigwigs schmoozing here and there, but most of the hundred or so guests in the ballroom seemed to be innocent employees and spouses. Just ordinary workers with kids and mortgages, and no inkling of Fuzzy Bunny's shadier operations.

I sighed and sipped my cranberry and soda. This wasn't going to be like yanking a single big ugly weed out of my garden. It was going to be like pulling chickweed: painstaking, tedious, and virtually impossible to eradicate.

The gardening metaphor made me relax into the memory of silence and solitude, the hot sun easing my back, the wholesome smell of moist earth...

"Arlene! How nice to see you again, my dear!"

I spilled my drink.

CHAPTER 31

I stifled some particularly vile profanity and choked out, "Excuse me" before hustling for the bar, ostensibly for some paper napkins.

Goddamn my shitty luck, and god*damn* Lawrence Harchman! What the hell was that slimy little pencil-dicked rodent doing here?

I dried my hands and crushed the sodden napkin in my fist before inhaling deeply, imagining both composure and my Arlene Cherry persona being drawn into my body.

Then I pasted on a sexy smile and turned to face him. "What a lovely surprise, Lawrence."

I sounded convincingly glad to see him. God, I was so full of shit it was no wonder my eyes were brown.

He smiled and drew his tubby little body up into the self-important posture I remembered far too well. "Yes, I'm surprised to see you here, too." There was an edge of double meaning in his tone. "Do you work for Fuzzy Bunny?"

"No." I kept my tone pleasant. "Nicholas Parr invited me."

"Nick invited *you*?"

He must have realized his emphasis was considerably less than flattering. He recovered smoothly. "What a small world! I thought I had met all Nick's friends. How delightful that we share an acquaintance." He peeled his arm away from the small, curvy blonde who was wrapped around him like a silicone-enhanced jellyfish, and patted her bottom proprietarily. "And this is my new wife, Tawny. Tawny, Arlene..."

He trailed off.

"Widdenback," I finished, and extended my hand. "Nice to meet you, Tawny."

Shit, I hadn't even thought it was possible to divorce and remarry in only five months. But maybe things got a little more streamlined when your wife got arrested for espionage, torture, murder, and whatever else they'd charged her with. I hid a shudder.

Tawny giggled and wiggled as if attempting to squirm out of her painted-on sequined dress. "Hi," she piped in a breathless little-girl voice. "I'm Tawny!"

Distracted by her freakishly overinflated lips, I muttered, "Yeah, I got that", before remembering I was supposed to be charming.

She giggled again, and I felt my intellect being slowly sucked away by the vacuum of her presence.

God, she couldn't be for real.

Slightly dazed, I turned back to Harchman. "Um, so, congratulations on your marriage."

He puffed out his chest, making the man boobs under his diamond-studded shirt unpleasantly perky. "Thank you. And how have you been since you vanished so... precipitately?"

I had been right; Tawny wasn't as dumb as she was pretending to be. Her vapid blue gaze sharpened, darting between us for an instant before fading into her bimbo act again. "Lawrence, honey, I have to go to the little girls' room." She patted his ass and pouted her overblown lips. "Don't forget about me while I'm gone."

"Of course I won't, my dear."

I tried not to watch while they cleaned each other's tonsils before Tawny sashayed away in her sky-high stilettos, her swivelling hips making me fear for the future of her spine.

Harchman watched her appreciatively for a few moments before turning back to me. His gaze roamed up my legs and perched on my boobs for a long moment before struggling to my face.

He leaned in to lay a moist hand on my arm. "I was terribly hurt when you ran away and left me waiting. I was so looking forward to seeing you in that red cherry-scented leather you promised."

"Lawrence, I'm so sorry." I leaned closer, dredging up the excuse I'd manufactured but never used back in the summer. "You remember John, the man who was mistreating me? While I was upstairs changing for you that day, he phoned and threatened me. I was so afraid, I just ran away-"

"Isn't that him over there?" Harchman interrupted.

Sick dismay twisted my stomach. What malicious bitch of luck would make Kane stride into the ballroom at exactly that moment?

"Uh... Yes..."

Kane glanced our way and nodded pleasantly before heading in the opposite direction.

Harchman's plump face drew down into a scowl. "Wait. Are you scamming Nick?"

"No!"

Goddamn it! Kane hadn't even been here thirty seconds, and our strategy was already shot to hell. My mind ricocheted through desperate excuses.

"Um... I didn't even know he was coming," I lied frantically. "It's a funny story, actually, um... we ended up working in the same building..."

Harchman's disbelieving expression shrivelled my inspiration to nothing.

"I don't know how Nick knows him," I finished lamely. "But we're not working a scam."

"You're lying," Harchman hissed. "You were working with him this summer to steal my drilling software, and you're planning something underhanded with him now, too. You used me! How dare you, you... you floozy!"

My jaw dropped and I stood speechless at his sheer gall for a second before fury suffused me. My hand shot out to seize a fistful of his shirtfront and jerk him toward me.

His squeak of alarm reminded me we had witnesses. I released him and shoved my face down so we were practically nose to nose.

"Listen, you little shit-weasel," I ground out. "Don't give me that bullshit! In the first place, you were all over me like fungus, Mr. Married Man. And in the second place, speaking of scams, how much have you made from all your Arlene Cherry videos?"

He took a quick step back and smoothed his rumpled shirt front with a shaking hand. "I don't know what you're talking about."

I got down in his face again. "How much, you little prick? You used *me*. That's *me* all over the goddamn internet, and I haven't seen a fucking penny! How much did you make on the movies?"

His eyes darted sideways and sweat beaded his upper lip. "Nothing, really. A pittance."

I smiled, slipped an affectionate arm around him and snuggled close to block any curious eyes.

Then I clamped a vise-like hand on his crotch.

"How. Fucking. Much," I grated, emphasizing each word with a hard compression that made him rise onto his toes and squeak like a doggy chew toy in a Rottweiler's teeth.

"Please," he whimpered. "P-please!"

Just for variety, I twisted instead of squeezing. "What's wrong, *Larry*?" I snarled. "You fucked me six ways from Sunday in those goddamn fake videos. Now you want to fuck me over financially. I'd think you'd be happy to have my hand on your balls." I clamped down hard. *"How fucking much?"*

His pink porcine face went bone-white, a layer of sweat lending it an appropriately lard-like sheen. "F-fifty-three thousand. That's all, I swear." His voice was almost as high-pitched and breathy as Tawny's. "P-please. I'll write you a cheque right now!"

"That's my boy." I released my hold and patted him on the shoulder. "Let's not have any more ugly talk about scams, shall we?"

"N-no, of course not. It was just a mista... misunderstanding."

"Good. Because I'd hate to have to tell the world how pathetically small your dick really is, after you looked like such a porn hero in those videos. I can imagine it might cause a certain amount of, hmmm... amusement? In your social circle?"

Harchman threw a panicked glance over his shoulder and groped in his suit jacket. "There's n-no need to be rash.

I'm sure we can settle this like civilized p-people." He withdrew a pen and chequebook and hurried to the nearest cocktail table.

The pen fell from his shaking fingers when he tried to write, but apparently the act of stooping to retrieve it restored some blood to his brain. He straightened, his eyes narrowing.

"How do I know you won't just blackmail me? Keep demanding more and more money?"

I leaned on the table and offered him a pleasant smile that made the blood drain from his face all over again. "You don't. But here's the deal. If you cut me in on half the proceeds from here on in, we'll be business partners. And then I won't have any reason to cause trouble for you. Fair enough?"

He relaxed visibly, colour returning to his face. "Of course. I was going to offer you a split anyway. I just didn't know how to find you. None of this... unpleasantness... was necessary."

"Well, that's just great, Larry. Because I don't like unpleasantness." I gave him another smile. "Now give me my fifty-three grand."

"I prefer 'Lawrence'. And you mean twenty-six five." He smirked, his smugness completely restored. "Fifty-fifty split, remember?"

I made my toothy smile just a bit pointier. "Fifty-three, you dickless little shit. Consider it an interest charge for late payment."

He huffed and scribbled out the cheque. "There's no need to be rude."

"Actually, Larry, there is." I tucked the cheque into my purse. "I'll be in touch mid-month, *every* month, for my cut." I showed him my teeth again. "Have a nice evening."

As I turned away, I spotted Tawny heading purposefully toward us. When she realized I was looking, her laser-sharp gaze softened into her bimbo blues once again, and she fluttered her fingertips at Harchman and me. By the time she reached us, she was all bubble-headed giggles again, but her timing was far too coincidental for my taste.

I wished her a pleasant evening and made for the ladies' room. Without anger to sustain me, my legs turned to rubber and my guts felt as though they'd been hollowed out with a spoon. I barricaded myself inside a stall and slumped down on the toilet seat, propping my head in my shaking hands.

Breathe.

In. Out. Ocean waves.

The washroom was a busy place. A constant flow of high heels tap-tapped in and out, borne on currents of perfume and gossip. The steady flushing of the toilets sounded like a space shuttle launch, and I stifled a groan and massaged my tension headache.

At last I couldn't take it anymore. Pushing my smile back into place, I exited the cubicle and washed my hands before abandoning the ballroom entirely.

It took a while to find a quiet corner. There seemed to be several Christmas parties in progress, and the corridors were dotted with couples and groups of happy party-goers. At last I found an out-of-the way niche and tucked myself into it. Drawing a deep breath, I let the silence descend on me like a blessing from heaven. I rolled my shoulders, trying to ease the burning of my rigid muscles, and breathed for a while.

After a few minutes, I revived enough to berate myself. I was here to do a job, not hide like a child. Other than the water-pistol Uzi, I hadn't heard a single whisper of anything even vaguely relating to weapons. I needed to get back out there and-

The murmur of approaching voices made me shrink back into my corner. A moment later, I realized how suspicious I would look hiding alone in a niche in an empty corridor. Dammit.

My mind racing, I seized the only semi-plausible excuse I could think of. Whipping my cell phone out of my purse, I held it to my ear just in time.

"...delivery of the prototype for testing. It sounds very promising for covert-" The speaker broke off as he spotted me.

Shit, this was the first useful conversation I'd heard all evening. And I'd gotten busted. Please don't let him realize I'd heard the word 'covert'.

"I miss you, too, sweetie," I assured my phone. "I wish you were here, but I guess I'd better get back to the party." I paused. "Love you, too, honey. 'Bye."

Tucking my phone back into my purse, I levered myself away from the wall and strolled toward the two men.

They seemed to be occupying more than their share of the corridor.

As I drew abreast of them, the white-haired man stepped in front of me. "Ms. Widdenback?"

Adrenaline surged into my veins. "Um... yes?"

I eyed him, measuring my chances of escape. About my height, but a hell of lot more muscle. The apparent age indicated by his hair was belied by a youthful face with penetrating blue eyes. His features were slightly too sharp to be classically handsome, but combined with those eyes and the hard fitness revealed by his well-cut suit, he bore a striking resemblance to a bald eagle or some other merciless raptor.

The man with him was taller, slimmer, and younger, and I didn't like my chances against either of them, let alone both at the same time. A glance down the quiet corridor made me curse my own idiocy. Go and get cornered in the only deserted part of the whole fucking hotel. Smooth move, Jane Bond.

The white-haired man smiled and extended his hand. "I'm Nick Parr. I'm glad you could make it to the party on such short notice."

A shock of fear stole my voice for an instant, but my smile and handshake were reflexive after years of business events I'd never wanted to attend.

By the time I finished shaking his hand, I thought I might be able to trust my voice. "It's nice to meet you. Thank you for inviting me. It's a lovely party." My voice rang false, but I hoped he'd chalk it up to the 'sweetie' I was supposedly missing.

He accepted my polite lies with an equally polite smile. "I noticed you talking to Lawrence earlier." His predatory gaze dissected my face. "He looked upset."

I nodded and kept my voice easy around the knots in my gut. "We have a joint business venture. I had to deliver some bad news."

A slow smile softened his sharp features. "Lawrence can be rather high-strung. Sometimes he needs careful... handling."

I couldn't prevent the twitch at the corner of my mouth. Parr's smile broadened into a rakish grin, and I smiled back automatically.

"So where are the cameras?" I murmured.

His eyes glinted amusement. "Everywhere. And I see you know John Kane, too."

My throat tightened. If Parr and Harchman were friends, Harchman would probably tell him exactly how I knew Kane. "That's a long story," I muttered. "Oh, excuse me a moment." I fumbled into my purse and peeked at my phone as if checking a text message while I stalled, thinking furiously.

No point lying or denying.

As I slowly closed my purse again, I realized this could work. I wanted Parr to believe I was Arlene Widdenback, fraud artist. What better way than to let Harchman vouch for my identity? And that might save Kane, too. Especially if Parr thought Kane and I were running a scam at Sirius.

I met his eyes again, ready to trot out my 'confession'.

"Do you know George Harrison, too?" Parr's question derailed my train of thought.

"Um... the Beatle? Isn't he dead?"

Parr laughed, a generous laugh from deep in his belly. "No. Well, yes, George Harrison the Beatle is dead. I meant George Harrison, the friend I was hoping to contact at Sirius Dynamics. I called to invite him to the party..." He inclined his head graciously. "...and thank you for providing his number. But I didn't receive a reply."

"Oh, that's too bad." The platitude rolled out while my brain ticked over all the people I knew at Sirius. Stemp had said it was safe to disseminate all the names on the list. But who the hell was George Harrison?

"I'm sorry," I said at last. "I can't put a face to that name. But I don't know everyone there."

Parr accepted that with a philosophical nod. "Unfortunate." He offered me a charming 'duty calls' grimace. "I'm afraid I don't have much time to chat tonight. I have to make a short speech, and then I have another engagement. But I would very much like to have a longer conversation with you. I'm booked solid for the rest of the week, but I'm flying down to Las Vegas on Thursday, and I hope you'll join me on my private jet."

He obviously noticed my instant of paralysis. "I'm sorry, I phrased that badly," he added hurriedly. "I'm not making an improper suggestion. My wife would undoubtedly take a dim view. Let me try again."

He smiled. "My wife and I are leaving on Thursday for our annual gambling holiday. Las Vegas is our first stop, after which we'll pop over to Ibiza and Monte Carlo. *We...*" He emphasized the pronoun. "...would be pleased if you would accompany us on our flight to Las Vegas. You and I can talk during the flight, and we will part company at the airport. I'll arrange for accommodations for you at the Venetian, and the jet will be available to return you to Calgary the following day."

Yeah, unless he figured out who I really was and realized what I'd just heard. Then 'parting company' would mean something a little more permanent.

I hesitated.

He glanced at his watch. "I'm sorry, I must go. My assistant will contact you on Monday. It was a pleasure meeting you, Ms. Widdenback."

Relief nearly melted my knees. Nearly two whole days to figure out what to do.

"Please call me Arlene." I shook his extended hand.

"Thank you, Arlene, and I hope you'll call me Nick." He gave me another charming smile and strode back down the corridor in the direction he'd come. His silent companion offered me a polite nod and followed.

I let out a shaky breath and collapsed against the wall, hauling out my faithful phone in an attempt to look as though I had another call. When I was capable of walking again, I hurried gratefully back to the bustle of the ballroom and made a beeline for the bar.

Nobly restricting myself to another non-alcoholic beverage, I turned to discover Kane in conversation with another man only a few yards away. For the first time since I'd arrived, my pulse rate slowed below crisis level. Thank God. I had survived a meeting with Nicholas Parr, and I wasn't on my own anymore.

I hid my relief and strolled casually in his direction. He excused himself from his conversation to give me a friendly nod, and we drifted to a relatively unoccupied spot in the room.

I raised my glass to my lips to murmur, "Cameras everywhere."

He nodded, apparently unsurprised. "So Harchman knows Parr." He didn't bother to conceal his lips, and I decided after an instant of panic that this was a perfectly plausible conversation for us to have.

"Yes. He'll probably tell him about that scam we tried this summer."

Kane nodded.

"Good evening, ladies and gentlemen." Parr had taken his place in front of a microphone on a raised dais at the end of the ballroom. "Welcome! I promise to keep this short, but before I begin, I'd like to introduce some of our distinguished guests this evening..."

I raised my glass to my lips again as Parr continued his speech. "I think Harchman's new wife is another plant from

Fuzzy Bunny."

"Makes sense." Kane took a sip from his own drink. "They'd want to continue to manage him subtly-"

He froze, his gaze riveted to the stage.

"What?" I hissed. I shot a look over to where several of Parr's 'distinguished guests' were filing onto the dais, nodding and smiling to the applause. I didn't see anybody I recognized, and I snapped my attention back to Kane's rigid face. "What? What is it?"

He reached out blindly as if to place his drink on the nearby table. He wasn't even close. It fell to the carpet with a sharp tinkle of ice and breaking glass, but he didn't spare it a glance. He was already forging through the crowd toward the stage.

CHAPTER 32

Adrenaline slammed into my veins and I hurried after Kane, muttering 'Excuse us' and 'Sorry' to the disrupted party guests.

Goddammit, what was he doing? I thought the whole point of being undercover was not to attract attention. And he was sure as hell attracting attention.

Parr's speech stumbled to a halt, and the guests on the dais turned to stare. The security guards at the door stiffened and began to push toward Kane, their hands diving into their lumpy suit jackets.

I ground my teeth and scurried to close the gap opened by his long strides. If he was going to attack somebody, I couldn't imagine what I might do, but maybe I could help somehow.

At the end of the row of guests on the stage, a beautiful dark-haired woman's eyes widened, her hand flying to her throat. In the sudden silence of the ballroom, the single word she uttered carried easily to every corner: "John!"

Kane shoved free of the crowd and vaulted up on the stage to crush her in his arms. Their passionate kiss left no question as to Kane's motives.

I trailed to a halt, my jaw sinking along with my heart.

Guess he didn't need my help.

Murmurs and titters rose from the crowd. Kane broke the kiss to caress her face with both palms as if cradling a precious treasure. They stared at each other for a moment before kissing again, their bodies entwining as though they would occupy each other's skin.

"Well." Parr's amused voice rose over the hum of the crowd. "I see at least one of our guests needs no introduction. That is Yana Orlov at the end. Yana has recently joined us from Moscow as our new director of operations."

At the sound of her name, the woman drew away from Kane's embrace, blushing, but it was clear that Kane was oblivious to everything but her.

Parr continued smoothly, "Next in line is Alex Peng, one of our valued manufacturing partners from China..." His voice faded into a buzz at the edges of my consciousness while I watched Kane guide Yana Orlov to the edge of the stage.

He jumped off the stage before reaching up to encircle her waist with his hands, lifting her effortlessly down into his embrace again. Arms around each other, they stood beside the stage, murmuring with their heads together. Her beautiful dark eyes welled up, and Kane wiped her tears away with a tender gesture, following his hand with kisses.

I was about to fade back into the crowd when Yana nodded in my direction with a questioning expression. Kane shook his head without turning, but she spoke urgently and he tore his attention away from her to meet my eyes.

He tried to draw her along with him but she held back, shaking her head and giving him a small push toward me.

He released her reluctantly and moved toward me with a

backward glance as if assuring himself that she was still there. When he reached me, he stooped next to my ear and spoke rapidly.

"I'm sorry."

"Sorry for what? John, what...?"

He grasped my shoulders to look into my eyes. "She's... I thought she was dead. Nearly a year ago. I thought she had died in a car bombing. I can't..." He broke off and stared at the floor for a moment before meeting my eyes again. "Don't get me wrong, what you and I had was..."

"It's okay," I said quietly.

"Yesterday I watched you kiss Arnie as if he was your whole world," he went on as if he hadn't heard me. "I can't compete with that, and I don't want to. You've always said I should find somebody else..."

I gripped his arms. "John. It's okay." When he stared into my eyes, I added, "Go. Be happy." I gave him a little push. "Go on. She's waiting."

His hands tightened on my shoulders for an instant. "Thank you."

He released me and returned to Yana without a backward glance, and I turned to push through the crowd in the direction of the bar, trying to ignore the whispers and curious stares.

Fortunately, the bartender was unoccupied when I arrived.

"Give me a shot."

He raised an eyebrow. "What kind?"

I rarely drank hard liquor, and my brain didn't seem to be working anyway.

"I don't care. Just give me a shot."

He shrugged and poured.

I tossed it back in a single gulp.

Whatever it was, it tasted like turpentine and burned like the fires of hell. "Jesus," I wheezed when I was capable of breathing again. "Fuck. Give me another."

The bartender's other eyebrow rose to join the first. "You sure?"

Apparently the caustic fluid had ripped away the lining of my throat. Or something had, anyway. My voice came out in a harsh rasp. "I *said*, give me another fucking sh-"

My brain kicked back into gear, too damn late. Shit, I had my car. And I had just made it impossible to leave for at least an hour, probably more, until I was sure I was sober enough to drive.

I groaned out loud and debated whether to beat myself senseless against the bar, induce vomiting before the alcohol hit my bloodstream, or just stand there and die of sheer stupidity.

"You okay?" The bartender eyed me with concern.

I blew out a long sigh. "Yeah. Forget the shot. Give me a cranberry and soda, please. And I'm sorry for being rude." I pulled a twenty out of my purse and laid it on the bar. "This is for you if you don't let me have any more booze."

He leaned closer, his brow furrowing. "Are you A.A.? Can I call somebody for you?"

"No." I shook myself back to a semblance of normalcy. "I'm not an alcoholic, I just have to drive tonight and that's my limit for the evening. Thanks, though."

"No problem." He handed me the glass.

I dredged up a smile and drifted back into the crowd.

Kane and Yana had vanished, and I could guess where they'd gone. Convenient that they were already in one of the nicest hotels in the city. Then again, they were so absorbed in each other, they could have been in the cheapest dive in Calgary and they'd never notice the difference. I spared a moment of self-pitying envy for the hot night that awaited Yana before determinedly rerouting my mind to the task at hand.

The booze trickling into my system was a blessing in disguise. If not for my flat-out refusal to drive under the influence of alcohol, I would have abandoned the whole effort on the spot. At least this way Dermott would get his money's worth from my surveillance.

An interminable half-hour later, I let out a sigh and wiggled my throbbing toes inside the confining boots. I had eavesdropped on more innocent and progressively inebriated people than I cared to think about. I had even initiated a few conversations from sheer desperate boredom, but learned absolutely nothing from the effort.

Parr had departed, and even if there were still some bad guys in attendance, I probably wouldn't be lucky enough to overhear any other useful tidbits unless I left the ballroom. Abandoned by Kane and without my gun, I just couldn't summon up the courage to do that again.

I vectored away as Jerkface and his mistletoe staggered in my direction. Just give me a nice quiet wall to hold up until I was sober enough to drive...

"Well, well. Arlene."

I halted without turning, briefly squeezing my eyes shut in martyrdom at the sound of the oily voice. When I opened them again, Hibbert was standing in front of me, wearing an expensive suit and his usual irritating smile.

"So I hear your boyfriend dumped you for another

woman." His smile broadened into a taunting grin. "Maybe you could have kept him if you learned to give better head. Come and see me later and I'll let you practice."

Suddenly all my hurt and fear and frustration had a visible target. Anger rose in a sizzling tide.

I closed my eyes again and counted to ten.

It didn't work. When I opened them, he was still there, his grinning face just begging for a knuckle sandwich.

I held his gaze and spoke slowly, the words straining out between my teeth. "The only reason I'd come anywhere near you is to rip your fucking ugly nuts off and shove them down your throat."

"Oooh, touchy!" He smirked. "I'd rather shove them down *your* throat. I could go for some teabagging."

The world went red.

Next thing I knew one of the gorillas had me by the arms and my hand hurt like hell. Hibbert sprawled on the elegant carpet, spitting profanity and bleeding all over his nice white shirt.

The gorillas were good. In seconds, they had hustled both of us into a small room and closed the door, leaving behind a cluster of eagerly chattering bystanders and a few spots of blood on the carpet.

"Call the cops." Hibbert's voice was muffled by his still-bleeding nose and the hand he'd clamped over it. "I'm pressing assault charges."

"It was self-defence," I retorted.

The hulking guard who'd grabbed me gave me a flat stare. "Lady, he never touched you."

"Not this time. But he threatened me with sexual assault. And he sure as hell assaulted me before."

The gorillas looked unimpressed, and I glared at

Hibbert. He flipped me a triumphant middle finger, and the guard's grip tightened on my arm as I jerked with the need to punch Hibbert all over again.

I drew a long breath and shot Hibbert a venomous look. "Okay. Go ahead and call the police. Lay charges. I'll tell Nick all about it on his private jet while we're flying to Vegas on Thursday."

Hibbert's victorious expression faded slightly. "You're full of shit. You're just a cheap whore. Parr wouldn't give you the time of day."

"And you're just a stupid two-bit thug who thinks with his sadly inadequate dick." Before he could explode, I added, "Call his secretary. She's setting it up."

Hibbert sneered, his confidence visibly returning. "Parr's secretary is male. You're full of shit."

I held his gaze. "Fine. Call *him*."

"Parr? I don't think so. I'm not going to bother a man like-"

"No, his secretary, you dumb shit!"

"Fine. I'm calling your bluff." Hibbert turned to the two guards who had been following the exchange like a pair of spectators at a tennis match. "Give me something to wipe my hands. I don't want to get blood all over my phone."

One of the gorillas handed him a box of tissues, and we all stood in silence while he took his time cleaning up. His nose still bled sluggishly, and he twisted a couple of tissues into plugs and inserted one in each nostril, wincing.

When he was done at last, he gave me a challenging stare. "Last chance, bitch," he mumbled through his makeshift packing. "But don't worry, you're going to make it up to me. You're going to suck my cock until-"

"Dial the fucking phone, asshole." My growl sounded

wholly confident, but I had no idea if Parr would have contacted his secretary yet. Probably not.

That meant police and explanations.

And Stemp was gone.

I clamped down on panic. Surely the emergency number he'd given me would reach Dermott. Surely Dermott would straighten things out with the police.

But if he didn't...

The thought of spending the night incarcerated made my pulse accelerate into a thundering rhythm. I held myself still and concentrated on controlling my breathing.

Stay calm.

"What?" Hibbert's face twisted into furious incredulity. "He *what?*"

Glorious relief flooded me as he punched the phone off and returned it to his pocket with short, stiff movements.

"Should we call the cops?" My gorilla posed the question with such perfect deadpan timing that I shot him a suspicious glance. His poker face was nearly impenetrable, but I detected the slightest glint in his eye. Apparently Hibbert did, too. He flushed an unpleasant shade of burgundy.

"No." The word sounded as though he was chewing on his tongue. He took a jerky step forward. "I'll get you for this, bitch," he snarled, and strode out.

I eyed the guards. "You heard that, right? He threatened me."

"I heard him." My gorilla shifted his grip on my arm to raise my hand for inspection. "Do you want some ice?" I realized my legs were trembling uncontrollably when he pulled a chair over. "Sit down. I'll get some from the bar."

I sank into the chair and inspected the small chunk of

skin peeled back from a shallow bleeding gash in my rapidly swelling knuckles. The second guard glanced over as I sighed and pulled off the loose bit.

"Jesus, don't do that!"

"Uh?" I dragged my attention up to his horrified countenance. "Why not?"

"It's gro... um... you wouldn't want to get an infection," he finished sheepishly.

I kept my expression solemn. "Right. Thanks."

My gorilla, obviously a resourceful fellow, returned with ice wrapped in a kitchen towel and a first-aid kit. He doctored my hand with professional efficiency before handing me the icy towel. "Keep that on it. It'll take a while for the swelling to come down. You really clocked him."

There might have been a hint of approval in his tone, but I was too tired to respond. "Thanks," I said instead. "I'm sorry to cause you so much trouble."

"No trouble. Would've been a boring night otherwise. The hotel says to take the towel home with you. You can stay in here until you're ready to go." He hesitated. "Unless you want to go back to the party?"

"I'd rather-" I bit off the words 'blow Hibbert', just in case they didn't realize death was preferable. "...not," I finished instead.

CHAPTER 33

Slumped in the driver's seat of my car at last, I reached wearily for a secured phone. It rang and rang on the other end, and I was about to give up when there was a click and a hoarse voice growled, "What!"

In my exhausted stupor, it suddenly occurred to me that I might have a wrong number. "Is this Brent Dermott?"

"Who the fuck do you think it is? What the hell do you want, Kelly?"

"Uh. Just checking in."

"Anything urgent?"

"No, I-"

"Then why the hell are you calling me? Report nine tomorrow morning, my office." The line went dead.

I stared at the phone, my fatigue slowly evaporating in the heat of angry embarrassment.

Okay. Fine. Next entry for the spy manual: Don't wake Dermott unless it's an emergency. Unlike Stemp, who always wanted to know the instant there was anything to report. And who was always alert. And who, if not strictly polite, was unfailingly civil.

I eased out a long, calming breath and started the car.

Hellhound pulled me into his arms as soon as I was inside his apartment. "Jesus. Finally."

I leaned into him and buried my face in his shoulder, the stress of the evening throbbing in my tense muscles.

"Hey, darlin'." He stroked my hair with a gentle hand. "Ya okay?"

"Yeah." I didn't raise my head.

"How'd it go?"

"Fine. I guess."

"What happened to your hand?"

"Punched a guy."

"Rip any nuts off?"

"Not quite. By the time I was done squeezing and twisting, he was ready to cooperate."

After a moment of silence, Hellhound asked, "Ya serious?"

"Yeah."

"Jesus. Remind me not to piss ya off."

I sighed and burrowed deeper into his shoulder. "Not my finest work. I made a couple of enemies I could have done without."

"Come here." He coaxed me over to the couch and lowered me onto it before dropping a kiss on my lips. "I'll get ya a beer."

"I can't. I have to drive back to Silverside tonight."

"Shit, darlin', it's damn near midnight an' the roads'll be bad. Go tomorrow instead."

"Can't." I toppled over to bury my face in the cushions. "Dermott wants me there by nine tomorrow morning."

"Dermott's an asshat."

"You don't even know him."

"Don't have to. He's an asshat if he expects ya to drive back tonight."

I sighed. "Yeah. But I still have to go."

Hellhound knelt beside the couch. "Okay, darlin', here's the deal. You're wiped out." He ran a gentle hand over my shoulders, kneading experimentally. "An' you're wound up like a fuckin' spring. I'm gonna go get ya a beer. You're gonna drink it. An' then you're gonna get in bed an' I'll give ya a massage, and then you're gonna go to sleep. I'll wake ya whenever ya wanna get up, but ya ain't gettin' back in your car 'til ya get some sleep."

"I love you," I mumbled into the cushions.

"Sorry, darlin', what?"

I sat up. "I said, that sounds about as close to heaven as I ever expect to come."

He grinned and headed for the beer fridge.

A slow hand stroked my skin, gliding over my shoulder and around the curve of my hip. I sighed and stretched, my eyes still closed. The hand coasted down my thigh before reversing direction. Warm lips and electric whiskers nuzzled my shoulder while the hand slid up to cup my breast. Dexterous fingers traced ever-decreasing circles until they reached their goal, and I moaned in sensuous bliss and rolled onto my back to offer better access.

"Mornin', darlin'." Hellhound's soft rasp dragged me from my dream. His mouth closed over my breast, his tongue flicking in jolts of pleasure while his hand migrated south to generate more exquisite sensations.

I groaned, the sweet ache coiling up inside me already. "Stop, Arnie. I can't."

"Sure ya can." Magic fingers reminded me that I could.

And in very short order, I would.

"No, I meant..." I caught my breath on a moan. God, those fabulous hands...

I tried again. "I meant, *you* can't."

He chuckled. "I ain't. Yet."

The hard length pressing against my thigh made it clear that if I didn't stop him while I still had a few vestiges of self-control, we both would. Enthusiastically.

I squirmed away. "God, Arnie, I want to. You have no idea how much I want to, but..."

"Shhh. Come here, darlin'."

I groaned and deflected his hands, my body aching for release. "Arnie, no. I've already had one man die in my arms. I won't take that chance with you."

He went still. "Shit, sorry, Aydan." He leaned over to kiss me gently, offering comfort instead of sex. "I shoulda thought of that. Guess I'm thinkin' with the little head instead of the big head."

I chuckled and slid out of bed before I could change my mind, my body protesting the deprivation. "It's okay."

He turned on the bedside lamp before tucking his arms behind his head to watch me. "Just 'cause I can't, doesn't mean you can't," he offered helpfully. "Come back to bed, darlin', an' I'll make it worth your while."

I wavered, my body's hungry need threatening to overpower my better judgement. As usual.

I pulled on my jeans with determination. "I can't. I don't have enough self-control when you're all hot and naked. And I'd better get going anyway. If the roads are bad, it'll be a longer trip than usual."

He sighed. "Okay, but hang on a sec." He rolled out of

bed. "There's somethin' I wanna give ya before ya go."

I gave him a lustful up-and-down look and yanked on my T-shirt before I could succumb. "And you have no idea how much I want it, but I really can't."

He laughed. "I wanna give ya that, too, but that ain't what I meant. Come on." He shepherded me out to the kitchen and reached into one of the drawers. "Here. I want ya to have this."

I stared at the key in his outstretched hand, my heart swelling to short-circuit my voice. "Are..." I cleared the hoarseness out of my throat. "Are you sure?"

"Yeah." He smiled. "If you're gonna keep gettin' Miz Lacey to let ya in anyway, ya might as well have your own key."

I hesitated, and he took my hand and closed my fingers over the key. "Don't freak out. I promise if ya use that key without callin' first, you'll prob'ly catch me ballin' some other chick."

I laughed and relaxed. "Thank God."

"Well, hell, darlin', if I'd known ya liked to watch, I'd have given ya a key sooner." He bounced his eyebrows.

I grinned and pitched my voice into a sultry purr. "What makes you think I'm only going to watch?"

"Mmm, kinky." He twisted his face into an expression of righteous indignation and gestured downward. "Now look what ya did."

I looked.

My willpower suffered a serious setback.

"See somethin' ya like?" His growl sent hot tingles all the way from my ears to my toes.

I dragged my gaze back up to his face. "Yes. I like you. Standing there alive. Cold and dead just doesn't do it for me."

He winked. "But hey, I'd be stiff."

"You'd be *a* stiff. Totally different thing." I let my gaze dip for one more rewarding peek. "And anyway, getting stiff has never been a problem for you. So hold that thought. I'll be back."

"Ya better be, after a tease like that." He grinned and followed me to the door. "Drive safe, darlin'." He dropped a kiss on my lips.

"I will. Thanks."

He sobered. "No. Thank you. Ya saved my ass. Again. I ain't gonna forget that."

By the time I parked in front of Sirius Dynamics, my eyes burned from staring at the dark icy highway and my arms and shoulders ached with the tension of gripping the wheel.

Goddamn Dermott, hauling me back here in the pitch fucking dark of early morning on shitty roads, after depriving me of sleep *and* multiple orgasms. Asshole.

Bereft of the warmth of my car, I shivered across the parking lot and into the lobby, wishing I'd had time to grab a second breakfast and a hot tea. But Dermott didn't sound like a patient guy, and it didn't seem like a good idea to be late for our very first meeting.

The guard in the security wicket looked as sleepy as I felt. Poor bastard, manning a booth in a largely deserted building.

He brightened slightly as I approached. "'Morning, Aydan. What are you doing here on a Sunday?"

"'Morning, Leo. Got a meeting."

He grimaced sympathy and I signed for my security fob,

feeling slightly comforted by the knowledge that I wasn't the only cranky tired person in the building.

"Is Dermott using Stemp's office?" I inquired.

Leo nodded, and I thanked him and headed for the stairs.

It was five minutes to nine but Stemp's door was still locked, so I hurried thankfully down the hall to the ladies' room. Pressure relieved, I washed my hands and verified with annoyance that I looked as exhausted as I felt. I made a face at my reflection and departed.

Beside the still-locked door, I propped myself against the wall, wrapping my arms around myself and sinking my chin on my chest. The weight of fatigue dragged my eyes closed, and I huddled in a miserable stupor.

I jerked awake when I started to slide down the wall, but my foot failed to get the wake-up call. Muttering curses, I shook it vigorously and hobbled around until the pins and needles subsided.

A glance at my watch returned my irritation full-force. Nearly nine-fifteen. That fucking asshole. Didn't even show up.

Well, fuck him.

I marched down the hall, seething with mental images of kicking Dermott's ass all the way to Calgary and back.

In the lobby, I stomped over to plant myself in front of the security wicket again. As Leo looked up, loud male voices and a blast of cold air on the back of my neck heralded the arrival of a couple more Sunday workers. Their offensively cheerful banter grated on my last remaining nerve, and I clenched my teeth and slapped my fob down on the security counter.

"What's up, Aydan?" Leo asked. "I thought you had a

meeting."

"Me, too," I snapped. "That fucking asshole Dermott called me all the way back here from Calgary this morning and then didn't even bother to show up. Dickhead!"

Leo gulped and shot a look over my shoulder. "Uh... I guess you haven't met. Aydan Kelly, Brent Dermott."

In my life before Sirius Dynamics, I would have sunk through the floor in sheer mortification. As it was, the extra dollop of shitty luck just pissed me off even more.

"Oops. Guess that was my outside voice," I snarled.

I turned to meet the glare of the large man behind me, obviously Dermott by his rising colour. His bushy eyebrows met in the middle. "What's your problem, Kelly? You on the rag or something?"

Red surged into the edges of my vision.

Perfect range. His feet were widely planted. I could drop him with a single kick to the balls.

"Here's your fob, Brent." Leo's voice held an urgent note, and I recognized the warning in it.

It didn't cool my anger, but at least it kept me from sending Dermott's nuts into orbit. I gave him a hard stare instead. "Do you want my report or not?"

Dermott signed for his fob and straightened to face me, returning a challenging stare of his own. "Yeah. You gonna start something with me?"

Stemp's comment about verbally abusing and assaulting my co-workers echoed in my memory and I clamped down with every ounce of my self-control. "No."

Dermott held my gaze for another moment before the corner of his mouth twitched. "But you'll finish it, is that what you're saying?"

I shrugged and kept silent.

He laughed. "Okay. Let's go."

Leo gave me a warning glance, and I returned what I hoped was a reassuring smile before trailing after Dermott.

Seated in Stemp's office, Dermott leaned back in the chair and regarded me with arms crossed over chest. "So?"

I kept my voice calm and level. "So it was Fuzzy Bunny's corporate Christmas party for their local office workers and some people from their other branches. The only conversations at the party seemed to be about legitimate business. But when I was hiding in a corridor, I overheard Parr talking to somebody about delivery of a prototype, and he used the word 'covert'. He also asked me about a name on the phone list, a George Harrison. And then he invited me to fly to Vegas on Thursday on his private jet."

Dermott's arms dropped, his eyebrows going up. "He's putting the moves on you already? Nice work."

"No, I don't think so. He said he just wanted to talk, and that's the only time he has available."

Dermott leered. "Talk. Yeah, right. Well, good. Get your stuff together for a nice little holiday in Vegas."

I hid my fear. I hadn't actually *expected* to avoid going. I had just been hoping really hard...

I sighed. "Except he might have realized I'd overheard his conversation."

"Well, did he or didn't he?"

"How the hell do I know?"

Dermott scowled. "Well, I guess you'll find out."

Not the words I'd been hoping for.

I applied my best stoic facade and pushed my credit card receipt across the desk. "Here are my expenses."

He scanned the receipt briefly before turning an outraged glare on me. "What the fuck, Kelly? You think we're here to cover your shopping therapy?"

I squelched my temper and held onto my calm voice. "I needed clothes for the party on short notice. I didn't have a choice." I slapped Harchman's cheque down on the desk with perhaps a little more emphasis than necessary. "This should cover it."

Dermott reached slowly for it, holding me in his scowl. When he transferred his gaze to the cheque, his eyebrows shot up. "What the hell is this?"

"A business transaction. You can expect regular monthly cheques from here on in. Probably not as big as this one, though."

His eyes narrowed. "You can't just go shaking down legitimate businessmen."

"I didn't shake him down." I hesitated. "Well, okay, I did. But it's legit. Kind of. It's my cut of the take from the Arlene Cherry videos."

"Oh yeah, those." I waited for a leer and a piggish comment, but none came. Instead, he eyed the cheque thoughtfully. "The Department can't cash this. It's a personal cheque to you."

"I'm sure the accounting department will figure something out."

Dermott gave me a piercing scrutiny. "Don't you think he owes you personally?"

"He sure as hell does owe me, the little prick, but I don't want his money." A vicious smile crept unbidden to my lips. "Actually, it was a rather satisfying exchange last night. Maybe Parr will give me a copy of the video footage for my viewing pleasure."

Dermott frowned as his gaze travelled to my bruised knuckles. "You nailed him in public on camera? Shit, he's a big-ass mover and shaker. What the hell were you thinking? And why isn't he pressing charges?"

"No, he wasn't the one I hit. I just grabbed him by the balls. He'll be too embarrassed to press charges. And Parr thought it was funny, so that worked for me."

"You had him by the balls." A grin spread over Dermott's face. "At a fancy party. On camera. To the tune of fifty-three large." His grin widened. "I gotta say it, Kelly. Ballsy. Really ballsy." He leaned back in the chair and laughed at his own joke, and I couldn't prevent an evil snicker at the memory of Harchman's squeaky discomfiture.

Dermott sobered. "Okay, I'll run the cheque by the bean counters and see what they say. So who'd you hit? Was that on camera, too?"

I sighed, all my amusement draining away. "Yeah. That was stupid. I punched Paul Hibbert in the face."

His brows drew together again. "Yeah, that probably was stupid. What happened?"

"Well, we had a... history... from before," I began.

"Yeah, I read your report," Dermott interrupted. "So?"

"So... he pushed my buttons. And I lost it on him. I threatened him with my brand-new 'relationship' with Parr so he didn't press charges, but..." I sank my head into my hands. "I made an enemy. Stupid." I braced for an abusive tirade.

"Well, it wasn't like he was your best bud before," Dermott said reasonably. "Did you make contact with Kane at the party?"

Surprise slowed the shifting of my mental gears. "Oh. Uh, yeah, I talked to him for a few seconds. We think Harchman's new wife is probably another plant from Fuzzy Bunny to keep him in line and maintain the operations they had piggybacked onto his business dealings before." I groped for a way to cover for Kane in case he didn't report in as scheduled. "Um, Kane met somebody he knew at the party. I think he's pursuing a lead there." Pursuing something, anyway.

"Okay." Dermott nodded and rose, extending his hand. "Good to meet you, Kelly. I like people who don't take any bullshit."

I shook his hand, noticing thankfully that he didn't crush my sore knuckles. "Um. Thanks."

"See you tomorrow," he said, and I nodded and dragged myself out.

CHAPTER 34

Home at last, I pulled off my boots and parka before sleepwalking directly through the house to do a fully-clothed nosedive into bed.

The complaints of my empty stomach woke me around noon and I staggered into the shower, eyes half-closed. After dressing and dragging myself to the kitchen for a late lunch of leftovers, I managed to get both eyes fully open, and my brain activity increased enough for me to realize the message light was blinking on my phone.

Yawning, I trailed over to punch the button. The first voice was Lola's, responding to my message about my friend in the hospital and hoping everything was okay.

The next message was from Spider, and I silently berated myself when he said he hoped my friend was okay, too. Shit, I should have called him. I blew out a breath. At least now I could give him good news and save him some worry.

I checked in with Lola first and then dialled Spider's number, my guilt and worry returning. Dammit, he was counting on me to help him figure out what to do about his moral dilemma over controlling Tammy. And it was Sunday already.

When he answered, I blurted, "Spider, I'm so sorry I

didn't call you."

"It's okay," he said hurriedly. "Lola said you were at the hospital with a friend. Is everything..." He hesitated. "How did it turn out?"

I rubbed my forehead, trying to press away the guilt. "Um, actually, I owe you an apology for that, too. It was Arnie..." I spoke rapidly over his indrawn breath. "...but he's okay now."

"Oh, thank God." His voice trembled with relief. "What happened?"

I explained in general terms about the fight before returning to my second apology. "...and I'm sorry, but I completely forgot to think about your situation at Sirius-"

"It's okay," he interrupted. "I didn't expect you to, and anyway, I've made a decision."

"Um... what did you decide?" I squeezed my eyes shut in a mixture of worry over the firm resolve in his voice and relief that it wouldn't be my responsibility.

"I'm just going to tell the truth." I imagined his raised chin and clear hazel eyes. "I can't morally do what they're asking me to do. That's all there is to it."

"Oh." I drew a deep breath. "Well, I'm glad you've come to a decision you feel comfortable with."

"I have." I could hear the smile in his voice. "Thanks to you."

"Me?" My voice was distinctly squeaky.

"Yes. You always do what you think is right, even when it could cost your life. Surely I can be brave enough to tell the truth to my employer."

"Oh." My throat closed up, and I cleared it and swallowed hard. "Um... thanks, but..."

"No, thank you. You helped me do the right thing. See

you tomorrow."

"Uh. Yeah... 'Bye." I hung up the phone and thudded my forehead vigorously with the heel of my hand. "Shit, shit, shit!"

The next morning I arrived at Sirius early and puttered anxiously in the lunchroom, brewing myself an unnecessary cup of tea before trailing down the hall to my office. I was perched on my small sofa when Germain arrived and sank into the opposite chair.

"'Morning, Aydan." He gave me his usual cheerful smile.

"Good morning. Have you seen Spider?"

"Not yet. Have you seen Kane?"

"No, not yet." I sipped my tea, trying to swallow my worry. "He was working on a lead on the weekend. Maybe he's not back yet."

Kane was the most dedicated agent I knew. He may have just rediscovered the love of his life, but it was hard to believe he'd skip work. Remembering the lovestruck look on his face at the party, it seemed possible. But still...

The worry escaped despite my best efforts. "I hope he's okay."

Germain and I exchanged a strained glance.

Unable to sit still any longer, I popped to my feet. "I'm just going to try Spider's extension and see if he's heard anything."

The phone rang only once before going to voicemail, and I hung up and flopped back onto the couch. "No answer."

We sat in awkward silence for a moment, and I seized on the first topic of conversation that came to mind. "So how was the self-defence workshop?"

"It was fun." He relaxed into a smile. "After the ladies got over their disappointment that Kane wasn't coming back."

I grinned. "I'm sure it didn't take them long."

He accepted the compliment with a smile. "It was good to have something to do over the weekend. The Silverside Hotel isn't exactly my resort destination of choice."

"No kidding-"

I broke off when Dermott stuck his head in the open doorway, shooting a frown at us. "What are you waiting for? Get to work."

"We need Kane and Spider," I said. Nerves twitched in my belly. "I haven't seen Kane, and Spider hasn't brought my network key up yet. Have you seen him?"

Dermott's frown deepened. "Kane won't be in this week, and Webb doesn't work here anymore. We should have a replacement for him by the end of the week. Go get the key yourself." He turned and strode away.

"But... wait!" I sprang up to hurry after him. "What do you mean, he doesn't work here? Where did he go?"

Dermott whirled, scowling. "What the fuck do you think I mean, Kelly? He doesn't fucking work here, and I don't give a shit where he goes. Now get to work! Get caught up on those decryptions and find out everything you can to get ready for your trip with Parr." He strode away and closed himself into Stemp's office with a slam while I stood gaping in the hallway, my heart sinking into my boots.

After a moment I turned to face Germain, who was propped against my doorframe looking as shocked as I felt. Guilt and fear struck me like a physical blow. "Shit, Carl, what are we going to do?"

He blinked and straightened. "Get to work, I guess. I'll

take over for Kane in the network, and we'll have to figure out some way to do it without Webb."

"But we need him!" I stood feeling as though I should be locked in combat with some unknown adversary. I made a pointless gesture with my uselessly dangling arms. "We can't do this without him. He knows everything!"

Fear rose in my throat, and I clenched my hands together. "He gets me out of the network when I'm lost. He pulls together the data I find and makes it all make sense. He's..."

I swallowed hard, and Germain made a calm-down gesture. "Steady, Aydan. We'll figure it out."

My throat tightened even more. "It's my fault," I whispered.

He shot a quick glance up and down the corridor. "Let's go for a walk."

Out on the sidewalk, Germain turned to study me, frowning. "What do you mean, it's your fault?"

"Spider didn't want to control Tammy without her knowledge. He talked to me about it and I promised to help him figure it out, but then I was at the hospital with Arnie-"

"How is he?" Germain interrupted.

"Better. He's home, and I think he'll be okay. Thank God."

Germain nodded, the tension easing from his face. "Good. But I don't see how Webb leaving is your fault."

"When I talked to him yesterday he said he'd decided to refuse on moral grounds." I scrubbed my hands over my face. "He said he wanted to be brave. Shit, Carl, I should have figured out some way around it! I should have talked him out of it, or, or... something!"

"Webb is an adult and he has to make his own choices,"

Germain said firmly. "And what if you did manage to talk him out of it? How would you feel if you convinced him to compromise his principles?"

I groaned. "Shitty."

He gave me a quick one-armed hug. "You can't protect everybody, Aydan. Sometimes there's just no win-win. It's not your fault. Come on, let's get back to work."

That didn't really help, but it wasn't like I had a choice. I sighed and we trudged back to Sirius.

In the lobby, I collected my security fob again and squared my shoulders to approach the heavy door to the secured area.

"Do you want me to get the network key for you?" Germain asked. "I don't mind the man trap."

The word 'trap' sent a chill down my spine. I drew a deep breath. "No, that's okay. I can manage."

"I know you can." His voice was gentle. "But do you really want to?"

I let out my breath. "No, but..."

"Then I'll get it for you."

I gave him a grateful smile. "Thanks, Carl."

He disappeared into the time-delay chamber, and I sank into one of the lobby chairs, my mind whirling with guilt and fear at the loss of both a brilliant colleague and one of the only friends I had at Sirius. How could I go on without Spider?

I was still staring into space and suppressing panic when Germain emerged from the secured area in animated conversation with Jack. Germain shot me a grin. "Jack's going to sit in for a while today. I thought she might be able to help."

Relief eased my shoulders as I rose to follow them to the

stairs. "Good idea. Thanks, Jack."

"I'm happy to help if I can," she replied with a smile, but the smile was mostly directed at Germain and soft roses glowed in her cheeks.

My answering smile came easily, my heart warming at the way their heads tilted toward each other when they resumed their conversation.

It was a long morning full of false starts and slow progress, but by noon we had evolved a workable system. Kane's and Spider's absence left an aching void, and I concentrated fiercely on the decryptions that had piled up again over the past several days.

When noon rolled around I stepped out of the network to clutch my pounding skull, clenching my teeth to capture the worst of the obscenities before they emerged. No firm hands eased my pain, and I severely forbade myself to whimper in self-pity.

Everything was as it should be. Kane had found his love at last, and he deserved a week off to celebrate, followed by years of happiness.

I hunched lower on the couch at the realization that his new lady-love probably wouldn't want him massaging my temples. But he probably wouldn't want to anyway. He might even quit the service to have the family I suspected he secretly wanted.

A groan escaped me.

"Aydan, are you okay?" Jack's concerned voice made me straighten into an imitation of normalcy.

"Fine. Thanks."

"Let's go grab some lunch." Germain spoke to Jack

before turning to me. "Do you want to join us?"

"No, thanks." I rose. "I'm going to drop by Spider's place and see, um... how he is."

"Give him our best wishes," Jack urged. "I hope he'll be happy in his new job."

I stared. "He has a new job?"

"Oh, I don't know." Jack looked flustered. "I was told he'd left, so I assumed he had gone to another position."

"Oh." I summoned up a smile. "Well, I guess I'll find out. See you later."

At Spider's house, I hesitated before knocking at the door. There was no answer, and I shivered when the cold wind swirled around to drop a powdering of fine snow down my collar. I tried the doorbell, hearing its lonely ghost of sound through the door.

I waited again before turning away with a sigh. Maybe he *had* gotten another job. Maybe he was happily set up in another office somewhere.

Shit.

I knew where he was.

I retraced my steps to the car and steered it in the direction of the small converted house that served as the office for Spider's cover business.

His lime-green Smart car was parked in front and the house lights glowed warmly through the snowy landscape when I pulled up in front.

Was that good or bad?

I hauled myself out of the car and up the sidewalk before I could worry anymore.

When I tapped on the outer door and poked my head inside, Spider looked up from his computer, his eyes reddened in a haggard face. "Hi, Aydan," he mumbled.

I hurriedly shed my boots and jacket, dread rising in my heart. "Spider, what happened?"

"I got fired."

CHAPTER 35

"What?" I stood frozen in the vestibule, staring. "I thought... I mean... Dermott said you didn't work at Sirius anymore, so I just assumed you'd quit."

"No." He sank his head into his hands and spoke to the desk. "I went in this morning to tell Stemp I wouldn't control Tammy without her knowledge, but Dermott was there instead. When I told him, he... he said some nasty things about being a diva and fired me on the spot. He said they'd clean out my desk and send my things over here this morning."

"Oh, Spider, I'm sorry!" I hurried across the room to hug him. "I forgot you were away on Friday. I should have told you Stemp was gone this week."

"It's not your fault," he muttered. "I should have known this would happen." He straightened. "And anyway, it's still the right thing to do. But Aydan..." He looked up with fear in his eyes. "I don't have a job now. Less than a week before Christmas. I haven't finished paying for Linda's ring yet. And I was keeping it in the secured area at Sirius so she wouldn't find it. What if they don't give it back?"

"You'll get it, Spider, don't worry," I comforted. "And if it doesn't come with your things for some reason, I'll get it for you."

A thump from the outer door interrupted me, and Spider shot to his feet. "That must be the delivery."

When he flung open the door, the delivery man was just arriving with a second box. He dropped it on top of the first and thrust a clipboard at Spider. "Sign here."

When Spider signed and handed back the clipboard, the man turned and strode down the sidewalk to his van without another word.

"Charming," I muttered. "Here, I'll give you a hand."

We manoeuvred the boxes into the house, and Spider fell to his knees and ripped them open to ransack their contents. I watched anxiously until his shoulders sagged with relief.

"Ah." He sank back on his haunches, lifting a small velvet box to peep inside. "Thank God."

The tension returned to his face as he looked up again. "But I still have to pay for it. And I don't know where to hide it. I can't take it home; Linda's such a neat freak she'd find it when she was tidying up. And I don't dare leave it here."

"Why don't you put it in the b-" I stopped myself, but Spider's face twisted as he caught my meaning.

"I don't have access to the bunker anymore. In fact, I'll probably get kicked out of this office, too, so they can put somebody else in place above it. Maybe they'll offer it to you. Your bookkeeping cover would work here."

I clutched a double handful of my hair in renewed chagrin. "How could he just fire you? With everything you know, and all you do for them? What a fucking moron! We'll fix it, Spider. I'll talk to him."

"No." His lips trembled, but his voice was firm. "I won't compromise on this, and I won't go crawling back to him. He's a... an *asshole!*" He flushed scarlet as he pronounced the unaccustomed epithet, but he met my eyes with defiance.

I sighed. "How can I help?"

He answered so promptly I suspected he had given it considerable thought already. "Could you please keep Linda's ring for me until Saturday? I was going to give it to her at the Christmas Eve party."

"Sure, I can-"

"But I need you to carry it with you all the time," he interrupted.

"Um... do you really think that's a good idea? I can just put it in a safe place at home."

"No." Spider gave me an imploring look. "I'm totally freaked out about this. I know you'll take good care of it. You have a gun and everything."

I determinedly squelched the twitch of my lips. "An armed guard probably isn't necessary." He opened the box and turned it toward me, and my jaw dropped. "Holy shit! Okay, maybe an armed guard would be a good idea." I stared at the glittering blue-white solitaire. "Holy *shit*, Spider, that sucker's enormous!"

He eyed me anxiously. "Is it too much? They say you're supposed to spend three months' pay on an engagement ring. I make..." He flushed. "...*made* pretty good money. And she's worth every penny!" His face fell. "But what if... I mean... now that I don't have a job... what if she..."

I gave him a quick squeeze. "She loves you. She wouldn't care if you were dead broke. And she'll love the ring. She'd love any ring you gave her, even if it was just a cheap little diamond chip. Trust me." I tightened my arm around his shoulders. "And you'll be working again in no time. A guy with your qualifications? You'll have to fight off job offers with a stick."

"But not here in Silverside. It's just a small town." His troubled gaze lingered on the sparkling ring. "And I just got my house rebuilt, and all my family is here, and Linda's family is here, and Linda's job is here."

I gave him a little shake. "Stop worrying, Spider. It'll all work out. No matter what happens, you won't lose your family and you won't lose Linda. Nothing else matters. You'll figure it out together."

He let out a breath, his shoulders relaxing under my grip. "Thanks, Aydan. You're right. So..." He eyed me hopefully. "Will you? Carry the ring for me?"

I released him to face him squarely.   "Spider, I understand you're worried, but I really don't think that's a good idea. I have to go undercover in Vegas later this week. You won't want me carrying it down there. I'm supposed to be back on Friday, but if anything happens..." I swallowed hard. If anything happened, it would be the end of me and his ring. "...I might be late to your party," I continued with stubborn optimism. "And you'll just end up worrying more. I'll put it in the gun safe in my basement."

His hands clenched around the small box. "But..."

"Or maybe you could give it to somebody else for safekeeping," I suggested. "Leave it with your parents. Or one of your sisters."

"No way." He gave me a rueful grin. "My mom and sisters can't keep a secret to save their lives. They'd blab two seconds after I showed it to them. And my dad wouldn't blab, but he's a lousy liar. My mom would know he was hiding something and she'd worm it out of him." He held out the box to me. "Please, Aydan. I really, really need you to do this for me. Just this one thing, and I promise I won't ask for anything else."

His beseeching look melted me despite my better judgement. "Oh, Spider, you know I'll do anything I can for you." I accepted the box with a sinking sensation and hesitated, wondering where to put it.

"Wait, I have a velvet pouch for it," he said as if reading my mind. "It'll be easier to carry than the box."

With the ring safely stowed in its tiny velvet sack, I double-knotted its cords and eyed it worriedly. Such a small, priceless thing. My hand hovered at the zipper of my waist pouch. What if somebody stole my waist pouch?

Spider watched me, his forehead crinkled with apprehension, and I sighed and tucked the tiny item into my bra instead. He blushed, but smiled. "Thanks, Aydan."

"You're welcome."

After a few more empty reassurances, I plodded back to my car, the almost-imperceptible sensation of the ring weighing like lead on my heart.

Back at Sirius Dynamics, I was heading for my office when Dermott beckoned from the doorway of Stemp's office. "Bit of activity at your place this morning. Looks like you have a secret admirer."

"What do you mean?" I eyed him warily as he ushered me around to look at his computer monitor.

A still view from my surveillance cameras filled the screen. He punched a key and the video played, showing Hibbert striding up my front walk with a white object swinging from his left hand.

The view switched to the next camera and my guts wrenched when the object resolved into a small body, its mangled fur matted with crimson.

"Is that a *cat?*"   My question was half-strangled by horror and rising bile.

"Analysts say jackrabbit," Dermott said shortly. "Judging by the injuries, they figure road-kill."

I swallowed hard and applied a tremendous effort to prevent my shaking legs from dropping me into Dermott's chair as Hibbert tossed the corpse onto my doorstep and strode away, grinning.

"That's fucking sick."

"Not as sick as if it was a cat," Dermott replied. "It's just a Fuzzy Bunny."

I heard the capital letters in his tone and nodded slowly. "Yeah, that makes sense. Asshole. He wouldn't know about the cameras, but he'd figure I'd know it was him and get the message."

Dermott switched the display off. "And what's the message?"

I grimaced. "The last thing he said to me: 'I'll get you, bitch'."

"That's original."

I matched his sarcastic tone as best I could with my paper-dry mouth. "That's our boy. Mr. Originality."

Dermott shrugged. "Analysts figure it's safe to move the carcass. The way he tossed it down, there's almost certainly no explosive device in it. He didn't take precautions with a mask or gloves, so there shouldn't be any biohazard. And it was stiff as a board. He probably found it frozen by the side of the road and picked it up just for you."

"I'm touched," I muttered, and swallowed another surge of nausea as I strode out, keeping my back straight.

Fresh air.

Hurrying down to the lobby, I tossed my fob into the

turntable at the security wicket and made for the door. The icy air gave me a bracing slap in the face, and I had just drawn a long thankful breath when my waist pouch vibrated. I sighed and pulled out my phone.

"Is this Arlene Widdenback?" The male voice was pleasantly modulated, with precise diction that managed to sound efficient without being prissy.

My heart lurched. Parr's secretary. It had to be.

"Um... speaking."

"Hello, Ms. Widdenback, this is Archibald Rankin, Nicholas Parr's assistant. I'm confirming your flight on Mr. Parr's private jet for this Thursday, departing at eight P.M."

"Oh, uh... good... hang on." I hurried back inside, dragging my chequebook out of my waist pouch. Appropriating a corner of the security counter, I planted an elbow on my chequebook for stability while I juggled pen and phone.

"Okay, eight, Thursday night, got it. I've never been on a private jet before. What do I need to do when I get to the airport?"

My marching orders in hand, I retrieved my fob a few minutes later and plodded up the stairs again, simmering in queasy fear. I'd probably have to go gunless again. And I'd be trapped for nearly three hours inside what amounted to an airborne ballpoint pen, with people who wouldn't hesitate to torture and kill me if I blew my cover. Assuming it wasn't already blown and this was just a convenient way to eliminate me.

The fear escalated into a full-blown panic attack, and I breathed through it. In. Out. Ocean waves.

Okay, panic attacks were cognitive distortions. All I needed to do was look at this objectively and identify the true risks.

Captivity, torture, and death.

Nope, objectivity definitely wasn't the answer here.

I went with denial instead. Thursday was days away. Anything could happen between now and then. Parr could change his mind. A terrible blizzard could sweep in and close down the airport. I could discover some hugely important piece of evidence in the network that would result in Parr's arrest and shut down Fuzzy Bunny entirely. I could be killed by a chunk of airplane lavatory ice falling from the sky.

Hell, anything could happen.

After a short sojourn in the ladies' room to regain my composure, I shuffled back to my office and slumped on the sofa to wait for Jack and Germain.

I spent the next day and a half immersed in the network, scouring every connection I could find until Jack finally called a halt late Tuesday afternoon.

"Aydan. *Aydan.*"

"Wha?" I mumbled into the sofa cushions, hugging my pounding head.

"We're stopping now."

I dragged myself upright and pried open one eye. "Just one more session, okay? I just want to-"

"No." She and Germain spoke simultaneously. They exchanged a warm glance before turning matching expressions of disapproval toward me.

"Aydan, you were beating your head against the couch so hard I thought you were going to concuss yourself," Jack said in her 'don't mess with Supermom' voice. "It's six o'clock.

You've had enough for the day, and we aren't going to let you hurt yourself. Whatever you're looking for, it can wait until tomorrow."

I was just opening my mouth to protest when Dermott poked his head in the door. "She finally out of the network?" He surveyed me with a frown. "Jesus, Kelly, you look like shit."

I couldn't summon up enough energy for indignation. My voice came out flat and lifeless. "Fuck you very much."

Jack gasped and coloured.

Dermott barked out a laugh. "Your boyfriend popped by with another present for you this afternoon. Want to come and see?"

"What is it, a horse's head?"

His mouth twitched. "Not exactly."

I groaned and dragged myself to my feet to plod for the door.

This time, the object in Hibbert's hand wasn't immediately recognizable. He placed it on my doorstep and strode away grinning as usual, and I squinted at the pale object barely visible against the snow. "What the hell is it?"

Dermott smirked. "Guess it's been a while for you, eh, Kelly? You don't recognize a cock when you see one?"

He zoomed in, and I recoiled. "Oh, for chrissake." I stared at the anatomically correct dildo rearing up out of the snow. "Well, it's better than road-kill rabbit. Is it going to explode?"

Dermott snickered. "Not unless it's more realistic than I think it is."

"Very funny."

He sobered. "No, I already had one of the bomb guys go out and collect it. It's just an unaltered silicone sex toy.

Apparently it's a common brand."

I sighed. "Yeah, I recognize it."

"Too much information, Kelly."

I shot him a disgusted look. "I meant, one of my bookkeeping clients owns a sex shop and I've seen that model there. It's one of the super-realistic ones that comes in skin tones of... um... various races..." I ran down. That probably was too much information.

"So do you want it for a souvenir?" Dermott asked, straight-faced.

"No. The veins gross me out. Let the bomb squad guys keep it. I'm sure they'll figure out some amusing use for it."

He grimaced. "It has *veins?* Okay, that really is too much information."

"Yeah, I thought so, too."

"So I assume this is another reference to a previous conversation?" He appraised me seriously. "Should I take a guess about what he threatened you with?"

I sighed. "Three guesses; the first two don't count. Thanks for getting rid of it." I turned to head for the door.

"Kelly."

I trailed to a halt. "Yeah."

"Watch yourself, okay?"

"I will."

CHAPTER 36

Wednesday morning, I hauled myself out of bed exhausted from screaming myself awake over and over. Shuffling out to my car, I jabbed a hostile middle finger at the sky, which had cleared overnight with the promise of fair weather for the next several days.

Slumped in my car, I thumped my forehead against the steering wheel. I hadn't found any solid evidence in the past nine months of searching, so I wasn't likely to find it before Thursday afternoon. And the fucking traitorous weather wasn't going to cooperate.

Time to face reality. I gave up hope for blizzards and evidence, and switched to fervently wishing for death by icy BM.

It didn't happen. By the time I drove home after another marathon session in the network, I could barely see the highway through my pounding headache. The headlights of the oncoming traffic sliced lasers of pain through my eyes and I fought to stay awake for the short fifteen-minute drive.

At home, I flung a few items into a suitcase and regretfully removed my pocketknives from my waist pouch. I couldn't take them through airport security, and if Parr was planning to kill me during the flight or immediately afterward, they wouldn't do me any good in a checked bag. And if he wasn't planning to kill me, I wouldn't need them anyway.

When I undressed for bed, I tucked Spider's precious velvet sack under the pillow next to my gun as I had done for the past three nights. Dreading the nightmares I knew awaited me, I slid into bed and diverted my mind to my latest moral dilemma.

My promise to Spider nagged at my conscience. It would be stupid to take the ring with me. My chances of survival were about fifty-fifty. If I got killed, the ring would be lost forever.

I flipped onto my side, yanking the covers irritably. But he trusted me. He was counting on me to do what he'd asked.

But dammit, I couldn't. I reared up to punch my pillow into submission.

I had to do what was best for him. I'd carry the ring with me in the morning as promised, but I'd stop off on my way to the airport and tuck it into my gun safe. Set up a timed email so if I didn't make it back, he'd know where to look.

Flopping back down again, I blew out a long sigh. If I lived, he'd never know I hadn't respected his wishes. If I died, at least the ring would be safe. And maybe he'd forgive me.

But I'd never know.

I rolled over again. It was the right thing to do. It was for the best.

I closed my eyes and let the black dreams take me.

The night seemed interminable, but morning felt too

early. I crept out of bed aching and exhausted, my hands trembling and my throat raw from screaming.

Thankful I'd done most of my packing the night before when I was actually less tired, I threw the last of my things into my suitcase and carried it out to the car. At least I could pick up anything I'd forgotten when I dropped off Spider's ring in the afternoon.

I spent the morning in the Sirius network chasing down every scrap of information I could discover about Parr's personal life and Fuzzy Bunny's upper management. My research made it even clearer how difficult it would be to make charges stick to Parr. He and his wife were involved in various philanthropic activities, his employees seemed to love him, and the local office had been voted one of Calgary's top ten places to work the previous year.

My swearing was especially heartfelt when I left the network at noon. When I opened my eyes at last, Jack looked shocked.

"Sorry," I mumbled.

"Remind me to keep the kids down in my lab on 'bring your child to work' day," she said faintly.

"Good idea," I agreed.

After a lunch I barely tasted, I scanned the contents of my suitcase one more time and decided I didn't give a shit. I was only going overnight. Or going to die; one of the two. Either way, my luggage just wasn't that important.

I had just zipped it up when Jack and Germain arrived for our afternoon session. Moments later, Dermott strode into my office, too, carrying a laptop case.

"Here you go." He set the case on the coffee table in

front of me. "And here." He opened his hand to reveal the portable network generator and a wristwatch. "Put your regular network key in your old watch the way you did when you were undercover at Harchman's. The new network key is in the other watch."

Jack's and my objections formed a chorus of dismay.

"I can't take classified technology right into Parr's hands!"

"That new key is almost completely untested and it makes her lose consciousness!"

Dermott scowled. "The chain of command already approved the generator and key for use outside the secured area-"

"A block away, not in Fuzzy Bunny's fucking back pocket!"

He shook his head like an angry bull and kept talking over my interruption. "It's approved by the chain of command. You need an undetectable way to communicate with us. And the new key is less obvious. You swear your fucking head off when you use the original key, Kelly. I can hear you all the way down the hall."

"If it's life or death I can keep quiet," I argued.

"Bullshit. Sometimes you can. And sometimes swearing is the best-case scenario. Worst-case, you have a fucking seizure and scream like a banshee from hell."

I stalled in mid-rebuttal, and he shot me a scowl. "Yeah, I read the reports, Kelly. At least with the new key, you're silent. And a few minutes of unconsciousness is better than a few minutes of screaming if you're doing covert ops."

That was unassailable logic. I shut my mouth and considered it.

"We don't know how long the unconsciousness will last,"

Jack protested. "The first time it was only a few seconds. The second time it was much longer. What if she becomes comatose the next time she tries?"

"So try it again now." Dermott gave her a hard look. "If she passes out for a few minutes, we'll know it's not getting much worse. If it's a lot longer this time, then she'll have to make the decision if the situation warrants it in the field."

Jack drew herself up, her gaze slicing him like blue lasers. "In my professional opinion-"

"I don't give a shit about your professional opinion," Dermott snapped. "When you're in the field, you do what you have to do." He turned back to me, ignoring the scarlet that flooded her face. "Kelly, try the new key now. That's an order."

I hesitated, fighting the instinctive urge to tell him to stick it up his ass. He might be a prick, but his logic was sound.

And a small and cowardly part of my mind whispered that if I was comatose, I wouldn't have to get on the plane with Parr.

I reached for the watch.

Jack's hand flashed out with the speed only achieved by mothers of small children. Wristwatch clenched in her white-knuckled fist, she faced Dermott with an icy rage that made her appear to tower over him despite her five-and-a-half foot stature.

"You *will not* bully her into this." Her tone sent a shaft of ice down my spine, and her anger wasn't even directed at me.

Dermott blinked, obviously surprised by the ferocity concealed by that soft and pretty exterior. Germain made a half-hearted gesture as if to step in, but wisely decided against it. He crossed his arms instead, his eyes sparkling with interest while he observed.

"He's not bullying me," I offered mildly. "I would actually like to try it again."

Dermott was smart enough not to betray any triumph. He remained silent and expressionless as Jack rounded on me.

"Aydan, this is untested technology. Sam might have been able to evaluate it more effectively than I can, but that knowledge died with him. I've only had a few months to get up to speed with your project, and I'm barely scratching the surface of everything there is to know. And we've lost Spider's expertise, too. This is unsafe, plain and simple. Don't do it."

"But... it would be so much better."

"Since when is unconsciousness *better?*" she demanded.

I ground my knuckles into my aching temples. "Trust me, it's better."

When I looked up again, her face betrayed her struggle. "Oh, Aydan, I hate to see you suffer. But what if you never regain consciousness? Or what if it damages your brain?"

I sighed. "Have you determined conclusively that using the original key doesn't damage my brain? The emergency room doctor said repeated concussions cause cumulative damage. And a concussion can't hurt worse than this. So how do you know I won't end up a vegetable anyway?"

Her lips trembled. "I wish you didn't have to do any of it," she whispered.

Then she straightened, tossing her hair back and lifting her chin. "All right." Her usual crisp tone was back. "Try it if you want, but there's no need to be irresponsible about it. Let me get my monitor so I can at least gain some useful data." She turned and marched out, ignoring Dermott completely.

He gave me a nod and a quirk of his lips before withdrawing, leaving Germain and me to avoid each other's eyes until Jack returned.

When she strode in again, case in hand, she shot a look at Germain. "Did you manage to talk her out of it yet?"

Germain blinked. "No. I, uh..." He shot me a glance of barely concealed alarm. "No. Sorry."

Jack sighed and turned without comment to hook me up to the monitors, and Germain eased back in his chair, looking wary.

A few moments later, Jack relinquished the wristwatch to me, her lips tightening. As I leaned back on the sofa, she laid a cool hand over mine. "Just go in for a few seconds. In and then out again. That's all."

"Okay."

I followed her instructions, stepping into the void of virtual reality for only a moment before turning back to the portal, flinching with the habitual expectation of pain.

None came, and I blinked up at Jack's worried face before casting a quick glance around my office. "I'm still sitting up. I didn't pass out." A smile grew on my lips. "And it didn't hurt."

She frowned. "I'm not sure. You went limp for an instant, but it might have just been the transition into the network."

I sat up a little straighter. "I'll try it again."

"Wait." She sank her chin into her hand, still frowning, her eyes focused on some invisible theory. After a moment she straightened. "All right. Just pop outside the Sirius network for a few seconds. Maybe it was the external access that did it before." Her brow furrowed again. "No, that can't be it. You lost consciousness after doing an internal sim before, too."

"So I'll try a sim," I volunteered. "Here we go…"

I stepped into the network again before she could object.

Hurrying down the virtual corridor into a vacant sim room, I stepped into my mountain simulation. My concentration was poor and the simulation was a lifeless postcard devoid of depth or scent, but I was too distracted to bother with details. I paced for a few moments before dissolving the sim to head for the portal again.

This time I woke horizontal, with two strained faces hovering above me.

"Aydan!" As soon as my eyes opened, Jack pounced. "Are you okay? Say something."

"Shit."

Germain laughed, a too-loud burst of relieved sound. "She's fine."

"Shit," I repeated, and hauled myself upright despite Jack's nervous fluttering. "How long was I out?"

"Twenty seconds." Her trembling fingers clamped over the pulse point on my wrist.

"Hmmph." I scowled at the watch on my wrist. "Maybe it was just the sim. I should try something else."

"No! It's obviously getting worse!"

I tugged a lock of hair, thinking. "But it's not worse than last time. Theoretically if I go in one more time, I'll only be out for five minutes, right? That's what happened last time. And I was fine as soon as I woke up."

"Theoretically!" Jack threw up her hands. "This is the most… I…" She glowered at me. "This is the most pathetic parody of scientific method I have ever had the misfortune to participate in. It's against every ethical-"

"I'm just going to give the external network a try," I interrupted gently. "Back in a bit."

Whisking into the external network, I hovered outside the Sirius firewall, hoping I hadn't just done something stupid. Well, stupider than usual.

A couple of minutes later, I retraced my route to step through the portal.

Horizontal again.

I sighed and sat up. "How long this time?"

Jack was frowning, but she didn't look as panicked as last time. "Twenty seconds again."

"Really?" Hope bubbled up. "So maybe I just need to get used to it. Maybe once I'm used to it, it'll get shorter, or I'll stop passing out altogether."

"Or maybe this was random chance and you won't wake up at all next time," Jack retorted.

"Yeah, well, there's that." I eyed the watch, wondering if the next chamber in this Russian roulette game contained a lethal bullet. "Guess I'll just try it again, then."

"Aydan, no. You can't just..." She stopped and raised her arms to let them drop helplessly against her sides. "Well, fine. I don't have a better idea."

Several tries later, I sat up again, hiding my delight at the absence of pain. "So?" I eyed Jack hopefully.

She sighed. "So the intervals seem to have stabilized between twenty and thirty seconds of unconsciousness. So far." She planted her hands on her hips. "A handful of tests is not a statistically significant sample."

"Yeah, I know, but it's a good sign, right?"

She scowled. "It's not a *sign*. It's a tiny smattering of data that is utterly meaningless in a larger context."

"Okay," I agreed, hoping to pacify her. "But that's as good as it's going to get for now, and I need to do some more research on Fuzzy Bunny before I leave in..." I consulted the watch, which Dermott had considerately set to the correct time. "Less than two hours." The words came out on a sigh, and I leaned back on the sofa again, closing my eyes.

"Wait!"

Jack's cry jerked me upright, my already rapid pulse bounding into overdrive. "Jesus, what?" I clutched my chest. "You scared the shit out of me."

"I'm sorry. I just didn't want you to go back into the network using the new key."

"Why not?" I frowned at her. "It's been fine. Twenty or thirty seconds, that's it. And no pain."

"Aydan..." She eyed me with unconcealed exasperation.

I groaned and hunched over to massage my throbbing temples. "Jack, please." I dragged my head up to give her an imploring look. "I've had a headache for the last three days and nights straight. I feel like there are evil trolls playing kickball with my brain. I only want to get through the next couple of hours and then with any luck Parr will blow my head off and put me out of my misery."

"Sorry," I added at her gasp of horror. "Just kidding. Graveyard humour. But honestly, the thought of having to go through another round of pain just..." I bit off the words 'makes me want to curl up and cry'. "...sucks," I finished instead. "Please just let me do this."

She sighed. "All right. It's against my better judgement, but..." She trailed off into another sigh, and I closed my eyes on her troubled face.

CHAPTER 37

"Aaaaydaaan..."

"Aaydaan..."

Shit. That probably wasn't good.

"Aydan!"

"'M okay," I mumbled, still trying to pry my eyes open.

"Aydan!" My shoulders shook vigorously and a hand patted my cheek.

I groaned and flailed a hand in self-defence. "I said, I'm okay." I finally managed to get my eyes open, to be confronted by Dr. Roth's face at close range. Behind her, Jack clutched Germain's hand in both of hers where they stood against a backdrop of emergency room cubicle curtains.

"Shit!" I jerked upright, squeezing my eyes shut when the room spun momentarily.

"Lie down."

Firm hands seized my shoulders, but I shook my head and opened my eyes again to concentrate on stabilizing the room.

"How long was I out?" I extricated my arm from Dr. Roth's grasp to check my watch. "Shit! I'm going to be late!"

I swung my legs over the edge of the bed, but Dr. Roth

planted both hands on my shoulders. "Not so fast. You were unconscious for twenty minutes. You're not going anywhere."

"I'm fine. It was just the..." I hesitated, not sure who might be within earshot outside the curtained cubicle. "...same tests we were doing before." I shot a look at Jack. "It was just a random reaction. I'll be okay, just like last time."

The colour was returning to her ashen cheeks. "It wasn't random. I ran some basic data analysis while you were unconscious." She sighed. "Despite the small sample size, I found a ninety-eight percent correlation in the data. It's a simple linear relationship. For every minute you spend in the network, you spend roughly fifteen seconds unconscious afterward."

She consulted her watch, steadying her wrist with shaking fingers. "And you're right on schedule. Eighty minutes in the network; twenty minutes unconscious." She leaned against Germain as though her legs wouldn't bear her weight. "Thank God."

His arm slipped around her as if it belonged there, and I turned my smile toward Dr. Roth. "So there you go. Simple four to one ratio, and then I'm fine." My optimism dissolved in a flood of renewed anxiety. "And I have to leave. Fifteen minutes ago."

I was half-way to Calgary before I remembered Linda's engagement ring, still tucked in my bra. I pounded the steering wheel and swore violently. Far too late to turn back to my farm now. It had taken me an additional fifteen minutes to talk my way out of Dr. Roth's clutches, and while

I didn't think Parr would leave without me, irritating him seemed like a bad idea.

A glance at the dashboard clock reminded me I was still behind schedule, and I pushed to ten clicks over the speed limit, hoping my all-wheel drive would carry me safely over any remaining icy patches concealed by the winter darkness.

When the orange glow of Calgary's streetlights bloomed ahead at last, I welcomed them even though they brought me closer to my fate with Parr. Shivers racked my body despite the stifling heat blasting from the vents. My stomach twisted itself into empty knots of hunger, and I yawned over and over, my burning eyes streaming with involuntary tears.

At last I gained the airport parking lot and spent several seconds peeling my aching hands loose from the steering wheel. Trembling in the seat, I berated myself all over again for forgetting to drop off Linda's ring. And I still had my gun, too.

I reluctantly unstrapped it and stowed it under the seat. Stupid place to leave it, but it wasn't like I had a choice. The ring was another matter. Leaving it at home in my gun safe would have been all right, but I couldn't bring myself to abandon it in my car. I couldn't imagine trying to explain to Spider that I'd walked off and left his precious purchase to be stolen from a public parkade.

I sighed. No choice. The ring was coming with me.

Once inside the terminal, I beelined to the washroom in defiance of my tardiness. I might be about to lose my life, but I refused to jettison the remains of my dignity by peeing my pants.

A glance at the hollow-eyed hag in the mirror made me glad Parr's wife would be on the plane. If I had been planning to ingratiate myself by seducing him, I'd have been doomed.

Well, more doomed than I already was, anyway.

My tired mind seized on the semantics of whether doom was already a superlative and 'more doomed' was redundant, and I navigated the airport procedure with half my attention while I wrestled with that conundrum. At least it distracted me from the terror that the airport security guards were somehow going to figure out that the innocent-looking USB device in my laptop case was classified technology.

Safely through security, I headed for the ramp, my mind buzzing with lies and nebulous plans to somehow trick Parr into telling me about his new secret weapon.

The interior of Parr's jet was enough to overcome my haze of fear and fatigue. I didn't try too hard to conceal my reaction as I goggled around the luxuriously appointed front cabin. After all, Arlene Widdenback the petty fraud artist wasn't necessarily sophisticated. And I sure as hell wasn't.

By the time the smartly uniformed and startlingly handsome blond flight attendant ushered me into a sitting room containing leather furniture, rosewood tables, and Parr, I had almost managed to close my dangling jaw.

He rose with a smile to shake my hand, carefully avoiding my discoloured knuckles. "Nice to see you again, Arlene."

Suppressing the idiot urge to hide the laptop case behind my back, I shoved down fear and a creeping sense of inadequacy to summon an apologetic smile. "Hi, Nick, it's nice to see you, too. I'm so sorry I'm late. I had an emergency right before I left."

"It's all right." He broke off as a tall, elegant woman appeared from the rear of the plane. "This is my wife, Eleanor. Eleanor, this is Arlene Widdenback."

"It's a pleasure to meet you." She extended a slim and impeccably manicured hand. I shook it, feeling like a coarse peasant meeting a queen. Her artfully shaded blonde hair was sleekly coiffed, her willowy figure accented by a creamy pant suit in some lustrous and expensive-looking fabric. And she wore pearls, for God's sake.

"Uh." I cleared my throat.

Thank *heaven* I hadn't planned to seduce Parr. Hibbert's insult rang in my mind. 'Just a cheap whore.' That was exactly how I felt next to Eleanor Parr.

"It's nice to meet you, too," I managed at last. "I'm sorry to delay your flight. I had an emergency, and I left late."

She made a graceful dismissing gesture. "Oh, nonsense, it's only a few minutes. Please, won't you sit down? And buckle in, please, we'll be taking off shortly." She eyed me with warm concern as I sank into one of the soft leather seats. "I hope your emergency was safely resolved. Are you all right? You look terribly pale."

"I'm fine. Thanks." I clicked the seat belt over my embarrassingly growling stomach. "Excuse me. I missed supper."

"Oh, dear!" She and Parr strapped in, and she reached over to pat my hand. "As soon as we're airborne, I'll have Thomas prepare a meal for you."

"That's okay, I don't want to trouble you," I began half-heartedly.

"It's no trouble at all. We'd be delighted."

At least if I was going to die, my last meal had been delicious. I sighed and pushed away the plate that bore only a few remaining drops of juice from a deliciously rare steak.

Eleanor Parr smiled from her seat across from me. "You look revived. Thomas..."

The handsome flight attendant bowed slightly as he appropriated the empty plate. "Yes, Mrs. Parr?"

"Please bring some fruit and cheese. And..." She hesitated, raising one elegantly arched eyebrow in my direction. "...coffee?"

"No, thanks. I don't usually drink caffeine."

"Herbal tea, perhaps?"

"Thank you, that would be nice."

I fought the sense of unreality that had enveloped me the whole time I had been chatting and dining aboard the luxury aircraft of the crime boss who had been my biggest fear for nearly a year.

Any minute now. Any minute he'd whip out a gun. Tie me up, beat and torture me...

I barely managed to control my twitch when Parr leaned forward. "Coffee for me, please, Thomas." He turned a twinkling smile toward his wife. "I have to stay alert while you spin my life's savings away on the roulette wheel tonight."

She chuckled and reached to squeeze his hand. "You suffer so greatly on my behalf."

He raised her hand to his lips. "And a privilege it is, too."

Watching them, I had to remind myself what Parr really was. No wonder suspicion never reached him. He was a frigging pillar of the community.

Sudden realization struck me. I was perfectly safe, at least for the moment. Parr couldn't afford to attack me on his own private jet. If Calgary airport security showed I'd left with him and Vegas airport security showed I hadn't arrived with him, it would be pretty plain where the responsibility lay.

The faithful Thomas offered me his deferent half-bow and a cup of chamomile tea, and I exhaled days of tension in the guise of blowing across the cup's surface.

Parr wouldn't do his own dirty work anyway. If anything was going to happen to me, it would happen after we'd parted company in Vegas. That made perfect sense. Just another unfortunate mugging in a crime-ridden city. No connection to Parr at all.

The realization that my potential demise was at least two or three hours away relieved me more than I had thought possible. My muscles turned to limp rags and an almost-palpable blanket of fatigue pressed me into the sumptuous leather upholstery.

My relief was short-lived. As Thomas placed a beautifully-arranged fruit and cheese platter on the shining table, Eleanor rose. "I know you two have business to discuss, so I'll leave you to it, if you'll excuse me."

"Of course." Parr rose, the epitome of good breeding, and remained standing until she had left the cabin. Then he reseated himself and leaned back in his chair, cradling his coffee cup and examining me with those incisive blue eyes. "So, Arlene, tell me about yourself."

"Um." Tension slammed back into my muscles. "What do you want to know?"

He smiled. "Why don't we start with work. What do you do for a living?"

"Um, I'm a bookkeeper."

I didn't sound very convincing. Was I supposed to sound convincing? Would a petty fraud artist just blurt out a confession? Hardly.

"Yes, and I understand Sirius Dynamics is one of your clients." He nodded encouragingly. "Do they keep you quite busy?"

"Um, yeah, but I have some other clients as well."

"Oh, are your other clients in research and development, too?"

"No."

That seemed rather abrupt, but he didn't seem taken aback. His expression of polite interest didn't waver. He didn't let it go, either. "What other clients do you work with?"

"Um. A restaurant. A bar." Dammit, Hibbert had probably already told him all this. I clenched my teeth. "A sex shop." It sounded completely sleazy when I said it out loud like that.

Parr grinned. "Ah. The hospitality industry."

"Yeah, something like that."

"So tell me about Aydan Kelly."

The suddenness of the question took me off guard. Adrenaline singed my veins. "Um, she's dead."

He swooped forward in his seat, a rapacious bird of prey. "Is she?"

"What... what do you mean? Of course she is. She died in a car accident. A few months ago."

"That's very interesting." Razor-sharp eyes slashed my cover identity to bleeding shreds. "Because I have some very sophisticated facial recognition software that says you are Aydan Kelly. Beyond a shadow of doubt."

My heart slammed into my ribs with a single sledgehammer blow before clattering emptily into the pit of my belly.

He had known all along. These last few months he'd just

been toying with me. Letting me think they'd believed my cover story.

And now it was all over.

CHAPTER 38

I stared at Parr for a moment, a deceitful deer frozen in the headlights of truth.

Then my bullshit factory jolted into emergency production. I leaned back in my chair, not bothering to conceal my trembling hands. "Okay. You got me." I eased out a shaky breath. "I'll tell you the truth. It's a long story..."

Which my frantic brain was spinning even while I hesitated as if reluctant to talk.

"I, um... I really am Arlene Widdenback. Aydan Kelly really is dead. We looked a lot alike. We were really good friends, and we sometimes switched places to fool people..."

Parr didn't hide his contempt. "Stop insulting my intelligence. You might have gotten Hibbert to swallow that story, but my facial recognition software doesn't lie."

I tossed my head, hiding my gulp of fear. "I didn't say it was lying. Your software identified my face all right. I was impersonating Aydan Kelly."

"Nice try." His lips twisted in a sardonic smile. "My sources tell me Aydan Kelly's driver's licence has had your face on it for the past ten years."

"Yeah." I gave him a challenging stare. "So what? Arlene Widdenback's driver's licence has had my face on it for the past ten years, too."

At least I hoped it had. Surely Stemp would have created airtight records.

Parr frowned. "True. But there is no official or unofficial photograph of Aydan Kelly on record that doesn't have your face on it. If there was, I would have found it. Believe me, my people are very thorough."

I drew a deep breath and hoped he couldn't see my jackhammer pulse beating in the veins in my forehead. "I told you it was a long story."

He leaned back, crossing his arms over his chest. "Do tell."

I gathered myself.

"My friend Aydan was in an abusive marriage-"

Parr interrupted me with an irritable hiss of breath through his teeth. "Don't waste my time. I've already heard the story of how she supposedly transferred her assets to you to hide from her ex-husband before conveniently dying in an implausible car crash. That's irrelevant. My software proves you are one and the same person."

Another wave of fear crashed over my faulty emotional wiring, short-circuiting into anger. I jerked upright in my chair.

"No, it doesn't, you dumb shit! Your software proves my face was on all of her identification. It's not the same thing. Now shut up and listen!"

Parr's eyebrows shot up and he barked out an incredulous half-laugh. Then he mimed zipping his lips and regarded me with a glint in his eyes that clearly said 'this better be good'.

'Or else' was easy to deduce.

I clung to the remains of my anger and honed it into a

cutting tone. "As I was *saying*... my friend Aydan was in an abusive marriage many years ago. When she finally got the courage to leave her ex-husband, she was afraid he would find her. That was when we decided to use my photo, and my address, on all of her official identification. It's easy to assume somebody else's identity when you have their full cooperation."

I shot a look at Parr, and he gave me a 'go on' nod. I threw myself into my newly-created story. "So her ex knew if he came looking for her, he was only going to find me. And he knew I had contacts. He wouldn't mess with me."

I drew a deep breath, thinking furiously. "So we just left it that way. We looked enough alike that she could use the ID without being questioned. And she was always pretty timid, so she just kept hiding behind it. Then when she started seriously dating her next husband, she explained it all to him. When he understood how scared she was, he just went along with it. He was a consultant and he had lots of business dinners and functions. Aydan was shy and she hated that stuff, so I usually went with Robert instead."

Inspiration struck. Arlene Widdenback was a con artist, after all.

"I liked the fancy events." I hesitated, hoping I wasn't overdoing it. "It was a good way to... meet... important people."

Parr quirked an eyebrow at me. "I understand those meetings didn't always go smoothly. Something about three fraud convictions...?"

I lifted my chin and viewed him down my nose. "Misunderstandings. That's all."

A sardonic smile flitted across his lips. "I see. Do go on."

Cautious hope rose. Was he buying it? Or was he just

toying with me again?

I snagged a grape from the fruit platter, hoping to moisten my dry mouth. "So when her second husband died, she came into some money. She was afraid her ex would find out and come after her, so she transferred it into my name. And then she died right afterward."

He shot me a skeptical look and opened his mouth, but I forestalled his comment. "And no, I didn't kill her," I snapped. "She was my friend."

"So you conveniently assumed her identity, took over her bookkeeping clients pretending to be her, and moved into her house." His icy tone sent shivers down my spine. "What a good friend."

I held his gaze. "Why wouldn't I? She was dead. It wouldn't hurt her. She had no heirs. And it comforted a lot of people when they 'found out'..." I made air quotes around the words. "...that it was all a big mistake and she hadn't died after all. That was a win for everybody except Aydan, and I couldn't change what had happened to her."

Parr eyed me in silence.

Please let him believe that. Or at least make him uncertain enough to think about it for a while.

"So Aydan worked for Sirius Dynamics," he said at last. "And when you tried to impersonate her after her death, they caught you with their security scanners."

Hibbert had obviously briefed him thoroughly. I took a deep breath, feeling as though I was scurrying across a barely-frozen lake with the ice cracking under my feet. Just keep moving and don't look down.

"Yes."

"Why do you suppose they didn't call the police?"

I repeated what I'd told Hibbert. "One of the higher-ups

likes me."

"And why are they letting you continue to use Aydan's identity without blowing the whistle?"

I tossed my head. "I don't know, and I don't care. They're paying me. That's all I care about."

"What about Samir Ramos?" The question snapped out like a whip.

Caught by surprise, I stared blankly at Parr. "Who?"

A moment later, recognition punched me in the gut. Shit, Samir Ramos. The spy I'd caught in the virtual network at Sirius back in March when this all started. The one who'd tried to abduct me before I even knew about Fuzzy Bunny.

Fortunately, Parr was speaking already. "Would Aydan use your identity without your permission?"

I frowned. "She had my permission. She could use it whenever she wanted."

His eyes narrowed. "Even if it put you in danger?"

"Well, yeah." I shrugged. "That was the whole point, wasn't it?"

"So you would die for your friend."

I played dumb. "I wasn't going to die. I told you, her ex wouldn't touch me."

"I'm not talking about her ex."

I gave him my best blank expression, and he sat in silence for a few moments, frowning into middle distance.

"So..." he said slowly. "Your shy, timid friend... who looked enough like you that you could pass for each other to casual acquaintances... who used your identity for years while carefully concealing her own... Did it ever occur to you that she was using you? Running a scam and setting you up to take the fall?"

A tendril of hope warmed my heart. Was he buying it?

I went for indignant. "No, of course not. Aydan would never do that."

"Oh, but she would." He spoke as if to himself. "She was projecting your identity to Ramos. And she's been flying under the radar ever since, quietly eliminating whoever gets in her way. Smart, smart lady. And she still has the fob."

His eyes focused on me with disconcerting suddenness. "She's still alive. She faked her death in that car crash."

Shit, that wasn't where I wanted him to go at all.

"Oh, no, I'm sure she didn't," I stammered. "She'd never do that. She would have called me if she was still alive. Even if she was hiding, she'd call me. I have all her money, and she'd need some. Besides, the police confirmed it was her body in the car."

"Hmm." He sank his chin onto his chest. After several long minutes of silence, he directed a frown at me. "Tell me about John Kane."

"Um..."

Parr had undoubtedly checked me out with Harchman by now. I reeled off the story I'd used with Harchman.

"I met Kane in a bar last summer. He said he was going to a fancy party and he needed a date to butter up the host. And he said he'd pay me. So I went."

"And he told Harchman you were his wife. But he called you *Aydan* Kane. Not Arlene Kane."

Parr had definitely talked to Harchman. I willed my pounding pulse to slow.

"Yes, he thought I was Aydan when we met in the bar." I shrugged. "Whenever anybody called me Aydan, I just went with it. I never knew where she'd used her ID, and I didn't want to get her in trouble."

A calculating smile tugged at his lips. "Oh, she was good.

Used you, and you had no idea…" He broke off. "So Kane thought you were Aydan, and expected you to go along with his scam."

I tried for discomfiture with a touch of defiance. "I didn't know it was a scam. He just said he'd pay me to butter up Lawrence. And I did." I pulled a frown and a faint shudder. "Then I discovered what he was really doing, trying to steal Lawrence's new drilling software. But by then it was too late. Kane… he's a mean son of a bitch. And big. Strong. Not like Aydan's ex."

Parr filled in the blanks. "So he abused you and forced you to play the game. Until you confessed your true identity to Lawrence."

I nodded, eyes cast down. "And then I ran." I tried a delicate little choke, my fingers fluttering to my lips. "And then Lawrence used me, too. Made those horrible videos…"

Parr laughed. "Nice acting, but you can skip it. You forget I saw the footage of your exchange with Lawrence at the party. I'm not falling for the cute little helpless act after I watched you twist his balls."

"Oh." I sat back in the chair and gave him a sheepish smile. "Sorry. Habit."

He eyed me, still grinning. "So what really happened?"

I shrugged. "Kane's a vicious bastard, but we got along okay as long as I didn't cross him. And Harchman is a slimy little shit. He made those movies without my knowledge and then cashed in on them."

"So Kane and Aydan were working at Sirius Dynamics together." Parr frowned and tapped his empty coffee cup thoughtfully against his thigh. "Probably running some kind of scam. How did he react when Aydan died and you took over?"

"He already knew about Aydan and me. He found out about our switch when I confessed to Harchman back in the summer." I tried another shudder. "I paid for that. Believe me, I paid."

He eyed me unsympathetically. "But you looked pretty friendly at the party this week."

"Yeah. I told you, we get along fine as long as I don't cross him. We had a bit of a thing." I hunched my shoulders. "Not as much as I thought, obviously."

"Mm." The coffee cup kept tap-tap-tapping. After a long pause, he said, "You do realize cars don't usually explode and burn when they're in an accident."

"Uh?" The non-sequitur took me by surprise, and I scrambled to figure out where he was going with this. "What do you mean?"

"I mean Kane probably killed your friend. Took what she had and then set up a car accident for her."

I didn't have to fake my gaping jaw. "What... no, he wouldn't have."

"Why not?"

"Um..." I came up completely blank. "I just don't think he would."

Parr eyed me with what might have been sympathy. "They both used you. Aydan set you up to take the fall for her scam. She wasn't quite smart enough and Kane got her, probably along with the item she stole from Sirius. And then he used you in her place. Now he's done with you and moving on."

I opened my mouth, but nothing came out. If I argued, I'd trip myself on one of my 'facts' and end up dead. And my network keys and the portable network generator would fall right into Parr's hands.

But if I didn't come up with an argument to exonerate Kane, Fuzzy Bunny would stop hunting me and start gunning for him. And I was pretty sure we both knew where he was.

Very likely making passionate love to their director of operations right at this moment.

Parr leaned forward. "I know where Kane is."

Shit, shit, shit, goddamn!

Rising panic choked my voice. "I... uh..." I swallowed the quaver and tried again. "I think the timing was wrong."

"What?" Parr shot me one of his predatory glances. "What do you mean?"

"Um..." My mind rocketed through possibilities. "I think the timing was wrong for Kane to have set up Aydan's accident. If he'd gotten what he wanted from her, wouldn't he have moved on right away? Why would he still be working at Sirius now?"

"Is he?" Those soulless eyes pinned me to my chair.

"Well, yeah." I successfully resisted the urge to gulp. "He's been off this week, but he'll be back on Monday."

"Ah." Parr's gaze went distant again. "Hm. Interesting..." His eyes snapped back into focus. "How would you like to do a small favour for me?"

"Uh... that would depend on what it was."

He smiled. "And what the compensation would be, no doubt. Hibbert tells me you're a businessperson first and foremost. By the way, why did you deck him at the party? You caused quite a stir."

I met his eyes steadily. "Did he tell you about our exchange at the Hogback?"

Parr's face froze in an expression of distaste. "The Hogback. I've regretted that purchase ever since I acquired the property, but Hibbert seems to have an unhealthy liking for it. What happened?"

"He thought he should receive a commission from your payment for the phone list. A commission that involved twisting my arm halfway out of its socket to get me on my knees in front of him." My lips peeled back in remembered revulsion. "I leave the rest to your imagination."

"Oh." Parr looked almost as disgusted as I felt. "Why didn't you press charges?"

"Uh..." I stared at him. Shit, of course an upstanding citizen would ask that. Protecting himself while cheerfully throwing Hibbert to the wolves. "Um... it didn't seem... wise. In the bigger picture."

Parr nodded as if in approval. "Hibbert has developed an unfortunate tendency to overstep his authority in unpleasant ways. It won't happen again." He smiled. "You hit him with a lovely right cross, though. I was impressed. How's your hand?"

I closed and reopened it slowly. "Sore."

"No doubt." After a short pause, he continued, "I find that Fuzzy Bunny is in need of a part-time consultant. I would like to offer you a retainer of fifty thousand dollars, for your services as and when required."

"And my services would be...?" I eyed him suspiciously.

"Oh, supervisory duties." He smiled. "And occasionally representing the company at social functions. Specifically, attending a wedding tomorrow."

My suspicion deepened. "What wedding?"

"The wedding of Yana Orlov and John Kane."

CHAPTER 39

"Wh... what?" The word barely cleared my lips.

"Our director of operations, Yana Orlov, is marrying John Kane tomorrow at the Little Chapel of the West at eleven A.M. I would like you to attend. To represent the company, as it were." Parr smiled. "And to keep an eye on Kane."

"I... I, uh... I doubt if he'd want me there."

Parr's smile went cold. "I don't care what he wants. I want to know what he's up to. As his business associate, you're in a position to find out."

"Um... ex-lover, actually," I said faintly, still trying to draw a breath around the gut-punch. "I think it might be awkward."

Well, of course he'd want to get married right away. He had thought he'd lost her. He was a decisive guy, and now that he'd found her again, he wouldn't waste a moment of their time together.

"All the better for you to banish the awkwardness by graciously wishing them happiness together," Parr said. "If you need an outfit for the wedding, use this company card." He extracted a credit card from his wallet and handed it over. "Get yourself something nice." His gaze politely avoided my hiking boots and waist pouch. "Now, if you'll excuse me, I'm going to join my wife for the remainder of the flight. If you'd like anything at all, Thomas will be happy to take care of you. A limousine will pick you up at the Vegas airport, and the details of the wedding and your return flight will be in your room at the Venetian. Archibald will be in touch to receive your report and the company credit card after you return to Calgary. Do enjoy Vegas."

He rose and left me staring blindly at the rosewood wall panelling.

The rosewood offered no epiphanies even after several minutes of intense contemplation, and I shook myself back to the present when Thomas appeared at my elbow.

"May I offer you a drink?" His blond good looks and sparkling smile were balm to my eyes, and the thought of a drink was pure heaven.

"Yes, please. Beer, if you've got it."

"Of course, we have several." He reeled off a list, but the names bombarded my aching brain meaninglessly.

"Thank you, that last one sounds good," I mumbled when the words stopped.

A few minutes later, icy bubbles tickled my tongue and I let out a heartfelt sigh. After a few delicious swallows, my brain ground into gear again.

Parr had believed me. Or was pretending to believe me, anyway. So I'd likely survive the trip.

I toasted that thought with a deep swallow of beer, and suppressed a belch while I considered the possibilities. I'd been too rattled to try to extract any information about the secret weapon from Parr this time, but I'd have other chances if the 'retainer' meant what I thought it did. And Stemp and Dermott were going to pee their pants in sheer delight over that.

My thoughts wandered to the memory of Kane and Yana locked in an embrace. I hoped my presence wouldn't spoil Kane's wedding day.

But why should it? We were friends, after all. Two detours into bed didn't count for anything. I had told him not to read any meaning into them, and he obviously hadn't.

So that was okay.

I tipped up the bottle and gulped its soothing contents.

By the time we touched down in Vegas a couple of beers later, fatigue and alcohol made rising from the soft leather seat a herculean task. I made it to my feet without actually swearing out loud, and managed to return Eleanor Parr's gracious farewell with a fair approximation of good manners.

The limo was an exercise in nauseated misery while we wallowed through the lights and traffic of the late-night Strip. When I finally reached my room after navigating the check-in queue and the interminable hallway, I trudged inside to fall face-first onto the bed.

When my complaining bladder woke me, the lights of the Strip still glared through the open draperies and the illuminated clock read two-fourteen. I hauled myself upright, easing the kink out of my neck and trying to convince myself that somebody else couldn't possibly have been eating shit with my mouth.

After a trip to the bathroom to scrub away the vile taste and rid myself of the processed beer, I staggered over to close the draperies and set the alarm. I was about to fall into bed again when I remembered Dermott would expect a report.

Damn.

At least it was an easy decision to choose the new,

painless network key. I plugged the network generator into the laptop and hesitated before setting the computer on the opposite side of the king-sized bed. Stretching out on my back on the other side, I briefly reflected that if for some reason I ended up comatose, at least I'd be comfortable.

Then I closed my eyes and slipped into the network.

Fearfully recalling my disorientation the last time I'd gone into the Sirius servers, I seeded tiny snippets of data all over the Venetian's network and along the data paths I followed through the internet. I'd lose most of them when the connections shifted as they always did, but if there were enough of them, I might find a few.

Please God, let me find a few.

Because there was nobody to call me home.

Too frightened to even consider that, I drove myself down the currents of data.

Sirius was well-concealed, as usual. By the time I found it at last, I had backtracked so many times and left so many data flags, my anxiety felt like jolts of electricity in my attenuated consciousness. Gathering my data bits, I quivered in the data flow for a moment before flinging myself at the server.

Chaos seized me, fear exploding my tumbled packets like a grenade. Hurling bits of myself to safety, I gradually gathered my scattered consciousness. Ignoring the disorientation, I focused on the Sirius server.

I was getting better at this. I wouldn't panic.

I launched myself at the server again.

And again.

And at last I was in.

Suppressing a sob of relief, I hurried down the blessedly familiar virtual corridors to file my report. The network was deserted at that hour and I hovered like a desolate ghost, wishing for the warmth of Spider's laughter or Germain's sturdy muscular presence.

Or Kane...

I shook off that thought.

I could have created constructs of them in the sim, but it seemed creepy to do that, and anyway, the embarrassing data records would be there for all to see in the morning if I did.

I dropped my file into the repository and slipped out into the internet again without making myself visible.

The trip back to the Venetian's network was equal parts terror and tedium. Terror when the data connections shifted like desert sand, leaving me lost in a trackless wasteland. Tedium while I slowly retrieved every one of my data flags, mindlessly searching and gathering until at last the portal appeared in the distance.

Several minutes later, I heaved a lungless sigh of relief and stepped through.

The alarm blared like the trumpets of Judgement Day.

"Jesus *Christ!*" I levitated several inches off the bed, my heart trying to batter its way out of my chest. Eyes still glued shut, I flailed ineffectually in the direction of the horrible noise and made solid contact with a backhand. The resulting crash generated blessed silence, and I fell back on the pillow, panting.

After a few minutes I managed to pat my heart back into my chest and pry my eyes open. The laptop sat black and silent on the opposite side of the bed. I didn't remember waking up after leaving the network, so either I'd been in a coma until the alarm went off or I'd fallen asleep right after regaining consciousness.

I made a mental note to ask Jack about that. Maybe I only regained consciousness if somebody shook me or there was a loud noise. That was a scary thought. If I hadn't set the alarm, would I still be passed out on the bed, not waking until the hotel staff barged in?

I pushed away my surge of fear. Never mind. I was awake now.

I headed for the shower, still quivering.

By ten o'clock I was back in the room, decked out once again in clothes I never would have chosen and hovering nervously in front of the mirror. I had thrown myself on the mercy of one of the Venetian's exclusive shops, and regretted it. This outfit lacked the winter coat and boots that I'd purchased in Calgary, but made up for them with an extra decimal place on the bill. I hoped Parr wouldn't freak out.

Sighing, I packed my suitcase and hesitated over the laptop. Parr's jet didn't leave until three o'clock, and I couldn't see schlepping my bag and laptop case with me for the next several hours. But I didn't dare leave the USB network generator with the laptop. The bell desk was undoubtedly secure, but...

No.

I hesitated for a moment before extracting the secured phone from my waist pouch to make room for the USB device. Then I dropped the phone and waist pouch into the capacious handbag I'd purchased, and hurried for the door.

The trip to the chapel was uneventful, but my heart pounded as though I'd been running beside the taxi instead of riding in it. When I stepped out of the cab at a quarter to eleven, the parking lot was empty and the doors of the small chapel were closed.

I eyed the building uncertainly. This was definitely the right place. Maybe they'd arrived early and the service was already in progress?

I drifted toward the chapel but trailed to a halt. What was I going to do, stick my face up against the window and gawk inside? That'd be a nice wedding memory for Kane.

I tried the door instead, and found it locked. That was a relief. Sort of. Either they hadn't arrived yet, or they'd come early and already left.

"Miss Orlov?"

The voice from behind made me start guiltily, and I turned to face the slim young man who was eyeing me questioningly.

"Um, no, I'm a guest."

"Oh. Well, they should be here shortly," he reassured me. "Why don't you wait in the pergola? I'll let you know when the ceremony is about to start."

I was several steps along the path and almost behind the building when the hushing of tires on pavement made me turn to see a black limo pulling up.

Frozen, I watched while Kane emerged and rounded the car to offer his hand to Yana. When they stood together on the sidewalk like the bride and groom figurines from a particularly high-class wedding cake, I swallowed the lump in my throat.

Kane's powerful shoulders and taut midriff were displayed to advantage in a perfectly-tailored dark suit and crisp white shirt, the distinguished silver at his temples frosting his dark hair. Yana's elegant white gown accented a perfect hourglass figure, and a short veil sparkled like snowflakes against the satin blackness of her chic coiffure.

Diamonds glittered at her throat and earlobes as she gazed up at Kane.

Completely wrapped up in her, he leaned down to whisper in her ear. She responded with a sultry chuckle, her hand gliding over his chest.

Feeling like a voyeur, I backed away, but the movement caught Kane's attention. He straightened, his brows snapping together. In a few long strides, he closed the distance between us.

"What are you doing here?" he demanded sotto voce.

"I..."

"Don't spoil this for me." Muscles rippled in his jaw and he gave me an imploring look. "Please."

I tried, but I knew I hadn't hidden my stab of hurt. "Of course I won't." My words came out stiffly despite my best efforts. "You should know I wouldn't."

Yana hurried over, casting an anxious glance from Kane to me, and I pulled myself together to offer the best smile I could manufacture. "Hi, Yana, it's nice to meet you. I'm Arlene Widdenback, and Nick Parr asked me to come and offer best wishes from him and his wife, and on behalf of the company." I dared a glance at Kane, but he was still frowning.

"Congratulations to both of you," I added. "I hope I'm not intruding."

"But of course not," she responded, a trace of accent giving her warm contralto an exotic appeal. "You are a friend of John's, too, yes?"

I nodded without looking at Kane. Maybe not so much anymore.

"Then you are most welcome." She embraced me lightly, air-kissing me on both cheeks. "Thank you for coming."

It would have been better if she had angrily dismissed me. I huddled in the back corner of the chapel, hoping Kane could pretend I wasn't there during the short ceremony.

The words were simple and meaningful, and the minister managed to sound utterly sincere despite my certainty that he said the same words every hour on the hour, three hundred and sixty-five days a year, for an endless parade of couples.

Kane said his vows in a strong, clear voice, his full attention focused on his bride, and she reprised the vows warmly, touching a delicate fingertip to her brimming eyes.

Then the deed was done and the minister pronounced them man and wife as though nothing greater had ever happened in the world.

And for them it hadn't. Their happiness glowed like the Vegas sun. While they shared a lingering kiss, I slipped out the chapel doors and around the corner to fumble in my bag for my phone.

I had just dialled the cab company when Yana hurried around the corner, towing Kane by the hand. "You are leaving so soon? Will you instead join us for lunch?"

A glance at Kane's stony face was all it took.

I turned back to Yana. "Thank you, but I can't. I have another appointment. But congratulations. It was a lovely ceremony, and I hope you'll have many years of happiness together."

She made some politely disappointed noises and air-kissed me again, and after a moment's hesitation, I offered Kane my hand. He took it with a brief, gentle squeeze, but his expression was remote.

I was glad when they turned back to their limo, leaving me standing alone outside the chapel.

CHAPTER 40

My remaining time passed too slowly. I ate lunch and bought a book, but it didn't hold my interest. The constant noise and flow of human traffic abraded my already-raw nerves, and after tolerating it for as long as I could, I phoned the limo service and asked them to pick me up early.

At the hotel bell desk, a cheerful attendant retrieved my bag and turned to the next customer.

"Wait." I flagged him down again. "Where's my laptop?"

"Oh, sorry, did we miss something?" He peered at the tag on my suitcase. "No, this says one item."

"I had two items. This and a laptop."

"Oh." He eyed me suspiciously. "Can you describe the laptop?"

Tension ratcheted up in my shoulders. "It was in a plain black case."

Yeah, like every other laptop on the planet. I racked my tired brain, but I couldn't remember what brand it was. The attendant was still waiting, his face registering equal parts cynicism and impatience.

I sighed and gave up. "I'm sorry, it was a company laptop and I don't even know what brand it was. I'll just leave you my contact information and if you've got a laptop left over after everybody else has claimed their luggage, give me a call."

I handed him my card with the dark suspicion that he'd simply appropriate the laptop at the end of the day, but at that point I really didn't care. I had the network generator and the network keys with me, and the laptop was just a bare-bones machine with no critical information on it. In a few hours I'd be home and I could make my report in person. I abandoned it to its fate and headed for my limousine.

Parr's flight crew allowed me to board early, and I scurried directly into the well-appointed bathroom to change back into my comfortable jeans and hiking boots. Sinking into one of the soft leather seats in the sitting room, I accepted another icy beer and sparkling smile from Thomas.

God, this was the life. I laid my head back and stretched my legs luxuriously. I was half-dozing when voices roused me.

Voices I recognized.

Shit.

Kane rounded the corner and stopped dead. "What are *you* doing here?"

The undisguised dismay in his voice stabbed a place that was already tender. I drew myself up. "Flying home. What are you doing here?"

"You *can't*..."

Yana slid her arms around him from behind, tucking herself under his arm. "Hello again, Arlene. Hello, Thomas. Do you have any champagne?"

Thomas gave his usual half-bow and dazzling smile. "Of course, Ms. Orlov."

She laughed, a husky, sexy sound that made me think of 1950s movie stars. "It's Mrs. Kane now. Wish us congratulations!"

"Congratulations, Mr. and Mrs. Kane." His smile widened. "This certainly does call for champagne."

"Yes," she agreed merrily. "Come, darling, we're blocking the aisle." She tugged Kane gently aside to allow another man to push past. The man nodded at us and continued through to the rear cabin without speaking, but he nonetheless gave off a friendlier vibe than Kane, who still stood rigid and glowering.

"Look, I'm sorry," I said, holding onto my temper with all my might. "Parr told me to be here. This is the only option I have."

Kane blew out a breath and nodded at last. Drawing Yana close, he took a seat with his back to me, pulling her down beside him to murmur in her ear.

"Fine. Asshole," I muttered, and dragged my book out of my bag to glare sightlessly at it.

I read the same words over and over without comprehension during takeoff. At last I gave up and started to turn a page every few minutes so it would look as though I was actually reading.

When the plane levelled off, Yana glanced back at me before whispering something to Kane. His deep chuckle did nothing to ease my irritation.

She rose, and I stared fiercely at my book, watching her in my peripheral vision while she headed for the serving cart Thomas had parked against the wall while he attended to the man in the rear of the plane.

Yana extracted a tall, slim bottle before moving back to whisper to Kane again, leaning down to kiss him. He made a playful grab for her, and she eluded his hands, giggling and shaking a reproving finger. "You wait here, darling. I have a surprise for you.   I'll be right back."   She gave him a seductive smile and vanished into the forward cabin.

I stared at Kane's broad back, wishing I could ask him what the hell his problem was. Thomas returned to his post at the serving station, and I dropped my gaze to glare at my book again, still fuming.

Okay, fine, so Kane was married to the love of his life now, but there was no need to treat me like an interloper. After all the times I had assured him I didn't want anything from him, surely he couldn't think I'd try to break up his marriage out of spite.

Yana strode around the corner, calling in her melodious contralto. "Oh, Thomas…"

He looked up with his usual smile. "Yes, Mrs. K-"

She pointed the bottle at him and he crumpled without a sound.

CHAPTER 41

Time slowed in a massive burst of adrenaline.

Thomas. Dead for sure. No mistaking that boneless collapse. Urine darkened his immaculate pants already.

Yana was still coming. The bottle swung toward me.

Kane launched from his seat.

I dove for the floor, away from the lethal bottle-thing.

Kane and Yana struggled at the edge of my vision but as I rolled, the man from the back ran in.

"Get her!" Yana's shriek told me everything I needed to know.

My old sports reflexes commandeered my body, rolling me to my feet. My momentum carried me forward and I ducked under his wide-armed grab, my hands locking onto his arm as I spun.

The arm-bar fell naturally into place with all my weight behind it. I felt rather than heard the deep ripping sound, like roots being torn from the earth. His scream was so sudden and horrible my hands flew off him as though I'd been burned.

He stumbled, falling forward, his useless arm collapsing under him.

His head wedged between two seats, his body still

dropping.

A deep pop held the finality I remembered too well from the frozen parking lot only a week ago.

His body went limp.

I backed away panting, scrubbing my hands against my jeans to erase the gruesome sensation of tearing muscles.

When I jerked my gaze away from the fallen man, Yana lay motionless at Kane's feet, her head twisted at an unnatural angle.

"Clear the back." His voice was a dry rasp, and he turned to vanish into the forward cabin.

My body obeyed even though my mind still didn't comprehend. The bathroom and small rear cabin were unoccupied. Beyond them, a king-sized bed flaunted itself in an opulent bedroom, and I mechanically checked closets and corners.

As I turned for the front of the plane again, it occurred to me that I'd have had no idea what to do if I'd actually found somebody.

Lucky I hadn't.

Still stunned, I tottered past Thomas's limp form. I couldn't look at him yet. Couldn't think about it.

Kane knelt next to Yana's body, reaching toward her face, and I turned away to give him some privacy.

A moment later, the sound of sudden movement and a shattering crash made me jerk around, fresh terror galvanizing my muscles.

Kane strode over to the laptop he'd thrown across the cabin. Snatching it up, he smashed it over and over against the table, gouging the polished rosewood and sending plastic shrapnel flying in all directions. Then he threw the remains to the floor and crushed them under his heel, stomping as if to grind them into oblivion.

As I stared open-mouthed, he crossed the cabin in two long strides and yanked me into a hard kiss.

Shocked, I pulled back. "What...?"

He kissed me again, his lips devouring mine.

I jerked away, my shock fading into angry confusion. "Hang on..."

Kane seized my face between his palms, and his eyes held a desperate appeal I'd never seen before. "Aydan, for God's sake," he said hoarsely. "Will you please just shut up and make love to me?"

Yana's dead eyes stared up at us accusingly, and suddenly I understood.

Kane's gaze followed mine. When he turned back to me, I could see his anger simmering just below the surface.

I touched his face, my heart breaking for him. "Okay," I whispered, and led him down the hall.

CHAPTER 42

In the bedroom I stripped without ceremony, and Kane's lips tightened as if in pain. When I went to him, the storm still raged in his eyes but his hands were gentle on my shoulders.

"I'm sorry," he mumbled. "You don't have to do this. I shouldn't have-"

I laid my fingertips over his lips. "Shhh." I kissed him softly, wishing the tenderness of my touch could take away his suffering. "I want to," I whispered against his cheek.

"Oh, God, Aydan."

Then his mouth was on mine, his hands moving over my skin. He muttered an impatient oath against my lips and withdrew far enough to tear off his own clothes before pulling me against him again, his erection jammed between us.

His hands slid down to cup my ass and I moved against him, feeding his hardness. He pressed me down on the bed, his hungry mouth finding my breast. I moaned and arched against him, but when I reached down to fondle him he stopped my hand.

"Wait." He fumbled for his pants, and I scooted further onto the bed, pulling him with me.

When he withdrew the condom from his pocket, we both hesitated.

The condom meant for his wife.

His dead wife.

The anger rose in his eyes again and I pulled him to me, trying to kiss it away. Kiss away the pain, if only for a little while.

His groan sounded like a sob.

A few kisses later, he poised himself above me, his eyes asking the question. I reached to guide him home, and he entered me on a long breath, his eyes closing.

A gasp escaped me. God, I didn't remember him being so huge.

He rocked into gentle motion, allowing me time to accommodate him. Running my hands over his bulging arms and shoulders, I watched him above me, moving with his rhythm. His strokes deepened, his muscles tightening, and I tried to find my usual warm, sweet tension.

It should be there. I should be ascending on his heat like a phoenix riding a blazing updraft, letting him carry me to that glorious apex right before the freefall of ecstasy...

His muscles flexed under my hands, reminding me of the gut-wrenching sensation of ripping tissue.

What was he thinking right now? Imagining Yana under him, one last time? Trying to forget the sensation of her life falling away in his hands?

His eyes opened suddenly, dark and vulnerable. He went still, looking deeply, seeing too much.

Or too little. Pain flared like fire in his eyes.

"I'm sorry." His voice was a rough whisper. "I'll stop."

I pulled him to me. "Don't stop, John. Take what you need. Just take what you need."

He collapsed, his arms locking around me, his face buried in my neck. "Aydan..." The word wrenched out of him and he drove deep, thrusting again and again.

I wrapped my arms around him, riding his hunger until he stiffened with a hoarse cry. The spasms shook him while he strained me close, his breath sobbing against my cheek.

At last he went limp, his face still buried in my neck, his ragged breathing slowing. I held him, rocking him softly, stroking his back and sprinkling kisses over his hair and temple.

After a few moments, his arms tightened around me. Then he pushed away, rolling over to sit on the edge of the bed. He pulled off the condom and threw it in the garbage as if it disgusted him.

"That was the most shameful thing I've ever done." He scrubbed his hands over his face and hung his head, locking his hands behind his neck.

"John, it's not shameful." I traced my fingertips over the puckered scars that marred his powerful back. "It's just a reaction-"

"Don't touch me like that." His voice was like a raw wound. "Not like you love me. Not now."

I pulled my hand away. "I'm sorry-"

"*Don't!*" It was almost a shout. He drew a ragged breath. "Don't apologize to me."

I opened my mouth but nothing came out. My hand hovered helplessly, wanting to touch him but forbidden.

After a moment, I gathered my clothes and left.

In the sitting room, I dressed rapidly under the empty gaze of dead eyes and tucked Spider's ring back into my bra. Then I knelt beside poor Thomas at last, straightening his splayed and cooling limbs and smoothing his smart uniform.

His handsome features were slack, but a ghost of his bright smile still lingered on his lips. I gently closed the lids over his dulling eyes and bowed my head to commend his soul to whatever place of rest he may have hoped for.

When I looked up, Kane stood fully dressed, silently watching.

I shot a glance at Yana's sprawled body. "John, go back to the bedroom. Let me..." I rose to approach the body.

"Leave her," he said roughly. "Aydan, we need to talk."

"Not here." I spread my hands, trying to guide him without touching him. "In the front cabin."

He nodded and turned away.

In the cabin, he gestured to a seat. "Please sit down."

I sat as directed, watching him worriedly while he paced, churning his fingers in his hair.

"I owe you an apology," he said abruptly.

"John, it's okay."

"Stop." He stared at me, tense lines scoring his face. "God, I can't do this when you look at me like that." He turned his back on me to stare out the window, clenching his hands behind him. "Aydan," he said hoarsely. "I need you to listen to everything I'm going to say without interrupting. Will you promise to do that?"

"That depends on what you're going to say."

His shoulders sagged. "God help me."

"John, just tell me. You know you can talk to me."

"Until you find out what I've done. Then you'll hate me. And I deserve it."

I locked my hands together so I wouldn't reach for him. "Why don't you let me decide how I'll feel? Just say what you need to say."

"All right." He spun to face me, his jaw set. "I lied to

you." The words grated out between his teeth, but his eyes beseeched me. "Yana never meant anything to me. I let you believe I was grief-stricken just to get you into bed."

My mouth dropped open.

"I knew you were pitying me." He clenched his fists. "I saw it in your eyes and I tried to stop, but God help me, Aydan, when you looked at me like that... When you said 'take me'..." He drew a ragged breath. "I lost all control. And all the time, you were just..." His face twisted. "...just... *enduring* me. Giving yourself to me out of pity and wishing I was Arnie. And I took you, God help me, I took you because I had to have you just one more time." He turned away to press his forehead against the window. "I'm sorry, Aydan. I'm sorry."

"Wait... what...? *Seriously?*" He flinched as my voice rose. "Seriously, John? I don't even... I..."

Words failed me and I lurched to my feet to grab him by the arm. "Look at me." When he turned his face away, I seized his chin. "Look at me, goddammit!"

He met my eyes reluctantly, bracing his shoulders as if expecting a blow.

"In the first place..." I stopped to gather myself. "Shit, I don't even know where to start! Okay, I was not *enduring* you and I was not wishing you were somebody else, I was just having a bit of trouble getting into the mood since I'd just killed a guy with my bare hands and I was pretty sure you hated me and you were pretending I was Yana."

He opened his mouth to speak but I overrode him. "And yeah, it was a pity fuck." He flinched at the words, and I jabbed a finger into his chest. "And that was your own damn fault for being such a damn good actor and making me believe you were upset. That whole thing with the laptop-"

"There was a listening device," he interrupted. "I had to make sure we weren't being recorded."

"Well, it worked for you, didn't it?"

His face twisted as though I'd knifed him in the gut, and my indignation faded. He was feeling bad enough already. And he could have just let me keep on believing the lie and avoided this whole scene.

"Goddammit, John..." I sighed. "Look, forget it. We all get carried away sometimes. I'm just going to choose to be flattered it was that important to you. And a pity fuck is nothing to be ashamed of. It just means there's somebody in the world who cares about you enough to take you to bed even if they're not really in the mood."

"But it was shameful to take advantage of your caring. I used you. I'm sorry." His voice vibrated with emotion and he dropped his gaze. "There's something else."

Exhaustion overcame me and I let my arms fall to my sides. "What?"

"I don't mean this to sound like an excuse. There's no excuse for what I did. But I wasn't acting. I truly was... *am* upset. Just not about Yana." He looked directly at me for the first time, and I could see the truth in the storm-grey of his eyes.

"Okay..." I swallowed rising fear. "What is it? What's wrong?"

"You know when we cleared the plane? You went aft, I went forward?"

I nodded, afraid to speak.

"You didn't find anybody alive." He hesitated. "Neither did I."

For a long moment, I just stared at him.

"The pilot and co-pilot are dead," he said gently.

"There's nobody to fly the plane."

CHAPTER 43

"There's nobody..." I had to stop and swallow. "...but we're still fly... oh. Autopilot?"

Kane nodded.

"But... you know how to fly, right?" I stared at him hopefully. "You're James Bond. You know how to do everything."

His hesitation made my heart sink to the bottom of my chest.

He gave me an apologetic grimace. "I'm an army guy. The only thing I know about planes is how to jump out of them. I was really hoping you were a pilot."

"Oh."

That seemed inadequate. After a moment, I added, "I'm not a pilot. Sorry."

"Oh."

The steady drone of the engines filled the silence.

"So, um..." I cleared the hoarseness out of my throat, holding off panic with details. "Do you know how autopilot works? Is it programmed to just turn off when we get to where we're supposed to land?"

"I don't think so. I once heard about a pilot who had a heart attack and the autopilot just kept the plane flying until it ran out of gas and crashed. But that was just a small private plane."

"Oh." I thought about that for a moment. "Do you know how much gas we have?"

"Enough to get to Calgary or maybe a bit farther, I assume. We aren't scheduled to land for another couple of hours."

"Right." I sank into the nearest seat when my knees decided to take an unscheduled vacation. "Um... I don't suppose there's a manual or something...?" A glance at his expression made my face heat up. "Okay, I know jets don't come with how-to-fly instructions. That was stupid."

He dropped into the seat across from me and gave me a twisted smile. "No stupider than me. I already looked."

I laughed out loud. "Thanks for that." My laughter died quickly. "So, army guy, I presume jumping out of the plane isn't an option?"

Kane leaned back, rubbing his hands over his face. "Even if there were parachutes, which there aren't, jumping out of a pressurized jet from thirty-five thousand feet at four hundred miles per hour wouldn't exactly work."

"I guess not." I drew a deep breath and let it out slowly, trying to convince my racing heart that we weren't in danger. Not until we ran out of gas or tried to land, anyway. "Okay. Well, I guess we'd better go and try to figure out how to use the radio. In the movies there's always some guy with nerves of steel in the control tower who magically teaches people to fly passenger jets in ten minutes or less."

I started to rise, but Kane put out a restraining hand. "Actually... I don't want to do that just yet."

"Okay... because...?"

"I think Fuzzy Bunny will be monitoring the flight and

radio transmissions, and if we call in an emergency, they'll know something has gone wrong. I don't want to alert them until it's absolutely necessary."

"Why would they... oh." The snatch of conversation I'd overheard at Parr's party suddenly made sense. "I bet that bottle-thing is the prototype Parr was talking about. And Yana was delivering it."

Kane's head snapped up. "*Parr* was talking about it?"

"I overheard him at the party. I was just about to tell you when you did your Oscar-winning performance with Yana." I couldn't quite suppress a hint of acerbity.

Kane flushed. "I wasn't trying to play you. I'm not that pathetic."

"So what's the story with Yana, then?"

He sighed and leaned back. "I met her when I was undercover in Moscow about sixteen months ago. I was tracking an arms deal. At the time, I couldn't find any connection to Fuzzy Bunny, but Yana was my suspect. So I got close to her. I couldn't tell if she was responding to me or buttering me up in return, but we had a..."

He gave me an uncomfortable glance. "...relationship. Then just when I thought I was getting close to cracking the whole thing wide open, she died in a car bombing. I thought. Obviously I was getting too close and she decided to disappear."

He grimaced annoyance. "My leads petered out, and I got recalled to Canada. Then you showed up with the network key in March. After that I went overseas again, chasing down whispers and hints about weapons and technology that all seemed to point to Fuzzy Bunny, but again, I couldn't find any concrete evidence."

Kane stared into middle distance for a few moments.

"Knowing what I know now, I'm still not sure I could have done anything differently. Anyway..."

He returned his attention to me. "When I got invited to Parr's party, I thought they'd flagged my name because of my involvement at Harchman's this summer. Maybe it was that, too, but as soon as I saw Yana, I knew I'd been set up. I had to pick up my old cover story. And I couldn't do or say anything out of character because when I was with her before, she planted a listening device on me. I had to assume she'd done the same again."

He frowned. "I didn't think you'd believe she meant anything to me."

"Why wouldn't I?" I gave him a rueful smile. "You're James Bond. A guy like you has a girl in every port."

"A guy like me..." He trailed off, looking incredulous. "That's what you think? You think I'm some kiss-kiss-bang-bang action hero who goes around seducing women in between blowing things up?"

"Um... well..." I made a hesitant gesture toward the rear of the plane. "If the condom fits. I mean, seriously, it reads like a Hollywood script. You save my life, kill the bad guy... um, girl, whatever... find out we're about to go down in a fiery plane crash, and the first thing you think is, you need to get laid before we die? Admit it, danger gives you a giant hard-on. And you've been in danger lots of times."

A flush climbed his neck. "It's a combat reaction," he growled. "The body diverts blood flow and all other resources to the muscles during a fight. When the fight is over, the blood goes... back..." His flush deepened. "To other places. And no, I don't screw whichever woman happens to be handy at the moment. In fact..."

He drew a deep breath. "I have one failed marriage,

which was largely my fault because I wasn't there for most of it. I have a series of failed relationships which ended badly when I couldn't come up with any plausible reason why I'd disappear for weeks at a time without calling. That's it. No grand passions. No secret lovers in exotic places. Just a long list of women who think I'm a jerk." His lips twisted in a bitter smile. "Welcome to the list."

My hand flew out to touch his arm. "You're not a jerk."

"No; I just took advantage of your sympathy so I could get my rocks off, with a total disregard for your needs. Hell, no, I'm not a jerk at all."

"Don't be so hard on yourself." I squeezed his arm. "If I'd known the whole story, I wouldn't have been so hard on you, either. I don't want you to feel guilty. We're friends. Friends forgive each other when they screw up." I considered that for an instant. "Let me rephrase that in a way that doesn't include the word 'screw'."

He winced, and I changed the subject. "So what did you find out from Yana? Did you know she was delivering the weapon prototype?"

"No, but I suspected she had something planned for this trip. That's why I pushed and cajoled her into getting married. It was the only plausible way I could follow her to Vegas. She tried to dissuade me, but she had to maintain her cover, too."

He frowned. "Though I still don't know exactly what she wanted from me. Why not just kill me instead of stringing me along?"

When I returned a puzzled shrug, he sighed. "I know I didn't act like it, but I was glad you were there. But saying those vows while you watched was probably the hardest thing I've ever done."

I didn't know what to say, so I kept silent.

After a moment, he continued. "When I hadn't caught her at anything the whole time we were in Vegas, I realized that whatever she had planned would take place on this flight. That's why I was so upset to see you on the plane." His hand closed around mine. "I almost lost you. Thank God she killed Thomas first. I didn't even identify that thing as a weapon."

I swallowed hard at the memory of Thomas's limp body. "Me neither."

"Nice takedown of the other guy, though." Kane gave me a piercing glance. "Aydan Kelly, bookkeeper."

"Don't start." I pulled my hand away and diverted the conversation. "I see why she'd want to kill Thomas and me, and maybe you to get rid of witnesses while she delivered the weapons. But why kill the pilots? She'd crash with the rest of us."

"No, she wouldn't." Kane rubbed wearily at the tense lines in his forehead. "Yana was a pilot. She must have been planning to take over."

"But... why? Don't the airports know who's flying the plane? Wouldn't they notice it was a woman's voice instead of a man's?"

Kane went still. "Yes... unless..."

"Unless she wasn't planning to land in Calgary at all," I finished.

"No, that doesn't make sense," he countered. "I don't know anything about flying a plane, but I know about filing flight plans. If she diverted without telling anybody, the airport would be on alert right away."

"But what if it was an emergency?" I asked softly. "Say, if the pilot died of a heart attack..."

"Or a brain hemorrhage," Kane finished. "That silent weapon. Doesn't leave an external mark. What do you want to bet it's some kind of beam that goes through skin and bone and vaporizes soft tissue behind it? I've never seen a guy drop like Thomas did. He was dead before he hit the floor."

My throat constricted. "Still smiling." My voice came out in a dry whisper, and Kane squeezed my hand.

"Did you know him?" he asked gently.

"No. But he seemed like a really nice guy. So young..." I swallowed. "So is Fuzzy Bunny expecting an emergency landing at Calgary? Or was Yana planning to double-cross them and use her 'emergency' to divert to a different airport and a different buyer?"

"That's the million-dollar question."

We eyed each other in silence.

I sighed. "Do we really care?"

Kane looked affronted. "Of course we care. We're not just going to give up."

"No, I didn't mean that." I eyed him cautiously. "Mind you, I hope you realize that you're going to have to be the one who lands this thing. I suck at video games. I can't see how this will be any easier."

"Oh, sure, make it my responsibility." He grinned, and I wondered if he was as scared as I was. Probably not. This was probably all in a day's work for him.

I recalled the naked appeal in his eyes when he'd kissed me. Or maybe not...

I dragged my attention back to the conversation at hand. "What I meant was, if we do manage to land, what does it matter whether Fuzzy Bunny knows Yana's dead and we know about the weapon? Maybe it's better if we broadcast a distress call to the world. That way if we survive, they won't dare try to get the prototype from the plane."

"True, but I want both." The predatory glint was back in his eyes. "I want to deliver the prototype weapon to Sirius for testing, and I want to nail Fuzzy Bunny for smuggling it into the country."

"Well, they're nailed anyway," I pointed out. "The weapon is on their corporate jet. They can hardly deny that."

Kane shook his head. "They can claim they knew nothing about it and Yana was acting alone. And it'll blow my cover for sure and probably yours, too. Nobody will believe an unarmed bookkeeper and an unarmed oil and gas consultant managed to kill two operatives." He hesitated. "Tidily, I might add... despite the operatives being armed with a devastating new weapon. It won't fly."

He grimaced. "And I'd like to rephrase that to something that doesn't include the word 'fly'."

He fell silent, drumming his fingers on the armrest and staring into space. "Okay, let's look at this from the other end," he said at last. "Whether or not there's another buyer is irrelevant. What matters to us is what Fuzzy Bunny is expecting."

He held up two fingers. "Two possibilities." He ticked off the first one on his forefinger. "One, if they're expecting an emergency landing, it means they'd plan to remove the bodies and the weapon under the cover of the emergency response. The runway would be swarming with vehicles and personnel if there was the possibility of a crash, and it would be easy to slip things by in the chaos if they had somebody on the inside."

"Or; two..." I added. "They're expecting a smooth, normal landing that doesn't attract attention, and the weapon would be removed from the plane in the service cart, probably with the excuse of restocking the bar. So they'd have somebody on the inside at food and beverage services."

"Except how would they explain the bodies?" Kane asked.

"Maybe they weren't expecting bodies. Maybe Yana planned to keep you on a string. If I hadn't been here, nothing would have happened. And Thomas would still be alive." My throat closed again.

"No," Kane said firmly. "Parr told you to be on the plane, so he would have notified Yana. If she knew you were working with Fuzzy Bunny, she wouldn't have any reason to kill you. And you had no way of knowing the weapon was on the plane unless she used it."

"Well, there's the answer."

We stared at each other for a moment before speaking simultaneously. "She had another buyer."

Kane sprang to his feet to pace. "She was going to double-cross Parr. He thought... thinks... this will be a routine flight to Calgary and the weapon will be removed by their contact in food services. But she planned to call in an 'emergency' and land at a different airport, where she'd be met by a chaotic emergency scene that would let her slip away with the weapon. Maybe even toss an incendiary device as she left, to destroy both the bodies and the plane."

We grinned at each other in triumph until reality filtered through.

"So..." I hesitated. "You're saying we can't call for help."

CHAPTER 44

Kane sank back into his seat. "Not if we want to nail them." He frowned. "You realize this is big, Aydan. It's a major airport security breach if they've been smuggling weapons via food services. We have to find a way to tell Dermott. Even if we crash and the weapon is destroyed, he needs to know about that leak."

Fear seized me all over again, and I fought to hold my voice steady. "Well, the radio's out, then. Even if we knew how to use it, they'll probably be listening." Inspiration struck. "How about one of Sirius's secured phones?" I was already on my feet when Kane demurred.

"It probably won't work. The secured system uses a ground-based cellular network. We're up high and moving fast."

"We could try it, though." I hesitated. "Our secured phones shouldn't interfere with the autopilot, should they?"

Kane shrugged. "You know more about computers and electronics than I do."

"I haven't a clue."

We eyed each other in silence. He extracted a phone from his pocket. "Should I try it?"

"What if it turns the autopilot off?"

We both stared at the phone as if it was a live grenade.

"It shouldn't," I added uncertainly. "They couldn't make the system that fragile. If it was, the commercial flights would confiscate everybody's cell phones before they got on board-"

Before I could finish my sentence, he nodded and pushed the button. My breath caught in my throat, but the steady roar of the engines didn't falter.

"It's ringing," he said. "...Dermott, it's Kane. Dermott! ...damn!" He lowered the phone to scowl at it. "It dropped the call."

"Try again!"

He lobbed the phone in the direction of the garbage receptacle. "Secured phone. Single contact only. That one's done."

"Do you have any more?"

"In my luggage. Not with me. You?"

"One in my purse." I headed for the sitting room, stepping callously over Yana's sprawled body and trying not to look at Thomas. Sinking into the seat I'd occupied, I dragged the purse onto my lap and extracted the phone.

Weighing it in my hand, I shot a look up at Kane, who had followed me in to lean against the wall. "Do you think we should waste it?"

He shrugged. "We might as well. The only way to slow down and get closer to the ground is to turn off the autopilot..." He didn't finish the sentence, and I clenched my teeth and pressed the button.

A garbled crackle that might have been a ring. Then another. The phone's case emitted a small creak under my clenched fingers. A final crackle, then silence.

"Hello?" I raised my voice, futility seeping into my skin

even as I did. "Hello! Dermott! Hello!"

A couple more staticky crackles, then nothing.

I got up and quietly dropped the phone into the garbage before returning to my seat.

Silence fell until I tried again. "There must be a satellite phone or something on board."

"Probably, but it wouldn't be secure." Kane frowned. "How about internet? A high-end plane like this must have satellite internet. You could..." His face fell. "No, I guess you couldn't. There's no brainwave-driven network."

My heart leaped. "But I have the portable generator and my network keys!" I sprang up to excavate my waist pouch.

"You brought the generator and keys on Fuzzy Bunny's private jet?" Kane's question held an 'are-you-nuts' inflection.

I grinned and held up the items in question. "Yep. You called it when you said Dermott's reckless. He made me bring them."

Kane blew out a breath, his shoulders relaxing. "I'm glad I didn't know that until now, but that's good news because I was completely out of ideas. Now we can secretly notify Dermott and call for help at the same time..." He trailed off, obviously noticing the dismay dawning on my face. "What?"

"Um. About that good news." My voice came out in a dry croak. "I don't suppose... you have another laptop?"

His eyes widened and he stared at the mangled electronic remains at his feet. His voice was almost as hoarse as mine. "You mean... you don't?"

"No. Mine got lost at the hotel."

"Oh." The word came out on a whoosh of breath as if he'd been punched in the stomach.

We stared at each other in silence.

My knees began to quiver, and I sank into one of the soft leather seats. "Well, then."

Kane sighed. "Well, then." He stared blankly at the service cart. "No scotch." He extracted a bottle of brandy instead and reached for a glass before shrugging and taking a swig directly from the bottle. "Drink?"

"Beer."

He handed it over, and I steadied the bottle with both trembling hands while I slugged back a few swallows in silence. Kane stood staring at nothing, the brandy bottle dangling from his hand.

"We'll have to call it in on the radio in about an hour and a half," he said finally. "We can't contact Dermott or mention Sirius; there are too many covert operations at stake. We'll just have to report that we've been hijacked and the pilots are dead. If we survive, we'll report the weapons and the security leak in person. If we don't..." He shrugged and took another drink of brandy.

I swallowed some more beer. "Do you know how to use the radio? I've never even seen one close-up."

"No, but it's probably not much different than a field set. I'll go and have a look."

He straightened and turned for the front of the plane, and I rose to hurry along with him. Somehow I wasn't in the mood for the company of dead people.

The cockpit wasn't an improvement.

The pilot and co-pilot slumped to opposite sides, their heads resting against the windows like slumbering passengers. Kane handed me the brandy bottle and dragged the bodies out before turning to study the ranks of buttons and screens.

I leaned around him to peer at the complex

instrumentation, renewed dread rising. "Um... not to be a downer or anything, but... I think the movies might have made it look a little more possible than it really is."

"Aydan." Kane turned, his face softening. "Look, I'm not going to sugar-coat this..."

"Don't say it," I begged. "I already know."

He sighed, and I stepped against him to hide my face in his broad chest. His arms closed around me and he pressed his lips against my hair while he held me as if his arms alone could protect me from the bonds of gravity.

I pulled away after a long moment despite the temptation to just stay in his arms until the plane fell out of the sky. Feigning intent interest in the control systems while I pulled myself together, I studied the screens and seats and pedals.

"*What's that?*"

Kane's gaze snapped around to follow the direction of my shaking finger. "What? Is that...?"

I swooped down on the smooth, slim object tucked beside the pilot's seat. "It's a tablet computer!" The sleek device trembled in my hands. "It has a USB port, thank God! Oh, please, God, let it be charged..."

The screen bloomed to life, its vibrant colours more beautiful than heaven itself. Kane and I exchanged a single wide-eyed glance before hurrying back to the cabin with our prize.

I sank into the nearest seat, barely breathing while I balanced the tablet on my knees and plugged in the network generator.

I looked up at Kane. "Wish me luck."

He stooped and kissed me hard. "For luck."

Drawing a breath to replace the one he'd just stolen, I

closed my eyes and concentrated on the network.

I wasn't sure if it was a true sensation or just my knowledge that the data signal was bouncing out into space and back again, but the data tunnel felt dark and barren as I rushed along it. A moment later the bustling vastness of the internet spread out before me and I dove into it like a dolphin riding the waves.

Bobbing up in buoyant relief, I tethered myself in the data flow and took my time spreading out dozens of tiny markers before turning back to share the good news with Kane.

"...Aydan! Goddammit! *Aydan!*"

My eyes snapped open to see Kane hovering above me, his face taut with the closest thing to fear I'd ever seen him display.

"I'm okay."

"Thank God!" He crushed me in his arms, pressing his lips against my hair. "Thank God. I thought... Thank God."

I hugged him. "I'm sorry. I forgot I was wearing the new key."

He said nothing, just held me tighter.

"I'm sorry." I gave him a squeeze before pulling away gently. "Jack and I did some more testing on the new key. It's about a four to one ratio of network access time to unconsciousness. I was so eager to get into the network it never even occurred to me that I was wearing the new one."

His composure didn't seem to be returning as easily as usual. He nodded wordlessly and released me. As I sat up, the sight of the tablet lying on the floor sent a chill of fear through me.

"Oh, God, John, I didn't break it, did I?"

He turned to follow the direction of my gaze. "I haven't a

clue. I didn't even look at it." His voice was still hoarse, and he rose as if using the last of his strength to reclaim the brandy bottle and take a longish swallow.

I could almost feel the alcohol burning my own throat when he croaked, "Please use your other key from now on."

"I will." I reached for the tablet with trembling hands. "Assuming the network generator still works."

The tablet looked all right. I gingerly set it on the floor beside the seat and unstrapped the new wristwatch to exchange it for my old one. Absorbed in fumbling with the strap, I started when Kane touched my arm.

"Don't go yet."

I glanced up worriedly, but he had regained his usual calm. "Now that we know you can do it, let's take a few minutes to organize our thoughts. I can't communicate with you while you're in the network, so you'll be doing all the work." His hand clenched. "I'll just be sitting here doing nothing."

"No, you'll be..." I groped for something encouraging to say. "...here to help me with the pain when I come out. I really missed you last week."

His frown eased. "Thanks." He opened his mouth as if to speak, but apparently thought better of what he'd intended to say. He stepped over to kneel near Yana's body instead, examining the fallen weapon without touching it.

I went to hunker down on the other side, carefully avoiding the business end.

On examination, it didn't look quite as much like the white glass bottle I'd mistaken it for, but it was still close enough to hide in a group of other bottles. There was even a threaded ring on the neck end that looked like a bottle cap. The end of it was flipped up, revealing what looked like a lens beneath.

"Sighting system," Kane muttered, hunching down to peer through it. "I can't tell if there's a trigger, though." He sat back, frowning. "There must be a way to activate the beam or ray or whatever it is. Can you see any irregularity? It just looks like a smooth cylinder to me."

"It looks smooth to me, too. But maybe it's something to do with the... I don't know what to call it... muzzle?" I pointed at the silvery bottom. "That's the end she was pointing at Thomas. Maybe it's automatic when a target is acquired?"

"That doesn't make sense. You couldn't carry it around if it automatically beamed out a death ray every time it acquired a target."

"Yeah, I guess you're right." I pressed my cheek against the carpet to peek through the lens. "And it must have some kind of built-in power supply. So it couldn't be on all the time or it would run down." I shot a nervous glance at the muzzle, pointed at the side of the seat. "Do you think it's on now?"

Kane's lips twisted. "Who knows? And I'm not planning to put my hand in front of it and find out."

"Well, we can't just leave it here. What if we hit turbulence and it starts rolling around?"

"Good point." He frowned. "It must have been safe enough in the beverage cart. Yana didn't seem nervous when Thomas brought our champagne."

I drew a breath of relief. "Right. So if we close the top and hold it by the neck the way she did and just put it back in the cart, it should be fine."

I reached for it, but Kane grabbed my hand. "I don't want to compromise any evidence. If there are fingerprints or anything else on it, we need to preserve them." He rose and moved to the closet to delve into his coat pockets. "Lucky it's winter where we're going."

He pulled on his leather gloves and squatted beside the weapon again. "Stand behind me. Just in case."

Pulse pounding, I obeyed, holding my breath while he carefully closed the cap and stood the weapon among the other bottles in the serving cart once again.

We both exhaled when it clinked into place without incident. Kane returned his gloves to his bag, and we sank into the soft leather seats again.

"All right," Kane said. "So give Dermott as much information as you can about the weapon and tell him our theory about Parr's smuggling operation. And maybe he can find somebody to give us some pointers for landing. Although..." The lines of strain tightened in his face. "I don't know how they could do that without using the radio. And you can't talk to me when you're in the network." He blew out a breath. "Maybe Webb can figure something out."

My heart clenched.

"What?" Kane demanded. "What is it?"

"Spider doesn't work there anymore." My voice was a bare whisper. "He got fired."

CHAPTER 45

I sank my head into my hands. "God, we're so fucked. I don't even know if I can get to Sirius and back again. I might get lost in the internet and you'll never know. You'll just be sitting here with my zombie body until the plane falls out of the sky."

Kane's arms closed around me. "That won't happen." He gave me a little shake. "It won't happen," he repeated. "You always find a way. And if you get lost, I'll guide you back." He smiled. "I'll search for camels."

After a lengthy and convoluted trip, I found the Sirius network and made my usual nerve-shattering trip through the chaotic tumble of data. By the time I slid into the familiar file repository after five tries, I had to fight the urge to curl up in the corner and tremble invisibly for a while.

Instead, I pushed my avatar into a visible form and fired off an email to Dermott: "Meet me in the virtual file room, now! Emergency!"

Then I waited.

Paced.

Dammit, where the hell was he? Everybody in Sirius had to carry a security fob, and I knew his would contain the built-in brainwave modulator that would get him into the virtual reality network. He should be able to appear instantly from anywhere in the building.

A sudden fear seized me and I checked the system time. Goddammit, Vegas was in a different time zone. In Silverside, it was nearly five o'clock on a Friday afternoon.

Shit, shit, shit!

Without much hope, I sent a slightly politer version of the same distress call to Jack and Germain, the only other people with a high enough security clearance to know about my project.

Jack would likely be home with her kids already. Germain... who knew? He might have even gone back to Calgary. With nobody to guard in the network, he wouldn't have any reason to stay.

I groaned aloud. How could I come this far only to fail?

What if I emailed Spider?

I considered that for a moment, but there wasn't much point. He had no access to Sirius, and if Dermott was already gone for the weekend, Spider wouldn't be able to find him anyway.

Despair trickled into my veins, and I slid slowly down the virtual wall to sit on the floor, my forehead pressed to my drawn-up knees. Alone in an abandoned network. I hadn't realized how much hope I'd been nurturing until it was snuffed out.

I clenched my fists in my hair. Dammit, I wouldn't quit. At least I could file reports on the weapon and the security leak. Even if nobody found them until long after Kane and I were greasy smears on the runway, that information could still help somebody else.

I was hauling myself to my feet when the door burst open and Jack, Germain, and Dermott dashed in.

The deluge of renewed hope almost swept me away. Tears burned the backs of my eyes as my heart leaped up from my toes to pound a triumphant tattoo against my ribs.

"What the hell, Kelly?" Dermott snapped.

"We have the prototype weapon." My words tumbled out. "But we're trapped on a plane and the pilots are dead and we can't fly." I made an attempt to untangle my narrative. "I mean, the autopilot is working but we don't know how to land-"

"What kind of plane?"

"What's the weapon?"

Germain and Dermott spoke simultaneously. Germain shot a look at Dermott. "Plane first. We need to keep them in the air."

Dermott nodded, and Germain's keen eyes focused on me again. "What kind of plane, Aydan?"

"A jet." At his frown, I blurted, "I don't know! It's white with a blue stripe..." I shook myself and drew a deep breath. "It's Parr's private jet. Or one of them, anyway. It's big, about the size of a regular passenger jet, with the cockpit in front... oh, Jesus, I know they all do, sorry... then some closets and a front cabin and a big sitting room and another cabin and a bathroom and bedroom in the back-"

"It's okay, Aydan, never mind," Germain said gently. "How long have you been in the air? When are you scheduled to land?"

"We've been up for less than an hour. We aren't scheduled to land for another couple of hours. Carl..." I hesitated, not sure I wanted to know the answer. "Will the autopilot... turn off? Is it programmed to do that?"

"No. Autopilot has to be manually disengaged."

"Oh thank God." I was about to slither down the wall

again when I remembered I was in a sim. With a wave of my hand I conjured up a chair and dropped into it. A moment later I realized my rudeness, and waved three more chairs into existence.

"Okay," Dermott said as he sat. "So we've got time. Good. Give me a full report."

I reeled off a blow-by-blow of the action and our deductions as quickly as possible, and took advantage of our virtual reality environment to create a simulation of the weapon.

Dermott leaned in to peer without touching it, as Kane had done. "How realistic is this simulation, Kelly? Any guts in it?"

"I don't know what the guts would be, but don't get in front of it. We're in a virtual reality sim. If any of us expects it to work..."

Dermott recoiled. "Shit. Get rid of it."

I waved it out of existence and leaned back with a sigh. "So I guess that's it until we have to try to land the plane."

Germain turned to Dermott. "We need a list of Parr's fleet and the flight plans for whatever they've got in the sky today so we can figure out what they're flying. And we'll need to contact the Calgary airport-"

"No," I interrupted. "We can't let them know there's anything wrong. That's why we didn't radio for help. We figure Fuzzy Bunny is monitoring all the transmissions, and we're pretty sure they have somebody planted inside the airport's secured perimeter. Probably food and beverage services, and who knows what else. If they find out things aren't going according to their plan, they'll just vanish."

"I'm sorry, Aydan, we have to notify the airport," Germain said. He hesitated. "I hate to say this, but your chances aren't good. It takes a lot of skill to land any aircraft, and the size of jet you're describing..." Jack squeezed his arm as if to silence him, her face white, and he shook his head before turning back to me. "Sorry, I have to say it. If we can find out what you're flying, I can probably guide you through the landing procedures-"

"Wait, you're a jet pilot?" I demanded.

He gave his usual self-deprecating shrug and nod. "Transport specialist. If it rolls, floats, or flies, I've probably driven or piloted it at least once."

I clutched my chest. "Thank God!"

He gave me a long look, his dark eyes filled with compassion. "But, Aydan, even if I give you instructions over the radio, your chances of landing successfully are slim. It would be criminally negligent not to notify the airport of an impending crash. If they know something's wrong, they'll clear the runways. If they don't, hundreds of innocent people could die with you. I'm sorry."

I groaned. "God, I wish the pilot was still alive. He was so good I never even felt it when we touched down yesterday. He probably could've surfed the net with one hand and landed the plane with the other."

"Yeah..." Germain's head jerked up. "Wait. What did you say?"

My pulse quickened under his intent gaze. "I said he probably could've-"

"Did he have a tablet computer? In the cockpit?"

"Yes." I swallowed, afraid to even wish. "Is that good?"

"Maybe. Maybe not." He made an equivocating gesture, but hope had ignited his eyes. "It might mean the aircraft has a computer control system. A lot of pilots use tablets to plot their courses, and sometimes the tablet software can communicate with the onboard system." He sprang up to pace. "If I had a way to access that... damn, but I don't know how I could. Maybe if you could tell me what was onscreen... but then we'd need a radio connection and that would blow your cover. Dammit!"

Inspiration exploded in my brain. I spun to face Dermott. "Get Spider! Hire him back! Offer him whatever it takes, but get him back, now! He can hack into the computer in the plane and Carl can fly us home!"

Dermott didn't hesitate. With a single nod, he launched out of his chair and sprinted for the portal.

"Aydan." Germain laid a gentle hand on my arm. "I don't want to be a wet blanket, but the tablet might not mean anything. And even if there is a computer control system, the interface might not work. And if I'm not actually in the cockpit..."

I tried to tamp down my hope and failed. "But even if the plane doesn't have computer control, most tablets have webcams. At least if we end up having to do it ourselves, we could put the webcam in the pilot's seat so you could see what we see."

He hesitated. "That might help," he agreed quietly.

I chose not to consider what that pause meant. "While we wait for Spider, I'm going to go back and tell John what we're doing so he doesn't worry." When Germain's brow furrowed, I gave him an imploring look. "I know you don't want to get our hopes up, but what harm can it do? In a couple of hours, we might be dead. We might as well enjoy a little hope while we can."

He nodded and gave me a smile that didn't reach his eyes. "You're right." He gave me a quick hug. "Go tell Kane."

Back in the internet, I retraced my path with slow determination, leaving my tiny markers in place and ignoring the frightened little voice that tried to convince me I might never find the Sirius servers again. Winding through labyrinthine data tunnels, I held my concentration steady, alert for the slightest whisper of camels.

And at last, there it was.

I raced down the pathway to my goal.

"Aaah! Jesus! Sonuvabitch!" When I stepped out the portal, the familiar agony seemed even more outrageous after the wonderful painlessness of the new key. I writhed and swore until Kane's strong hands locked around my temples, extinguishing the pain.

I went limp and pried my eyes open. "Thank you. You have no idea how much I missed that."

He smiled, but the expression had to fight its way past the tense lines in his face. "Did you get through?"

"Yes." I sat up. "We might have some good news."

"I could use some."

I gave him a smile. "I just got Spider re-hired. And the plane might be computer-controlled, and if I can bring Spider in through the network, he might be able to hook it up to Sirius, and if he can, Carl might be able to land the plane for us."

"Those are a lot of 'might's and 'if's."

But some of the tension went out of his shoulders nonetheless.

I squeezed his hand. "I have to go back to Sirius now. I hope it won't take Dermott long to get Spider there, but I don't know how long it'll take me to find Sirius again. I might be a while."

"All right. I'll keep doing the camel searches."

He sounded as calm and confident as ever, but a tiny inflection in his voice suddenly reminded me how horrible it must be for him to be forced to sit doing nothing, surrounded by dead people and watching my oblivious body while he waited to die in a plane crash.

I laid a hand on his. "I didn't get my kiss for luck last time," I said softly. "I could use one."

"So could I." His arms closed around me and his lips met mine in a slow, gentle kiss.

A kiss that gave instead of taking. No demand or expectation behind it. A kiss that could stop time itself.

He broke the kiss to gather me in, tucking me close to his heart. His lips moved against my hair. "Good luck."

I tightened my arms around him before pulling away.

"Thanks." I slipped back into the network without meeting his eyes.

It took a long, long time to find my way back to Sirius in spite of my markers. When I finally burst into the file repository after four shattering attempts, I could only lie curled in a trembling ball, abjectly grateful for my invisibility while I shook with tearless sobs.

I allowed myself only a few moments before yanking my emotions back under control. Rising, I drew a deep breath and faded into visibility.

"Aydan!" Spider flung himself at me, hugging me fiercely. "Oh, Aydan..."

His greeting undid me completely, and I made good use of virtual reality to banish my tears to invisibility.

"Hey, Spider," I said when I thought I could trust my voice. "Good to have you back."

I gently disengaged myself from his hug to take stock. The sim had been furnished while I had been lost in the internet. Germain was barely visible behind a bank of computer screens. Jack had her own desk and computer, and when she looked up her eyes burned like blue flames above her stark white cheeks.

Spider slid behind a third desk littered with computer gear and within seconds he was riveted to his screen while he typed furiously.

Dermott stood to the side, feet widely planted, arms crossed, but not as if in anger. He looked more like a man physically restraining himself from rushing into some kind of action.

Germain looked up from his monitors. "Welcome back," he said. "Webb's got me patched into the Calgary control tower."

He made a 'calm-down' gesture as my eyes widened. "Without their knowledge," he added. "I've pulled specs and flight simulator data for your aircraft. The good news is, it's a 737." He hesitated, apparently realizing the model would mean nothing to me. "It's one I can fly," he said instead. "The bad news is, I've never flown that specific model, and we can't bring in a qualified pilot even if we could find one in time because..." He waved a hand at our virtual file room and grimaced. "Well, classified. Obviously. And, uh... its base model doesn't have the kind of computer control I was hoping for."

I felt the blood drain from my face, and he hastened to add, "But it's a custom build and Webb is still tracking down the manufacturer's as-built drawings. Don't give up hope yet."

"Got it," Spider rapped out. "Over to you now."

Germain vanished behind his screens again. A moment later he hissed a fierce, "Yes!" When he looked up, his eyes blazed with triumph. "It's got the upgraded module! Get on it, Webb. Get me in."

Spider rose, looking worried. "I don't know how this is going to work, Aydan. I need you to carry me along the network like you did before so I can get to the tablet operating system. Then you'll have to get out of the network at that end so you can plug the tablet into the plane's computer control module. And I don't know if I'll get kicked out of the network when you leave. Probably."

"Then it's too dangerous," I snapped.

Spider shook his head, opening his mouth, but I overrode him. "I'm not going to do it. You're our only hope and I'm not going to take a chance on losing you somewhere in the network. I'll go back now and get the tablet plugged in and then come and get you." I turned to Germain. "Tell me what to do."

Despite Spider's protests, everyone ganged up to overrule him, and a few moments later Germain had shown me what to do using his simulation.

"Back in a flash," I promised, and dove back into the network.

The return trip was a little easier since the internet connections hadn't had as much time to shift. I stepped back into my physical body again, spitting violent profanity and clutching my skull.

Kane had barely begun massaging my temples when I pulled away to drag myself to my feet and stumble toward the cockpit.

"We have a plan," I threw over my shoulder as Kane hurried behind me. "I just need to plug the tablet into the plane's control system, and then I can go back and bring Spider through the network to hack into it."

He stopped my hand as I reached to connect the cable. "That won't override the autopilot, will it?"

I froze. "I... don't think so." I eyed the plug fearfully. "Carl would have said something if it was going to... wouldn't he? He said the autopilot had to be manually overridden."

"But what if there's something on the tablet that overrides it?"

My hand began to tremble and I scowled at it, willing it to steady. "Carl would have warned us if there was." I drew a deep breath. "But maybe you should sit in the co-pilot's seat just in case. If the autopilot turns off, you should be able to just hold all the pedals and levers and stuff right where they are and we'll keep on flying. Right?"

"Right," Kane said grimly, and slid into the seat, poising his hands and feet. "Do it."

CHAPTER 46

I clenched my teeth and plugged the cable into the cockpit computer module.

Nothing happened.

Kane and I both sagged with relief.

"Okay," I croaked, and sat abruptly on the floor when my knees gave out. I shuffled backward on my butt to prop myself against the bulkhead behind me, pretending I'd meant to do that. "I'm going to get Spider now," I said. "I'll have to use his network key, so don't worry when I pass out."

"Thanks for the warning, but I'll worry anyway." He slid out of the seat to kneel beside me. "Good luck."

His arms closed around me, and I stepped back into the network before I could cling to him.

The trip back wasn't any easier. I found the Sirius servers more quickly this time, but my frazzled consciousness couldn't breach them. Time and again I threw myself into the violent turbulence only to be repulsed and terrifyingly scrambled.

At last, I huddled at the edge of maelstrom, my non-existent heart galloping beneath breaths that would have been sobs if I'd had a body. I hugged my data bits closer as if to coalesce into a black hole of despair.

So close.

So damn close.

Everybody at Sirius poised to help. Kane holding steady with lion-hearted courage on a doomed airplane.

And me, useless me, crouched in defeated and terrified limbo.

My incompetence would kill Kane. I couldn't go back and face him.

But I couldn't hide like a coward in the network, waiting for my existence to wink out while he plummeted to his death accompanied only by my unresponsive body.

Sudden deep anger flooded me. I hadn't signed on for this shit. I hadn't asked to be responsible for someone else's life. Or someone else's death. I hadn't volunteered to be beaten and tortured and terrified, and I sure as *hell* hadn't volunteered to be some repulsive cyber-mole, grubbing around in the sordid tunnels of the internet and never seeing the light of day.

And there was no damn way I was going to let the peaceful life I'd planned and worked for be torn away, defiled and discarded by a bunch of criminal assholes. No, goddammit, those fuckers weren't getting my life!

And they weren't getting Kane's either.

My boiling consciousness whirled into a nuclear warhead of white-hot rage and punched through the servers as if they were tissue paper.

My imagery was unfortunate.

I tumbled into thunderous noise and chaos, jerking into a ball until the din faded and no more debris fell from the sky. Then I slowly uncurled and dragged myself to my feet in the wreckage of the virtual file room.

"*Shit!*" I snapped a terrified glance around the rubble.

"Spider! Carl! Jack!"

"What the *fuck*, Kelly!" Dermott rose from a heap of debris, spitting dust and ire.

"I'm okay," Spider quavered, emerging from under the remains of his desk.

"Me, too," Germain seconded, rolling off Jack from where he had apparently thrown himself to protect her with his body. "Jack, are you all right?"

"I'm fine."

I hadn't thought she could get paler, but I'd been wrong. Her skin was nearly transparent.

"Fix this shit!" Dermott snapped.

"I'm sorry..." I stared helplessly at the destruction.

"It's okay," Spider said hurriedly. "I'll just roll back the sim." A moment later, the desks and computers miraculously restored themselves, and my jelly-like legs gave way entirely.

"What the fuck, Kelly?" Dermott repeated.

"I'm sorry." I looked up at him from my seat on the floor. "If I leave from this network, I can get back in just fine, but when I'm coming in from outside, it's really hard. I couldn't get through. And then I... kind of... um, overdid it."

He scowled. "No shit."

"Are you all right?" Jack came over to kneel beside me. "You look terrible."

I didn't bother to return the compliment. "I'm fine. Let's go, Spider." I hesitated. "If you're still okay with it..."

"Of course I am." He didn't look as certain as he sounded. "Just carry me along like you did before. When we get there, though, I might need to control you. And don't forget, we'll have to come back here when I'm done."

I bolstered my courage with the smouldering remains of

my anger. "Okay, let's go. Take my hand."

We slipped into the network, and cold dread seized me.

My markers had shifted again.

Questing back along my path, I clung to the best semblance of certainty I could muster. I didn't think Spider would intentionally read my mind, but if he did by accident, I didn't want to share the fear that gnawed at me.

Just find the next marker.

And the next.

And the next.

At last, a thin stream of camel searches trickled across my path, and I blessed Kane's homing beacon.

Then we were rushing through the long, dark tunnel into space and back. At the end of the tunnel, the network generator's portal looked like the gates of heaven to me. Now, let Spider do his work.

Seized by sudden immobility, I fought panic.

This was good. This was right. Spider was doing what he needed to do.

Stay calm.

A tornado of claustrophobic terror battered me. Trapped! Imprisoned in endless limbo...

I clung to control.

Stay calm.

Calm.

I lost track of time while I concentrated all my will on remaining still and pliant under Spider's control.

At last the terrifying sensation lifted and we rocketed back toward Sirius, the data tunnels gloriously easy to navigate under Spider's guiding presence. The passage through Sirius's servers was barely a blip, and a moment later we stood in the virtual file room again.

Spider dropped my hand and blinked back into visibility. I followed his lead and stood panting and shaking, struggling to regain my composure while he hurried to his desk and dropped into the chair, his fingers flying across the keyboard.

"I'm in," he said a few minutes later. "Patching you into the system now." He looked up. "Carl? Have you got it?"

A slow smile spread over Germain's face. "Got it. Looks like a direct interface."

"So..." My voice trembled, and I cleared my throat. "So what does that really mean?"

Germain sobered. "Well, it means I can control the aircraft through its computer interface. IFR only, of course."

"What does that mean?"

"It means I can only use the instruments, I can't actually see where I'm going."

I swallowed. "That can't be good."

He gave me a reassuring smile. "It's not as scary as it sounds. Most commercial flights are IFR."

"But... can you land it like that?"

His smiled slipped. "Technically, yes."

"Wait, hang on a sec," Spider mumbled, tapping busily at his keyboard. "How about..." A few more keystrokes. "...this?"

He turned his monitor toward us.

Germain frowned. "What? That looks like the ceiling of a cockpit."

"It is." Spider grinned. "I just hacked into the webcam on the tablet. When Aydan gets back into her body, she can point the tablet out the front windshield so you can see forward."

Germain relaxed. "Nice. That will help. Okay, Aydan, here's the deal." He glanced at his watch. "In exactly one hour from now, I'm going to disengage the autopilot and begin a descent." He paused. "Hey, Webb, can you do two-way communication on that thing so I can talk to them in the cockpit as well?"

"I can." Spider's brow furrowed. "But I'd rather not. I want all available bandwidth to your control systems. If our internet connection is compromised..." He pressed his lips shut, but I got the picture.

Germain blew out a breath. "Okay. In an hour I'll start the descent, so don't be afraid when the engine noise changes and you start to go down. If you can point the webcam to the front, that'll help, but I want one of you in the co-pilot's seat just in case I need you to do something. I'll communicate with you via the tablet if that's the case."

"I've set it up so the tablet will display what the webcam is seeing," Spider put in. "Just point the tablet forward so you can see on the tablet what you want Carl to see here."

I nodded, afraid to trust my voice.

"I'm going to be communicating with the tower as if I'm the pilot," Germain continued. "A few minutes out of the airport, I'm going to report smoke in the cabin. That will give us priority landing sequence and alert them that they might have an emergency situation on their hands. It'll give them a chance to scramble the emergency equipment and clear the runway."

Dermott spoke for the first time. "That can also be our excuse for the bodies. I'll arrange for a coverup with the autopsy reports anyway, but if you can safely generate some smoke before you leave the plane, do it. It'll make the coverup easier if the emergency response team finds some smoke. Take the weapon with you when you abandon the aircraft. I don't think you'll get searched if it's an emergency landing, but even if you do, you should be able to just carry it out. Nobody will suspect it's a weapon."

"One more thing." Germain hesitated. "There's a chinook blowing into Calgary right now, so it'll probably be a bumpy ride. Don't be scared; it's just normal turbulence."

"Great." My voice came out in a croak. "Fabulous."

Silence fell.

"Everybody clear?" Dermott asked. "Kelly?"

I drew a deep breath. "I think so. But, Spider, you're saying I can't come back through the network again?"

"Not unless you absolutely have to. I don't want to take a chance on disrupting Carl's control of the plane."

Another deep breath. "So we won't have any way to communicate with you from here on in."

"No, you can talk to the webcam," he said. "It'll be running the whole time anyway, so we'll see and hear everything that's going on in the cockpit. It's just that I don't want any extra communication unless it's absolutely necessary."

"Oh, good." I eased out a sigh and hesitated. "Well... thanks, you guys. If anything happens, I just want you to know-"

"We'll see you in a few hours," Germain interrupted firmly.

I shoved a smile onto my face. "Sounds good. See you later."

"Good luck, Aydan." Spider hurried over to hug me, and Jack did the same, her eyes brimming with unshed tears.

"Good luck." Her voice trembled.

"Thanks." My own voice wavered on the edge of control.

"Get the hell out of here, Kelly, you're using up the bandwidth," Dermott growled. I straightened, and he gave me a hard look. "Get your ass back here in one piece."

I nodded and vanished before my face could betray me.

CHAPTER 47

Alone again in the data tunnels, I crept back the way I'd come, retrieving my markers and concentrating on the route. Most of the connections Spider and I had used in our headlong flight were still available, and I made my way back to the network generator's portal with relative ease, guided home by Kane's steady searches.

"...Aydan... come on, Aydan..."

I dragged a leaden arm up to restrain the hand that was gently patting my cheek. When I opened my eyes, Kane's face whirled sickeningly above me and I clamped my eyes shut again.

"'M'okay," I mumbled. "Just... a minute..."

Safely back. Thank God.

Well, as safe as one can be in a plane with dead pilots.

I drew a deep breath and pried my eyes open again. As soon as the spinning stopped, I struggled to my feet. "It worked. We're connected, and they can see and hear us through the tablet. Now we just have to point the tablet forward so Carl can see where he's flying."

Kane eased out a breath. "So he's flying the plane now?"

"Not yet. We're still on autopilot. He'll start our descent in..." I consulted my watch. "Just under an hour."

Kane leaned over the pilot's seat, where the tablet lay. "And they can see us through this thing?" He picked it up and tilted it so his own face appeared on the screen. "Hey, Germain, thanks for the lift. See you in a few hours." He grinned at his reflection before laying the tablet back on the seat. "Okay, how can we set this thing up?"

I studied the tablet for a few moments. "I'm afraid to prop it up right in front of the window. That's not what he'd normally see from the pilot's seat." I frowned. "Is there a first-aid kit on board?"

Kane's brows snapped together. "Why, are you hurt?"

"No, but I bet there's medical tape in the kit."

"Good thinking."

In short order, we had secured the tablet to the headrest of the pilot's seat and wedged a couple of rolled-up bandages behind it to tilt it in the proper direction.

Kane stood back to survey our handiwork, hands on hips. "So that's it? That's all we need to do?"

"Until we start the descent in about three-quarters of an hour. Then you get to sit in the co-pilot's seat."

"Why me?"

I tugged him away from the cockpit, acutely aware that the team could hear everything we said. "Because you're James Bond and I'm just a bookkeeper. Come on, let's go get a drink."

In the sitting room, I offered Kane the brandy bottle, but he shook his head. "No, thanks. I don't drink and fly."

"Funny guy." I put it back on the counter and popped open a beer instead. "Lucky I don't have to do anything. I can just sit here and get snockered."

The beer wasn't as enjoyable as I'd hoped. We sat in silence, avoiding each other's eyes while I sipped without enthusiasm. Stress wound up in my shoulders.

After a few minutes I set my bottle aside. "We can't just sit here doing nothing."

Kane twitched his shoulders irritably. "All I've done is sit here doing nothing for the last hour and half. If you have any suggestions, I'd love to hear them."

The walls of the cabin seemed to close in and I sprang up, unable to stay still.

Trapped in a hurtling cylinder of impending death. Absolutely powerless.

My pulse bounded into a rapid rhythm. Yana's dead eyes seemed to watch me cynically while I paced in tight circles. Her troubles were over. Bitch.

"Aydan." Kane rose to lay his hands on my shoulders, stopping my increasingly agitated pacing. "Why don't you sit down and finish your beer?"

"Because if we actually get onto the ground in one piece, I need to be sober to drive my car." I reached for yoga breathing.

Stay calm. In. Out. Ocean waves.

Like water sloshing back and forth inside a bottle, trapped...

"Aydan, are you all right?"

I gritted my teeth. "I'm okay. I'm just..." I glanced up at him and looked away hurriedly. "I was fine while I was doing something, but now I'm... claustrophobic."

Saying it out loud made it worse. My breathing quickened, went shallow.

"Aydan!" The urgency in Kane's voice jerked my attention back to him. His hands tightened on my shoulders. "Aydan, I really need you to stay calm. Can you do that for me? Please? I hate this, too. I hate having to sit here and depend on somebody else to save me." He hesitated. "If you lose it, I... it'll make it even harder."

"I won't lose it." I spoke through my teeth. "But I really need to run... or hit something." My fists clenched at the thought. "God, I wish I knew martial arts so I could spar with you like Carl does. Blow off some steam."

Kane sounded as though he was holding onto his patience by a thin thread. "Aydan, less than an hour ago I saw you kill a man with your bare hands."

"Don't start with me! Just don't start!" I jerked loose from his grip.

He shifted his weight to the balls of his feet, giving me a dangerous grin. "Come on. Take a shot."

"No."

"I know you can," he prodded. "And after what I did to you, I deserve it. Go ahead. Hit me."

I scanned him, my raw nerves quivering under the strain. Edgy energy sizzled in the tautness of his muscles, his eyes blazing with grey fire.

He could destroy me with a single blow.

I could destroy him with a few words.

We could annihilate each other, leaving nothing but smoking ruins long before the plane crashed into the ground.

"I've got a better idea." My words came out low and breathless. I stepped forward and pulled him into a hard kiss.

He reacted instantly, yanking me against him and crushing my lips with his. My unspent adrenaline ignited in a firestorm of lust. Fumbling with the button on his pants, I body-pushed him in the direction of the bedroom.

His hands locked onto my shoulders and he held me at arm's length. "No." His voice trembled, his eyes dilated almost black. "No, I'm not going to do this again."

I gripped his arms. "Shut up and fuck me."

"Aydan." He squeezed his eyes shut before opening them again to look into my face. "It wasn't good for you last time when you didn't even know anything was wrong. I'm not going to use you now when I know you can't enjoy it."

"I knew damn well something was wrong," I snapped. "At least now I know you want me, not Yana. And the only alternative is for me to punch you, and I damn sure won't get an orgasm from that. So what have I got to lose?"

"Aydan, we've only got half an hour-"

"Give me five minutes."

"You're..." His grip on my shoulders softened, his lips quirking up. "Really? We're about to die in a plane crash and all you can think of is, you need to get laid?"

I growled and captured his lips.

Locked together, we stumbled into the bedroom. His tongue met mine, pressing into my mouth as if he couldn't wait to be inside me. I caught my breath as he pulled me one-handed against his growing hardness, his other hand slipping under my top to unhook my bra.

I unfastened my jeans, shoving them down as he transferred his grip to the front of my bra. Raising my arms, I let him pull off both T-shirt and bra in a single smooth motion.

Spider's precious velvet pouch fell, and I pulled away and knelt to scoop it up.

"Oh, don't tempt me," Kane growled. He fell to his knees behind me, his jeans rough against my ass while his hands found my breasts.

I gasped and ground against the hard ridge behind me as he rolled my nipples between his fingertips, sending electricity sizzling down to melt in the heat between my legs.

"Oh, God, John..." I reached behind me, fumbling backward at the button on his jeans.

"Wait."

When he pulled away and stood I let out a desperate whimper, my body aching with the hunger for him. I turned, kneeling in front of him, and his eyes went black with desire. I reached for his zipper but he backed away, breathing hard.

"Dammit, Aydan, I don't have another condom."

"I don't give a shit. We might be dead in an hour."

His fists clenched. "But we might not be."

I dragged myself to my feet, trembling with adrenaline and need. "John, please..."

"Check the bedside table," he rasped. "I can't... can't get close to you or I'll..."

I was already ransacking the drawers. "Thank *God!*"

I had barely turned, box in hand, when his arms were around me again. I tossed the box on the bed and pulled his shirt off, revelling in the hard planes of his massive chest and corrugated midsection.

He kissed me again, pressing my lips open, his hand cupping my breast before his mouth moved down to close over my begging nipple.

I cried out, my body hypersensitive with adrenaline. The hot need coiled up inside me and my fingertips tracked the landing strip of hair below his navel, finding his zipper to free another enormous erection.

I backed toward the bed and pulled him down with me. When I wrapped my hand around his length, he sucked in a sharp breath before gently staying my hand.

"Not this time," he rumbled. "This time it's your turn."

He kissed his way down my body, lifting my leg over his

broad shoulder. His five o'clock shadow rasped against the inside of my thigh, an electric jolt of sensation. I moaned and shivered as his hot breath caressed me.

The first delicate touch of his tongue slammed shock waves through my body and I strained up to him in helpless supplication. His hands locked around my hips, holding me while his strokes grew stronger until the world contracted to nothing but his hot mouth and the sound of my rising moans.

Then the glorious waves claimed me and I bucked helplessly against the pillows, the spasms shaking me again and again until at last I lay limp and panting.

His rumble vibrated against my skin as he paved a trail of kisses back up my body. "That's more like it."

"John..." My voice was a breathless whisper, my eyes still half-closed. "I need you... inside me... Oh, please, now..."

He rolled on the condom and paused, devouring me with hot eyes.

I didn't wait.

Pushing him onto his back, I swung astride and slid onto him without hesitation, knowing I was ready to take him as deep as he wanted to go.

He gasped as I rocked into motion, the exquisite tension building inside me already. His body matched my rhythm, meeting me to drive deeper, pushing me closer to the brink.

I arched back to ride him hard, searching for that perfect place, letting my heat spiral higher.

"Aydan!" His voice was a rough whisper. "I... need... can I...?"

I looked down into his voracious eyes. "God, yes!"

His arms closed around me, his body twisting beneath

me, and in a moment I was on my back. As he slid into me again, I wrapped my legs around him, greedy for every ounce of sensation. He groaned and slowed his rhythm to deep, powerful thrusts that drove me higher and higher, my muscles tensing around him.

"Oh... God... John... please... *yes*..." My words tumbled out between gasps, my entire being caught up in the blazing whirlwind.

An inarticulate cry wrenched from his lips, and he drove home again and again until the explosion of orgasm shattered me into brilliant shards of ecstasy. Locked in his arms, my climax spiralled still higher while he reached his own release with a few more hard thrusts, his body straining into me for long moments before slackening at last.

He collapsed and we lay panting, limp arms and legs tangled together in sweaty sheets. Eventually I regained enough breath to gasp, "That might have been a little more than five minutes."

Kane's lips turned up against my cheek and he chuckled. "Not by much." He rolled over and cuddled me close.

I tucked my head into the hollow of his shoulder, wrapping an arm around him. "God, you have no idea how much I needed that. Thank you."

If we hadn't been entwined, I might not have noticed the slight stiffening of his shoulders. His voice came out as relaxed as ever. "My pleasure. Literally."

I rolled up on my elbow to look down into his face. "What's wrong?"

"Nothing." He reached up to kiss me gently. "You blew my mind. As always." He reached over to the bedside table and dangled the little velvet pouch above his chest. "Are you going to tell me what this is? I noticed you carefully put it on the table the last time you got undressed, too."

I appropriated the small sack and smirked at him. "It's a secret."

He grinned. "Lucky I'm a spy. It's a ring, isn't it?"

I sobered, the weight of responsibility crushing me down to his chest with a long sigh. "Yes."

"An important ring." He stroked my tangled hair back from my face, eyeing me seriously.

"Yes." I laid my cheek on his chest. "Spider bought it for Linda. For a Christmas engagement. And he begged me to carry it with me. But now..."

The warm lassitude evaporated from my body, and I pulled away from Kane's embrace and got out of bed to retrieve my clothes.

"Come back to bed. We've still got time." His warm baritone rolled over me like a velvet wave of seduction, and I hesitated.

He smiled, irresistible laugh lines crinkling around his eyes, his chiselled body and tousled hair making him look like an earthbound angel from a delightfully naughty heaven.

But the small bag weighed in my hand like a sinking heart.

I sighed and pulled on my underwear, tucking the ring back into my bra.

"It's always going to be like this with you, isn't it?"

The resignation in his voice made me stop to look at him with my pants halfway up my legs.

"This." He gestured to the tangled sheets. "It doesn't mean anything to you. It's just another way to blow off steam. And then it's 'thanks for a good time', and you get dressed and walk away. Right back to Arnie."

I yanked my pants up. "I'm not going to have this

conversation. In case you forgot, we're in a bit of a fix here and in another fifteen minutes or so we have to be in the cockpit."

He rolled to his feet and disposed of the condom before pulling on his underwear. "I haven't forgotten." He reached for his pants. "I'm just saying…"

"Just don't, okay?" I pulled on my sweatshirt and secured my waist pouch around my hips.

He froze, his shirt bunched in a white-knuckled fist. "Dammit, Aydan, if not now, then when? We might have less than an hour to live. Can you please just take a few minutes to be completely honest? For once?"

"I've always been honest with you," I snapped.

He stood for a moment as if carved from stone before slowly pulling on his shirt. "Then how about being honest with yourself?"

"What the hell is that supposed to mean?"

"In the hospital, you kissed Hellhound as if nothing else mattered. When I got there the next morning, you were asleep in each other's arms as though there was no safer place in the world. You won't even stay in bed with me for five minutes, let alone sleep in my arms. When are you going to admit you're in love with him?"

I clutched a couple of handfuls of hair. "I can't believe we're having this conversation again. Look. I'm going to say this once more, slowly, and hope you get it this time. Arnie is completely fucked up. I am completely fucked up."

Kane shook his head, opening his mouth to speak, but I made a savage silencing gesture and kept talking. "Yes, I love him, but all I want from him is a casual night together every now and then. I think he loves me, but he will never trust himself enough to have a committed relationship with anyone. The only reason I let him get close is because I know he'll never want a relationship. The only reason he lets me get close is because he made me promise to shoot him if he ever lost control."

Kane's jaw dropped. I gave him a twisted smile. "So, yeah, Arnie is my safe place, and I'm his. But that's all it is, and that's all it'll ever be."

CHAPTER 48

I was turning away when Kane spoke. "Why are you so dead set against being in a relationship again?"

I turned back, weariness dragging at me. "Why do I need a reason?"

"There has to be a reason. Seeking companionship is a normal human thing. Avoiding it is-"

"Completely fucked up," I snarled. "Yeah. I thought we'd already established that. Now, can we please-"

"Aydan, that's a cop-out!" He planted his fists on his hips. "You hide behind that excuse because it means you never have to look any deeper!"

Frustration seized me. "Oh, for chrissake!" I flung my hands up and glared at him. "Fine! You want to know what my problem is? You want to know why I don't even want to think about having a relationship with you or anybody else? It's because of *this* goddamn shit!"

The hurt that twisted his face wrenched my heart. Fury at myself and at him drove the words out of my mouth. "You're exactly like my fucking ex! You use your emotions to make me do what you want; to punish me if I don't! You push and demand and corner me and I can't let that happen again, I can't get trapped in that..."

My anger vanished as quickly as it had come, and I dropped to the bed, the old terrible memories bowing my shoulders like the weight of rotting corpses.

After a short silence, Kane spoke, his voice gentle. "But, Aydan, all people have emotions. It doesn't mean they're trying to control you. Arnie has emotions, too, but you feel safe with him."

"I'll never be trapped with him. I'll never wake up and realize I've been gradually twisted into a person I don't even recognize. Someone so crippled that happiness and love and even hope is gone and the only thing left is endurance..." My voice choked into silence.

The bed dipped as Kane sat beside me, his arm closing around my shoulders. "But Aydan, you know you can trust me. You've already trusted me with your life, over and over."

"It's easy to trust you with my life. If it's the wrong decision, I don't have to live with the consequences."

His silence made me look up. He was staring at me, open-mouthed. "I... never quite thought of it like that," he said faintly.

I shrugged and blew out a sigh before meeting his eyes. "Look, John, think about it. I freak out if I feel manipulated, whether you're trying to do it or not. Do you really want to be in a relationship where you have to walk on eggshells all the time? Believe me, I've lived like that, and I wouldn't wish it on my worst enemy." I dropped my gaze to the carpet again.

He squeezed my hand. "But Aydan, when we both understand what's happening, we can work together to change it. It's never going to be perfect. We just have to keep trying."

Hopelessness overcame me, and I met his eyes again.

When I spoke, my voice came out flat. "But that's the problem. I tried so hard, for so long... It's just... I've got nothing left. It's gone. And it's not coming back."

His hand fell away from mine. The last remnants of my heart crumbled to ashes as the hope died in his eyes.

"I'm sorry," I whispered.

He rose and turned his back to stare out the window.

I curled down around my aching chest, closing my eyes. Finally, he understood. It was done.

"I'm not." Kane's voice barely penetrated my lifeless shell.

His voice rose. "Aydan, dammit, I'm not! I'm not sorry at all!"

His triumphant tone made me uncurl to look up at him. He was smiling, his eyes blazing with courage and unquenchable life. He pulled me to my feet and into his powerful embrace. His lips claimed mine in an exultant kiss.

He pulled away, cupping my face in his hands. "I will never be sorry for this. Whether we die today, or whether we survive and go our separate ways, or whether we figure out some middle ground together, I will never be sorry."

He kissed me again, the heat of his body thawing my frozen misery, and my arms wrapped around him in return. He broke the kiss to smile down at me. "Now let's get this bird onto the ground."

I tightened my arms around him, hiding my face. "Thanks," I whispered to his chest.

The note of the engines changed and I pulled away, relief and fear warring for ascendancy. "That's your cue. Go fly the plane."

"As if."

We headed forward and I trailed to a halt in the sitting

room, frowning. When Kane shot me a questioning look, I motioned him ahead. "I'll be right there. I just have to figure out a way to make some non-dangerous smoke when we're landing. Carl's going to call it in so we get priority landing sequence and emergency vehicles."

He nodded and headed down the corridor while I contemplated my options. I had no way of starting a fire, and open flame seemed like a bad idea anyway.

But there was a small electric cooking element in the serving counter. If I put something on the element and turned it on...

I began opening drawers and doors. Steak would have been nice and smoky, but there was none left in the fridge. Must have been a special thing just for the Parrs. I briefly considered laying a dishcloth across the element. That would make some good smoke.

But, no, if it actually caught fire...

I shuddered.

The first vibrations of turbulence bumped the deck beneath my feet, and I hurriedly settled on a packet of crunchy cheesy snacks. Using aluminium foil, I fashioned a rough retaining ring around the element. When I was ready, I could pour the snacks directly onto it.

Next I studied the fire extinguishers just in case my cheesy smoke got a little too thick. Besides, if there was smoke on board, surely they'd expect the crew to have the fire extinguishers out. That might help Dermott's coverup.

The plane bumped a little more vigorously, and I headed for the front of the plane to stick my head into the cockpit.

"How's it going?"

"Fine, flying a jet is easy," Kane joked, but his hands hovered tensely near the controls and his smile looked pasted-on.

I drew a deep breath and let it out slowly. "Must be nice to be so talented."

He grimaced, dropping the pretense. "Go look at the emergency exits. We should evacuate the plane as though we're afraid of the smoke. I already checked the ones at this end, but maybe you should use one of the rear ones. Make it look good."

"Okay. I'm going to generate some smoke in a few minutes with some stuff on the burner in the serving station, but don't worry, I'll be standing by with the fire extinguisher just in case." I was glad my voice sounded calm and level despite the pounding of my heart.

"Wait. Could you grab my coat, please? Put the weapon in the inside pocket and bring it to me."

I frowned. "Are you sure you want to do that? What if it goes off? Or beams, or whatever it does?"

The lines of strain deepened around his mouth. "It's a chance I'll have to take." He hesitated. "There's always a possibility we might have to evacuate for real if the landing doesn't go well. I don't plan to waste time trying to locate the weapon."

My heart lurched, and I turned away before he could see my reaction. "Be right back."

Coat in hand, I pulled on one of Kane's gloves before squatting beside the serving cart to gingerly tuck the weapon into the coat pocket. Holding the coat at arms' length, I carried it back to prop it cautiously in the pilot's seat, making sure the bell end of the bottle pointed away from Kane. He nodded his thanks, and I withdrew again to reconnoitre the exits.

Beside the serving station, I glanced at the diagram on

the over-wing hatch, thankful for all the times I'd booked an exit-row seat on commercial flights for the extra legroom. The flight attendants had given me the briefing often enough. It seemed pretty straightforward.

I swallowed the tightness in my throat. It wouldn't be a real emergency. Germain would land us safely and we'd just be faking it. Pretending to be terrified.

I was doing a great job of that already.

I made my way into the bedroom at the back of the plane, taking an uncertain step sideways as the plane yawed.

The rear exit door looked more complicated. The big lever made sense, but there seemed to be another release lever beside it to disengage a locking system. I frowned at it. It didn't look like rocket science, but who knew?

The plane dipped suddenly, my stomach soaring in space for an instant before catching up to my body, and I hurried forward again. The floor vibrated as though we were driving over a rough road, and another tricky little yaw made me sidestep to compensate.

"I have a whole new respect for flight attendants," I said to Kane as I arrived at the cockpit. "They walk around during this kind of turbulence just like they were on solid ground."

He nodded, his lips twisting in a mirthless smile as he stared out the windshield. Germain's voice crackled over the radio, exchanging a stream of incomprehensible jargon with the air traffic controller. I caught the words 'smoke in the cabin'.

"That's my cue." My pulse sped up to vibrate in my throat. "Okay, I'm going to go and turn on the element. I'll take the fire extinguisher and strap into one of the seats in the sitting room so I can supervise my smoke." I didn't sound quite so calm anymore. My voice trembled, and Kane reached back to squeeze my hand. I noticed a tremor in his grip, too.

"See you on the ground," he said confidently.

"You bet."

Back at the serving station, I tackled one of the little bags of snacks, tugging at the slippery plastic with shaking hands. The packet split abruptly, spraying snacks all over the counter and carpet.

"Shit!" I dropped to my knees to gather them before stopping to thud my forehead against my hand. Just get another bag, stupid.

"Everything okay?" Kane's strained voice drifted from up front.

"Fine. Just dropped my snacks."

I grabbed another bag and tried again, successfully containing the goodies this time to pour them into my foil ring. Then I hefted a fire extinguisher out of its bracket and turned the element on high before I could chicken out.

Sliding into the seat, I fumbled the seat belt closed one-handed, unwilling to tear my gaze from the cooktop or relinquish the fire extinguisher.

A few curls of smoke rose, and the disgusting smell of scorched carbohydrate drifted to my nose. The plane began to buck and vibrate in earnest, and I eased out a long breath.

I'd ridden flights into Calgary's wild chinook winds lots of times. Nothing unusual. It just meant we were getting closer to the ground. Closer to safety, I corrected myself firmly.

The bottles in the serving cart clanked and tinkled and the bulkhead above the serving station flexed, creaking. I sent a silent prayer toward the front of the plane. Surely the weapon would be okay. It shouldn't go off even if it was bumped.

Please let that be true.

The smoke thickened, and I yanked my attention back to the element. The snacks were blackening. Good. Just a little longer and then I'd turn the element off.

Another heart-stopping drop and lurch made the serving cart bounce, the bottles crashing together on its bottom shelf. In the next yaw it rolled partway across the floor, and I realized with chagrin that Thomas would have undoubtedly secured it for landing if he'd still been alive.

The smash of breaking glass jerked my attention back to the cooktop. As if in slow motion, the shards of the fallen brandy bottle breached my aluminium foil, shoving it over the edge of the counter in a wave of brandy. The alcohol leaped up in bluish flame and the snacks ignited like matches.

CHAPTER 49

"Shit!"

I tried to spring up from my seat, forgetting my seatbelt. I swore again, whipping the fire extinguisher into position and yanking the pin.

The wavefront of burning alcohol raced down the front of the serving station to the carpet, igniting the snacks I hadn't cleaned up earlier.

"*Shit!*" I pointed the nozzle at the base of the flames and clamped down on the lever. The plane bounced again, spoiling my aim. Burning brandy and flaming snacks splashed and scattered, setting dozens of tiny bonfires in the carpet.

"SHIT-SHIT-SHIT!" I yanked the seatbelt free and lunged to my feet.

"What's wrong?" Kane's shout sounded from the front of the plane.

"*Fire!*"

The plane's unpredictable motion fought me. Staggering, I struggled to direct the nozzle, but only half the flames were out when the spray diminished to a trickle. The acrid smell of burning carpet filled the air, smoke collecting on the ceiling already.

Kane lunged into view on the other side of the flames, fire extinguisher in hand.

"Breathing mask by the rear fire extinguishers!" he shouted, sweeping the nozzle back and forth. "Put it on and bring them!"

I turned to race aft but the plane bucked while I was off balance, slamming me to the floor. A cacophony of shattering glass made me twist in time to see the serving cart on its side, blue flames racing from its smashed contents in a deadly wave across the floor to lick at the rosewood panelling.

"Mask!" Kane shouted. "Get in the bedroom!" A fit of coughing silenced him. Smoke thickened between us and I stared for a frozen instant before scrambling up.

Choking smoke jolted me into a recollection of basic fire safety. I dropped to hands and knees again to scuttle below the deadly cloud.

I stood only long enough to rip the plastic case from its bracket beside the fire extinguishers before dropping to the floor again. Coughing, I tore the case open, deciphering the cryptic pictogram instructions with agonizing slowness. Another fit of coughing seized me and I hunched lower, searching for cleaner air and fighting dizziness. I dragged the apparatus over my head, yanking my hair out of the neck seal and jerking the cords.

Blessedly smoke-free air filled my lungs and my coughing eased, my throat burning. I hauled myself to my knees, bracing against the bounce and roll of the floor. Grabbing the fire extinguishers by feel, I turned to face a wall of black smoke.

Panic gibbered at the edges of my mind. The neck seal squeezed my throat like threatening hands. My frenzied heartbeat resounded in my ears, almost drowning out the engine noise muffled by my hood.

I wrestled the panic down.

Move.

I crawled unsteadily along the pitching deck, dragging the fire extinguishers and following the wall of the plane by leaning a shoulder against it.

It seemed like miles in the smoky limbo. Was I going the wrong way?

I couldn't be. The wall was still on my right. I hadn't turned around.

Kane's extinguishers must be spent by now.

He needed me.

Move faster.

Orange flickered dully through the pall of smoke. A moment later, my hand landed on a bulky object that yielded under my weight.

A leg.

Kane!

I dropped the fire extinguishers to haul desperately on his leg before realizing the flames were too close.

Where his head would be.

Sobbing screams tore my throat. I slammed my hands to the floor, scrabbling frantically for the fallen fire extinguishers.

Too slow, too slow!

At last, my hand struck a smooth cylinder. I fumbled it into position by feel and blasted at the orange glow until the nozzle's stream dropped off. The flames faltered, then recovered.

I jerked at his foot again, sweat and tears pouring down my face. He was too heavy.

His shoe came off in my hand and I pitched backward. The impact slammed reality into my brain.

The flames were nearly down to his waist.

I was too late.

Mindless wails of horror and grief filled my hood. The pitch of the deck increased.

Final descent.

The heat was increasing, flames creeping closer.

Kane would want me to save myself.

And Spider was counting on me.

I flung out arms and legs in the smoke-filled darkness and made contact with the wall again. Jamming my shoulder against it for guidance, I hauled myself to hands and knees to crawl uphill toward the bedroom, still hugging Kane's shoe. Tears choked me, the breathing mask so terrifyingly confining I could barely keep from tearing it off.

Bedroom.

Close the door. Basic fire safety.

My face almost on the carpet, I followed the dim glow of the floor-level emergency lighting to the exit door. Helpless sobs convulsed me while I huddled beside it, clinging to the shoe as if it could somehow save me.

The plane shook like a rat in a terrier's jaws.

A terrifying bang. The floor leaped under me.

Another impact, then a third, the unmistakable feel of landing gear slamming onto the runway.

The engines screamed. The hard braking shuffled me across the floor toward growing heat.

I flung out my arms and legs, bracing against the deceleration, digging useless fingers at the too-short carpet. The shoe slipped from my grasp.

All I had left of him.

Beyond rational thought, I grabbed for it with both hands. Momentum took me.

A short tumble.

A hard blow to my side.

Pushed against the hot wall as if by brutal hands.

Long seconds later, the force decreased enough for me to roll away. The floor stopped bouncing and the engine noise subsided.

Wheezing hysterical sobs, I clawed my way back to the unseen seam of the exit hatch.

Hauled myself up, my frantic hands racing over the wall panel. The lock release had to be here somewhere. I'd seen it earlier...

Darker. Getting darker.

Dizziness weakened my knees.

My hand smashed down on the release lever at last. Shoved it into place.

My shaking legs barely carried me to the door. I hauled on the big lever with the last of my strength.

The hatch swung open. Icy air against my hands.

An inflatable slide unfurled, bouncing with macabre gaiety like a midway ride in hell. My knees gave way and I pitched down the steep slope to slam into heartless tarmac.

Get up. Get away from the plane.

My body refused to move.

Lights flashed and voices shouted.

A horrible flying sensation and a bumpy ride recalled the too-fresh terror of the plane. I clung to Kane's shoe, my only anchor in the incomprehensible chaos.

More lights. More shouting. A hard yank on my hair when the breathing mask was pulled off.

Someone tried to take the shoe and I fought with what

little strength I had left. When it was wrenched from my grasp the wail of a lost soul filled the air, a cry so inhuman I didn't even realize it was coming from my own lips until a mask clamped over my nose and mouth and muffled it.

I closed my eyes and went limp, letting the black cancer consume my soul.

I had killed Kane. As I'd always known I would.

The flames flared again behind my eyelids, the indistinct silhouette of his burning body wavering through the smoke. The monstrous guilt strangled me.

Time blurred. Faces and voices came and went, delivering barrages of meaningless words and pointless questions.

Sometimes I spoke empty words back to them; other times not.

At last the commotion abated and the bright lights went away. Someone brought the shoe back and I clasped it against the place where my heart had been.

Quiet enfolded me.

I sank into its barren embrace.

"Hey, darlin'."

Hellhound's soft rasp roused me, but I kept my eyes shut.

"Aydan." Gentle fingertips caressed the hair away from my forehead. "Talk to me, darlin'."

How could he bear to look at the woman who had murdered his brother?

A slight tug between my hands. "Hey, Aydan, what's with the shoe?"

My eyes flew open, my hands clenching on the hard

leather. Hellhound's bruised features hovered above me, his black-on-black fatigues stark against the pale emergency-room curtains behind him.

His rigid face softened enough to attempt a smile. "That's better, darlin'. Ya had me worried. Doc says you're okay, just banged up a bit. How ya feelin'?"

How could he even ask that? I closed my eyes, willing myself to die.

"Hey." Another tug.

I opened my eyes again, clinging fiercely to the shoe.

"Hey, Aydan." He leaned down to brush a feather-light kiss onto my forehead. "Talk to me, darlin'. Tell me about the shoe, okay?"

Unable to meet his eyes, I stared down at the sooty object.

And saw it clearly for the first time. Slow realization penetrated my brain.

It was too small.

And Kane had been wearing boots.

A tremor seized my hands, spreading through my body like stone-dropped ripples in a pond. I stared up at Hellhound, afraid to ask, afraid to know. My grip tightened on the shoe until my knuckles popped, searing pain through my hand.

"J-John...?" It came out as a bare whisper. "Is... he...?"

"He's fine, darlin', got a bit of a bang on the head, but he's fine." He touched my bone-white knuckles. "Ya wanna tell me about the shoe now?"

Tears flooded my eyes and cascaded down my cheeks.

Hellhound gathered me close. "It's okay, darlin', it's okay." He muttered gentle nonsense, stroking my hair while I wept in his arms with Thomas's shoe crushed between us.

CHAPTER 50

"I said safely generate some smoke, not burn down the whole fucking plane! What the hell was that?" Dermott glowered across his desk.

I studied my hands, clenched in my lap. "Sorry. I should have put the brandy bottle back in the cart and secured the cart. And I should have realized how flammable those cheese snacks were."

"Didn't you see that video on the internet a couple of years back?" Dermott demanded. "You can use those fucking things for campfire starters, for shit's sake!"

I slid lower in the chair. "I know that now."

"It wasn't Aydan's fault." Kane's firm baritone restored some strength to my spine. "She couldn't have known about the snacks, and I didn't think to secure the cart, either. And I'm the one who took the brandy bottle out."

I shot him a grateful glance, giving silent thanks once more that his concussion hadn't been as severe as Hellhound's. The bandage on his forehead gave him a rakish appearance, especially when he grinned like that.

In fact, everybody except Dermott was grinning, but I thought he was having a hard time holding onto his scowl.

I was right. A moment later, his lips quirked up, too.

"That was some nice cover, though," he said. "I'll hardly have to tweak the accident report at all. There wasn't much left of the bodies for the medical examiner to look at, and you made the flight crew look like heroes when you said they gave you the breathing masks."

"Thank God you knew about those," I said to Kane.

"I didn't." He shot a grin at Germain. "As soon as you yelled 'fire', Germain connected over the tablet and told me about them."

"Thank you!" I sent an admiring gaze Germain's way before realizing Jack was already doing that. And doing it a lot more attractively than I could.

Germain smiled. "I'm glad you got to them in time. In an aircraft, the smoke is usually more deadly than the actual fire."

"How did you get out, though?" I asked Kane. "I thought the whole plane was on fire. The bedroom door was hot to the touch."

"I closed myself into the cockpit and went out the window as soon as we were down."

"Thank God you're both okay," Spider blurted. "Thank God."

I grinned. "I'll second that motion."

Dermott eyed Jack. "You've got the weapon locked up in the secured area? Started any testing yet?"

"Bare preliminaries." She returned his gaze coolly. "I've only had it for twelve hours. But it's secure, and I'll do a thorough analysis next week."

"Twelve hours?" I shot a frown at Kane. "We were still in the hospital twelve hours ago. How did you...?"

"I didn't." He smiled. "I handed it off to Hellhound and he brought it."

The light dawned. "That's why he was at the hospital so soon after we got there. And wearing fatigues."

Dermott nodded. "We inserted him at the airport as soon as we knew when you'd be landing. Even if you hadn't made it out of the plane, he would have been first on the scene to look for the weapon."

"But he shouldn't have been on active service," I protested. "It's only been a week since his head injury. The doctor said at least two weeks."

Dermott shrugged. "We only had an hour to get somebody in there. He was the only weapons specialist available on such short notice. You do what you have to do."

I digested that for a moment.

"So, um..." I eyed Kane's bland expression for a moment before turning back to Dermott. "How high a security clearance does Arnie have, anyway?"

Dermott returned a deadpan stare that would have done Stemp proud. "That's strictly need to know, Kelly. And you don't need to know. You got the network keys and portable generator secured?"

"Um." I reined in my curiosity and refocused. "Yeah. Spider took them down for me as soon as we got here."

Dermott leaned back in his chair with a sigh. "Okay. Then let's get the hell out of here while we've still got a few hours of Christmas Eve left. Monday is Boxing Day so if nothing else blows up between now and then, we'll do a briefing Tuesday morning at nine with Stemp."

We abandoned the office with alacrity and Dermott strode off down the hall. As he vanished into the stairwell, Spider turned to me with a grin. "And we've got a party to go to!"

The others began to drift away, and inspiration

illuminated Spider's eyes. "Hey, wait, hang on." He turned his buoyant smile on them. "I know it's really short notice, but can you guys come? Linda and I would love to have you. The more the merrier."

Jack's smile bloomed. "Thank you, I'd love to! My ex has the kids until tomorrow and I always feel blue spending Christmas Eve alone."

"Beats the hell out of watching TV in a hotel room," Germain seconded. "Thanks!"

Kane hesitated. "I appreciate the invitation, but my dad flew into Calgary this morning. He's visiting with Arnie now, and I was planning to drive back there tonight to join them."

"Your dad would probably prefer that you got some rest." Jack shot a pointed glance at Kane's bandaged head. "It would be nearly ten by the time you got there anyway. You should take it easy tonight and leave in the morning instead."

Kane grimaced. "Is there an echo in here? That's exactly what he said at the hospital before we left."

Jack laughed. "You should listen to your dad. And to me."

Kane shrugged, smiling. "All right. I know when I'm outnumbered."

"Great, then let's go!" Spider beamed at us and we all turned to head for the stairs.

Under cover of the general exodus, I slipped the small velvet sack into his hand. He blew out a long breath. "Thanks, Aydan. Thanks for everything. For getting my job back. For keeping the ring safe."

I grimaced. "Safe isn't the word I would have used. I hope you're going to put it back in the box. The velvet still smells like smoke."

"I will. I have the box with me." He turned wide hazel

eyes on me. "I'm so... I feel like I'm going to explode, I'm so excited. And scared. Maybe this was a dumb idea. Maybe I should have proposed in private." His lips trembled. "What if she says no?"

"She won't." I squeezed his shoulders. "Come on, let's go do it. Then you can enjoy the party."

The festivities were already under way when we arrived. Lights and garlands brightened the small living room, and a decorated Christmas tree sparkled in the corner. Spider's two boisterous older sisters circulated, offering cups of eggnog and singing along to the Christmas carols on the stereo. His parents smiled in the background while a group of young people I didn't recognize bantered noisily.

Lola greeted me with a hug, wearing a spangled blue sweater almost as bright as the Christmas tree. Another couple about my age nodded and smiled a greeting from behind her, and I recognized Linda and Lola's fine bones in the diminutive woman. I surmised they were Linda's parents, but Spider didn't give us time to chat.

He leaned down to whisper in Lola's ear, and a moment later she stuck two fingers in her mouth and let fly with a whistle that could have summoned cabs all the way from New York.

Silence fell, and Lola shouted, "Hey, Linda, where are you?"

"Here, I'm here." Linda emerged from the kitchen, looking like a teenager playing Mrs. Santa in a red-and-white ruffled apron and a Santa hat perched at a jaunty angle on her shiny dark hair. Her smile sought Spider as always, and she scooted across the room to insert herself under his arm.

"What's up?"

Spider gently disengaged his arm and turned to face her. "Well..." He was trembling visibly, his face pale. "I... I tried and tried to think of some way to make this special..."

Linda sobered, her eyes widening.

"I thought about all kinds of fancy ways to do this," Spider continued. "But..." He gestured at the room full of people and decorations. The Christmas carols were the only sound in the silence. "This is what's *really* special." His voice trembled, and he swallowed audibly. "Family... and friends... and you."

He sank down on one knee, extracting the ring box, and a faint 'aaah' whispered from the watchers. Linda's eyes began to fill.

"Will you share it with me?" Spider gazed earnestly at her. "Forever?"

She was already starting to nod when he opened the box and offered it to her. "Will you marry me?"

"Yes! Yes-yes-yes!" She flung herself at him.

He let out a yelp and overbalanced, landing on his butt on the floor. Linda pounced, smothering him with kisses, and a shout of laughter rose to the ceiling.

"Yippee! That's my little brother! And my new sister!" Spider's sister bounced to her knees to fling her arms around both of them.

"Dogpile!" The second sister landed atop the heap.

Laughter and shouts of congratulations rocked the small house, and in the bedlam I quietly ignored the vibration of my waist pouch. I knew who was calling me. Archibald Rankin and Fuzzy Bunny could wait.

Kane grinned beside me, and we all joined in the applause when the ring was finally extracted from its box and fitted on Linda's finger to be duly admired.

"Mistletoe!" One of the irrepressible sisters pointed ceilingward.

There was mistletoe indeed. Lots of it, scattered in various places throughout the room. Smooching ensued, and I relaxed into the almost-palpable joy. In a quieter corner, I noticed Jack and Germain taking advantage of the tradition, and I nudged Kane and inclined my head in their direction.

He smiled. "That's nice to see. Germain's been on his own for a long time." His gaze met mine and he sobered, but the smile still lingered in his eyes. "Merry Christmas, Aydan."

I moved just a bit nearer. Not touching, but close enough so I could feel his warmth.

"Merry Christmas," I whispered.

Book 8 is available!

Visit my Books page at dianehenders.com/books for progress updates and announcements.

A Request

Thanks for reading!

If you enjoyed this book, I'd really appreciate it if you'd take a moment to review it online.

Here are some suggestions for the "star" ratings:

Five stars: Loved the book and can hardly wait for the next one.

Four stars: Liked the book and plan to read the next one.

Three stars: The book was okay. Might read the next one.

Two stars: Didn't like the book. Probably won't read the next one.

One star: Hated the book. Would never read another in the series.

You can help prospective readers by writing a few sentences about what you liked or disliked about the book.

Thanks for taking the time to do a review!

About Me

Before I started writing fiction, I had a checkered career: technical writer, computer geek, and interior designer. I'm good at two out of three of those. Fortunately, I had the sense to quit the one I sucked at (interior design).

When my mid-life crisis hit, I took up muay thai and started writing thrillers featuring a middle-aged female protagonist. ('Walter Mitty', you say? Nope, never heard of him.)

Writing and kicking the hell out of stuff seemed more productive than more typical mid-life-crisis activities like getting a divorce, buying a Harley Crossbones, and cruising across the country picking up men in sleazy bars; especially since it's winter most months of the year here in Canada.

It's much more comfortable to sit at my computer. And Harleys are expensive. Come to think of it, so are beer and gasoline.

Oh, and I still love my husband. There's that. So I stuck with the writing.

Diane Henders

And here's my "professional" bio, in case you need something more suitable for mixed company:

Diane Henders is the Kindle best-selling author of the NEVER SAY SPY series: Sexy thrillers packed with tension, laughs, profanity, and sometimes warm fuzzies.

The first book in the series, NEVER SAY SPY, has had over 450,000 downloads to date, and stayed on Kindle's 'Women Sleuths' Top 100 list for 60 consecutive months.

Diane enjoys target shooting, gardening, auto mechanics, painting (art, not walls), music, and martial arts; and loves food and drink almost as much as she loves her husband. They live in the wilds of British Columbia, Canada, where they get all the adrenaline rush they could ever want by growing fruit trees in bear country.

Want to know what else is roiling around in the cesspit of my mind? Drop by my blog and website at dianehenders.com, check out the extras, and don't forget to leave a comment in the guest book to say hi – I love hearing from you! Or you can connect with me on Facebook at:
https://www.facebook.com/authordianehenders.
See you there!

www.ingramcontent.com/pod-product-compliance
Lightning Source LLC
Chambersburg PA
CBHW030926020726

47498CB00001B/124